SHERLOCK HOLMES AND THE RUNE STONE MYSTERY

Other Minnesota Mysteries by Larry Millett
Published by the University of Minnesota Press

The Disappearance of Sherlock Holmes
The Magic Bullet
Sherlock Holmes and the Ice Palace Murders
Sherlock Holmes and the Red Demon
Sherlock Holmes and the Secret Alliance

SHERLOCK
HOLMES
AND THE
RUNE STONE
MYSTERY

Larry Millett

A Minnesota Mystery Featuring Shadwell Rafferty

University of Minnesota Press
Minneapolis
London

The Fesler–Lampert Minnesota Heritage Book Series

This series is published with the generous assistance of the John K. and Elsie Lampert Fesler Fund and David R. and Elizabeth P. Fesler. Its mission is to republish significant out-of-print books that contribute to our understanding and appreciation of Minnesota and the Upper Midwest.

Map illustration by Lorelle Graffeo

Originally published in 1999 by Viking Penguin

First University of Minnesota Press edition, 2012

Published by the University of Minnesota Press
111 Third Avenue South, Suite 290
Minneapolis, MN 55401-2520
http://www.upress.umn.edu

Library of Congress Cataloging-in-Publication Data

Millett, Larry.
Sherlock Holmes and the rune stone mystery / Larry Millett.
—1st University of Minnesota Press ed.
ISBN 978-0-8166-7704-7 (pb : alk. paper)
1. Holmes, Sherlock (Fictitious character)—Fiction. 2. Rafferty, Shadwell (Fictitious character)—Fiction. I. Title.
PS3563.I42193S5 2012
813'.54—dc23
2011051269

Printed in the United States of America on acid-free paper

The University of Minnesota is an equal-opportunity educator and employer.

To John Mallander (1947–1999),
whom I will always miss

Contents

Acknowledgments

I received help from a number of people in writing this book. Kate Parry, my editor at the *St. Paul Pioneer Press*, was kind enough to let me go off in search of rune-stone lore, and the story I produced for the newspaper in 1998 turned out to be the germ of this book. Arlene Fults, executive director of the Rune Stone Museum in Alexandria, Minnesota, shared with me her knowledge of the famous artifact and its contentious history. Two other Alexandria residents, Gilmore and Marjorie Moe, provided a memorable tour of Rune Stone Park, which marks the site of the stone's discovery in 1898.

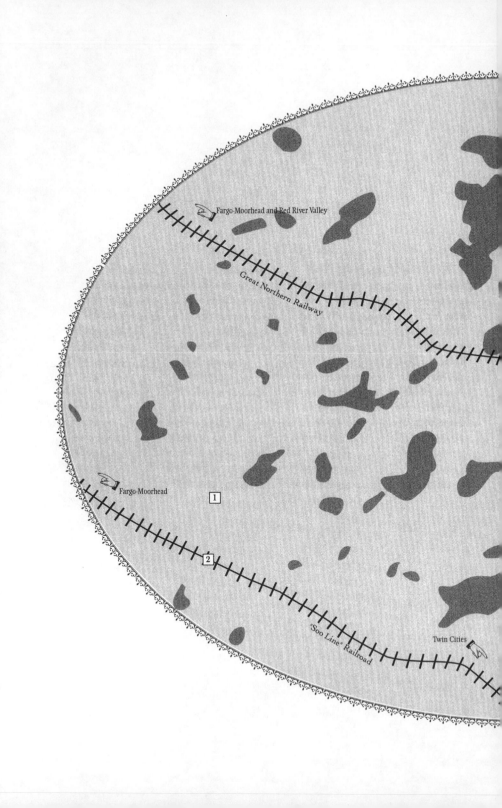

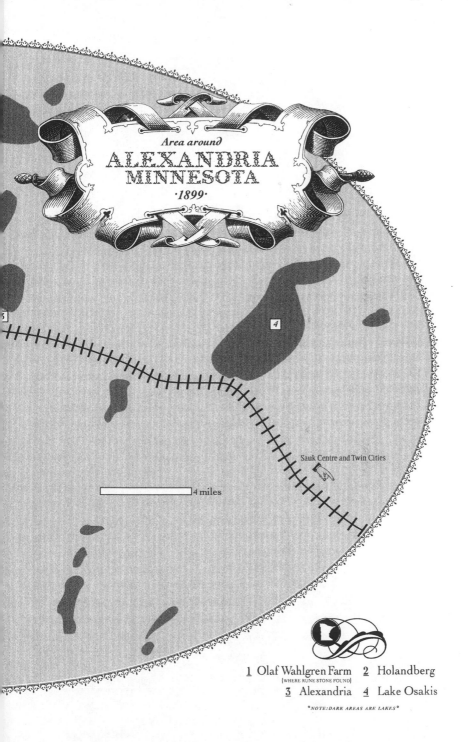

Area around
ALEXANDRIA
MINNESOTA
·1899·

4

Sauk Centre and Twin Cities

4 miles

1 Olaf Wahlgren Farm   2 Holandberg
[WHERE RUNE STONE FOUND]
3 Alexandria   4 Lake Osakis

°NOTE:DARK AREAS ARE LAKES°

Introduction

THE BOOK YOU ARE ABOUT TO READ RECOUNTS THE THIRD adventure of Sherlock Holmes and Dr. John Watson in Minnesota, following on the heels of *Sherlock Holmes and the Red Demon* (published in 1996) *and Sherlock Holmes and the Ice Palace Murders* (1998). One of the central themes of this newly discovered adventure is what Watson calls "the power of coincidence" and its unpredictable role in human affairs. Coincidence, as it turns out, is also very much a part of the story behind the discovery of the long-lost manuscript for *Sherlock Holmes and the Rune Stone Mystery*.

The story begins in the spring of 1899, when Holmes and Watson were drawn to western Minnesota to investigate the so-called Holandberg rune stone, a highly controversial artifact that had been unearthed several months earlier on a farm not far from its namesake village. Among the people Holmes and Watson may well have encountered on their visit was a newspaperman named Albert Carlson. Although mentioned only briefly in *The Rune Stone Mystery*, Carlson wrote extensively about the case for his newspaper, the *Clarion*, published in the town of Alexandria, just a few miles from Holandberg.[1]

More important for the purposes of history, Carlson also came into possession of what is now the only known copy of *Sherlock Holmes and the Rune Stone Mystery*, which Watson appears to have completed sometime toward the end of 1901. Exactly how Carlson obtained the manuscript is a mystery, since neither his will nor any other document he left behind after his death mentions the manuscript. Nor is there anything in Dr. Watson's papers at the British Museum that would shed light on the issue.

Absent any firm evidence, it is only possible to guess how the manuscript found its way to Carlson. The most likely scenario — which admittedly qualifies as little more than rank speculation — is that Watson sent the manuscript to one of the principals in the case, several of whom lived in Alexandria, and that at some point (perhaps not until many years later) this person in turn gave it to Carlson.

Watson, of course, was a tireless writer who devoted himself to chronicling the many adventures of his dear friend Sherlock Holmes. The great detective, however, did not always share the good doctor's enthusiasm for memorializing their cases through the written word. It is thus well known that some of the duo's most celebrated cases — the tantalizing affair of the "giant rat of Sumatra" being one notable example — were never committed to paper by Watson, presumably because of objections on Holmes's part.[2] In other instances, Watson "wrote up" an adventure knowing all the while that its publication would inevitably be delayed, perhaps for decades, because of the sensitive nature of the investigation.

Such seems to have been the case with *The Rune Stone Mystery*, even though the events it describes were well publicized by newspapers and magazines of the time. I have found references to the case in such major newspapers as the Chicago *Tribune*, the New York *Sun*, and even the *Daily Chronicle* of London, one of Holmes's favorite publications.[3] Such prominent American magazines as *McClure's* and *Harper's Weekly* also devoted articles to the case. Carlson's stories in the *Clarion*, however, remain to this day the most thorough journalistic account of the rune stone affair.

Yet despite ample opportunity to do so, Carlson never attempted, insofar as is known, to publish or in any way promulgate Watson's manuscript, the value of which he most certainly would have understood. From these circumstances it can be inferred that Holmes, for reasons known only to himself, insisted on suppressing the manuscript during his lifetime. My own theory is that Holmes did not want the manuscript published because he believed the rune stone investigation had been, in the end, a failure on his part. While this may have been true in a specific legal sense, I would contend that the case in fact displays some of the most brilliant work of Holmes's career, even if he thought otherwise.

What is certain is that the manuscript of *The Rune Stone Mystery* remained in Carlson's possession until his death, in 1936, at the age of eighty-seven. Probate court records in Douglas County, where the city of Alexandria is located, indicate that Carlson, who left behind no children or other close relatives, gave the bulk of his modest estate to charity. He did, however, donate a number of items—including scrapbooks, old photographs, and three boxes of miscellaneous documents—to the Vikingland Historical Society in Alexandria. One of these boxes, as it turned out, contained the manuscript of *The Rune Stone Mystery*, along with instructions that it was not to be opened until twenty years after Carlson's death. It is not clear why Carlson placed this embargo on Watson's manuscript, but his decision proved to have long-term, unintended consequences.

The director of the society's museum in 1936 was an elderly woman named Catherine Bisson. Known for her devotion to local history and her great probity, Bisson honored the embargo religiously, and so the manuscript stayed in its box, which was consigned to a dusty storage room at the society's small museum in Alexandria. Unfortunately, by the time the embargo was ready to be lifted, in 1956, Bisson had long since died and Carlson's box of documents had been forgotten. The box was to remain unopened for the next forty-two years, until fate finally intervened in 1998.

Early that year, the society's board of directors, with the aid of a state grant, approved a plan to enlarge and renovate the aging museum. This plan was designed in part to create adequate space for a special centennial exhibit documenting the history of the Holand-berg rune stone, which now resides permanently at the museum. Among other things, the renovation project entailed expanding the museum's main exhibit hall into an area formerly occupied by the storage room. With workers prepared to knock out its walls, the room's contents had to be carefully sorted, an onerous duty that fell to Leeander Peck, the museum's current director. Intrigued by the long-expired embargo on Carlson's box, Peck opened it and so discovered the manuscript you are about to read.

A dedicated Sherlockian in his own right, Peck realized the significance of his discovery and at once contacted the Minnesota Historical Society, which in turn got in touch with me. As the editor of Holmes and Watson's two earlier adventures in Minnesota, I was asked to evaluate the manuscript. I did so, using techniques and procedures I have described in detail elsewhere.[4] From these tests, I was able to determine beyond any reasonable doubt that the manuscript came from the hand of Dr. Watson.

Readers of this latest adventure will, I think, find much of interest in it, including a second appearance by Shadwell Rafferty, the St. Paul tavern keeper and detective who was of such great help to Holmes and Watson in their ice palace case of 1896. Rafferty, a genial and engaging character with a core of solid steel, is once again in top form during the adventure of *The Rune Stone Mystery*. Another, far more sinister character from the past also reappears in this case, creating a world of trouble for Holmes, Watson, and Rafferty.

I am pleased now to offer you this magnificent trio in *Sherlock Holmes and the Rune Stone Mystery*.

— Larry Millett

Sherlock Holmes
and the Rune Stone Mystery

Chapter One

"THE WHOLE THING IS NOTHING BUT A CRUDE HOAX"

Coincidence, Sherlock Holmes once remarked to me, is the tribute reason must occasionally pay to fate. In the case of Holmes, that payment was made with surprising regularity, for coincidences of one kind or another played a crucial role in many of his investigations. The amazingly fortuitous circumstances behind the capture of Pemberton, the Ipswich strangler, serve as but one example in this regard.[1] Although Holmes believed as strongly as any man in the rule of reason, he eventually came to accept, if not to embrace, the unpredictable power of coincidence. Or, as he liked to say, "lightning has a way of finding the rod." And surely there was never a higher or more visible rod than Sherlock Holmes, who by his very nature seemed to attract those sharp strikes of fate which can so strongly illuminate human affairs.

It was just such a strike—a coincidence so startling that I would not have believed it had I not witnessed it with my own eyes and ears—which set in motion one of the most curious cases ever undertaken by Holmes. Known to the world as the Holandberg rune stone affair, the case continues to inspire fierce debate on both sides of the

Atlantic, as evidenced by the recent, and much talked about, article in *Harper's Weekly*. The affair was most unusual because it involved two distinct but interconnected mysteries—one historical, and the other of the immediate human kind, written indelibly in blood and betrayal.

That Holmes solved both of these mysteries there can be no doubt. Yet it is also true that the case failed in the end to satisfy that deep thirst for justice which is his only real satisfaction in this world. It is thus no surprise that the rune stone affair continues to trouble Holmes and that he ponders it often during those gloomy periods of inactivity which so try his noble soul. I also find myself thinking back frequently to the final days of the case and to the improbable nightmare in which it culminated amid the bleak and sullen flatlands of the Red River Valley. Confronted with villainy of a rare and deadly kind, we were, I realize now, fortunate to escape with our lives.

The beginning of the rune stone case can be dated to the morning of March 15, 1899, when we were, as is our weekday habit, in our rooms at 221B Baker Street. The day had begun with Holmes in one of his splenetic moods, which were invariably brought on by pro-longed periods of idleness. Like a gifted but irritable child, Holmes needed constant stimulation, absent which his mind would turn inward on itself in most unpleasant ways. Unfortunately, he had found no case worthy of his talents since the Milverton blackmail affair at the beginning of the year, and as winter turned into spring he became increasingly out of sorts.[2]

On this particular morning, he sat at his desk, the usual collection of newspapers spread in disarray around him as he searched for some nugget of information, however trifling, which might lead him to the golden mother lode of a truly challenging problem. The prospects did not appear promising, however, for after a few minutes he launched upon the sort of lament I had heard all too frequently in recent weeks.

"My dear Watson," he began, "I fear there is absolutely no hope for me. I am a ship without a rudder adrift on an empty sea. The criminals of London, it would seem, have suffered a collective failure of the imagination, for which I must pay the price. Even this absurd business of the diplomat's stabbing at Kings Cross Station, which *The Times* finds so fascinating, is of little consequence. Indeed, a satisfactory solution would require but an hour of my time, if that."[3]

"No doubt," I murmured, hoping that Holmes might lay the matter to rest and return quietly to his newspapers.

Holmes, however, was in no mood to suffer alone in silence. "As for the rest of *The Times*, it is a desert, Watson, a desert without feature or termination, a vast aridity in which there is not one precious drop of hope for a thirsty detective such as myself. It is enough to make me wish that the late Professor Moriarty might return from the grave, or from whatever dark portion of the hereafter he may be occupying, and embark upon some interesting mischief. At least Moriarty had the gift of imagination to go with his talent for crime."

"Really, Holmes, I do not think that summoning the spirits of the dead will be of much benefit to you," I said, putting down a medical text I had been reading and going over to the window to look out upon the teeming life of Baker Street, which was bathed in bright sunshine. "It is a beautiful day, and heaven knows we have enjoyed few of those this winter. Perhaps you should go out for a walk. The exercise would do you good."

Holmes shook his head as he turned to the back page of his newspaper. "It is mental, not physical, exercise which I require, Watson. A walk would—"

He abruptly stopped and I could see by his furrowed brow that something in *The Times* had caught his attention.

"What is it, Holmes?"

There was no answer for a moment; then Holmes looked up and said: "A rune stone, Watson. They have found a rune stone in Minnesota. How curious!"

I should note here that the study of runes—that distinctive alphabet used by the Norsemen of old—had become one of Holmes's latest passions. Some months earlier, he had gone to visit his friend Lomax at the London Library and returned with a stack of dusty tomes, several of which were written in the Scandinavian languages. When I asked Holmes why he had suddenly turned to the study of ancient Norse writing, he replied that "the runes are in many ways a mystery, Watson, and as I have nothing more productive to do at the moment, I propose to give them my full attention. I may even be able to clarify one or two points which have long baffled the leading scholars in the field."

I learned later, however, that Holmes had in fact acquired his interest in runes during the sojourn in Scandinavia which followed his duel to the death with Professor Moriarty. Holmes seldom spoke of his activities during this period, but I gradually deduced from various small hints and passing remarks that he had spent several months in Sweden, where the study of runic writing, as might be expected, is quite advanced in the universities.

Although I knew little of runes myself, I was naturally surprised to hear from Holmes that a stone with runic writing had been found in Minnesota, a place with which Holmes and I were already far too familiar.

"I must suppose it is a hoax, not unlike that of the Cardiff Giant," I said as Holmes handed me *The Times*. "I cannot imagine that the Vikings could ever have reached a place so distant from their homeland."[4]

Holmes nodded and said: "There is also the inconvenient fact that Minnesota is at the very center of the North American continent and therefore a thousand miles from salt water. You are right, Watson, it may well be a fraud, but if *The Times* is to be believed, it must be a very clever fraud, and therefore one that is not without certain points of interest. Here, take a look at the article."[5]

I dutifully perused the story, which read as follows:

A large stone chiseled with what is said to be medieval runic writing has been discovered in a remote inland region of North America. The stone was found last November, clasped within the roots of a tree, by a farmer in the western part of Minnesota, a state in the far northern portion of the American Midwest. Only recently, how-

ever, has word of the finding spread to scientific circles, where it has occasioned much excitement and discussion.

According to a translation made by a professor at the University of Minnesota, the stone tells of a group of thirty Norse explorers who entered the region in the year 1362 but met with tragedy when ten of their members were murdered by natives. In light of the recent history of archaeological forgeries, the supposed discovery will undoubtedly be greeted with skepticism by Swedish runologists, who are regarded as the world's leading experts in such matters. Nonetheless, it has been reported that several leading American scholars are already convinced as to the authenticity of the stone, which would of course be an artifact of immense significance if it is indeed genuine.

"I should like to see that stone," said Holmes after I had finished reading the story. "It would present a novel problem in detection, do you not think, Watson?"

"I suppose. But as I recall, you vowed after the ice palace affair that you would never again set foot in Minnesota. Have you changed your mind?"

Holmes shrugged and said: "It has been three years since that business, Watson, and as the poet tells us, 'distance lends enchantment.' But it hardly matters, since we shall not be going all the way to Minnesota merely to satisfy my curiosity about a stone that will probably turn out to be an obvious piece of fakery."

Barely an hour later, the unlikely power of coincidence took us into its grasp.

It was just before noon when Mrs. Hudson, our redoubtable if long-suffering landlady, announced that there was a man downstairs who wished to see Holmes. "His name is Mr. Ohman," she said, "and he sounds like some kind of Swede." Mrs. Hudson, like others of her class, was intrinsically distrustful of foreigners, and she pronounced the word "Swede" with something approaching disgust.

Mention of our visitor's name had quite the opposite effect on Holmes. The languor which had consumed him of late appeared to vanish in an instant. He rose from his chair, where he had been gazing idly out the window, and rushed over to the door. "Ah, Mrs. Hudson, you are my salvation," he said, reaching out for her hand and giving it a kiss, which greatly startled the poor woman. "Please, send the gentleman up at once."

The man who appeared moments later at our door was in his early forties, tall and slender, with an oblong face, short blond hair, a closely trimmed beard covering the pugnacious thrust of his chin, and keen blue eyes beneath round wire spectacles. He carried a leather attaché case, but he did not have the look of a businessman or diplomat, for his dress—a wrinkled brown coat, a rather frayed white shirt, and a pair of baggy gabardine trousers—was that of a man indifferent to the niceties of fashion. His disheveled appearance, combined with a kind of willful abstractness in his gaze, suggested that he might be a scholar or academician of some kind, which in fact he was.

"Professor Ohman," said Holmes, greeting our visitor with a hearty handshake. "How good to see you again. I presume you have come about the rune stone."

The professor stared at Holmes with blank astonishment, a look Holmes often induced by virtue of his seemingly uncanny, though in fact quite simple, deductions.

"Yes, yes, I did," Ohman said. "But how on earth . . . ?"

By way of response, Holmes went to his desk, picked up *The Times*, and showed the startled professor the article about the Minnesota rune stone. "It was merely a guess on my part," Holmes admitted, "but I thought it not unlikely that your visit was somehow related to the same topic."

"I fear I have not read *The Times* today," Ohman said. "Perhaps I should have."

"Better yet, why don't you sit down, Professor, and tell us your tale," said Holmes, ushering the tall Swede to a seat by the window. "First, however, let me make the proper introductions. Dr. Watson, this is Erik Ohman, professor of medieval studies at Uppsala University. Professor Ohman is a man of many accomplishments, but is perhaps most widely recognized as an authority on runes."

"A pleasure to meet you," I said. "I gather that you and Holmes are quite well acquainted."

"Indeed we are," said Ohman with a smile. His English, though quite heavily accented, was excellent (I later learned that he had studied for two years at Oxford). "Mr. Holmes and I once spent a most enjoyable fortnight in Uppland examining runes."

It was now Holmes's turn to smile. "So we did. I was at that time going under the name of Sigerson. Indeed, it was Professor Ohman who suggested that alias, which I used on my subsequent travels. It was also through the professor that I was able to do a small favor for the king of Sweden."[6]

"I would describe it as much more than a small favor," said Ohman. "To this day, Oskar II remains deeply grateful for your assistance, as well he should. The man is a damn fool, if you ask me. Still, I am instructed to send you his warmest greetings."[7]

"And I in turn send my best wishes to him," Holmes replied with a slight bow, giving no indication that he was surprised by the professor's intemperate remarks about the king. "Now, let us sit down, and you can tell us what other instructions you received from Oskar, for I must assume your visit is not simply for the purpose of renewing our old acquaintance."

"You are right," said Ohman as we drew up our chairs. "The king, bless his royal heart, is now faced with what he considers to be a most difficult decision, and he would like your help."

Holmes leaned back in his chair and said: "I see. This decision, I presume, has to do with the rune stone discovered in Minnesota."

"It does," Ohman acknowledged with a shake of his head. "The crux of the matter, Mr. Holmes, is this: the king, subject to approval from the Riksdag, is prepared to purchase the rune stone, for a sizable amount of money, so that it can be put on public display at the royal museum in Stockholm."

"How much money?" Holmes asked.

"The amount has not been officially settled upon, insofar as I know. I am told, however, that the king is prepared to pay up to the equivalent of ten thousand English pounds for the stone."

I let out a soft whistle, for that was indeed a great deal of money. "But why would the king be willing to spend so much for a mere stone with some runic lettering?"

Ohman said: "Why indeed! The only explanation is that the king is a perfect fool. God knows what special form of madness contaminates royal blood, but if it were up to me we would be done forever with kings and all they represent. If I have said it once, I have said it—"

Holmes interrupted: "A thousand times, Professor. Your feelings regarding the Swedish monarchy are well known to me. I should be more interested at the moment, however, in hearing specific reasons as to why King Oskar is so taken with the Minnesota rune stone."

"Of course, of course," Ohman muttered. "Please accept my apologies. Very well, I will explain the situation as best I can. You must understand that Oskar, like many of his subjects, is an enthusiastic believer in the notion that the Vikings discovered North America. He has devoured the ancient sagas and is also familiar with the work of Carl Rafn and the other historians of his ilk.[8] The king was also much excited by the replica Viking ship which was built for the World's Fair in Chicago. As you probably know, that ship was sailed successfully across the Atlantic, thereby giving much encouragement to those who believe that Norsemen could have made an early voyage to the New World. Even so, there is much dispute as to whether the Vikings did in fact reach North America long before Columbus. The king believes the rune stone could prove the theory of Norse discovery once and for all. If so, then the stone is a supreme prize, not only for the king but for the Swedish people."

"Has King Oskar actually seen the stone?" Holmes asked.

"No. It remains in Minnesota. But the king has received a copy of the stone's runic inscription, and he is inclined to think the writing is genuine."

"Obviously, you think otherwise."

"I do. The whole thing is nothing but a crude hoax, as far as I am concerned. I would not spend a farthing for the stone, if it was up to me."

"Why do you say that?" I asked.

"For one thing, the lettering employed on the stone shows suspicious variations from the standard futhork of the fourteenth century."

Anticipating my next question, Holmes said: "The futhork, Watson, is the name of the runic alphabet used during the Middle Ages. The name is derived from the first seven characters in the alphabet, which has sixteen characters in all."

Holmes now turned his attention back to Ohman and said: "Please, continue, Professor. What else makes you suspect that the stone is a fraud?"

"The place of its discovery. Do you know anything about Minnesota, Mr. Holmes?"

"I am not unfamiliar with the state of that name," Holmes replied dryly as he gave me a conspiratorial wink. He went on to tell Ohman about our two previous visits to the state, in 1894 and 1896.

"Well, then, you know more about the state than I do," said the professor. "Of all the places where one might have expected to find genuine Viking artifacts, it is about the least likely in my opinion, because of its great distance from the sea. On the other hand, Minnesota is a very likely place for a fake rune stone to turn up, because the state is teeming with Scandinavian immigrants, most of whom probably have at least a smattering of knowledge about runes. Indeed, I am told that Professor Carl Rosander's encyclopedic book, which includes a section on the runes, can be found on half the farmsteads in Minnesota, as can the popular grammar written by C. J. L. Almquist, who also provides an illustration of the futhork."[9]

Holmes paused to light his pipe and said: "I presume you have conveyed your doubts to the king, Professor Ohman."

"In no uncertain terms," replied Ohman, "but he remains convinced that the stone will ultimately prove to be authentic. You see, he has fallen under the spell of Magnus Larson."

This name was unfamiliar to me, but not to Holmes, who said: "You have begun to intrigue me, Professor. How did the famous novelist become involved in this business?"

"Before you answer that question, I should like to know who this Larson is," I told Holmes.

"He is a writer, highly regarded by his fellow Swedes. I first ran across his books in Stockholm. As I recall, he is writing a series of novels about the experience of Swedish immigrants in America."

"You are right again, Mr. Holmes," said Ohman. "But what is most interesting is that Larson was in Minnesota last fall, supposedly doing research for his next book. In fact, he was staying only ten miles away from the farm where the stone was discovered. I find that to be a most amazing coincidence."

"It certainly raises questions," Holmes acknowledged. "Are you suggesting that Mr. Larson perpetrated the hoax, if that is what it was?"

"I think it entirely possible. The man in my estimation is a mountebank. Oh, he claims to be an historian and an expert on runes, but in fact his only real talent is for writing fiction. Nonetheless, he has managed to convince the king that he, the mighty Magnus Larson, will prove beyond any possible doubt that the stone is genuine."

"And just how will he go about doing that?" Holmes asked.

Ohman shrugged and said: "Who can say? I am sure he will weave some magical story and buttress it with all manner of supposed proofs. Given how gullible many runologists seem to be these days, I fear he will find numerous supporters. I know Mr. Larson quite well—I once debated him during a runology conference in Stockholm—and he is a man who craves notoriety above all else. If he can somehow convince the king and the rest of the world that the stone is genuine, well, he will be very famous. It makes me sick to think of such a thing."

Ohman paused for a moment, as though the thought of Magnus Larson achieving such renown was simply too much to bear, and then said in a quiet voice: "I am sorry for going on like this, Mr. Holmes. I know it is the facts you want, not my opinions. Perhaps I should back up a bit and tell you exactly how the rune stone was found and what happened thereafter."

"You have read my mind, Professor," Holmes said. "By all means, let us hear the tale."

❀ ❀ ❀

Over the next half hour Ohman, who had collected numerous newspaper articles about the rune stone, provided us with a full account of its discovery and the events which followed:

On the morning of November 15, 1898, while trying to grub out an aspen tree on a hilly portion of his land near the small community of Holandberg, a farmer named Olaf Wahlgren encountered a large stone tablet wrapped in the tree's roots. It was only after he cut away the roots that he saw the runic message carved into the stone, which was of a type known as graywacke and which was quite common to the region. Appearing to be mystified by his discovery, Wahlgren showed the stone to a neighbor, who suggested that the strange letters might in fact be runes. Word of Wahlgren's peculiar find spread quickly, and a local man with some knowledge of runes soon attempted the first translation. Several days later, Larson—who was staying in the nearby town of Alexandria—appeared at the farm. He quickly confirmed that the writing on the stone was runic and then made a translation which became widely accepted by people in the area.

"I have read that Mr. Larson was so excited by the stone that he made a cash offer for it only days later," Ohman told us. "Farmer Wahlgren was no fool, however, and apparently decided to keep the stone until more could be learned about it."

Within a couple of weeks, articles about the stone and its inscription were published by various newspapers in St. Paul, Minneapolis, and elsewhere. In preparing their articles, the newspapers consulted with linguistic experts at several universities, most notably a certain Professor George Hagen at Northwestern University just outside of Chicago.

"I do not know Professor Hagen," Ohman said, "but if he is typical of most American runologists, he has much to learn. Still, he is said to be a highly regarded scholar. He made his own translation of the stone—one which was virtually identical to Larson's—and then declared the stone to be genuine beyond a doubt. I even have a newspaper article in which he describes the stone as 'the find of the century.' What nonsense! As you can imagine, the professor's widely quoted opinion, which I am certain will in time be proved utterly wrong, did wonders for the stone's credibility, at least in America."

"And I suppose it also whetted King Oskar's interest in the stone as well," Holmes said.

"It did," Ohman acknowledged. "It also fortified the king's confidence in Magnus Larson."

Ohman went on to relate how Larson had first contacted King Oskar in December to tell him about the stone and to urge its purchase. By February of 1899, after the exchange of numerous letters and telegrams, Larson had convinced the king of the stone's significance and obtained approval to buy it on behalf of the Swedish government, contingent upon "irrefutable proof" of its authenticity.

"I assume such 'proof' has yet to arrive," Holmes said.

"You assume correctly," Ohman replied. "But I am sure that even as we speak Mr. Larson is working on his grand fairy tale for the king. He may have a problem, however, which is that there appears to be some competition for the stone."

"What do you mean?" Holmes asked.

"Well, according to the newspapers I've been reading, there is at least one other party—a certain Mrs. Frank Comstock—interested in acquiring the stone from Olaf Wahlgren. This Mrs. Comstock is said to be the widow of a rich farmer in the area. The poor woman must believe the stone is real. One account claims she has already offered five hundred dollars for the stone."

Displaying a rare smile, Ohman added: "It is a terrible thing to say, Mr. Holmes, but I hope she buys the damn thing. She would save me—and the king—a great deal of trouble by doing so."

"I am surprised that a farmer such as Mr. Wahlgren wouldn't jump at the chance to make five hundred dollars on the stone," I noted. "He probably doesn't earn that much in a typical year."

Ohman nodded and said: "You are right. I can only conclude that he has gotten greedy and thinks there is an even larger fortune to be made from Mr. Larson. In any case, that is where the situation stands today. The stone remains in Wahlgren's possession while Magnus Larson continues to gather evidence in an effort to show that it is indeed genuine. He has promised the king he will have such evidence by the end of next month."

"I see," said Holmes, who stood up and went over to the window near his desk. He gazed out at the city for a moment, then turned around and said to Ohman: "Now, sir, let us come at last to the point. What is it that you—and King Oskar, of course—would like me to do? Certainly, you do not need me to determine whether the stone's inscription is genuine. You are a far greater expert than I in such matters. Besides, I should think that the language of the inscription will always be controversial, given the debates which have long raged over the runic alphabet and its proper interpretation."

"What you have said is true, Mr. Holmes," Ohman acknowledged. "That is why I believe the stone's authenticity can only be proved, or disproved, in another way. What is needed is hard proof from the scene of its discovery: proof that the stone was indeed found in the manner described by Olaf Wahlgren, proof that no one locally might have produced the inscription, proof that the chisel marks are not of recent manufacture—proof, in short, that the stone itself cannot under any circumstances be a modern forgery. I should add that the king is in agreement on all of these points."

Holmes smiled and said: "Why, it sounds, Professor, as though what the king needs above all else is a good detective."

"He does, and there is one name at the top of his list. He has authorized me to ask you if you would be willing to take on this assignment. It would, of course, entail a trip to Minnesota."

Holmes turned to me and said: "Well, Watson, what do you think? Are you prepared for a third adventure in the New World?"

I will not deny that the prospect of yet another trip to Minnesota was hardly pleasing to me. Our previous visits there had put Holmes in great jeopardy, and I did not relish the idea of tempting fate once again so far from home. Yet I also knew that life for Holmes would soon become unbearable unless he could find a case to satisfy his craving for adventure. The rune stone affair, I suspected, would be just such an adventure; and so I told him: "I shall go wherever you go, Holmes."

"Very well then," said Holmes with his customary decisiveness.

"We will look into this affair, and if there is fakery involved, you may rest assured that Watson and I will ferret it out."

"That is wonderful news," Ohman replied with a broad grin. "I shall wire the king at once and let him know that you are on the case."

Holmes nodded and said: "Incidentally, do you happen to have a copy of the rune stone's inscription with you? I should like to see it."

"I have a copy in my case," Ohman said, and he brought it out at once for our inspection. Written on a sheet of foolscap, the inscription was entirely meaningless to me, but Holmes pored over it with the enthusiasm of a schoolboy trying to decipher some secret code. I have included a copy of it here, along with a translation provided by Professor Ohman:

8 GOTHS AND 22 NORWEGIANS ON EXPLORATION FROM

VINLAND THROUGH THE WEST. WE HAD CAMP [BY] 2 SKERRIES

[ISLANDS] ONE DAY'S JOURNEY NORTH FROM THIS STONE. WE

WERE [OUT] AND FISHED ONE DAY. AFTER WE CAME HOME [WE]

FOUND 10 MEN RED WITH BLOOD AND DEAD. A V M SAVE [US]

FROM EVIL.

[WE] HAVE 10 MEN BY THE SEA TO LOOK AFTER OUR SHIPS

14 DAYS' JOURNEY FROM THIS ISLAND. YEAR 1362.

"It is quite a haunting story in its own way," said Holmes, "if there is any truth to it."

As it turned out, however, a strange story of another kind was about to play itself out, and the travails which may or may not have been suffered by ancient Viking explorers were soon to be the least of our worries.

Chapter Two

T he Cunard Line's schedule was such that it was not until March 20 that we were able to depart on our journey. Holmes used this waiting period to immerse himself more deeply than ever in the mysteries of the runes. Indeed, by the time we left for New York on the *Campania*, he was able to write the entire futhork with great ease and had also become what he described as a "fair translator" of runic writing. Holmes also made a point of acquainting himself with various archaeological controversies and hoaxes, especially those in America.

"I am now well posted on the Davenport Tablets, the Newark Holy Stone, the Grave Creek controversy, and the remarkable petroglyphs of Dighton Rock," he reported to me not long before we left for America. "I can only conclude from the evidence of these dubious artifacts that what the late Mr. Phineas T. Barnum liked to call 'humbug' is a flourishing industry in America."[1]

"Then I take it that you are already certain that the Minnesota rune stone is a fraud," I said.

"No, Watson, I am not," Holmes replied to my surprise. "It is rather like the famous case of the little boy who cried wolf. The mere fact that there have been numerous other cases of fakery does not mean the rune stone must inevitably fall in that category. I shall maintain an open mind, but I shall—in one way or another—get to the truth. Of that you may be certain."

Before we left, Holmes took one other preparatory step. He sent a telegram to our friend and patron in St. Paul, James J. Hill, who was most pleased to hear that we would be making yet another visit to Minnesota. Although the railroad baron thought the rune stone to be a "perfect piece of nonsense," he nonetheless offered to collect articles relating to the artifact and make them available to Holmes upon our arrival in St. Paul.

The wonders of modern transportation are such that only nine days after leaving our apartment in London we found ourselves sitting once again in the sumptuous library of James J. Hill's mansion in St. Paul. Both our Atlantic crossing and our forty-hour rail trip from New York had been accomplished without incident. Holmes, who was not an enthusiastic traveler, had been poor company the entire distance, preferring his books to any sort of conversation. I therefore felt some measure of relief when we finally reached St. Paul, where I knew Holmes would emerge from his shell once the prospect of an active investigation lay before him.

Upon our arrival, we were met at the Union Depot by Joseph Pyle, Hill's longtime confidant and editor of the St. Paul *Daily Globe*, one of several large dailies which flourished in the city. Pyle was a well-tested, thoroughly reliable man who had been of particular help to us during our investigation of the ice palace murders three years earlier. Now, he shook our hands with his usual vigor and enthusiasm.

"My God, but it is good to see the two of you again!" he said, smiling broadly. "I trust you had a pleasant journey."

"We did," Holmes said, speaking for himself.

"Well then, we'd best be on our way," Pyle said. "Mr. Hill is anxious to see you. I have a carriage waiting, and you'll be pleased to know that it is much warmer than it was on your last visit."

"For which we are most thankful," I said, recalling the bitter subzero cold which had assailed us in January of 1896 during the ice palace affair, when the magnificent crystalline structure at the center of St. Paul's celebrated winter carnival became the scene of awful criminality and grisly death. The very thought of that case, which had taken Holmes and me to the heart of a dark conspiracy reaching to the highest echelons of power in St. Paul, still caused chills to run down my spine. In expectation of more biting cold, I had brought along my heaviest coat, but I was now pleased to discover that I did not need it, for the cool, damp, and cloudy weather we encountered in St. Paul was almost identical to the conditions we had left in London.

As we made our way through the commercial portion of the city, which seemed to have changed little since our last visit, Holmes inquired about Shadwell Rafferty, with whom we had corresponded regularly since the days of the ice palace case. Rafferty's long and entertaining letters, which he sent punctually the first of every month, had kept us so well informed of the goings-on in St. Paul that it almost seemed as though we had never left the city.

"Shad's just fine," Pyle told us. "Got his nose in all sorts of business, as usual. I sometimes wonder how he finds time to run that saloon of his, but I guess that with Shad, anything is possible. I was hoping he could meet us today, but he's off fishing somewhere. Word has it that he's out to catch a record pike up north. At least that's what I'm told by George Thomas, whom I'm sure you remember."

"How could we forget that noble barman?" said Holmes, referring to the large, handsome black man who was Rafferty's chief assistant. "Indeed, had it not been for his timely intervention, I might still be spinning in circles on Mr. Rafferty's back!"

Pyle could not help breaking out in laughter at the mention of this incident, which had occurred when Holmes attempted to subdue the drunken Rafferty and was tossed around like a rag doll for his troubles.

"By heavens, that was a sight, Mr. Holmes!" said Pyle. "You were hanging on for dear life! You might still be spinning if George hadn't come to the rescue. Fortunately, Shad has had no encounters with John Barleycorn since that memorable evening, so I don't think you need worry about taking another spin."

After a short ride through the gray, chilly city we arrived at Hill's mansion, which occupied a prominent site on the steep bluffs overlooking the commercial district and the Mississippi River. The mansion itself looked as grim and imposing as ever, with its massive walls of dark red sandstone and its great, many-chimneyed roof. Once we had pulled beneath the porte cochere and alit from our carriage, the Empire Builder himself greeted us at the front door. Before long, the four of us were seated in his comfortable library, sipping fine French brandy and smoking excellent Cuban cigars.

Hill himself looked just as I remembered him, for like some great rock-bound mountain he seemed impervious to the advance of age. Time had not eroded his stocky and powerful body or the great smooth dome of his forehead, nor had it weakened his most notable feature—the imperious gaze (he had but one good eye) which took in the world with the hard, haughty confidence of a king.

After we had exchanged the usual pleasantries, Hill—as was his wont—got down to business at once.

"I have had Joseph gather some material for you," he told Holmes, handing him a thick folder of newspaper and magazine clippings. "But I am surprised that you would come all this way to investigate what strikes me as an obvious fake."

With a slight smile, Holmes replied: "I must tell you that Dr. Watson, who is otherwise such a romantic, shares your sentiments, Mr. Hill. Even so, I am willing to give the stone the benefit of the doubt. I will tell you this, however. If the stone is a forgery, it appears to be a surprisingly good one, and that alone merits my attention. Besides, as Dr. Watson will tell you, I have had little to occupy my attention in recent weeks, and I therefore thought it not inappropriate to take on this curious matter, especially since the king of Sweden requested me to do so."

Holmes now explained our visit from Professor Ohman and King

Oskar's desire to resolve the issue of the stone's authenticity once and for all.

"I don't suppose you'd let me print up some of this in the *Globe*," said Pyle, though I think he knew what the answer would be.

"No, Mr. Pyle, I do not wish our presence here publicized in any way," Holmes said. "The king wants to be as discreet as possible in this matter, as do I."

"Too bad," replied the newspaper editor. "It would be an incredible story."

Hill, whose many possessions included the *Globe*, now intervened: "Joseph, will you never stop dreaming of a scoop? I swear, there must be something in the blood of journalists which causes them to pant like hungry dogs at the prospect of beating their competition. However, you need not worry, Mr. Holmes, your secret is safe with us."

"A fact which I never doubted," replied Holmes in his most gallant manner.

"Very well then," said Hill, "I suppose you and Dr. Watson are eager to go about your business. What can I do to help you?"

"At the moment, I shall require nothing more than a pair of railroad tickets to Holandberg, the community near which the rune stone was found. Can it be reached by your Great Northern?"

"Nearly," replied Hill. "It is about ten miles from the much larger city of Alexandria, which is one of our main stops in the western part of the state."

"How long a trip is it?" I asked.

"About 120 miles," said Hill. "If you catch the morning train, it shouldn't take you more than four hours. Once you're in Alexandria, I can have a carriage and driver ready to take you to Holandberg. I presume you wish to meet the farmer—Wahlgren, is that his name?—who claims to have found the rune stone."

"I do," said Holmes. "I am anxious to hear Mr. Wahlgren's story. I shall also want to see the stone and the site where it supposedly was uncovered. What time is the morning train?"

"Nine a.m. sharp," said Pyle.

"Then we shall be on it," Holmes said. "Incidentally, do you happen to know whether Magnus Larson, who is apparently the stone's chief defender, is still in the vicinity of Holandberg?"

"I believe so. In fact, as I recall there was a mention of him in one of the more recent articles," said Pyle as he began paging through the folder filled with clippings. "Ah, here it is. According to a story dated March 24 in the Alexandria *Clarion*"—which was the very same newspaper from which Ohman had obtained so much information—"Mr. Larson is most definitely in Alexandria. The article says, and I quote, 'Mr. Magnus Larson, our distinguished Swedish visitor, told the *Clarion* this morning that he will soon reveal new evidence proving conclusively that the rune stone is genuine. "The scoffers will be forced to swallow their ugly words," he said, adding that because of the rune stone Alexandria will one day be regarded as the birthplace of America.' "

Pyle handed the article to Holmes, who read it in its entirety, then said: "Mr. Larson does not appear to be a man bashful in the presence of hyperbole."

"So it would seem," Pyle agreed with a smile.

The dinner bell now rang and we made for the dining room, where Hill's wife and large family joined us. The younger children in particular were full of questions for Holmes, who regaled them with stories of our many adventures, and it was nearly nine o'clock by the time we left the table. Although Holmes showed no signs of weariness, I went to bed at once, knowing that the next day would be long and demanding.

When I arose early the next morning, I found Hill and Holmes already at the breakfast table, discussing bulls and how best to breed them. The details were quite earthy, but that did not deter Hill, for whom the subject obviously held great interest. In fact, he described the reproductive activities of his most cherished bull—a Jersey named Berkeley Duke of Oxford—in such graphic terms that one of the female servants fled the room.[2]

"Tell me, Dr. Watson, have you ever watched a bull mate?" Hill asked as I piled buckwheat pancakes, a rasher of bacon, and fried potatoes on my plate.

"I cannot say I have had occasion to witness such a thing," I replied, "but I think I am reasonably well acquainted with how it is accomplished."

"By Jove, that is an excellent answer, my dear Watson!" said Holmes, who appeared to be enjoying the conversation immensely. This was most peculiar, since I had never known Holmes to be interested in animal husbandry, and so I wondered how the topic had come up in the first place.

The answer was not long in coming, for after a few more passing remarks, Holmes said: "I have heard, Mr. Hill, that you maintain a farm in the Red River country to the north. Perhaps as a result you have come in contact with a woman named Mrs. Frank Comstock, who I understand owns a large farm in that region, presumably with her husband."

"I don't know the lady, but I certainly knew Frank Comstock," Hill said, in a tone of voice which left little doubt as to his opinion of the man. "He was nothing but a plunger, one of those fellows who farmed as a hobby while he tried to make his fortune at the Chicago Board of Trade buying and selling commodities. Like all of his breed, he had little regard for the future of the Northwest."

"Since you speak of him in the past tense," said Holmes, "am I to presume that Mr. Comstock is dead?"

"He is, and I can tell you all about it, because that wife of his tried to sue the Great Northern," Hill said, his famous temper now beginning to show itself. "You see, Frank Comstock, who was probably drunk at the time, fell off one of our trains and managed to kill himself. It happened last year — up near Alexandria, as a matter of fact. As I said, I don't know his wife, but she found a lawyer quick as could be and tried to sue the Great Northern. Claimed negligence and all the usual nonsense. Well, our attorneys put a stop to that. She didn't get a penny and she didn't deserve one! People need to be careful aboard trains, and if they are not, then they must face the consequences."

The topic of lawsuits clearly irritated Hill—I recalled him giving a somewhat similar speech during the course of the Red Demon affair—and Holmes wisely decided not to intervene while the great man, like one of his locomotives, vented excess steam. It was only after Hill had calmed down that Holmes made further inquiries about Mrs. Comstock.

"Well, in any event," he said, "I suppose the lady still has the farm, which must be quite valuable in its own right."

"It is," Hill said. "Comstock built up one of the largest bonanza farms in the Red River Valley. I believe he had about twenty thousand acres under cultivation, all in wheat."

Turning to me, Hill added: "Why, it is likely, Dr. Watson, that the wheat in the pancakes you're now enjoying came from Comstock's farm, or one like it. The bonanzas are far and away the largest provider of wheat to the Minneapolis millers."

"And just what are these bonanza farms?" I asked.

To my surprise, the answer came from Holmes: "I have been doing a little reading on that very topic, Watson. The bonanzas are extremely large, highly mechanized farms, many of which were founded after the Northern Pacific Railroad, which had large land grants in the area, encountered severe financial problems during the Panic of 1873. Faced with the prospect of imminent failure, the railroad offered to exchange its bonds for its one reliable asset—land. As a result, a number of bondholders and speculators came into possession of huge tracts of virgin prairie in Minnesota and North Dakota. To make their newly acquired land pay, these investors then turned to wheat growing on a vast and unprecedented scale."[3]

Hill shook his head in admiration and said: "You are an amazing man, Mr. Holmes. I could not have given a better explanation myself. Comstock, from what I've heard, owned plenty of Northern Pacific bonds, and that's how he ended up as a gentleman farmer, though I doubt he ever turned a spadeful of dirt himself."

"Are these huge farms still operating?" I asked.

"Some are," Hill said, "but many of them have already been subdivided, because the land can be sold at great profit. Comstock, on the other hand, always held out. I suppose he thought he'd get a better price by waiting. Or maybe he needed the land as collateral, since he was a trader first and a farmer second."

"What else can you tell me about the gentleman?" Holmes inquired.

Hill cast a knowing look at Holmes before responding with a question of his own: "And just why are you so interested in Frank Comstock, Mr. Holmes?"

Holmes now explained Mrs. Comstock's interest in purchasing the rune stone, a fact of which Hill had been unaware and which clearly struck him as odd. Said Hill: "I can't imagine why she'd want to get involved in a piece of foolishness like that stone."

Holmes now consulted his pocket watch, rose from his chair, and said: "Ah, Watson, you had best work quickly on those bonanza pancakes of yours. It is nearly eight, and we must be packed and ready to leave by half past so that we do not miss the train."

Hill, too, arose, for it was already past the normal time he left for his office. "Well, good luck to you gentlemen," he said, "though I think you are on a fool's errand. Still, if there is anything you should need while out in the prairie country, you know where to reach me."

Holmes gave a slight bow and said: "As always, Mr. Hill, your hospitality is nonpareil. I am hopeful, however, that our 'fool's errand' will prove to be rather more interesting and productive than you might expect."

"We shall see about that," said the Empire Builder, "but I fear the two of you are in the position of Berkeley Duke of Oxford trying to mate with an infertile cow: that is to say, you will expend much effort but achieve no fruitful result."

"Well," replied Holmes with a smile, "let us hope that, like the Duke, we at least enjoy ourselves in the process."

When we had finished packing and were ready to leave for the depot, Holmes took me aside and said: "I think it best that we travel incognito from this point on, Watson, so as not to unduly arouse the natives. I see no reason not to use the names we employed on our previous visits to Minnesota. Therefore, I shall be John Baker and you shall once again present yourself to the world as Peter Smith."

"Very well," I said, "and what shall our occupations be? In Hinckley, as I recall, we masqueraded as correspondents for *The Times*. I should think that arrangement would also be suitable this time."

Holmes shook his head. "No, Watson, we shall need a different, more convincing cover for this affair. Here, what do you think of this?"

Holmes now handed me a business card which he apparently had had printed in London before our departure. It said: JOHN BAKER, ASSISTANT CURATOR, SCANDINAVIAN ARCHIVES, BRITISH MUSEUM.

"Very impressive," I said. "But what shall I be?"

"Why, you shall be an assistant to the assistant curator."

"But I know nothing about Scandinavian art or history," I protested.

"I, on the other hand, do," said Holmes, "so you shall have to let me do all of the talking."

"As you would do in any case," I said, a remark to which Holmes's only reply was a small, crooked smile.

At the depot, which was not as busy as it had been on our arrival in St. Paul the day before, we were able to board our train without delay, and soon we were on our way west to what Hill had called the "prairie country." I was anxious to see this landscape, for the American West always fascinated me, as it did, I suspect, most visitors from the close and crowded quarters of Europe.

It took us more than an hour, however, to break free of our urban bounds, since our first stop was in Minneapolis, which we reached after crossing the Mississippi River near the Falls of St. Anthony. A great number of new passengers boarded at the depot here, and our car was full as we departed for points west and north. At last, however, we began to reach more open country, though we stopped every eight to ten miles at the small towns which had sprung up along the tracks.

These towns, platted in most cases by the railroad itself, all looked much alike, and I cannot say that they were especially impressive.

Each town was organized around a central street lined with wooden or brick store buildings seldom more than two stories high. A few streets intersected or paralleled this main thoroughfare to form the standard American gridiron. Here could be found the town's modest dwellings, almost invariably built of wood and always set amid substantial yards, since it is a well-observed fact that Americans, especially those in the western regions of the country, demand ample space for themselves. The charm of the English country village was nowhere evident in these communities, though Holmes reminded me that most of the towns we passed through were probably thirty years old at best.

Still, almost every one of these remote and rather drab towns was marked by an exceptional object which commanded the skyline much as a church or castle would in Europe. But the only lord served by these tall wooden structures — known as elevators — was grain. Holmes shared my fascination with these agricultural goliaths, which were quite unlike anything I had ever seen in England, and said we would have to make it a point to tour one of them before returning to St. Paul.

If the towns we passed through seemed monotonous, the landscape was even more so. Late March and early April, Pyle had informed us before we left, was not the lovely early spring season in Minnesota which it was in so many other places, and I could see now what he meant. The ragged, open land all about us was brown and barren, with trees bereft of foliage and small patches of snow still scattered amid the scrawny windrows sheltering farm fields. I could only imagine how desolate this landscape must have seemed to its inhabitants during Minnesota's long winters.

After we had passed the bustling city of St. Cloud, however, the terrain grew more attractive as our train wound past low wooded hills and numerous small lakes. I noticed that these bodies of water had not yet been emancipated from their wintry mantle of ice and remarked on this fact to Holmes, who said: "I have noticed the same thing, Watson. It makes me wonder just what sort of fishing expedition our friend Mr. Rafferty has undertaken, since the ice appears to be too thin to support a man and too thick for a boat."

"Let us just hope he is not out on the ice," I said, thinking back to our life-threatening excursion across the frozen Mississippi three years earlier.

"Mr. Rafferty, I am sure, can take care of himself," Holmes replied. "But you have my word of honor, Watson, that I shall not set one foot on anything that even resembles a frozen lake, pond, or river."

It was just after one o'clock when we reached Alexandria, which was the largest town we had seen since St. Cloud. We had hardly gotten off the train when a small but well-built man dressed in a black trenchcoat came up to greet us. The man had a face as round as a pumpkin and soft brown eyes which took us in with a look verging somewhere between sympathy and wonderment.

"I'm George Kensington," he announced. "I own the livery here in town, among other things. Would you by chance be the English gents coming to look at the rune stone?"

"We are," Holmes said.

"Well, then, I guess you haven't heard."

"No," said Holmes, as mystified by this statement as I was, "we haven't."

"Then I must tell you. They found Olaf Wahlgren dead this morning, his skull split down the middle like a ripe watermelon. Someone took an ax to the poor man, they did. As for that famous rune stone of his, well, it's gone. Now ain't that something!"

"Indeed," said Sherlock Holmes, a gleam of excitement in his eyes. "Indeed it is."

Chapter Three
"JUST WHO EXACTLY MIGHT THE TWO OF YOU BE?"

"**W**ell," said I after hearing this dreadful news, "what are we to do now?"

"Really, Mr. Smith, I am surprised you should ask such a question," replied Holmes with an unseemly grin. "We must go at once and see if we can be of any help to the authorities. Mr. Kensington, how far is it to Olaf Wahlgren's farm?"

"Just under ten miles."

"Then by all means let us go there as quickly as possible. Time is wasting."

"As you wish," said Kensington, setting his team of fine roans into motion with a shake of the reins.

It took but a few minutes to put the rather limited charms of Alexandria behind us and reach the open countryside to the south, which was characterized by short, steep hills interposed among numerous small swamps. Wherever possible, farmers had established their fields, but it must have been hard and unpromising work, for the rough and rocky landscape did not have the look of an agricultural paradise. I mentioned this observation to Kensington, who quickly concurred:

"You're right, sir. Most of the land hereabouts is better suited to grazing cows than growing corn or wheat, but that doesn't stop the Swedes and Germans and all the rest from trying to eke out a crop. They'll all die poor, if you ask me."

"And what of Mr. Wahlgren?" asked Holmes. "Was he one of those poor farmers of whom you speak?"

"Now, sir, I do not wish to speak ill of the dead—" began Kensington before he was cut off by Holmes, who said:

"The dead deserve our honesty just as must the living, Mr. Kensington. So do not hesitate to speak what is on your mind, since Mr. Wahlgren is now no doubt in a better place, where the opinion of mankind, whether kindly or harsh, is utterly insignificant."

"Well, that is quite a way of putting it, sir, but I guess you are right," said Kensington. "What I will tell you is this: Olaf was cleverer than most, I would judge, but not clever enough to get himself a prime piece of land. That farm of his is about the worst property in the county. It's nothing but gravel hills and swampland. But I don't say you can blame him. He arrived late at the dinner table, so he got the leftovers."

"Most interesting," murmured Holmes, though I could not see why he was so fascinated by the poor quality of Wahlgren's farm. "When exactly did Mr. Wahlgren arrive in the vicinity of Holandberg?"

Kensington scratched the back of his head and vigorously rubbed his chin, as though pondering some especially intricate problem in the higher realm of calculus, and finally said: "It was about eight or nine years ago, as best I can recollect. The county abstract clerk could give you the exact date, I'm sure, but it must have been right around 1890. Now, most of the best land in the county was gone by 1880, '85 for sure, so Olaf just had to make do with what he could get."

"I see. I take it, therefore, that his farm was not particularly successful."

This comment drew a snort from Kensington. "You take it right, sir. Fact is, the place was always pretty much of a sty. And with four mouths to feed, well, it was tough to eke out a living."

"Ah, so he was a married man. Do his wife and children survive him?"

"The children do," Kensington replied. "His wife—a dear woman she was—died, well, it must have been six years ago. The influenza took her just like that. Then, last fall, not long after Olaf dug up the stone, his son—that would be Olaf Jr.—just up and left one day. I guess he couldn't stand it on the farm anymore. Can't say as I blame him. Last I heard, he was supposedly out west somewhere. So that just leaves his daughter, Moony."

"What a strange name," I noted.

"It's not her real name," Kensington said, sounding apologetic. "Moira is the name she was born with, but everybody calls her Moony."

"And why is that?" Holmes asked.

Kensington said: "Well, I guess if you ever met her, you'd understand. She's a sweet child, and the wife and I love her dearly. It's just that she's a little different, that's all. People who don't know any better call her slow, but they're wrong. Like I said, she's just different."

"I see," Holmes said. "Tell me, how old is she?"

"Sixteen. In fact, we had a nice birthday party for her at our house just last week."

This last statement obviously intrigued Holmes, for he thought for a moment and then asked: "Will young Moony be out at the farm now, do you suppose?"

The question appeared to surprise Kensington, who said: "Oh, no. Didn't I tell you? She lives with Elsie—that's my wife—and me. Has for several months. I guess we're the only family she has now. Poor child."

"How did she happen to come into your household, if I may ask?"

For the first time, Kensington seemed reticent, and he stared out straight ahead over the horses, as though surveying the horizon for an answer, before he finally said: "It is a thing I would rather not talk about, sir. There were problems with her father. He did not treat her right in my estimation, and when she came to us, we took her in. She is happy now, and that is all that matters."

"But she is, I take it, aware of her father's death?"

"We have told her," Kensington replied curtly, his tone of voice leaving little doubt that he wished to hear no more upon the subject of Olaf Wahlgren's daughter.

Holmes understood this at once and moved to other matters. After readjusting the heavy woolen blanket across our laps, which provided some protection from the chill, he said: "Tell me, Mr. Kensington, what do people hereabouts think about the rune stone? Did they believe it to be real, or is it simply regarded as a forgery concocted by Mr. Wahlgren in an attempt to enrich himself?"

"Well now, that is a good question, sir, a very good question. I would have to say opinion is divided, yes it is. Some folks think Olaf was just trying to pull a fast one, that's for sure, but plenty of others are happy to believe he made a great discovery. The Swedes in particular are of a mind that the stone is the genuine article. The local Norwegians, on the other hand, can pretty much be counted on to be against whatever the Swedes are in favor of. The Germans, as far as I can tell, don't much care one way or the other. But there's been lots of arguing back and forth, and always will be, I suppose."[1]

"And what of you, Mr. Kensington? Where do you stand amid this great controversy?"

Kensington turned back toward Holmes and gave him a sly, knowing smile. "Where I stand, sir, depends on where I am. If I am out among the Swedes, why, I am all for the stone. But if I am in town among the skeptics, well then, I am as big a doubter as any. You see, there is no advantage to arguing about the stone, none at all, because you can't change anybody's mind. It's a religious thing with people hereabouts, sir, and you might as well take sides with the Catholics or the Lutherans as argue over that stone. At least, that's my view of the matter."

"Mr. Kensington, it is obvious you are a wise man," Holmes said, "and I salute your wisdom. But I am curious about one thing. You mentioned to us earlier that the unfortunate Mr. Wahlgren's skull was, as you put it so colorfully, 'split down the middle like a ripe watermelon.' Am I to take it that you saw the poor man's body?"

"Why, of course," replied Kensington, who reached down under his seat and removed a tall black hat, which he promptly placed upon his head. "I guess you gents would have no way of knowing that I'm also the only undertaker in Douglas County, not to mention director of the local historical society and member of the town council. Why, I took the deceased's body into town not long before I picked you up."

This unexpected revelation was, of course, akin to manna from heaven for Holmes, who immediately peppered Kensington with all manner of questions regarding Olaf Wahlgren's murder. Over the next hour, as we made our way to the victim's farm along roads that became increasingly bumpy, Kensington was able to fill us in on virtually all the salient features of the case.

He told us that Wahlgren's body had been found at about seven o'clock that morning in his barn. "One of his neighbors, a farmer named Lars Olson, came over to borrow a tool of some kind. Lars got no answer at the house, so he went over to the barn, figuring he'd find Olaf there. Well, you can imagine the shock he got when he saw the body. None of the farmers hereabouts have telephones, so Lars rushed as fast as he could into Holandberg and roused the town constable, who dialed up Sheriff Boehm in Alexandria."

"What time did the sheriff arrive at the murder scene?" Holmes inquired.

"Right around half past eight," Kensington said. "I know because I came with him. So did a couple of other fellows from town. We found the body sprawled out by a manure pit at the rear of the barn. Like I said, there was no mystery about what killed him. His skull was split almost clean in two by a bloody ax we found near the barn door. You might be interested to know we also found a shotgun next to Olaf's body."

"Really? Could you tell if it had been fired recently?"

"Didn't smell like it. But it was loaded, I'll tell you that."

Holmes then went on to ask a number of questions about Wahlgren's head wound. He learned that the wound had already clotted by the time the sheriff arrived, leading Kensington—who had some experience in such matters—to conclude that death must have occurred several hours earlier.

"Did the sheriff—Mr. Boehm, I believe you said his name was—conduct a search of the barn and other areas of the farm for evidence?"

"He did," Kensington confirmed. "Gus Boehm is nobody's fool. We went through the barn and the house and all the outbuildings with a fine-tooth comb. Didn't find anything amiss. Of course, we didn't find the rune stone, either."

"Where had the stone been kept before it disappeared?"

"Well, the fact is, nobody seems to have any idea where Olaf put the stone, so I guess there's no way of knowing for sure if it was stolen. But I'll tell you this: I don't think he owned anything else worth getting killed over."

"Just how big is the stone?" Holmes asked.

"Oh, it's got some size to it. I'd say it's about two and a half feet high, maybe half as wide, and about four to six inches thick."

"And how much would a stone such as that weigh?"

"It's not light, that's for sure," Kensington replied. "I suppose it would weigh at least a couple of hundred pounds."

"Thank you. Pray, continue."

Kensington went on to tell us that the sheriff's preliminary investigation at the farm had turned up no obvious clues beyond the bloody ax. As a result, Kensington had been instructed just after ten in the morning to remove Wahlgren's body to Alexandria, where the county coroner would perform an autopsy.

Holmes was about to ask another question when we came over a slight rise and saw a farmstead directly ahead. A number of wagons and at least one carriage were parked around in the yard, where a surprising number of people could be seen milling about.

"Here we are," said Kensington, coaxing his team forward at a faster pace. "It looks like Olaf's place has become quite an attraction."

❖   ❖   ❖

As we pulled into the narrow road leading up to the house, I could see that Kensington had not exaggerated the woeful condition of Wahlgren's farm, which despite its short tenure on the land had already acquired a look of profound dilapidation. The largest structure on the property was a wooden barn which showed no evidence of paint and which leaned noticeably to one side, suggesting that the first good wind might send it crashing to the ground. Nearby, the rusting blades of a tall metal windmill rattled in the breeze, and I wondered how Wahlgren could have endured its constant racket.

Wahlgren's small house, which was about a hundred yards along a diagonal path from the barn, looked equally decrepit and forlorn, its paint peeling badly and one corner of its sagging front porch propped up by a long wooden plank. The yard between these two shabby structures was littered with equipment and resembled nothing so much as an outdoor museum devoted to the display of rust in all its stages of progression. Elsewhere, small piles of wooden debris—boards, shingling, parts of old posts—added to the atmosphere of disorder and decay, as did the ill-kept barbed-wire fencing around a pasture south of the barn.

"Mr. Wahlgren's farm is not exactly an advertisement for the unbounded joys of the pastoral life," Holmes remarked as we alit from our carriage, which Kensington was forced to park well back from the house because several wagons were blocking our way.

"I guess that's one way of putting it," Kensington said. "Anyway, I'll introduce you to the sheriff, assuming he's still here."

"That would be most helpful," said Holmes, who clearly was itching to make his own inspection of the scene of the crime. It would not, however, be the sort of pristine environment favored by Holmes, for I could see at least a dozen people wandering to no apparent purpose amid the bucolic disarray of Wahlgren's farmyard.

As we walked down the road to the house, I was surprised to find that no one asked for our identification or otherwise challenged our approach. Holmes was also struck by this situation and said to Kensington: "I find it odd that the authorities have not cordoned off the farm so that there will be no contamination of whatever evidence may be present."

Kensington responded with a shrug and said: "I can't explain it either. Gus is usually pretty careful about such things. But I guess there's never been a murder like this in Douglas County."

"Well then, perhaps we can be of some assistance to the sheriff," Holmes said. "I have not mentioned this to you before, out of respect for my friend's modesty, but it so happens that Mr. Smith spent several years working for Scotland Yard prior to joining the staff at the museum."

I had no warning that Holmes would depict me in this manner, and I could only suppose that he had decided to play one of his infernal games at my expense.

Kensington appraised me with a rather skeptical look, then said: "Is that a fact? I would sure like to know, Mr. Smith, what Scotland Yard would do in a case like this."

I was not entirely without ideas in this regard and was about to reply when Holmes, who could be unspeakably rude at times, cut me off.

"What I am sure Mr. Smith was going to say is that the first step would be to look at the scene of the crime and study it in the most minute detail. Isn't that right, Mr. Smith?"

Since Holmes had invested me with newly discovered powers, I decided to use them. "No, Mr. Baker, I think our first step should be to introduce ourselves to the sheriff and find out what he has learned thus far. Now, Mr. Kensington, if you would kindly lead us to the sheriff, both Mr. Baker and I would be most grateful."

I cannot adequately describe the look which Holmes now gave me other than to say it was of the kind he might normally have reserved for the contemplation of an especially large and venomous snake. I merely smiled in return.

We found Sheriff Gustavus Boehm inside the farmhouse, where he sat at a small table in the kitchen sorting through a stack of papers, which appeared to be receipts of some kind.

"God, what a mess," he said, ignoring our entry for the moment as his eyes swept the kitchen, which was indeed in a state of considerable disarray. Dirty dishware was piled up all about, while a miscellany of objects—an old dustpan filigreed with spiderwebs, a stack of yellowed newspapers, a screwdriver with part of its handle broken off—lay scattered like so much flotsam and jetsam on the room's rough plank floor. "All these Swede farmers are alike," Boehm now complained aloud, still ignoring our presence. "They buy a few pigs and they start to live like them."

The author of this rather insulting statement was, to my surprise, strikingly handsome, with long, curly brown hair, a well-tended mustache above thin lips, and the sort of sharp, chiseled bone structure one often found in men drawn to the military life. The sheriff was also quite young, and I put his age at not much past forty. When he finally looked up at us, Boehm's dark brown eyes registered a kind of irritated curiosity, and he said in a flat baritone:

"Well, what have you dragged in now, George. Looks like a couple of tourists."

"I suppose you might call us that," said Holmes affably, "but we are tourists with a special itinerary. You see, we have come all the way from England to examine the famous rune stone. But I fear that may prove more difficult than we thought."

"You've got that right," said the sheriff, "unless you happen to have a magic wand that will show me where Olaf hid the thing. Now, just who exactly might the two of you be?"

Holmes introduced us, emphasizing our supposed credentials as authorities on runic writing.

Boehm received this information with no apparent enthusiasm, his dark eyes flashing back and forth between Holmes and me, as though he were trying to memorize our features. Then he said: "Well, I don't think there's anything for you here now."

"Perhaps not," said Holmes, still displaying his friendliest manner. "But if you do not mind, Mr. Smith and I would like to look around a bit. We have, after all, come a long way to see this very farmstead. And with so many other people already here, I fail to see how we could cause any harm."

The sheriff considered this request momentarily and then said: "All right, go ahead and satisfy your curiosity. But don't touch anything in the barn or I will be very unhappy with you. And I assure you I am not a man to be trifled with. Understand?"

"Perfectly," said Holmes. "We shall be most careful."

"The sheriff seems to be a rather strong-minded man," Holmes remarked to Kensington as we stepped back out onto the porch.

"He is that," Kensington agreed. "A lot of folks around think he's maybe a bit too strong-minded. He'll be gone next year."

"What do you mean?" I asked.

"I mean he'll never get re-elected. Gus has made a lot of enemies. He seems to enjoy his power just a little too much, and the Swedes in particular don't like a man who gets uppity. I've also heard he owes quite a bit of money around here. He plays poker all the time, but doesn't like to pay when he loses."

We now turned our attention to the crowd idling about the farmyard. It consisted largely of men in overalls who had formed into small knots and were talking in hushed tones. What few words I could hear were in a language which I assumed to be Swedish.

"And who are all these people so busily destroying whatever evidence might have been left behind by the murderer?" Holmes asked.

"Locals mostly," Kensington replied. "Something like this doesn't happen but once in a lifetime, so everybody's curious. I expect folks will be coming by all day, as long as Gus lets them. This business will be the talk of Douglas County for years to come."

"It is too bad they cannot do their talking elsewhere," Holmes muttered and then said to me: "Well, Mr. Smith, please avail us of your expertise. Do you think we might want to take a look inside the barn, where the murder occurred?"

"An excellent idea," I said. "Why don't you lead the way, Mr. Kensington."

Built of rough planks and culminating in a high, double-sloped roof of the Dutch kind, the barn was smaller than others we had seen in the area, no doubt reflecting Wahlgren's poor status as a farmer. There was no guard posted at the open door, and we went inside at once. The interior was cool and dark, the only light provided by the door opening and rows of small windows along either side. I noticed at once the barn's dense, earthy aroma—a mixture of hay, manure, and strong animal scents which brought back memories of a summer I had spent in Berkshire as a lad. Holmes, however, had no time for such pleasant recollections and immediately went about the business of inspecting the place where Olaf Wahlgren had met his violent end.

The barn's main level contained stalls for Wahlgren's draft horses and the few dairy cows he maintained, all of which had apparently been sent out to pasture. There was also a small room where harnesses and other equipment for the horses was kept. Next to this room was a workbench, above which various hand tools were affixed to the wall with hooks. Holmes made a point of examining these tools, particularly several chisels of the kind that could be used on stone. Near the center of the barn was a ladder leading to the hayloft above, and Holmes climbed up to inspect this space as well.

Once he had come back down, he told Kensington: "Show me where the body was found, and please be as precise as possible."

Kensington led us to the rear of the barn, where the light was exceptionally dim, and pointed to a spot on the dirt floor. "Right here the poor man was," he said.

As it so happened, this spot was just a few feet from the barn's manure pit, which exuded a stench so powerful that I had to bring a handkerchief up to my nose. Manure was scattered in small piles around the sides of the nearly empty and surprisingly deep pit. Neither Holmes nor Kensington appeared to be in the least affected by the terrible odor, however. Holmes by this time had found and lit a kerosene lantern, and he made a brief study of the manure pit, presumably looking for any signs of blood or tissue, before bending down to examine the place where Wahlgren's body had been discovered. The lantern's glow revealed a large crimson stain on the floor, as well as an elongated pattern of smaller splotches nearby.

"Well, Mr. Smith, what do you make of this?" Holmes asked in a rather imperious way.

"I should say Mr. Wahlgren was killed here. The large bloodstain is where he fell and where his head wound bled profusely. The other splotches are blood which splattered at the time he received the fatal blow."

Holmes raised an eyebrow and said: "Your Scotland Yard experience has served you well, Mr. Smith, for I have no doubt you are right."

After examining the bloodstains for several minutes, Holmes stood up and said to Kensington: "Tell me, sir, has anything in this part of the barn been disturbed, to your knowledge, since you first saw the body this morning?"

Kensington slowly looked all around and said: "No, I don't think so, except for the gun, of course."

"You mean the shotgun found by Mr. Wahlgren's body?"

"Yes."

"Where is that weapon?"

"The sheriff put it over there," Kensington said, pointing to a double-barreled shotgun which was leaning barrel-up against the side of a nearby horse stall. "But I don't think you should touch it. You know what Gus said."

"I do," acknowledged Holmes. "Still, there comes a time when a man has to live a little dangerously, don't you think?"

Without another word, Holmes went over to examine the weapon, breaking it open and sniffing for any sign that it had been recently fired. After he had returned the gun to its place, he said: "I agree with your earlier conclusion, Mr. Kensington. It does not appear that Mr. Wahlgren had a chance to use his weapon to defend himself."

"That's what the sheriff figures, too," Kensington said. "Olaf must have heard something in the barn, got his shotgun out, and then gone to investigate."

"So it would seem," Holmes agreed, "though one would think that a man armed with a shotgun would stand an excellent chance against an assailant armed only with an ax. Unless . . ."

"Unless what?" I asked.

"Unless there is another possibility," said Holmes, reverting to his familiar cryptic manner. Turning back to Kensington, he said: "Now, what about the numerous footprints visible in the dirt floor? Were they here this morning as well?"

Kensington stared down at the floor with a rather quizzical expression and replied: "That I can't say, sir. But as there were quite a few people here this morning, my guess is that they made most of the footprints you see."

"How unfortunate," said Holmes with something close to a sigh. "But there is nothing to be done about it now."

Chapter Four

"ROCHESTER KNOWS"

I t was well past three o'clock by the time we finally left the barn and walked out into the brisk afternoon air. A day which had seemed uncomfortably damp and chilly in the morning now took on the quality of a wonderful tonic, for the barn's fetid atmosphere had become almost more than I could tolerate. I took several deep draughts of fresh air, saw that a few stray shafts of sunlight had burned through the clouds, and for an instant thought myself the most fortunate man in the world.

Such simple delights as these, however, were lost upon Holmes, who ignored the beneficial change of atmosphere and remained deep in thought as we made our way across the farmyard toward Wahlgren's house. The crowd of curiosity seekers had by now expanded to perhaps double its former size, so that the farmyard had become a kind of fairgrounds where men in overalls, work boots, and wide-brimmed hats gathered to gaze upon the mysteries of violent death. Holmes looked upon these curiosity seekers with an irritation bordering on contempt.

"What do these people expect to find here?" he asked no one in particular. "Why don't they go home and tend to their own affairs?"

"It is just natural curiosity," I said.

"Well, I wish they would go elsewhere to be curious," said Holmes. "Murder should not be accounted a form of entertainment."

Back inside the house, we found George Kensington warming himself by the kitchen's wood stove, which someone had taken the trouble to fire up.

"Ready to head back to town?" he asked.

"Not quite yet," said Holmes. "Is the sheriff still here?"

"He went out to talk to one of the fellows in the yard. He should be back any minute."

"Good," said Holmes, striding past the startled Kensington toward a door which appeared to lead into the house's front parlor. "Mr. Smith, would you be so kind as to whistle if you see the sheriff coming. I certainly do not wish to miss his return."

"Of course," I said as Kensington gave me a questioning look.

"Really, I don't think—" he began, but then abandoned his protest, for by this time Holmes had already vanished into the parlor.

"It will be all right," I said, stepping toward the door to watch for the sheriff. "Mr. Baker is a most circumspect man. I am sure he will cause no trouble."

Having uttered this confident prevarication, I went out on a small porch in front of the kitchen to make sure Sheriff Boehm was still occupied elsewhere. I knew that Holmes, whose skill at quick searches was extraordinary, would need but a few minutes to complete his work.[1] A few minutes, as it turned out, was all that he had, because I soon saw Boehm coming toward the house. I stepped back inside and gave out a loud whistle. By the time the sheriff came through the door, Holmes was sitting at the kitchen table, chatting with Kensington.

"Ah, Sheriff, it is a pleasure to see you again," Holmes said, rising from his chair. "Mr. Smith and I simply wish to bid you a good day and thank you for your help. You have been most kind. We will be returning to Alexandria shortly, although we would first like to examine the site where the famed rune stone was found. I trust you would have no objections?"

Boehm, who seemed preoccupied with some other matter, said he would not, although he again warned us not to disturb any evidence, a caution that seemed peculiar given the large number of curiosity seekers already at the farm.

Once we were outside, Holmes asked Kensington how far it was to the place of the stone's discovery.

"Oh, it's no more than a quarter of a mile," Kensington told us. "It's at the south end of the farm. The easiest way to get there is on foot, unless you gents have any objections to walking."

"None at all," said Holmes. "Please, sir, lead the way."

It required but a short hike through fields and pastures, as Kensington had promised, to reach our destination. The wooded hillock from which Wahlgren had supposedly pulled his unlikely treasure lay just beyond a small pond still covered with a thin coating of ice. To the south of the pond I could see the house and barn of a neighboring farm, which did not look any more prosperous than Wahlgren's.

"That's Nels Fogelblad's place," said Kensington, as though reading my mind. "Nels actually lives much closer to where the stone was found than Olaf did."

"Perhaps we should have a talk with this Mr. Fogelblad," Holmes suggested. "He may have seen or heard something last night."

"That's what the sheriff figured, too," said Kensington. "Trouble is, Nels has been out of town since Monday. Went to see some relatives in Minneapolis."

"How unfortunate," said Holmes as we circled around the pond (neither Holmes nor I wanted any part of ice after our experiences on the Mississippi three years earlier) and then climbed a narrow trail toward a poplar grove which crowned the hill like a thick head of hair. Although quite steep, the hill was not very high, for I judged it to be no more than fifty feet above the surrounding terrain.

Noting how rugged and undeveloped this section of land was, Holmes asked whether Wahlgren had been able to put it to any productive use.

"No, there was nothing he could do with it," said Kensington, who was panting like an old hunting dog as he led us up the hill. "This part of the farm was kind of a wasteland—too steep for plowing and too wooded for pasturage. But he was slowly clearing out the trees up here so that his cows could graze. That's how he came upon the stone."

When we at last reached the hilltop, where a stiff wind rattled the bare branches of the poplars, I could see miles of countryside to the south—rolling brown fields, black stands of trees, icy white ponds— all beneath a lowering slate-gray sky. A few farmsteads were also visible, but they looked small and insubstantial against the immensity of the landscape. It was, I thought, a profoundly melancholy scene, largely bereft of the improving hand of man. London, with its teeming life, seemed from this vantage point to be not merely somewhere far, far beyond the horizon but on another planet altogether.

I doubt that Holmes felt any similar sensations, however, for part of his genius was his ability to concentrate with a kind of fierce intensity on whatever problem lay before him. The stone was his only interest now, and he looked on eagerly as we neared the discovery site. I had half expected to find a monument or some other marker to commemorate the scene of Wahlgren's momentous find. Instead, there was nothing except a hole in the ground perhaps three feet deep and about the same circumference.

"Well, there it is," Kensington announced. "The cause of all these troubles. Doesn't look like much, does it?"

Holmes stared at the hole and then, to my surprise, jumped down into it and began digging furiously at the hard soil with his hands.

"What on earth are you doing?" I asked.

"Looking for roots," Holmes replied nonchalantly. After several minutes of digging, he said: "Ah, here we are. I believe I have found one of the smaller lateral roots, which looks as though it was chopped in two with an ax. I see no evidence of the taproots, however. Tell me, Mr. Kensington, how large was this tree?"

"Funny you should ask. There's been lots of debate on that very subject. Olaf claimed it was a large poplar, maybe sixty or seventy years old, but others have said it was a young tree. The thing is, poplars grow like weeds around here, and it's hard to tell how old they are because they shoot up so fast."

"I see. Do you know what happened to the tree?"

"Not really. But my guess is that Olaf cut it up and hauled it away. Heaven knows where it is now."

"A pity," remarked Holmes, who held up one arm so that I could pull him out of the hole. After dusting off his trousers and his long black raincoat, he said: "It is depressing how little regard for evidence everyone seems to have in this matter, Mr. Kensington, but I suppose I should be used to it by now. Let me ask you this, sir: how did Mr. Wahlgren typically grub out a poplar tree?"

"All the farmers around here do it pretty much the same way," Kensington explained. "You dig around the tree and cut off all the shallow roots, then you dig deeper until you can see the main roots, which go straight down, more or less. Once you've found those taproots, you chop them off with an ax, and then you use a winch and cable to pull the tree right out of the ground. It's a job, I can tell you that."

"I see. And where exactly did Mr. Wahlgren find the stone as he was undertaking this arduous procedure?"

"It was clasped in one of the taproots, or at least that's what he said. It was lodged in there so tight that the stone came right out of the ground with the stump."

"And there are witnesses to this? That is, did anyone in addition to Mr. Wahlgren actually see the stone clasped in the roots?"

"Fogelblad did, that I know. When Olaf saw the writing on the stone, he called Nels over right away. As you can see, Nels's house isn't more than a few hundred yards away."

"So I have noticed," said Holmes. "Now, besides Mr. Fogelblad, did anyone else see the stone in the position in which it was found?"

"You mean in the tree roots?"

"Precisely."

Kensington considered this question for a moment, then said: "I don't think so. The story I heard is that Olaf, with Nels's help, chopped away the roots until the stone dropped free. In fact, you can even see a mark on the stone where Olaf accidentally struck it with his ax. At least that's how it was explained to me when the stone was on display at the bank in town."

"And how long was the stone at the bank?"

"Well, let's see. It was there at least a couple of weeks, right in the lobby. Magnus Larson—he's the famous novelist, you know—even had a translation printed up to go with the stone. Of course, folks already knew what the message said."

"How so?" Holmes inquired.

"Well, old Einar Blegen came over to Olaf's farm the day after the stone was found and translated it right on the spot."

"Really," said Holmes. "I have not heard of this Mr. Blegen. Who is he?"

"Oh, Einar's a character, he is. Used to be a preacher, but then got to spending too much time with the bottle, or so it was rumored. Personally, I never saw him in his cups. He claims he was a professor back in Sweden, which is why he supposedly knows all about runes."

"He sounds like a most interesting fellow. I shall have to make it a point to talk with him. Does he live nearby?"

"He's in Holandberg. Lives over the tavern there. You'll have no trouble finding him, I'm sure."

Holmes nodded and said: "Thank you for your help, Mr. Kensington. I believe we are finished here. It is getting late, and I should like to be back in Alexandria before dark."

On our way back to town, Holmes asked Kensington if we could talk that evening to Moony Wahlgren. "She is, unfortunately, the only member of the family left here now," he said, "and she may be able to tell us something about the stone."

At first, Kensington was very reluctant, but Sherlock Holmes is a very hard man to resist. By the time we reached Alexandria, just as the sun dropped beneath the horizon, Kensington agreed to let us talk to the girl and gave us directions to his house. We were to stop by at seven o'clock.

"But you must not press or badger Moony in any way," Kensington cautioned, a note of sternness entering his voice for the first time. "I will not tolerate that."

"You have our assurances that we will treat her with nothing but the kindness I am sure she deserves," Holmes promised.

Our friend James J. Hill had already made reservations for us at the Douglas House, which was reputed to be Alexandria's best hotel, and it was there that Kensington dropped us off. I had come to like Kensington a great deal, as had Holmes, who gave him an extra twenty dollars as a token of our appreciation.

The Douglas House occupied a brick-fronted building along the town's main street and offered a restaurant which was said to be quite good by the rather crude gastronomic standards of the region. Our rooms turned out to be small but not uncomfortable, and after we had washed and changed clothes, we went downstairs for supper.

The hotel's plain but spacious dining room was virtually empty ("It appears people here like to eat early," Holmes noted), and we took a large table near the front window, which offered a view of the town's dark and, at this hour, quiet main street. I was famished, having had nothing to eat since morning, and asked our waiter for a large plate of buttered rolls at once.

"And be quick about it if you would," Holmes told the man with a grin. "Otherwise, I fear my friend will be gnawing at the furniture shortly."

We quickly ordered up a substantial dinner—pork ribs in heavy sauce, boiled and seasoned potatoes, creamed asparagus, thick slabs of black bread said to be the specialty of the house, and cold Pilsner beer of the type favored by Americans.

Once I had eaten a few rolls and downed a glass of beer, I felt much refreshed. I then asked Holmes, who did not seem especially hungry, if he had found any significant clues at Wahlgren's farm, since he had made no comments in that regard on our way back to town.

"There were a number of suggestive features about the barn," he said, not bothering to explain, however, what these features were. "But Mr. Wahlgren's parlor proved to be, if anything, even more interesting."

"Ah, so you found something."

"Indeed I did, Watson. Since I knew I would have little time to conduct my search, I decided to look for anything in the room which might have some possible connection to the rune stone. My eyes at once fell on a certain book, one of no more than half a dozen sitting rather forlornly on a small shelf against the back wall of the parlor."

"What attracted you to this particular book?"

"Its title. The book was written by a man named Carl Rosander and is called *Den kunskapsrike Skolmästaren*. In English it would be entitled 'The Knowledgeable Schoolteacher,' or something to that effect. As it so happens, I am familiar with the book, which I came across during my travels through Scandinavia. It is a sort of one-volume encyclopedia, Watson. I believe it first came out in the 1850s and that there was a second edition in the 1880s. It is a very popular book in Sweden. More importantly, it has an excellent section on runes."

I now began to see why the book had so interested Holmes. I said: "I take it that you believe this book might have been used by Mr. Wahlgren to help him carve the stone."

"An engaging theory," replied Holmes. "However, the fact is that a number of the runes carved on the stone cannot be found in the book."

"Really, Holmes, how do you know that?" I asked, for I did not see how he could have examined the book in such detail during his brief search of Wahlgren's parlor.

"It is quite simple, Watson. You see, I happened to acquire a copy of the book some years ago while pursuing my study of runes. Before we left for America, I checked its runic alphabets against the message on the stone, a copy of which, you may remember, was provided to us by Professor Ohman. There are least six runes on the stone which cannot be found in Mr. Rosander's encyclopedia. But the book did yield other valuable information, such as this."

Holmes now removed a folded sheet of paper from his coat pocket and handed it to me. "I found it pressed between two pages in the section of the book on runes. What do you make of this, Watson?"

The document was a legal agreement which read as follows:

IN CONSIDERATION OF THE SUM OF TWO HUNDRED DOLLARS
($200.00), MR. OLAF WAHLGREN WHO RESIDES NEAR THE TOWN
OF HOLANDBERG IN DOUGLAS COUNTY, MINNESOTA, HEREBY
AGREES TO SELL TO MR. MAGNUS LARSON THE RUNE STONE
FOUND ON NOVEMBER 15, 1898, ON MR. WAHLGREN'S PROP-
ERTY, SUBJECT TO SUCH OTHER CONDITIONS AS SHALL BE
AGREEABLE TO BOTH PARTIES.

There were three signatures at the bottom: Magnus Larson, Olaf
Wahlgren (in an almost childlike scrawl), and Einar Blegen (who
listed himself as a notary public). The agreement was dated January 30, 1899.

I read over the document a second time, making sure I had missed
nothing, and said: "I must say this is very strange, Holmes. If Mr.
Wahlgren had already sold the rune stone, why was he murdered?"

"An excellent question, Watson. Here are several others: Where is
the stone now? Does Mr. Larson in fact have it? Or, for some reason, was the sale never completed? Clearly, we shall have to talk
with Mr. Magnus Larson as soon as possible. First, however, there is
someone else who requires our attention."

"You mean the Wahlgren girl?"

"Yes, but there is another person as well. You see, the sales agreement was not the only item I found in the book. Next to it was another slip of paper, which I am sure you will find intriguing."

Holmes unfolded the small piece of paper and laid it before me on
the table. It was a handwritten note which said:

Olaf,
  *You must not fail to meet me. March 30, 10 p.m. sharp, room
208, Douglas House. Do not be late.*

The note bore no signature.

"My God, that is tonight," I said. "Who do you suppose it is from?"

"We will know soon enough," said Holmes, who then returned the slip of paper to his coat pocket without further comment.

George Kensington lived in a small, plain white house near the end of one of the straight, wide streets which ran parallel to Alexandria's main thoroughfare. As the house was no more than half a mile from our hotel, we had made our way there on foot, enjoying the crisp night air and the magnificent display of stars spangling the vast prairie sky, which had been scoured clear of the day's clouds by a fast-moving cool front. The town itself was remarkably quiet, and as we walked along past the slumbering houses with their big dark yards and shadowy trees I felt a deep sense of calm unlike anything I had ever experienced amid the roar and bustle of London. What I did not know was that this calm would prove to be very short-lived, for events were soon to overtake us in a relentless and, at times, terrifying rush.

Kensington greeted us at the front door after Holmes, consulting his watch, had rapped upon it at precisely seven o'clock.

"Come in, gentlemen," he said amiably. "We're all ready for you."

He took our coats and ushered us into a small parlor, decorated with the usual knickknacks along with an unusually large collection of framed and mounted photographs, most of which appeared to be of his family.

"Please, sit down," he said. "I'll let my wife know you're here. Incidentally, Moony says she is looking forward to your visit."

"I am pleased to hear that," said Holmes, taking a seat in a large wooden rocker while I occupied a side chair nearby. "We very much look forward to meeting her as well."

Kensington then left, returning momentarily with his wife, Elsie, a large, jolly-faced woman with doughy, dimpled cheeks and sparkling hazel eyes. He introduced her to us, after which she insisted that we sample the sugar cookies she had brought in on a tray. Although Holmes, in my experience, had little taste for sweets, he took the cookie enthusiastically, bit into it with gusto, and immediately pronounced it "most excellent."

He added: "Why, Mrs. Kensington, I feel compelled to tell you this cookie is better than any I have ever had in London, or Paris, for that matter. I must have the recipe before we leave."

As Holmes was hardly a gourmand, this request struck me as odd, until I saw the wide smile which spread across Mrs. Kensington's face. I then recalled one of Holmes's frequent observations, which was that "when dealing with the female of the species, flattery is not merely useful but essential."

Holmes's display of charm had its desired effect, for after a few more minutes of pleasant small talk he had put both the Kensingtons entirely at ease. As a result, he soon was able to steer the conversation toward the topic of Moony Wahlgren.

"I am truly anxious to meet her," he remarked, "for she sounds like a most interesting child."

"Yes, 'interesting' is as good a word as any to describe Moony," Kensington acknowledged. "All right then, I suppose we should go on up to her room. But please don't forget that you must be gentle with her."

"Of course," said Holmes.

We followed Kensington up a narrow stairway to the second floor, which consisted of a long room with steeply slanting side walls and a pair of windows at either end. A kerosene lamp burned near the front windows, and by its glowing light we got our first glimpse of Moony Wahlgren, who sat hunched over a small desk, drawing on what appeared to be a large sheet of paper. She wore a calico dress with a lace collar and puffed sleeves, and a small silver locket around her long, thin neck.

She looked up as we approached, and I was struck at once by her features, for she had the kind of face which once seen, can never be forgotten. Neither beautiful nor plain, she was, for lack of a better word, distinctive in appearance. She had long, high cheekbones, a wide brow beneath straight blond hair which fell to her shoulders, a small mouth with unusually thick lips, a narrow, beaklike nose, and, most remarkably, enormous, blank blue eyes which seemed to gaze right through us, as though focused on some unseen world beyond our ken.

"The gentlemen from England are here," said Kensington softly as we drew beside the desk.

I will never forget her first words, uttered in a flat, matter-of-fact voice which was almost comic in its childlike directness. "I would like to see the queen," she said. "The queen is a large woman."

I could not imagine how to respond to such a peculiar statement, but Holmes showed no such perplexity. "I am sure the queen would like to see you someday, too, Moony. And you are right, she is a large woman."

"Not as large as Mama," the girl said. "Mama was very large. Mama is dead."

Said Holmes: "I am sorry to hear that."

"Papa is dead, too. You"—here she glanced over at Kensington—"told me. Too bad."

As the girl showed no interest in learning our names, Holmes did not offer them. Instead, he looked down at her drawing, which turned out to be an extremely intricate picture of what I could only assume was the rune stone. The stone itself was rendered in delicate pencil strokes, while the inscription was depicted more boldly, the runes skillfully shadowed in a way which made them almost look carved into the paper. It was, I thought, a superbly executed drawing, of which even Cruikshank or Paget might have been proud.[2] Yet the drawing was also odd in one respect, for it showed only a partial inscription, with the runes in the last line gradually fading away, as though someone had tried to erase them.

"You are a very fine artist, Moony," Holmes said, bending over to inspect the drawing more closely. "May I ask what this is a picture of?"

"Papa's stone," she said. "It is very pretty."

"Yes it is," Holmes agreed. "Did Papa carve it?"

The girl looked up at Holmes, her eerie eyes giving no clue as to what she might be thinking or seeing. "I like stone," she finally said. "I like the sky. Do you ever touch the sky?"

"No," said Holmes. "Do you, Moony?"

"Oh yes. I touch it every day. The sky is clean and blue. I like clean things."

What, I wondered, would Holmes say now, for it was abundantly clear by this time that the girl was more than just "different," as Kensington had described her to us. Indeed, I began to doubt that she understood anything Holmes asked her.

Holmes, however, seemed enormously taken by the girl, and said to her: "I like clean things, too. Did your papa like clean things?"

"Papa was dirty. Papa and the other one, they were dirty."

"Yes, some people are dirty," said Holmes. "That is too bad. People should be clean."

The girl nodded, looked down at her drawing, then gazed back up at Holmes and said: "I caught them."

Holmes said: "Yes, I bet you did. Where did you catch them, Moony?"

"In the box. I caught them in the box."

"I see. What were they doing, Moony? What did you catch them at?"

"I caught them," she repeated. "Rochester knows."

"Of course he does," Holmes said.

The girl nodded in agreement and said: "Rochester took the box. Rochester knows."

"Could I talk to Rochester?" Holmes asked.

With no advance warning, the girl now stood up and said: "I am tired. Good night."

Then, to my astonishment, she began to unbutton her dress despite our presence.

"We'll be going now," said Kensington as, out of modesty, both Holmes and I averted our gaze. "Good night, Moony."

"Good night," she said as we made our way to the stairs and left Moony Wahlgren to her own strange dreams.

Chapter Five

"ONE MIGHT AS WELL HAVE STOLEN THE *MONA LISA*"

"**W**hat an extraordinary young woman!" marveled Holmes as we walked back to our hotel. "I do not believe I have ever met anyone quite like her. Her mind would be a fascinating study for Dr. Freud, don't you think, Watson?"[1]

"I cannot say," I replied. "But I am not sure the poor child has any kind of grip on reality."

"To the contrary, Watson, I am of the opinion that she is well aware of 'reality,' but simply chooses to ignore it. Indeed, that drawing of hers was amazingly realistic. No, I am inclined to believe the young lady knows much more about the rune stone than she told us."

"So you think she is deliberately hiding something?"

"Not at all," said Holmes, taking out a match and lighting his favorite briar pipe. "As I see it, Miss Wahlgren is the possessor of a most peculiar but acute intellect, one that moves along an entirely different path from yours or mine. Or, to put it another way, we are on one set of tracks and she is on another, and so we passed in the night. Once I find a way to locomote, as it were, on her track, then I think we shall learn a great deal."

"I trust you are right," I said. "Still, the girl was a complete mystery to me. Who do you suppose is this Rochester she mentioned?"

"I have absolutely no idea," Holmes confessed. "Nor, it seems, does anyone else in the household."

This was true, for after our interview with the girl Holmes had spent some time quizzing the Kensingtons about her reference to "Rochester." But neither of them had ever heard her utter the name before.

"Well, let us set aside the mystery of Miss Wahlgren for the moment," said Holmes as we turned a corner and neared the Douglas House. "Now, we must see if we can discover whom her late father intended to meet in room 208 tonight."

"But surely whoever it was must know by now that Wahlgren is dead," I pointed out.

"That is a reasonable assumption," Holmes agreed. "Nonetheless, we must make inquiries, just in case."

When we reached the hotel, just after eight o'clock, Holmes immediately went to the front desk to speak with the night clerk, a lanky young man with thick round glasses and an eager manner.

"I am supposed to meet a gentleman in his room tonight," Holmes announced. "His name is Mr. John Watson. I believe he is in room 208, but I fear I may have the wrong number. Would you be so kind as to check for me?"

"Certainly," said the clerk, consulting a log book at the desk. "No, sir, I am afraid there is no one by that name in 208."

"Are you certain?" said Holmes, sounding quite distressed.

"I am certain. There is a Mr. Moriarty in 208."

"Really? Why, I believe I know him. Would that be Mr. Paul Moriarty of St. Paul?"

"No, sir. This Mr. Moriarty is from London, England."

"I see," said Holmes. "Well, I must have been mistaken. Thank you."

"My God, Holmes!" I said as we turned away from the desk. "You don't think—"

"No," Holmes cut in, "I do not."

Showing no sign of concern, Holmes went directly up the wide staircase to the second floor, and for a moment I thought we were returning to our rooms. But instead, Holmes went the opposite way down the hall.

"Where are we going?" I asked.

"To see Mr. Moriarty," Holmes replied.

"But the meeting with Mr. Wahlgren was not to have been until ten o'clock."

"It never hurts to be early," said Holmes, stopping in front of room 208 and, without hesitation, rapping loudly on the door.

After a moment, I heard heavy footsteps within. Then came the sound of the door chain being removed, after which the door itself began to swing open.

But before the occupant could make himself known to us, Holmes said in a stentorian voice: "Mr. Rafferty, how good of you to join us."

Holmes was right, of course, for it was indeed our good friend Shadwell Rafferty who now greeted us with a wide and mischievous smile.

"Ah, I feared you would see through my little trick," he said, feigning mortification that his ruse had failed to deceive Holmes. "Alas, there is no foolin' Sherlock Holmes, and that's a fact! What a pleasure it is to see the two of you again!"

Although we had not seen Rafferty for over three years, our bonds of friendship with him were permanent and powerful. We had first met him in January of 1896 during our investigation of the convoluted ice palace affair in St. Paul. Rafferty, who owned one of that city's most popular saloons and also dabbled in what he called "discreet investigations," had quickly earned our admiration for his skill as a detective and for his enormous courage in the face of danger. Twice during the ice palace case he had saved Holmes's life, and he had rescued me from dire peril as well. All the while he had maintained an air of genial ease, as though saving lives was a no greater matter to him than discussing politics with a patron at his tavern.

But what had especially attracted Holmes to Rafferty was his agile intellect. He possessed what Holmes called "a mind of the finest type," wedded to an indomitable will which had enabled him to triumph time and again over the inescapable tragedies of life. Yet to my way of thinking what made him an indelible character was the sheer power of his presence. He was one of those rare people who seemed to galvanize the air around him with the exuberant glow of his personality, and to be with him was to feel splendidly and joyfully alive. Holmes inspired the same intensity of feeling, yet one of the happy miracles of his relationship with Rafferty was that the two of them did not, like electric wires brought in contact, create destructive sparks, even though they clearly relished competing with each other.

Now, as we exchanged handshakes with Rafferty in the hallway, I could not but feel a great sense of pleasure that he would share our latest adventure. My pleasure was soon nearly squeezed out of me, however, for mere handshakes were not enough for Rafferty, who insisted on wrapping us in bear hugs. Given Rafferty's enormous size and strength, his display of affection was a rather painful experience, but I gladly tolerated it, as I think did Holmes, although he seemed a bit embarrassed by our friend's effusiveness.

"It is good to see you again," said Holmes with genuine sentiment. "By the way, how is that pup of yours?"

The "pup" was a bull dog which Holmes and I had given Rafferty just before our departure from St. Paul in 1896. The grateful Rafferty had promptly named the dog "Sherlock."

"Oh, he is just fine," said Rafferty. "You'll be interested to learn, Mr. Holmes, that Sherlock has lived up to his name, for when it comes to detectin' things—especially things he might enjoy eatin'—he has no peers in the canine world."

"I am pleased to hear that," said Holmes. "I must say the years seem to have been kind to you as well."

Indeed, Rafferty looked hardly different from when we had last seen him, in February of 1896, at the conclusion of the ice palace affair. Since then, his long red beard had acquired a bit more gray and he had added a few pounds to his formidable bulk, but there had been no lessening in the glint from his keen blue eyes or in the tone of his deep, rolling voice, which radiated warmth and fellowship. And, of course, he retained the diagonal scar over his left eyebrow (acquired in a knife fight in the Nevada silver mines) which added a note of piratical swagger to his otherwise genial appearance.

Nor had our friend lost his penchant for colorful attire, for he wore a maroon jacket over a checkered waistcoat, dark blue pants with pale yellow stripes along the sides, and brown-and-white brogans that somehow seemed far too small for a man of his daunting size. Had I not known better, I might have mistaken him—especially in view of the striped pants—as a country bandmaster out for a night on the town.

Although Rafferty was now well into his fifties, it quickly became clear to us that he still exhibited an abundance of that youthful zest we had found so appealing during our adventures with him in St. Paul.

Inviting us to sit on the room's only two chairs, he rolled up onto his bed, stretched his long legs as far as they would go, put his hands behind his neck, and said: "Now then, I need to know, Mr. Holmes, for purposes of the historical record, as it were, just how you found me out. Was it something I said in that note I left for you? Or did somebody spot me here and spill the beans?"

Holmes smiled and said: "It was your handwriting on the note, Mr. Rafferty, which gave you away. You see, once I have seen a man's handwriting—and I had occasion to observe yours several times in St. Paul—I never forget it. Your *f*'s, in particular, are quite distinctive."[2]

"Next time, I will have to print," said Rafferty with a grin.

It was now Holmes's turn to query Rafferty, for we were eager to learn how he had managed to reach the murder scene ahead of us. After posing this question, Holmes added: "I am sure your account will be most informative, Mr. Rafferty, and no doubt entertaining as well."

"Well, I don't know about that, Mr. Holmes, but I will say my presence here is something of a coincidence."

"Dr. Watson and I seem to be running into coincidences wherever we turn these days," said Holmes, "so I cannot say I am surprised to see you here. But please, continue."

"All right, here's the tale. Last Saturday, after a much-too-busy night at the saloon, I decided the time had come to undertake a little fishin' expedition. Anglin', Mr. Holmes, is like prospectin' for gold, only more relaxin'. Both are exercises in boundless optimism and so deny the hard reality of the world. At least that is what I've always thought. Now it so happens I know a fellow up at Osakis, which is not far from here, who has a knack for snaggin' plump pike, so I rang him up and asked if he'd like to go out fishin' for a few days. He was agreeable, and so I took the train up to Osakis and out we went on the ice—it's still solid in the lake's shallower bays—to try our luck."[3]

"And did you catch anything, Mr. Rafferty?" Holmes asked with an air of bemusement.

"I am sorry to say that the pike of Lake Osakis were bein' uncommonly elusive, so I had little to show for my efforts by the time I happened to call up George Thomas—he's my barman back in St. Paul, as you remember—on Wednesday night."

"Let me guess what happened next," said Holmes. "Mr. Thomas had heard from our friend Joseph Pyle that Dr. Watson and I were in St. Paul and were going out to Alexandria today. Therefore, you decided to join us."

"Exactly," said Rafferty. "Of course, what I didn't know was that this Wahlgren fellow was goin' to get himself murdered. Heard about it right away when I got into town just after nine this mornin'. So I decided to head out to the farm to see what I could find out. Hitched a ride with one of the curiosity seekers goin' down there from town."

"And you obviously spent enough time on the scene to plant that delightful note for us," said Holmes. "A clever touch, Mr. Rafferty. How did you manage to keep Sheriff Boehm at bay while you searched Mr. Wahlgren's parlor?"

Rafferty gave out a hearty laugh and said: "The sheriff's not exactly a friendly fellow, is he? I could see right away that he wouldn't like me pokin' around in the house, so I just waited until he went outside for a while. Funny thing is, he didn't leave anybody guardin' the house, so I just slipped inside, waltzed right into the parlor, and started lookin' around. Found a few documents of the usual sort in the desk there — elevator receipts, tax statements, doctor bills — Mr. Wahlgren seems to have had a bad back. 'Twas nothin' of any note, in other words. Then I started rummagin' through some of his books and hit pay dirt when I discovered that purchase agreement for the rune stone. Of course, I figured you and Dr. Watson would be down to the farm soon enough yourself, so I thought I'd play a little joke and leave that message for you. I knew you'd find it."

"I shall take that as a compliment," said Holmes. "Now, Mr. Rafferty, did you also manage to make your way into the barn where Mr. Wahlgren was murdered? If so, I should be interested to hear your impressions."

Rafferty thought for a moment, then sat up on the bed, lit one of the cheap, vile-smelling cigars he liked to smoke, and said: "I found the manure pit quite intriguin', as I'm sure you did, Mr. Holmes."

I looked over at Holmes and could tell by a slight raising of his eyebrows that Rafferty had struck a salient point.

"Go on," said Holmes.

"Well, it's like this: As I was nosin' around the barn, I was thinkin' to myself just where an old bird like Olaf Wahlgren might have hidden the rune stone. I knew he would have stashed it away, for that is how these rustics think. They don't trust banks and they don't trust city folk and, truth be told, they don't trust their neighbors either, so if Mr. Wahlgren had somethin' he thought was valuable, he'd hide it away. At least that's the way I reasoned."

"And you reasoned well," said Holmes.

"Ah, but where would he hide it? Now that was an interestin' question. If it was something small and easy to tote around, why, he could go out and bury it just about anywhere on the farm and no one would be the wiser. Probably every farmer within a hundred miles of here has got a stash of coins somewhere beneath a rock or a post or a tree on his farm. The rune stone's a different matter, however. It's big and heavy—at least two hundred pounds, I'm told—which means it's not the sort of thing that could be easily carried around by one man, especially if he has a bad back. So Mr. Wahlgren, I figured, would want his valuable stone nearby. And that's when I started lookin' at that manure pit."

"But what led you to look there?" I asked, remembering how Holmes had also examined the pit with an unusual degree of interest.

Holmes provided the answer: "I think it had to do with the manure which was piled around the pit, Watson. Am I correct, Mr. Rafferty?"

"You are," said our Irish friend. "I spent some time workin' on a farm as a lad and shoveled my share of dung. Now, there's no mystery about cleanin' out a manure pit. You just shovel the manure into a cart and then haul it out to be spread on the fields. But the one thing you wouldn't do is shovel it out and leave it in piles around the pit, unless—"

"You were looking for something at the bottom of the pit," said Holmes.

" 'Tis the only logical conclusion," Rafferty agreed. "Whoever dug out that pit was probably the killer and was probably lookin' for the rune stone, which would have fit in there very nicely under a thick layer of manure. 'Twas a brilliant spot for hidin' the stone when you think about it, since most folks would not be especially anxious to go rootin' around in such a malodorous and disagreeable place."

"I can find no flaw in your reasoning, Mr. Rafferty," Holmes said, "although I would suggest one other possibility, which is that Mr. Wahlgren himself was preparing to remove the stone for some reason when he was surprised and murdered by an intruder, or perhaps intruders."

Rafferty's eyes lit up at this last remark. He said: "Ah, I see you're thinkin' along the same lines I am, Mr. Holmes, for it's likely more than one man was involved in the killin'. That gun is the giveaway."

"Could you explain what you mean?" I asked Rafferty.

" 'Tis just this, Dr. Watson: a man with a shotgun, investigatin' trouble in his own barn in the dead of night, is bound to be very careful. And yet the evidence suggests that Mr. Wahlgren was surprised from behind by his killer. Now, there are any number of ways that could've happened, but I'm thinkin' that maybe Mr. Wahlgren found somebody at the manure pit, told him to get his hands up, and then got struck down by an accomplice somewhere in hidin'. 'Twould explain why Mr. Wahlgren wasn't able to defend himself despite bein' well armed. But I guess we'll have to find the murderer, or murderers, before we know for sure."

"We will indeed," said Holmes. "But first, Mr. Rafferty, I should like to acquaint you with how Dr. Watson and I became involved in this most vexing matter."

"I was hopin' you'd get to that soon," said Rafferty. "I'm all ears."

Holmes now briefly explained our involvement in the case, going back to our visit from Professor Ohman in London and our agreement to authenticate the rune stone for King Oskar. He also described our curious interview with Moony Wahlgren.

Rafferty received this information with great interest, especially the news that Magnus Larson was supposedly working on behalf of the Swedish king. Said Rafferty: "Will wonders never cease! I knew, of course, that Magnus Larson was a big supporter of the rune stone—it's been in all the newspapers—but I didn't know he was workin' for royalty. Did I tell you, by the way, that I talked to Mr. Larson—or tried to—this afternoon?"

"My, but you have been busy today, Mr. Rafferty!" said Holmes with a touch of sardonicism. "What, may I ask, did the famous Swede tell you?"

"I got nothin' from him," said Rafferty, shaking his head and, to my relief, stubbing out his execrable cigar in an ash tray on the bedstand. " 'Twould be easier to pry open a clam with tweezers than to get useful information from him."

"I am surprised to hear that," said Holmes. "I did not think any man could resist your charms, Mr. Rafferty."

"Well now, come to think of it, he actually did tell me a thing or two," Rafferty said. "Let's see. He told me to go to hell, to mind my own business, to stay out of his way, and to never, ever bother him again. Had my sainted mother been handy, why, he probably would have wished her eternal damnation for good measure. Oh, he's a mean, ornery character, he is. You can see it in those icy blue eyes of his. But he's also smart as blazes, or so it's said. At least, that's the case when he's sober, for I'm told that when the sun goes down he turns into a regular tosspot."

"Well, perhaps I shall have to try my luck with Mr. Larson tomorrow," said Holmes. "In the meantime, we are faced with at least three difficult questions beyond the obvious one, which is who murdered Olaf Wahlgren. There is, to begin with, the question of what happened to the stone itself. Presumably it was taken by Mr. Wahlgren's murderer and has now been hidden away by that person. Of course, there is also the possibility that the stone remains somewhere on the farm and that the thief did not find it. In that event, it may never turn up. However, I prefer to think that the thief got what he was looking for. If he did, then this would suggest that the thief and murderer is either someone who lives nearby or who has found a place not far from here to secrete the stone."

"That seems a great deal to presume," I noted.

"Not really, Watson. You must remember that the stone is a heavy and cumbersome object. The killer must have had a wagon to haul it away, unless he was an enormously strong man such as our friend, Mr. Rafferty, and could carry it on his back. But I am inclined to think the use of a wagon is more likely. If that was indeed the case, then there is a limit to how far the stone could have traveled, since the roads hereabouts are quite poor and a wagon trip to some distant locale would take days, if not weeks."

I now had another thought. "What about shipping it out by rail from Alexandria or Holandberg?"

"Ah, Watson, now you are thinking like a detective," said Holmes. "Let us hope that it occurs to Sheriff Boehm to begin examining all packages weighing more than two hundred pounds which leave this area over the next few days."

" 'Twould be the obvious thing to do," said Rafferty. "But just in case the sheriff is asleep in the pilot house, I'll do some checkin' of my own at the local freight stations tomorrow."

"That would be most helpful," Holmes said. "Still, I doubt our thief would be quite so stupid as to try to ship out the stone by rail, at least for the time being. Unfortunately, finding the wagon used to haul the stone will be all but impossible. There were so many wheel marks in Mr. Wahlgren's farmyard that I could not distinguish one from the other. All of which suggests that we will have to use other means if we hope to find the stone."

Holmes, who had gotten out his pipe, paused for a moment to light it, drew in the smoke, and then said: "That leads to the second question, which is this: what does the thief intend to do with the stone now that he has it?"

Rafferty couldn't resist breaking in: " 'Tis an intriguin' question all right, and so far I've not found a convincin' answer."

"I must confess that I don't quite understand," I said. "Doesn't the thief intend to sell the stone?" Hardly had I uttered these words than I realized my mistake. "But of course. How can the thief sell such an object when everyone knows that it was obtained by theft and murder?"

"Precisely," responded Holmes. "One might as well have stolen the *Mona Lisa*, or so it would seem."

"True enough," Rafferty observed, "though I would note there are certain art collectors—I know one or two myself—who would purloin the *Mona Lisa* if they could hide it in the attic, just for the pleasure of possessin' it. Maybe there is just such a person who covets the rune stone."

"Perhaps," Holmes acknowledged. "But if he exists, we have few means to find him at present. Still, I have no doubt that whoever stole the stone, or ordered it to be stolen, fully intends to profit from it. The question is how."

" 'Tis a mighty poser," Rafferty agreed, "and it's complicated by the fact that Mr. Wahlgren might not even have owned the stone, given that agreement he made with Magnus Larson. Speakin' of which, I'm wonderin' why Mr. Larson, if he bought the stone, didn't take possession of it."

"It would be interesting to know whether any word of the agreement ever became public," Holmes said.

"From what I know, it didn't," Rafferty told us. "You see, one of the first things I did when I got into town today was to go over and have a chat with the editor of the *Clarion*, Mr. Carlson. As far as he knows—and there isn't much around here that escapes his attention—Olaf Wahlgren has had possession of the stone all along. Mr. Carlson, I'm sure, would have known if the stone had been sold."

"Well, it would seem we shall have plenty of work to keep us occupied tomorrow," said Holmes, signaling to me that it was time to leave. "Perhaps if we all spend some time thinking tonight, we will have better answers in the morning."

Chapter Six

"HER NAME WAS MARY ROBINSON"

There have been only a few times in my life when the hand of fate seemed to descend from the heavens and slap me across the face, as if to say, "Look, sir, your life can change in an instant, and you must never forget it." One such occasion came when the Jezail bullet tore through my shoulder at Maiwand and missed killing me by mere inches. Another occurred at the Criterion Bar in London, where I was spotted by young Stanford, an unlikely chance meeting which was to lead to my introduction to Sherlock Holmes.[1] Now, far from home on the western prairies of Minnesota, I was about to have another encounter with the unexpected.

It happened at around one o'clock of the following afternoon, which was a Friday and also the last day of March. I had slept late, as is sometimes my wont, and by the time I got down to the hotel dining room, I found out from my waiter that Holmes and Rafferty had already finished their breakfast and had gone out on unspecified business. Having no better plan, I ate a leisurely breakfast, found a copy of the *Clarion*, which contained a long and quite sensational account of Olaf Wahlgren's murder, and then waited in the lobby for Holmes and Rafferty to return.

They did so just before noon, and both had news—albeit not especially revealing—to report. Holmes had spent the morning talking to anyone he could find about the name "Rochester." He had canvassed the local merchants, stopped in for his talk with the *Clarion*'s editor, and even stopped people on the street to make inquiries. But no one seemed to know a person bearing the mysterious name which Moony Wahlgren had mentioned to us. Rafferty, meanwhile, had busied himself conversing with the Great Northern freight agent in Alexandria and had also talked by telephone with other agents in nearby communities.

"If a two-hundred-pound package of a certain dimension gets shipped out, we'll know about it," said Rafferty, who had offered a twenty-dollar gold piece to the agent who could provide such information.

After a quick lunch at the hotel, Rafferty went off to attend to what he called "another little matter," while Holmes and I walked over to the railroad depot. There, Holmes wrote out a telegram to be sent to James J. Hill, informing him of our progress in the investigation. Since Holmes required several minutes to compose his message, I decided to wait for him out on the train platform. I found a chair, lit a cigar, and enjoyed the splendid weather, for the day had turned out to be sunny and surprisingly mild. It was then that I received one of the great surprises of my life.

As I waited, I heard a train coming in from the west, its whistle sounding as it approached the depot. The train soon pulled into the station and several passengers began to disembark. I paid no particular attention to this scene, and was in fact staring up at the sky when I was startled by a loud thud, which turned out to be the result of a heavy trunk being dropped by one of the porters. Glancing toward the front of the platform, where I had heard the noise, I saw a woman in a fur overcoat and wide-brimmed hat alighting from the train. A young man was at her side, holding several pieces of luggage. One look at the woman—her statuesque figure, the cascade of auburn hair beneath her hat, her distinctive profile—left no doubt as to her identity.

I ran at once into the depot, where Holmes had just finished sending his message.

"My God, Holmes," I said, "she is here! You must come and look!"

"What is it, Watson?" said Holmes calmly. "I have not seen you so excited in ages. Who is here?"

I then collected my wits sufficiently to name the woman I had seen. Holmes was not a man easily taken off guard, but in this instance even his cool, probing eyes widened in astonishment. "Are you absolutely sure?" he asked.

"I am sure."

"Show me," he commanded, turning from the desk and running toward the platform. By this time, the train, having disgorged its passengers and taken on a few new ones, was already leaving the station. But Holmes was able to catch a fleeting glimpse of the woman as the carriage which she had entered moved slowly away from the depot, toward the main part of the town.

"Come along, Watson—we must not lose sight of her," Holmes said, and we fell in behind the carriage, which was proceeding at a moderate pace, though moving faster than we could walk.

Fortunately, the depot was but a ten-minute walk from Alexandria's main business section, and so we had no trouble keeping the carriage in view until it stopped in front of the Douglas House.

"It appears the lady will be joining us this evening," said Holmes. "How convenient!"

We watched from a distance as the woman, helped by her young companion, stepped down from the carriage and entered. After waiting a few minutes, we followed her into the hotel.

The clerk on duty was a doughy-faced little man with that supercilious air which seems to be the birthright of every functionary who has ever ruled over some insignificant little fiefdom.

"I just saw a woman come in who was wearing a fur coat and a wide-brimmed hat," Holmes told the clerk. "I am sure I have met her before, but I can't for the life of me remember her name. Would you happen to know who the lady is?"

"I might," said the clerk, "but I don't see where it's any business of yours. How do I know you're not some kind of masher?"

"You do not," replied Holmes icily, "but then how do I know you are not so incompetent at your job that you are about to lose it? Now, sir, you will tell me the lady's name, as I have asked. If not, then I shall have to spend the rest of this day, and subsequent days, making your life miserable. It is not a task I look forward to, but one at which, I assure you, I am very good. I also happen to be well acquainted with the proprietor of the hotel" — this was a lie — "and I do not think it would take me long to remove you from your job, should that be required. Now, sir, what will it be?"

The clerk, confronted with a vastly superior will, instantly lost his nerve, like a bully who finally meets the one boy in the schoolyard who will not back down. "Of course, sir, of course," he said. "I was merely trying to protect the lady's interests. But since you are obviously a gentleman, I see no reason why you should not have her name. The woman you caught sight of is Mrs. Comstock, Mrs. Frank Comstock, of Fairview Farms, near Moorhead. Do you know her, sir?"

"Oh, yes," said Holmes, "oh, yes indeed. Only when I knew her, her name was Mary Robinson."

Although over four years had passed since our first encounter with the lady, she was one of those women who remain forever vivid in memory, not only because of her striking appearance but also by reason of her exceptional, if not necessarily virtuous, character.

I remembered down to almost every detail the day we had first met her, in her flaming red brothel on the outskirts of Hinckley, in the days before that doomed city and the lives of over four hundred men, women, and children were consumed in the holocaust of September 1, 1894. Holmes's private interview with her, while I was being harassed unmercifully by a pair of brazen young strumpets

known as the jack pine twins, was, he later admitted, "one of the singular incidents" of his life, perhaps in more ways than I ever knew.[2]

Yet in the years since the tragic case of the Red Demon, which
Holmes accounted one of the great failures of his career, he seldom
talked of Mrs. Robinson or of her connections to the brutal and
twisted figure who had claimed so many innocent lives. And, in
truth, Holmes had little reason to mention her name, for what
were the odds that a woman so clever, so treacherous, and—it must
be admitted—so beautiful would ever cross our paths again somewhere in the vast spaces of America? No, it was a thing impossible
to imagine—and yet here she was, a gorgeous specter from the past
come back to haunt us, carried into our midst by that vast moving
hand which no man can anticipate or control.

"What room is the lady in?" Holmes now asked the thoroughly
cowed clerk.

"She is in 221, sir, the finest suite we have."

"A most coincidental number. Thank you," said Holmes, whose
agitated look suggested that he was trying to decide what to do next.
After a moment's hesitancy, he turned away from the clerk and said
to me: "We must talk with her at once. I see no other choice."

As we walked upstairs, I could sense that the unforeseen involvement of Mrs. Robinson—or, as she must now be known, Mrs.
Comstock—in the rune stone case had brought about in Holmes an
intense mixture of excitement and apprehension. Like Irene Adler,
Mrs. Comstock was that rare woman who by virtue of her rigorous
intellect and faultless intuition had proved an able adversary for
Holmes. Indeed, her escape from Hinckley had been managed so
brilliantly that even Holmes, for whom the fair sex was normally
accounted an unworthy foe, could do little but salute her ingenuity.
And, of course, there was the letter which followed, a missive
Holmes had read with both disgust and admiration, and which convinced him that further pursuit of the lady would be futile.

I wondered now how Holmes would respond to this unexpected
and formidable opponent. Thus far, the rune stone case had been
well within what might be called conventional bounds, except per-

haps for our encounter with Moony Wahlgren. Now, however, a diamond—hard, beautiful, and dangerous—had entered the field, and I had no doubt that Mrs. Comstock's glowing if perilous presence would inevitably affect Holmes's calculations.

When we reached room 221, Holmes paused, as though collecting himself for an especially trying ordeal, then rapped on the door.

It was opened, but only a small way, by the young man we had seen with Mrs. Comstock. He could not have been more than twenty-five years of age and sported long golden locks which reminded me of those I had seen in photographs of the unfortunate cavalryman General George Custer. The young man also had a cavalryman's face, lean and leathery, with blank gray eyes, a short nose, and thin lips shadowed by a light mustache. His attire matched his "western" features, for he wore a fringed buckskin jacket and a large hat of the kind which Americans call a "Stetson." High boots, denim pants, and a large silver belt buckle completed his accouterments.

"Who are you?" he asked with a distinct air of challenge.

"Friends of Mrs. Comstock," replied Holmes. "We should like to pay our respects to the lady."

"She ain't interested," said the young man, who appeared to be unfamiliar with both good manners and proper grammar.

Then I heard the lady's voice, which was at once firm and musical, a throaty contralto that must have seduced many a man: "Who is it, Billy?" she asked.

"Some men," he replied, keeping his eyes on us. "They say they know you."

"Well then, let them in," she said, after which her companion grudgingly swung open the door for us.

She was standing at one of the room's big windows, looking down at the street below, and then she slowly turned around to look at us. I shall never forget that moment of recognition, for in her extraordinary violet eyes I saw a kaleidoscope of emotions—astonishment, fear, anger—followed by a kind of hardening which suggested the beginnings of infinite calculation.

I also saw at once that age had not diminished the lady's beauty.

Although she was now perhaps in her forty-fifth year, she remained the kind of woman whom no man could fail to notice and, I daresay, covet. Her long, proud face, marked by prominent cheekbones and full lips, was just as I remembered it, as was the remarkable luster of her flowing red hair. Her attire was also elegant, for she wore a high-buttoned pink dress with a white lace collar and a long shawl edged by white fur.

"Why, Mrs. Robinson," said Holmes, "you look as beautiful as ever. What a pleasant surprise to see you again!"

"And for me as well," she said in a calm voice which gave no hint of the apprehension I had briefly seen in her eyes. "What a small world it is! Please, come in and sit down. We will have some tea. Billy, why don't you go downstairs and fetch us three cups, as hot as they can make it. Orange pekoe would be nice, I think."

"Are you sure—" the young man began.

She cut him off at once: "Now, Billy, don't argue with me. You know better than that. I will be perfectly fine with these distinguished gentlemen. Now run along."

After the young man had left, Mrs. Comstock seated herself on a small divan near the windows while Holmes and I occupied two nearby chairs.

"I see you are still using Jicky," Holmes remarked, referring to the expensive French perfume which had been the lady's signature in Hinckley.

"There is no reason to change when one has a good thing," the lady said with a smile. "I have, however, taken on a new name since we last met. I am now Mary Comstock. But I expect you're already aware of that, Mr. Holmes."

"Why do you say so?"

"Because I know you," said the lady. "Since I have only just arrived in town, there can be but two possibilities to account for your showing up so quickly at my door. One is that you knew I was coming. The other is that you saw me by chance, perhaps at the railroad station or as I entered the hotel. In either case, you would have made it a point to learn my new identity before making your appearance."

"You flatter me, madam," said Holmes with a slight bow.

"I would expect nothing less of you," she said. "You are, after all, the world's greatest consulting detective. But I must say I am surprised to find you here. I presume it has something to do with the rune stone."

"It does," Holmes acknowledged. "I have heard that you, too, are attracted to the stone. May I ask why?"

"Let us just say that I have an interest in antiquities, as did my late husband."

"I would call a bid of five hundred dollars for the stone more than an interest," said Holmes. "It seems a pity that poor Mr. Wahlgren did not accept your offer. Had he done so, he might be alive today."

"So it would seem," Mrs. Comstock said. "I saw the news of his death in the newspapers. A tragic thing! But now that you are here, Mr. Holmes, I am sure you will bring the murderer to justice, just as you did the Red Demon. Of course, I can only hope and pray that four hundred innocent people will not have to die first."

It was a stinging rebuke, and Holmes knew it, his face reddening—something I had seen happen to him only once or twice before. For a moment, I feared he might lose his customary composure and lash back at Mrs. Comstock, who was far more culpable for the deaths in the Hinckley fire than Holmes could ever have been. But Holmes, to his enduring credit, mastered his anger and said in a steely voice:

"There will be justice beyond this world, Mrs. Comstock, and when the trumpets summon you, you shall have to answer them."

"Perhaps," she said, "but I am inclined to think that the only justice for any of us is the justice we make for ourselves in this world. Only time will tell whether you are right, Mr. Holmes, or I am."

"Then I shall look forward to that time of judgment," said Holmes. "But let us return to more mundane matters. I must say I find it to be quite a coincidence that you have come to Alexandria on the day after Mr. Wahlgren was murdered."

"Coincidences are part of life, Mr. Holmes. I would not read too much into it, if I were you."

"Thank you for that advice, madam. I shall do my best to keep it in mind. Incidentally, can you tell me when you made the offer of five hundred dollars for the rune stone to Mr. Wahlgren?"

"It was some months ago. I do not recall the exact date."

"And did you make the offer directly to him, or did you perhaps go through an intermediary?"

"I am afraid that is my business and not yours, Mr. Holmes. And since the offer was rejected, I hardly see that it matters."

"Do you know why Mr. Wahlgren turned down such a generous offer?"

"You would have to ask him."

"Unfortunately, as you know, he is dead."

"Then it would appear you have a problem, Mr. Holmes, wouldn't it?"

I thought this last remark to be insufferably arrogant, but Holmes refused to be baited. Maintaining his usual calm and reasoned manner, he said: "I always enjoy a good problem, madam, and you may be assured I shall work on solving it. Now then, you mentioned your husband earlier, and I must admit that I was surprised to hear that you had remarried. Of course, I was saddened to learn of your husband's sudden death last year. You must have loved him very much."

Mrs. Comstock gave Holmes a long, bemused stare and said: "Love, I fear, is much overrated. It is for most women little more than a cruel disease which ruins their lives. As for men, it is merely an irritating itch which must periodically be scratched, though I would note that your friend Dr. Watson seemed rather reluctant in that regard the last time I saw him. A pity. I was so sure he would like the jack pine twins."

"Really, madam," I protested, "I see no point —"

"Dr. Watson is still rather embarrassed by that little episode," Holmes interposed. "But I am sure he will get over it in time. Now then, madam, am I to take it that your all-too-brief marriage to Mr. Comstock was purely a matter of convenience?"

"Aren't all marriages, when you come right down to it, Mr. Holmes?"

"Having never been married, I am hardly in a position to comment on that subject. Still, as I understand it, Mr. Comstock was quite a wealthy man."

"Yes, Frank enjoyed some success in the world. I trust you find nothing wrong with that."

"Not in the least. May I ask how long you were married?"

I had been waiting for Holmes to ask this question, and I was most curious to hear the lady's answer. My curiosity stemmed from the fact that in her letter to Holmes after the Red Demon affair, she had mentioned going to a remote place and taking on a new line of work and a new identity. It occurred to me that Fairview Farms could have been that place, which would mean she must have married Comstock within months of making her escape from Hinckley. Then again, I thought it unlikely that she would have been happy for long living on a farm in this far, cold country.

My assessment proved correct, for Mrs. Comstock now said: "Frank and I were married last year." Then she added: "You seem terribly interested in my late husband, Mr. Holmes. Is there a particular reason?"

"I am a curious man by nature," Holmes replied smoothly. "I suppose you could call it an occupational hazard. Besides, your husband obviously was not the usual sort of businessman, and unusual people always interest me. I find it fascinating, for example, that your husband, who made his fortune as a commodities trader and farmer, would suddenly take an interest in an artifact as suspect as the rune stone."

"And why is that?" asked the lady, her eyes studying Holmes's face the way an eager cartographer might pore over an especially valuable and interesting map.

Holmes, whose eyes remained equally fixed on Mrs. Comstock, replied: "It is simply an observation based upon my experience with men of Mr. Comstock's type. They are usually interested in business and little else."

"Frank, as you have said, was not the usual sort of businessman," Mrs. Comstock said, neatly parrying Holmes's verbal thrust and at the same time leaving him little latitude for further debate on the topic of her husband's interest in the stone.

"A point well taken," Holmes admitted. "In any event, it sounds as though Mr. Comstock was a most intriguing gentlemen. How sad it is that he fell off that train! Tell me, did anyone see the horrible accident?"

"No, Frank was alone. As you said, it was very sad, but life is always a risky enterprise, don't you think, Mr. Holmes?"

"I agree, madam. In fact, I might go so far as to say that without risk, life would offer little of interest to a woman such as yourself. Indeed, I am wondering whether it was some 'risky enterprise' which brought you here to Alexandria."

The lady's mouth curved into a small, enigmatic smile before she said: "No, I am here merely to take care of a few minor business matters involving the farm."

"I should be curious what those matters are," said Holmes, showing a slight smile of his own.

"Then I am afraid your curiosity will have to keep for a while," Mrs. Comstock replied evenly, "since I do not make a habit of discussing my personal business matters with others unless there is some reason to do so. I am sure you understand."

"Of course," said Holmes, just as Mrs. Comstock's virile young companion, carrying a small tray, returned with our cups of tea, which he sat on a small table in front of the divan.

"Thank you, Billy," the lady said, and then pointed to a chair against the far wall of the room. "Why don't you take that seat over there. These gentlemen will be leaving shortly."

"Yeah, sure," he said, giving us a sullen stare.

"I fear we have not been properly introduced," said Holmes, standing up to intercept the young man before he could take his assigned place. "I am John Baker, and this is my friend Peter Smith. We are old friends of Mrs. Comstock's. And you are—?"

"Billy Swift," said Mrs. Comstock. "My apologies for not introducing you. Billy is the foreman at Fairview Farms. These gentlemen, Billy, are indeed old acquaintances. They are from London and are quite the world travelers, or so it would seem."

"A pleasure to meet you," said Holmes, extending his hand, which Swift shook quickly, as though Holmes might be carrying some dread contagion.

"Yeah, same here," Swift muttered, and then shook my hand with equal alacrity before retiring to his chair across the room.

Giving the young man an appraising stare, much the way a farmer might judge a prized bull, Holmes said: "I can imagine that a large and fertile farm such as yours requires a good deal of plowing. It must be a hard if rewarding task for the young man."

"It is," said Mrs. Comstock. "But Billy is quite expert. I have found that there is no substitute for youth when it comes to such work, as I'm sure you understand."

Holmes now prepared to ask another question, but Mrs. Comstock, who was obviously beginning to tire of the game, suddenly took the offensive. "It seems we have talked enough about my affairs, Mr. Baker. Perhaps we should talk about yours. I find it odd that something as minor as this rune stone matter could bring you halfway around the globe. I should think your work in London would be sufficient to keep you well occupied, but that apparently is not the case."

"London has been disappointing of late," Holmes said. "I was therefore most pleased when Mr. Smith and I were asked to come to America to investigate the rune stone."

"Well, I wish you good luck," said the lady as she arose from her chair and extended her hand toward Holmes. He bent over to kiss it, and as he did so, I had the queer sense that some powerful current had suddenly passed between the two of them.

Slowly lifting his head to look at Mrs. Comstock, Holmes said: "You possess a most extraordinary presence, madam, most extraordinary."

"As do you, Mr. Baker," she replied. "I have business to attend to now, but I trust that we will meet again soon."

"Oh yes," said Holmes before we turned around to leave. "I have no doubt that we shall meet again."

"Well," I said to Holmes as we went back down to the hotel lobby, "the lady does not seem to have changed one bit."

"You are right, Watson, and that is what worries me. She is up to something, for unless I am mistaken she is deeply involved in every aspect of this rune stone business."

"How do you know that?"

"Call it male intuition," said Holmes with a wan smile.

Chapter Seven
"WELL, I GUESS I WIN"

"So, Mr. Holmes, who is your new lady friend?" Rafferty asked when he joined us for supper that evening in the dining room of the Douglas House. Baked ham, potatoes au gratin, black-eyed peas, and apple pie were the featured items on the menu, and Rafferty—who was a trencherman of the first order—was already well on his way toward polishing off his meal when he brought up the topic of our visit with Mary Comstock.

I sensed that Holmes had expected the question, for he knew as well as anyone that Rafferty sopped up information as readily as he did the food on his plate.

"Wherever did you hear such a thing?" Holmes replied in a bantering way. "I must say, Mr. Rafferty, that I am beginning to think you have spies everywhere. Or am I merely imagining that such is the case?"

"No, 'tis true," Rafferty admitted with a grin. "Why, I venture there are fifty people in this town I know by first name, maybe more."

Rafferty's incredibly wide web of friendship was, by now, something of a standing joke between Holmes and me, dating back to our time in St. Paul in 1896, when we had become convinced that the big Irishman knew virtually everyone in that city.

"All right, Mr. Rafferty, let us hear the story," I said. "How is it that you are acquainted with so many people here?"

"Well now, there's no mystery in that," he told us. "The fact is, I used to be a drummer in this territory long ago."

Holmes, who always found Rafferty's tales amusing, said: "You were a drummer, Mr. Rafferty? I had not heard about this aspect of your long and varied career. Were you selling whisky, perchance?"

Rafferty mustered a look of mild annoyance and said: "Oh no, Mr. Holmes, I never sold whisky. 'Twas Bibles I peddled."

"Bibles?" Holmes and I echoed, almost in perfect unison, for the idea of Rafferty selling the Lord's word seemed about as likely as the Archbishop of Canterbury distributing tracts promoting devil worship.

"You need not look so surprised," Rafferty said, appearing to be genuinely offended by our skepticism. "Though I personally am not a man inclined toward religion, I hold no grudge against it, and there's good money to be made sellin' Bibles. This was back in the eighties, before I opened my saloon at the Ryan. Sold Bibles all around Minnesota and the Dakotas. Met a lot of folks, as you might imagine, and sold more Bibles than any drummer in the territory."

Holmes shook his head in amazement. "Mr. Rafferty, you offer no end of wonders. Did you go directly from selling Bibles to operating a saloon?"

" 'Tis true," he admitted, giving no indication that he saw anything irregular about this peculiar change of occupation. "You see, Mr. Holmes, 'tis my firm belief that most men are lookin' for one thing in life, and that is solace from their worldly cares. Life's a ragin' sea of troubles, and most men will jump ship sooner or later unless they've got somethin' to soothe the pain in their gut. Religion works for some, a glass of good whisky for others, which is why I've always contended that tendin' bar is not much different from bein' a priest, except for the hours you keep."

"I am not sure most ecclesiastical authorities would subscribe to that notion, Mr. Rafferty," Holmes said, "though your argument is not without a certain logical appeal."

"Why, thank you kindly, Mr. Holmes. And now that you have learned a little secret from my past, perhaps you can tell me one of your own. Word has it that you seemed to know Mrs. Comstock, who I understand was the lady you and the good doctor paid a call on this afternoon."

Holmes now told Rafferty about our experiences with Mary Comstock—then Mary Robinson—in Hinckley and also gave an account of our interview with her in the hotel.

Rafferty took in this information in his usual easygoing way and then said: "The lady sounds like a regular Tartar in skirts. I would like to meet her sometime."

"I am sure you will," said Holmes, "for I do not think Mrs. Comstock is through with us, nor are we through with her. But tell me, Mr. Rafferty, what of our plans for tonight? Has everything been arranged?"

"It has, Mr. Holmes. I've been doin' a little detectin' about town, and the consensus among the drinkin' crowd is that, this bein' Friday night, Mr. Larson will almost certainly spend the night at his favorite waterin' hole here in town, the Majestic Tavern."

"Good. Then we shall have to join him. What do you say, Watson? Are you up for a pleasant night of drinking and fellowship at one of Alexandria's finest taverns?"

The idea of spending the night in bed, under a warm blanket, sounded far more appealing, but it was apparent that Holmes and Rafferty, for whatever reason, had other ideas.

"I go where you go, Holmes," I said. "I am sure we will all have a wonderful time."

As it turned out, these were not the most prescient words I ever uttered.

The Majestic Tavern, described by Rafferty as "a middlin' stand-up joint," was located only two blocks from our hotel.[1] Rafferty, who had considerable expertise in all matters related to saloon keeping, told us that the Majestic's chief claim to virtue — and the main reason for its popularity in town — was that its owner, a Swede by the name of Ericson, poured an "honest drink."

" 'Tis well known," Rafferty informed us as we walked toward the tavern just before ten o'clock, "that water is the dishonest barman's best friend, for if applied properly it will grow profits just like manure grows corn, and that's a fact! There's an art to it, of course. Too much water and your customers, who may not be the most forgivin' sorts, will find you out for sure and either take their business elsewhere or take you to the hereafter with a noose around your neck. Saw just such a thing in Deadwood once, and while I do not condone lynchin' I cannot say I shed a tear for any cheatin' barman who is jerked to Jesus. Of course, if you're dilutin' is so subtle that you manage to put but a drop or two in the bottle — well then, you have gained nothin' but dishonor for the risk you have taken."

Holmes found this speech quite intriguing and told Rafferty: "Your expertise in this matter is most astounding, sir. It leads me to wonder whether you have any practice in this black art."

"Those are fightin' words, sir," Rafferty replied, only half in jest. "A man who would dilute a good bottle of whisky should burn in hell, in my estimation, and will surely do so if the devil is performin' his duties."

"My apologies," said Holmes instantly. "I have no doubt that your fine tavern is known throughout the Northwest for the honest drink you pour. Now, however, let us turn our attention to the situation at hand. Is everything in readiness?"

I was rather puzzled by this question, but Rafferty seemed to understand it perfectly. "It is," he replied.

"Excellent," said Holmes. "Very well then, let us see what marvels the Majestic may hold for us this evening."

The Majestic, we soon discovered, did not live up to its name. The tavern occupied the ground floor of a nondescript wooden building a block off Alexandria's main street, and as we neared it we could hear sounds of laughter and conversation echoing through the walls.

Holmes, as usual, led the way, marching through the front door as nonchalantly as if he were arriving for a night at the opera.

Inside, we hung our coats on a big row of hooks near the door (though Rafferty, saying he was chilly, declined to shed his long overcoat) and then surveyed the establishment's decidedly limited splendors. The tavern consisted of a large, square room with a plank floor below, a tin ceiling above, flimsy walls decorated with peeling paper, and a long wooden bar at the rear. Prints of fishing scenes mounted on the walls comprised the sole attempt at decoration. Not surprisingly, the place reeked of cigar smoke and beer, and I noted with disgust that the floor was stained with innumerable expectorations which had missed their intended mark in the randomly placed spittoons.

Despite its evident lack of appeal, the tavern was packed with hard-looking men in simple work clothes who stood at small tables or before the bar. Electric lamps provided the illumination, and in their glow Holmes and I—both attired in well-cut suits—were instantly conspicuous. Rafferty, of course, stood out by the sheer bulk of his presence, as did one other man, who occupied a place near the center of the bar, facing the crowd of drinkers.

Rafferty had done his best to describe Magnus Larson for us, but in the flesh the man was even more commanding than my imagination had made him out to be. Well over six feet, he was broad-chested and muscular, with a thick blond beard and long golden locks which swept down to his shoulders. When I got a better look at him, I was struck by his wild eyes, which were the deep, piercing blue of an alpine lake. His broad nose, however, was red and splotched, no doubt as a result of his incessant drinking. I put his age at no more than forty-five, given the limited progress of the gray strands flecking his hair and beard. His most remarkable feature was a very high forehead, which was so cut through by deep creases that it inevitably suggested the rugged fjords of his homeland.

His attire was also most distinctive, for he wore a long red tunic, cinched with a black belt and adorned with primitive decorations which I took to be of Scandinavian origin. He was, in short, a perfect

Viking of a man, and had he suddenly produced a sword and shield and waved it menacingly at the crowd, I should have at once taken him for some ancient Nordic raider improbably restored to life in the last years of the nineteenth century.

He was declaiming upon history as we made our entrance, and his lordly basso boomed across the room like a cannon over water: "Columbus, curse him, was but a follower, gentlemen, and he no more discovered America than the Pope discovered religion. The whole rotten story of 1492 is nothing but a pack of wop lies, and you should not believe it for a moment. No, gentlemen, it was your forebears, Vikings with the hearts and souls of giants, who sailed from Greenland and first set foot on this mighty continent. History will one day prove it so — you can mark my word on that. And now, barkeep, I propose you fill my glass and we drink to the noble Vikings of old!"

As Larson uttered these last words, earning a loud hurrah from the tavern patrons, he finally caught sight of Holmes, Rafferty, and me. Setting down his tall glass of beer, he gave us a long disbelieving stare, as though he were looking upon some unprecedented wonder. "Well now," he said, his powerful voice easily cutting through the din of the room, "what have we here? Is that you, Mr. Rafferty, the bothersome Irishman?"

"I am at your service, sir," said Rafferty with a slight bow, "and I appreciate the lesson in history you have just provided, though I would put in a word for St. Brendan, if you don't mind."[2]

Larson raised his glass in a mock salute and said: "By all means, sir, by all means, give the Irish monk his due, though in my opinion the Celts are more to be trusted with fancy than fact."

Then, looking directly at Holmes and me, Larson said: "I see, Mr. Rafferty, that you have brought along some gentlemen of leisure to mix with the lower elements. Who are these well-dressed fops you have dragged into this den of iniquity?"

The other conversation in the bar had now come to a halt, and all eyes were on us. Gesturing toward Holmes and me, Rafferty said: "These are indeed gentlemen, Mr. Larson, and they have braved the stormy North Atlantic to come here all the way from England. I would like you to meet Mr. John Baker and Mr. Peter Smith, experts from the British Museum who hope to examine the famous rune stone."

"You don't say," said Larson. "Experts, are they? Well, will you consent to join me for a drink, gentlemen, or are you of the dry persuasion?"

"I have no brief against enjoying a drink now and then," replied Holmes with a tight, chilly smile. "I suppose it would do us no harm to join you."

"Well then, step right up," said Larson, who spoke with a pronounced accent which did not at all resemble that of a Swede. Indeed, he sounded much more like the rude hacks we had encountered in Manhattan on our way to Minnesota.

I would have found this most unaccountable had not Holmes informed me much earlier that Larson, the son of Swedish immigrants, was a native of New York City. Holmes had gleaned this knowledge through "digging," as he called it, prior to our voyage across the Atlantic. Among other things, he had learned that Larson was twenty-two years old before he made his first visit to Sweden and was thirty when he finally settled down to live there. And even though Larson had excellent command of Swedish, he wrote his novels first in English and then translated them back into Swedish. "He is more American than Swedish," Holmes had told me, "though he now makes a great show of his Scandinavian heritage. Indeed, he likes to call his books 'an epic of my people.' "

Holmes had also learned that Larson, despite the success of his novels, was such an improvident spender that he was virtually penniless when he left Sweden in the summer of 1898 to do what he called "research with the people" in America. In fact, according to Holmes, Larson's departure had less to do with literary research than with an urgent need to escape a horde of angry creditors snapping at his heels.

Once we had joined Larson, the bartender—a dour character whom I assumed to be Ericson, the Majestic's owner—asked what we wanted to drink.

"We shall have some of that beerlike substance which Mr. Larson is imbibing," said Holmes, whose haughty manner hardly seemed designed to put Larson at ease. Three large glasses of beer were soon placed before us, after which Holmes said: "I am surprised to see, Mr. Larson, that you are not mourning the tragic death of your friend Mr. Wahlgren. After all, you must have known him quite well."

"I knew him," Larson agreed. "Not that it is any business of yours. The fact is, my friends and I have been drinking all evening to the poor man's memory."

" 'Tis supposed to be a regular Irish wake then," chimed in Rafferty, "though without the comfortin' presence of the corpse. That does not seem to be much of a wake to me, Mr. Larson."

Holmes, as though hoping to irk Larson even further, quickly added: "You are right, Mr. Rafferty. It is hardly a proper send-off for a friend. I must say, Mr. Larson, that I find your indifference rather odd, since it is said you have been one of the chief promoters of Mr. Wahlgren's rather unlikely discovery."

Larson turned his icy blue eyes on Holmes and said with considerable irritation: "I do not wish to talk of Mr. Wahlgren, sir. He is gone and that is that. As for how I do my grieving, that is none of your concern, sir. Nor do I need any lessons in bereavement from your fat Irish friend, thank you. I am, however, interested in you, Mr. Baker. Just what sort of expert are you?"

"My specialty is ancient and medieval Scandinavia," replied Holmes, "with particular attention to runic writing. That is why I wished to see the famous rune stone here. Naturally, it is a most intriguing discovery. The British Museum, in fact, might be interested in buying the artifact, if it can be proved genuine, which I very much doubt will happen. However, I am told that you, also, have shown some interest in buying the stone."

"Where did you hear that?" Larson demanded.

"It is merely a rumor about town," Holmes said with a shrug. "Am I to assume it is false?"

"You can assume whatever you damn well please," replied Larson, who appeared to be well lubricated with alcohol, judging by his bellicose demeanor and a slight slurring of his speech. His eyes now bored in on Holmes and he said: "Let us talk about runes, sir, since you claim to be such an expert on the subject. You have no doubt seen a copy of the stone's inscription, or you would not be here. What does a great expert such as yourself make of the inscription?"

Holmes coolly returned Larson's gaze and said: "I cannot be certain what to make of it, which is why I hoped to examine the stone itself. Still, I have much experience in such matters—the good plowmen of Sweden, as you well know, are famous for their love of runic forgery—and I should be surprised if your stone proves to be anything but a hoax."

"Specifics, sir, give me specifics," said Larson, who clearly was offended by Holmes's blunt and skeptical comments. He now removed a small, thick notebook from his back pocket and waved it about like a talisman. "Do you see this? It is all the evidence I need. I've spent months collecting information about the stone, and it is all right here in black and white. These are the facts, sir, the facts, and not the opinions of some supposed expert. And the facts point to one conclusion and one conclusion only: the stone is genuine. So, I say again, give me specifics, sir, or I will have to assume you are nothing more than a two-bit English mountebank with his nose up a place it shouldn't be."

"As you wish, Mr. Larson," said Holmes, ignoring the Swede's final insult. "If it is specifics you want, you shall have them. I would begin by noting that there are a number of problematic runes—the double use of the *r;* the reversed capital *K,* the highly irregular *n,* the very odd dotted *a,* and the peculiar *j,* among others. No such runes can be found in the standard futhork or in verified medieval examples of runic writing in Sweden. Therefore, these runes—and the stone into which they are carved—must be viewed as extremely suspect. The stone's pentadic numerals are also peculiar, as is the use of the word *oppagelsefarb,* which in my judgment is a blatant modernism. In other words, Mr. Larson, there are many reasons to question the stone's authenticity."

Holmes's dissection of the inscription's flaws left Larson fuming, no doubt in part because of the rather arrogant manner in which it was delivered. I must confess that I, too, was surprised by Holmes's response, since in our previous conversation he had always seemed willing to maintain an open mind as to the rune stone's credibility.

"By God, sir, every one of your objections can be readily answered!" Larson said, pounding his fist so hard upon the bar that glasses from one end to the other rattled and shook, as though a minor earthquake had rumbled through the tavern. "First of all—"

"Please, spare me," said Holmes dismissively. "I have heard all the usual defenses, and they are invariably founded on nothing more substantial than a thin tissue of speculation."

Larson was so angry now that I thought he might strike Holmes, but instead he waged his assault with words. "You so-called experts are all alike," he sneered at Holmes. "You are little men with little ideas, and you are so intent upon promoting the old lies that you have closed your minds to new possibilities. Why shouldn't the Vikings have been here five hundred years ago? They were the best sailors in Christendom, with the best boats, and for all I know they might have traveled all the way to the Rockies before they were through. The stone which has now been stolen is proof, sir, proof of who discovered this continent, and if you are looking for something suspicious, then you might consider who stole it and for what reason. That is what I say, sir!"

This spontaneous oration, to which our fellow tavern patrons had listened in astonished silence, was greeted with a boisterous round of cheers. "A drink for Mr. Larson!" someone shouted. At once other voices joined the chorus. "*Ja, ja,* a drink for Mr. Larson!"

Holmes waited for the uproar to subside, and said: "I shall buy you that drink, Mr. Larson, for I admire a man who speaks his mind fearlessly and with great skill, even when he is completely wrong. And, if you are interested, I will also make you a proposition."

Larson, who was a bit unsteady on his feet, lurched toward Holmes until the two men stood eye to eye, barely inches apart. "A proposition, you say? You are beginning to sound like some cheap Bergen whore, sir, or have I misunderstood you?"

This crude remark drew peals of laughter from the tavern's drinkers, who now circled around us as though anticipating the bloody ritual of a prize fight.

Paying no heed to this latest insult, Holmes calmly asked Larson: "Tell me, sir, are you a betting man?"

"And what has that got to do with anything?" Larson replied suspiciously, rocking on his heels as he tried to maintain his balance.

"Merely this," said Holmes, raising his voice so that his words rang out across the tavern. "I believe, sir, that you are delusional about the rune stone, which is almost certainly nothing but a clumsy fake concocted by a few local farmers to entertain themselves on a long winter's night. But I see I cannot convince the great Magnus Larson"—he pronounced these last three words with acidic contempt—"of what should be obvious even to a child. Therefore, I propose a simple contest—a duel, as it were—by which we will settle our little disagreement, here and now. Are you man enough for that?"

Holmes's provocative speech won the attention of the crowd, whose ragtag members now eagerly looked toward Larson to hear his response.

With a contemptuous snort, Larson stepped back from Holmes and said: "A duel, sir, is that what you wish? Well, why not! What will it be, Mr. Baker? Pistols, knives? No, I think not. The more I look at you, sir, the more I see one of those fairy Englishmen wearing breeches and waving a little sword."

Once again, the crowd reacted to Larson's sneering insult with the utmost glee. I, however, had endured quite enough of the famous author and was about to deliver a good sound punch to his bearded jaw when Rafferty grabbed me by the arm. "Oh no, Doctor," he whispered in my ear. " 'Tis not the time for fisticuffs."

Holmes, meanwhile, remained the picture of composure. "Actually, I am rather good with an épée," he informed Larson. "But there would be scant pleasure in slicing up a fool such as yourself. No, I have quite another weapon in mind." He turned to the bartender, Ericson, and said: "Two bottles of your best akvavit, if you please."

The crowd was now enrapt in the little drama unfolding before them, as was Larson himself, who looked on with undisguised curiosity as Ericson produced two quart bottles of the pale yellow liquor and placed them on the bar.

Holmes picked up one of the bottles, studied it for a moment, and handed it over to Rafferty. He then said: "Well, Mr. Rafferty, does it meet with your approval?"

I was now at a complete loss and could only wait with the rest of the crowd to find out what would happen next.

Rafferty carefully examined the bottle, like a jeweler studying a fine diamond, then removed the stopper by wrapping his coat around it to keep his hand from slipping. Finally, he raised the bottle to his nose and sniffed the contents. " 'Tis one hundred proof, no less," he said, "or Shadwell Rafferty is not the best saloon keeper in St. Paul."

"Good," said Holmes, taking the bottle back and holding it up in front of Larson. "Well, sir, here is my proposition. If you are prepared for the challenge, I intend to drink you under the table tonight, with as much of this delightful substance as is required for the job. And before you fall to the floor in a blathering stupor I expect to hear from you an apology for your impertinence, which I have begun to find very tiresome."

I could not believe what I had just heard. Although Holmes would occasionally take a glass of brandy or a pint of bitters, he was in general most abstemious when it came to liquor, and during our years together I had never seen him overindulge in ardent spirits. And yet here he stood, proclaiming his intention to outdrink a huge tosspot of a man who obviously possessed an enormous capacity for alcohol.

"Really, Mr. Baker," I said as a malevolent grin spread across Larson's face, "I am not sure this is a wise idea."

"Not now," said Holmes irritably, brushing me aside. "Well, Mr. Larson, are you up to the challenge?"

"Ha! The question should be whether an English swell such as yourself is up to it," came the instant reply. "Why, I will take great amusement in seeing you laid out on the floor with your fancy suit, puking your insides all over it. Ha! Bring us shot glasses, Mr. Ericson, for we are going to have fun tonight." Turning to the crowd, he added, "Come on, boys, three cheers for the Englishman, who will soon regret his arrogance."

The crowd immediately urged the contestants on, and so began what must be accounted one of the most curious episodes in my long association with Sherlock Holmes. The rules of the contest, if it could be called such, were simple. Separate rows of shot glasses were set out on the bar before Holmes and Larson, and each man was to pour a drink, down it in one gulp, then wait for the other man to do likewise. This would be repeated until, as Rafferty put it, "one of the gents retires to a comfortable spot on the floor."

I was aghast at the whole idea, not only because I knew Holmes's limited tolerance for alcohol but also because of what he would be drinking. I had sampled akvavit only once — during the ice palace affair three years earlier — but its bitter, acrid taste had left an enduring impression. It was, I thought, the most vile liquid I had ever consumed, and I simply could not imagine how Holmes proposed to drink glass after glass of it.

Holmes, however, appeared quite ready for the task. Pouring out his first drink, he raised it high so that everyone could see, saluted the crowd with a "Here's to you" — one of many Americanisms he seemed to have mastered — and then downed the horrid liquid in a single gulp.

Larson quickly followed suit, and before long he and Holmes were consuming one shot after another, much to the enjoyment of the crowd which had gathered tightly around them to watch the tawdry contest.

Initially, Holmes and Larson said nothing to each other, but after a goodly number of drinks had gone "down the hatch," to use Rafferty's phrase, the two contestants began to shed their mutual animosity. Indeed, as the night wore on, and more shot glasses were emptied, Holmes and Larson became quite friendly, engaging in the sort of nonsensical banter which drunkards — but not onlookers — find so amusing. Amid all of this inane palaver, Holmes loosened his tie and removed his coat, and I noted with alarm that he had become wobbly on his feet and was beginning to slur his words.

Hoisting what must have been his tenth glass of akvavit, Holmes offered a toast to Larson: "To a fine drinking man, Magnus Larson. You can handle your liquor, sir, and you have my compliments."

Larson, who appeared to be in the same reeling condition as Holmes, responded with a toast of his own: "To you, sir, to you. Why, I thought we'd be wiping you off the floor by now, but for a skinny English dog you are a fine drinking man. A fine man."

Two more shots soon went down, by which time Holmes, weak and unsteady on his feet, seemed to be holding himself up at the bar by sheer force of will. His head, meanwhile, bobbed around like a balloon atop his long neck, and I could only imagine the befogged state of his magnificent intellect. And then, to my utter dismay, I heard Sherlock Holmes giggle — a sound so inconceivable that I now believed he had lost complete control of himself.

Holmes's bizarre giggling proved contagious, and soon Larson was laughing uncontrollably at nothing in particular. When his insipid laughter finally subsided, Larson put one arm over Holmes's shoulder and began singing at the top of his lungs in Swedish. This impromptu aria was accompanied by lascivious gestures, which suggested to me that the song was not of the kind suitable for the ears of women and children. Holmes soon joined in the song, and the spectacle presented by the two men was so painfully absurd that I begged Rafferty to put a stop to it.

"No, Doctor," he whispered, " 'twould not be right to deny a gentleman his pleasure, even if he is Sherlock Holmes."

Both men were now staggeringly drunk, and once they had finished their song they began shouting incomprehensibly to the crowd, after which they launched into a brief dance, whirling each other around and otherwise acting like shrieking madmen. How they managed to stay on their feet for these absurd gyrations was quite beyond me, but when it was over they both wobbled back to the bar for yet another drink.

Holmes duly downed his shot and, in words so slurred I could barely understand them, told Larson: "Let us toast the rune stone, my friend — a toast to the greatest piece of fakery in the history of America!"

Larson, whose earlier bellicosity had vanished in a soft warm sea of alcohol, raised his glass and replied: "A toast, sir, but to the truth:

the damn thing is real, don't you see, real as this drink before me. You have my word on it, kind sir, my word."

Holmes, swaying and reeling as though he were being buffeted by some unseen wind, responded by letting out a long, noisy burp. He then reached for his bottle of akvavit, which was nearly empty. With trembling hands, he somehow poured another drink, which he slowly brought up to his lips. Finally, he said: "So the stone is real. You have convinced me, sir. You are a genius to see such a thing, a genius, sir! I suppose that is why you were smart enough to try to buy it from that fool Wahlgren."

Larson nodded eagerly and reached for his own bottle. "Sure, I made a deal, but it's no good now, no good at all. That damn farmer! He signed the paper and then he reneged, the son of a b — — h. And now the stone's gone. It's hidden out there somewhere on that lousy, stinking farm of his. You can bet on that."

Holmes gave a sympathetic nod and said: "People are no damn good, my friend, that is what I say. An honest man such as yourself tries to make an honest deal and what does he get? A kick in the teeth, that's what, because a crook like Wahlgren just can't be trusted. Why, the old cheat got what he deserved, that's what I say."

"Exactly," Larson said, gulping down another shot. "But I'd sure like to find that damn stone, I can tell you that. Otherwise, there'll be no money for any of us."

Holmes gave a long, sad shake of his head. "No money," he repeated several times, then said: "You're right, Magnus, right as rain. Oskar won't pay if you don't have the stone."

"Oh no, you don't understand," Larson replied, pulling Holmes close and putting both hands over his shoulders, as though addressing his dearest friend in the world. "It's the other king, the one in Chicago. The Match King. He's the one with the money—lots of it. He's the one who wants the stone."

"Well then, let us drink to the Match King," said Holmes, sliding out from Larson's grip and tottering back to the bar, where he poured yet another glass for himself, spilling half of it as he did so. Then, in a shaky voice, he said: "Yes, a drink to the Match King, to Mr. — "

His face a study in alcoholic confusion, Holmes paused, presumably trying to dredge up a name from his bedimmed memory, and finally said: "Say, Magnus old boy, what did you say his name is, that Match King fellow?"

But Larson, who was rocking back and forth on his feet like a big tree branch caught in the wind, did not seem to hear the question. Instead, he gave Holmes a loud slap on the back and said out of the blue: "A woman, sir. That is what I need, a woman. Oh yes, and I know one, too. Have you seen her?"

"Certainly I have seen her," said Holmes loudly. "Yes, I have seen her many times. Many times . . . yes, of course . . . I have seen her."

Holmes began to slump over on the bar, and I thought for a moment that he would pass out. But even though his train of thought appeared to be on the verge of derailment, he somehow got his head back up and said: "Yes indeed, I have seen the woman . . . seen her many times . . . ah, what did you say her name was again?"

"Why, Mary Comstock, who else?" said Larson, grinning like a satyr. "Now, there is a woman a man could get lost in, and I would not mind making the journey! She could do things, things that—"

These were to be Larson's last words of the evening. Turning to look at the crowd, his eyes so fixed and glassy that I wondered if he could even see anything at all, he suddenly went down to his knees and then toppled over onto the floor. After that, he did not move.

Holmes, who looked in no better shape than his vanquished foe, stared at Larson's prostrate form, looked up at the disbelieving crowd, and said with a giggle: "Well, I guess I win."

Rafferty immediately took charge of the situation. "Mr. Smith," he said, "would you please take a look at Mr. Larson to see if he's all right? After that, 'twould be best if we leave at once."

I bent down to examine Larson. His breathing, as might be expected from so much alcohol consumption, was shallow and labored, but he appeared to have a good pulse and I did not think him to be in any immediate jeopardy.

"He just needs to sleep it off," I told Rafferty, "though I imagine he will have an awful headache come morning."

"Good. Then if you will be so kind as to help me with your gigglin', smirkin' friend here, we'll say our farewell."

We each grabbed Holmes under one arm and more or less dragged him from the tavern, by which time he had broken out into an old English drinking song whose words I would be embarrassed to repeat.

Chapter Eight

"HE IS ALSO SAID TO BE THE RICHEST SWEDE IN AMERICA"

Holmes kept at his obscene song until we were well out of view of the Majestic, and I could only imagine what sort of a ruckus he would raise once we reached our hotel. As we turned onto Broadway, which was Alexandria's main street, Rafferty looked behind us, suddenly let go of Holmes, and announced: "All right, we're in the clear."

To my surprise, Holmes instantly abandoned his dreadful caterwauling, firmly removed himself from my grasp, and said in a completely normal voice: "Well, my dear Watson, what did you think of our little show?"

In truth I did not know what to think, so flustered was I by Holmes's rapid and unexpected return to sobriety. "I . . . I am pleased to see you . . . so . . . so well," I stammered. "But how in God's name could you have consumed so much alcohol and still be—"

Here I found myself searching for a word, which Rafferty, who had broken out in gales of laughter, gladly provided: "Standin'? Is that what you're tryin' to say, Doctor?"

"Why, yes, I suppose it is."

Holmes, who obviously was not the least bit intoxicated, slapped me on the back and said: "It was all trickery, Watson, courtesy of our fine friend Mr. Rafferty."

Rafferty, who was now doubled over and laughing so hard that I feared he would spring a hernia, finally straightened himself up and, by way of explanation, produced a large liquor bottle from inside his capacious coat.

He said: "Now you know why I didn't take off my coat inside the lovely Majestic, even though the place was stinkin' hot. You see, this is the bottle of akvavit—a most foul and despicable liquor, to my way of thinkin'—which the barkeep brought out for Mr. Holmes. Take a look, Doctor, and tell me what you observe."

We were standing near a street lamp, and in its soft glow I could clearly see that the bottle was full. "You switched bottles," I said. "But how—"

"—did I do it?" Rafferty interrupted, completing my thought. " 'Twas simple enough. You see, among the many minor skills I've acquired along the undulatin' road of life is a bit of a talent for sleight of hand. Learned it from a card sharp in Virginia City by the name of Edgar Valdez. Edgar had hands so fast he could steal the drawers off a Pinkerton man, with the poor fellow being none the wiser, and that's a fact! Poor Edgar got shot in the end, of course—most of those sharpers did—but he taught me a few tricks before he rode the box to Boot Hill. Are you beginnin' to see the picture now, Doctor?"

I thought back to the events at the Majestic and remembered how Rafferty had examined the bottle of akvavit, then wrapped his coat around it to pull out the stopper. Of course! It was then that he had switched bottles, replacing the one from the bar with a similar bottle presumably kept in his pocket. Rafferty quickly confirmed that this was indeed the case.

" 'Twas not a hard thing to do. After Mr. Holmes and I planned our little ruse this mornin', I stopped by the Majestic late in the day to scope the place out and have a chat with Mr. Ericson. While exchangin' thoughts about the finer points of bartendin' with that gentleman, I learned what brand of akvavit the establishment serves to its thirsty customers. I then had no trouble obtainin' a similar bottle at one of the town's other waterin' holes."

"And the contents of this substitute bottle," I said, "were then emptied and replaced with colored water."

"Not entirely," said Holmes. "In the interest of verisimilitude, Mr. Rafferty insisted upon mixing in enough akvavit with the water to provide a semblance of the real thing and its alcoholic odor. However, I can assure you, Watson, that even at a dilution rate of ninety-five percent, akvavit is hardly a pleasant libation. But it had to be done, since Mr. Rafferty and I agreed that Magnus Larson was far too clever a man to tell us anything unless his tongue could somehow be loosened. It was Mr. Rafferty who came up with the idea of the drinking contest. It was, if I may say so, Mr. Rafferty, a stroke of genius."

"Well, I don't know about that, but it seems to have worked pretty much as we intended. Too bad, though, that Mr. Larson went to sleep before we could squeeze a little more out of him."

"That is true," agreed Holmes, "but I am nevertheless quite satisfied, for we learned four things of great value. First, we now know that Olaf Wahlgren, for reasons as yet not entirely clear, reneged on his sales agreement with Mr. Larson. This confirms that the farmer kept the stone and must indeed have been murdered on account of it. Second, we learned that Magnus Larson has apparently abandoned any attempt to sell the stone to King Oskar and the Swedish government. The mystery is why he did so. Third, we have new information that there is a man in Chicago—presumably a very rich one—who wants to buy the stone. Unfortunately, we do not know the man's name, other than that he seems to be known as the Match King. Finally, we now have proof that a relationship of some kind exists between Mr. Larson and Mary Comstock. What we do not know is the exact nature of this relationship and what, if anything, it may tell us about the murder of Olaf Wahlgren."

"Sounds like we have some busy days ahead of us," said Rafferty. "The questions you pose, Mr. Holmes, are mighty posers indeed, though I'd be especially eager to learn why Mr. Larson is no longer interested in sellin' the stone to the king."

"There is one idea which comes immediately to mind in that regard," said Holmes.

"Ah, then maybe you are thinkin' what I'm thinkin'," said Rafferty.

"And what would that be?" I asked.

"There is no point in speculating about Mr. Larson's motives at this point," cautioned Holmes. "Mr. Rafferty is correct. We now must go to work if we are to find good answers. There is still much that we do not know about this entire matter."

"I can't argue with you there, Mr. Holmes," said Rafferty. "But I will say this: Magnus Larson certainly had a very good motive for murderin' the farmer."

"He did," Holmes acknowledged. "And yet I think it is premature to point the finger of guilt at him, since I found him to be quite convincing when he said he wished he knew where he could find the stone. Still, I should like to know where Mr. Larson was on the night when Mr. Wahlgren met his unfortunate demise."

"I'll do some checkin' on that very matter," said Rafferty. "But chances are he was imbibin' somewhere during the course of that night, maybe even at the lovely Majestic. From what I've heard, Mr. Larson can be counted on to stay until closin' at whatever tavern he happens to be patronizin'."

"What time do the taverns here normally close?" Holmes asked.

Rafferty said: "If memory serves me right, closin' time is eleven o'clock on weekdays and midnight on Fridays and Saturdays."

Holmes thought for a moment and then said: "Assuming that Mr. Larson was out drinking on Wednesday night and that the tavern closed at eleven o'clock, he would have had time to hurry out to Mr. Wahlgren's farm in order to murder him at, say, one or two in the morning. Of course, this also assumes that Mr. Wahlgren did not die before about midnight. We shall have to talk with the coroner to see whether the time of death has been precisely established."

"I'll handle that," Rafferty volunteered. "You see—"

Holmes interrupted: "You know the coroner—is that what you were about to say, Mr. Rafferty?"

"Well, as a matter of fact—"

"Enough said," remarked Holmes with a smile. "Talk with the coroner, tomorrow if possible, and let us know what you find out."

"It will be my pleasure," Rafferty replied.

As there seemed to be a lull in the conversation, I now sought the answer to a personal question, for the more I thought of how Holmes and Rafferty had duped me, as well as Magnus Larson and the tavern patrons, the more peeved I became.

"Now that the business at the Majestic is done with," I said, "I should like to know why the two of you did not inform me of your plan."

Rafferty, dropping his eyes in a way no doubt intended to suggest deep contrition, replied: " 'Twas me you have to blame for that, Doctor, and no one else. Mr. Holmes, of course, has complete confidence in your discretion, as do I. But I was worried, I don't mind tellin' you, about how the whole little game would play out. I knew that if anybody in the tavern got wise to what we were doin', we'd be in the devil's own trouble, for drinkin' men can get mean in a hurry. So, I figured you'd be our canary in the cage, as it were."

"Your canary? What on earth do you mean?"

"Just this. In the old days, when miners went down into the shafts, they'd take along a canary as a kind of insurance policy. Canaries, it is said, like good sweet air, but if the air is at all bad, why they keel over and die, poor creatures. If that happened, the miners knew the time had come for them to get out pronto. Well, Doctor, I figured you'd be our canary, for if Mr. Holmes could fool you—his most loyal and valued friend—with his carryin' on, then we'd be all right. But if you started gettin' suspicious, then we'd have to assume that maybe other folks were as well, and then we'd start thinkin' about beatin' a fast retreat."

"In other words, my dear Watson, you were our sentinel," said Holmes, "upon whom our safety depended."

I failed to find this explanation very satisfactory. "I do not take it as a compliment that you and Mr. Rafferty view me as your guardian canary," I told Holmes. "But as the two of you seem to so enjoy your silly little scheming, I suppose there is nothing more to be said about it."

❀   ❀   ❀

Although it was fast approaching midnight by the time we reached the Douglas House, neither Holmes nor Rafferty displayed the slightest hint of weariness, despite a day that had begun very early for both of them. I could only marvel at the energy which they brought to our investigation, for I was by this time more than ready to turn in for the night. This was not to be, however, for barely had we stepped into the lobby when Holmes, who at times seemed gifted with a kind of infinite wakefulness, announced that he must make a telephone call at once.

"It is very late, Holmes," I noted. "Whom would you call at this hour?"

"There is a gentleman we know in Chicago who is very much a creature of the night," Holmes responded. "Perhaps our luck will hold and he will be by his telephone. Why don't you and Mr. Rafferty enjoy a cigar while I see if our friend Wooldridge is available."

I now knew who Holmes was attempting to reach, for Clifton Wooldridge was indeed a friend, although one we had not seen since before the days of the ice palace investigation. Wooldridge was the most famous police detective in Chicago, known for his relentless pursuit of criminals and his ability, as he himself phrased it, to "make the big collar."[1] He had given Holmes and me a memorable tour of Chicago's vice-ridden Levee district after we had come to that city to investigate what turned out to be a minor matter on behalf of Potter Palmer, the real-estate and hotel mogul. Holmes and Wooldridge had remained in periodic contact since that time.

As Holmes went over to a small table near the front desk where the telephone was located, the desk clerk caught Rafferty's eye and motioned him over.

"There is a message for you," he said. "Came in about ten o'clock."

Rafferty took the message, which was on a piece of the hotel's stationery, quickly read it, and then slipped it into his pocket.

"Thank you, my boy," he said, but made no comment to me about the message itself.

While Holmes attempted to place his call, Rafferty and I took his advice and retired to the lobby, where we found comfortable chairs and smoked. Rafferty—who, as might be expected, was a marvelous raconteur—entertained me with tales of his days as a miner and, later, a freight-wagon driver in Nevada, during the era of the fabulous Comstock Lode.

"After they found the 'Big Bonanza'—which was in '73, as I recall—why, they were haulin' so much ore out of the mines you could have paved the roads with silver and nobody would have given it a second thought.[2] Dangerous work, though. Bushwhackers everywhere, not to mention the usual variety of gunslingers, cardsharps, four-flushers and bowie-knife artists, like the fellow who left that little souvenir on my forehead. Say, Dr. Watson, did I ever show you my secret weapon?"

"I don't believe so," I said, curious as to what new wonder Rafferty was about to reveal.

"Well, come on up to my room. You'll appreciate it."

I glanced over at Holmes, who by now was talking rapidly into the telephone.

Rafferty saw the same thing and said: "Looks like Mr. Holmes has made his connection. Knowin' him, he'll be talkin' for a while. We'll have plenty of time to look at my little beauty."

I followed Rafferty up to his room and watched as he reached down under his bed, pulled out a long leather case, and opened it to reveal the largest pistol I had ever seen. Its partly round and partly octagonal barrel must have been two feet long and was attached to a heavy nickel-plated frame with a walnut grip. But it was only when Rafferty took out what he called the "skeleton stock"—a sort of metal outline of a traditional wooden rifle stock—and attached it to the grip that I realized the pistol could also be used as a rifle.

"A beauty, isn't it?" said Rafferty, who, I was beginning to see, was a genuine connoisseur when it came to guns. (I later learned that he owned more than twenty-five of them and usually carried at least two on his person.) "It's called a pocket rifle, Doctor. Made by the Stevens Arms Company out of Chicopee Falls, Massachusetts.

Got my first one in Virginia City back in '73 or '74, after they'd just come out."3

"But why would you need a pistol that doubles as a rifle?" I asked. "Wouldn't one of each suffice, if, say, you were guarding a shipment of silver?"

"Certainly. But there are times when it's not convenient to be carrying a rifle around, such as when your hands are full of bags of silver bullion. That very thing happened to me once out at a freight station in the desert. Left my rifle in the wagon, and a bushwhacker who was lyin' in wait took a shot at me from a few hundred yards, figurin' I was easy prey. He wanted the bullion I was carryin', of course. But the poor fellow didn't know I had Mr. Stevens with me. I got down behind a pile of dirt, pulled out my secret weapon, and waited for the bushwhacker to come in for the kill. Dropped him at over a hundred yards, clean through the forehead."

"Impressive shooting, Mr. Rafferty," I said.

"Well, the fact is, I didn't have much choice. The Stevens is a single-shot weapon, Doctor, and reloadin' could have been fatal in that situation. Like to take a closer look at it?"

"I don't see why not," I said, picking up the weapon, holding its skeletal metal stock against my shoulder and squinting down the sights. "What caliber is it?" I asked

"This one's a .44," Rafferty said, "but they come in a variety of calibers. I should tell you that the beauty you're holding isn't the same one I had back in Nevada. This is a special model, with a screw-on barrel. Had it made for me a couple years back by Harry M. Pope himself, the best riflesmith in America."4

"Well," I said, handing the weapon back to Rafferty, "let us hope you will not have to use Mr. Stevens, as you call it, any time soon."

"You never know," said Rafferty as he returned the gun to its case. "Mr. Stevens saved me once, and it could happen again."

In fact, this was to prove true, though in a way neither Rafferty nor I could ever have anticipated.

❖   ❖   ❖

By the time we returned to the lobby, Holmes had just gotten off the telephone, and there was a glimmer of excitement in his eyes when he rejoined us.

"Mr. Wooldridge has more than lived up to his reputation as Chicago's greatest detective," said Holmes after he had pulled up a seat beside us. "The pieces are beginning to fall into place."

"Well then, let us hear where you have filled in the puzzle," said Rafferty.

"Very well, let us begin with the so-called Match King, Mr. Rafferty. I now know who he is, for Mr. Wooldridge identified him as a well-known figure in the Chicago business community named Karl Lund. He is commonly called the Match King because his company is said to be the world's largest producer of that useful item. Indeed, I am informed that the box of matches I now have in my pocket"—here Holmes showed us some matches he had picked up at the hotel—"were supplied by Mr. Lund's company. More importantly for our purposes, he is also said to be the richest Swede in America."

"Is he now?" said Rafferty. "And would he happen to be interested in antiquities?"

"Mr. Wooldridge says he is indeed. In fact, Mr. Lund's estate on Lake Michigan supposedly contains an enormous collection of Viking and Scandinavian artifacts. You will also be interested to hear that Mr. Lund is known to be extremely secretive, a recluse who keeps his collection under lock and key and seldom if ever admits visitors to his estate."

"In short, he's just the sort of man who might be willin' to buy the rune stone and ask no questions about how it was obtained," said Rafferty.

"Exactly," said Holmes. "There is something else you should know about the mysterious Mr. Lund. According to Detective Wooldridge, Mr. Lund is known to be a frequenter of Chicago's most beautiful and expensive courtesans."

"And why is that significant?" I asked.

"For this reason, Watson. When I talked to Mr. Wooldridge, I asked if he had ever come in contact with Mrs. Comstock, whose late husband, as we know, made his fortune in Chicago. Mr. Wooldridge was not familiar with anyone named Mary Comstock, but when I described the lady, he recognized her immediately. He reported that she was going under the name of Anna Robinson when she first came to the attention of the Chicago police in the summer of 1895. At that time, she was suspected of 'entertaining high-class gentlemen,' as Mr. Wooldridge put it, at one of the big hotels."

"So it appears her profession did not change after leaving Hinckley," I said.

"Not in the least. She merely moved her base of operations. In any case, she soon developed an influential clientele, which included a number of the city's aldermen. Thus protected from prosecution, she was by 1896 living in luxury in a large apartment overlooking the shores of Lake Michigan, according to Mr. Wooldridge. The lady's customers were said to include many of the city's wealthiest businessmen, and rumor had it that she received one hundred dollars a night, or more, for her services. I do not think it at all unlikely that Mr. Lund was one of those high-paying customers."

"Ah, this is gettin' juicy now," said Rafferty. "If the lady is well acquainted with Mr. Lund, then maybe she made an arrangement to sell him the rune stone."

"A distinct possibility," Holmes agreed.

"Of course, she'd first have had to convince him that the stone was the genuine article. And to do that, I'm thinkin' she'd have needed a confederate, somebody with credentials as an expert on runes."

"Magnus Larson," I said.

Holmes smiled and said: "I see we are all thinking alike. Unfortunately, we have no proof at the moment that any of this is true."

Rafferty thought for a moment and then said to Holmes: "Perhaps your Mr. Wooldridge in Chicago could be persuaded to have a nice long chat with the Match King."

"I suggested that very idea," said Holmes. "But Mr. Wooldridge informed me that such an interview would be impossible unless there was substantial evidence of wrongdoing. Mr. Lund guards his privacy to the utmost degree, and has the money, and the necessary lawyers, to keep the police at bay. No, I fear he will not be of much help to us."

"So what do you propose to do now, Mr. Holmes?" Rafferty asked.

"I propose to conduct our investigation here with all possible vigor, Mr. Rafferty. In the meantime, Mr. Wooldridge will gather what additional facts he can in Chicago. I shall be especially interested to learn more about Frank Comstock and when he married the former Mrs. Robinson. I am also curious as to why Mrs. Comstock, if her husband was so wealthy, now finds it necessary to engage in a scheme to sell the rune stone."

"Perhaps she is not as rich as we think," I opined.

"An intriguing thought, my dear Watson," said Holmes, rising from his chair, "and one I shall consider during the rest of this night. Perhaps we will all have some fresh ideas in the morning."

"We will have more than that, much more," said Rafferty. This statement, which Rafferty had uttered with unusual gravity, caused Holmes to return to his seat.

"All right, Mr. Rafferty, what is it?" Holmes asked. "I have the feeling you are about to spring a little surprise on us."

"Could be," he said, a sly twinkle in his blue eyes. "You see, I haven't told you, but I have a little birdie here in town."

Holmes said: "Really? And who might this 'birdie' be?"

"Ah, now, that must be a secret for the time bein', Mr. Holmes. This birdie of mine can be rather shy, as I'm sure you must understand."

"I see. Nonetheless, am I safe in assuming that this birdie of yours can talk?"

"Oh yes, there is nothin' wrong with its voice. It sent me a very interestin' message tonight."

"I have no doubt that it did, Mr. Rafferty. Would you care to share with us the song it warbled into your ear?"

"Be happy to. What the birdie told me is that Nels Fogelblad will be comin' back to Alexandria tomorrow on the afternoon train from Minneapolis. The train arrives here at just after three o'clock."

"I see. Then perhaps we should try to have a talk with Mr. Fogel-blad as he arrives."

"I think it should be even sooner than that," said Rafferty.

"Why?"

"Well, my little birdie told me something else, Mr. Holmes. The fact is, not only is Mr. Fogelblad coming back to town, he's also pre-pared to show the sheriff where the rune stone can be found."

Chapter Nine
"I KILLED NO ONE"

Rafferty's surprising statement prompted a barrage of questions from Holmes, few of which our friend could answer.

"I don't know the whys and wherefores," Rafferty finally told an exasperated Holmes. "All I know is that Mr. Fogelblad has supposedly stated that he is in possession of the rune stone and will lead the authorities to it as soon as he returns to town. I have no idea how he got his hands on the thing, but I imagine we'll find that out when we talk to him tomorrow."

Holmes considered these words for a moment and said: "Do you think there is any chance that Sheriff Boehm will permit us to interview Mr. Fogelblad tomorrow before he turns over the stone?"

Rafferty emitted a low grunt and said: "Not likely, Mr. Holmes. You've met the sheriff. He's a dark and suspicious man and not at all generous when it comes to sharin' information with civilians like us. That's why I believe we'll have to take matters into our own hands if we're to get to Mr. Fogelblad. Matter of fact, I just happen to have a little plan I've cooked up."

Over the next several minutes, Rafferty outlined his scheme, which was at once simple and audacious. Still, I could not help but wonder why Rafferty and Holmes thought it so vital for us to speak with Fogelblad before Sheriff Boehm interviewed him.

When I posed this question to Rafferty, he said: "The reason, Doctor, is that I'd be willin' to bet the best bottle of Irish whisky in my tavern that the sheriff will tell Mr. Fogelblad to keep his mouth shut from now on. I've talked to a few people around town about Sheriff Boehm and they all tell me the same thing: he doesn't brook any interference with his business, and will be happy enough to throw a man in jail just for lookin' at him the wrong way. In the case of Mr. Fogelblad, I suspect the sheriff may even specify that he is not to talk to us for any reason. Bein' a good Swede, that shouldn't be much of a challenge for Mr. Fogelblad."

"You are undoubtedly right, Mr. Rafferty," said Holmes. "Therefore, the sooner we can intercept Mr. Fogelblad and find out what he really knows, the better off we will be."

After discussing a few minor details regarding Rafferty's plan, Holmes finally went up to bed just after one in the morning. I gratefully followed, while Rafferty, who was inclined to insomnia, remained down in the lobby, saying he wished to do a little "freelance cogitatin'," as he so quaintly termed it.

"Well, I trust you will get some sleep tonight," I said to him before I went up to my room.

"Don't worry about me," he replied, lighting one of his awful cigars. "They say there is no rest for the wicked, which is why I figure that those of us who are tolerably good had best stay busy as well. Pleasant dreams, Doctor, and a good night to you."

The next morning, a Saturday, was the first of April, or April Fools', a designation which was to prove all too accurate before the day was done. Holmes had arisen early, as had I, since I did not wish to be left out, as I had the morning before, on any trickery he and Rafferty might be plotting. Rafferty, however, was nowhere in evidence when we went downstairs for breakfast. Holmes was not in a talkative mood and seemed content to read the local newspaper while I enjoyed my breakfast of bacon, hard-boiled eggs, and thick slices of toast slathered with strawberry jam.

It was only after I had finished my meal and ordered a second cup of strong black coffee that Holmes spoke up. "The *Clarion*, I fear, will not prove of great benefit to us in this investigation," he said. "Its editor shows little imagination and seems content to regurgitate the most basic of facts regarding the rune stone affair. Too bad! A good journalist here might find much of interest to write about and perhaps could even be of signal use to us."

Holmes, as I well knew, had always maintained a close, if at times thorny, relationship with the press, which he skillfully manipulated for his own purposes. He was on especially good terms with Lanier, the crime reporter for the *Daily Telegraph*, who on several occasions had gone so far as to "plant" certain items at Holmes's request.[1] Still, Holmes had learned through hard experience that the press was an unpredictable beast, which could be docile one moment only to turn ferocious the next, and more than once he had found Fleet Street more a hindrance than a help to his investigations.

"Journalists are invariably useful to the professional detective," Holmes now continued, in the manner of a professor delivering a lecture. "Yet one must always be cautious when it comes to the press, since as a rule the rude scribblers of the fourth estate have one great failing, which is that they pay little heed to the hierarchy of information."

"What do you mean?"

"Only this, Watson. You see, for journalists one piece of information is as good as the next, since they are above all else stokers who must constantly feed words into their busy printing presses, which are as voracious as the firebox of a locomotive. The presses need constant fuel, and it is the newspaperman's job to scavenge it wherever and however he can. As a result, everything and anything must be tossed to the hungry beast, with little regard for its value as information.

"Recall, for example, the Rathburn and Son swindling case, which I was able to clear up simply by reading a rather insignificant-looking story in the *Evening Chronicle*.[2] All I needed to know was there, but the *Chronicle*'s correspondents, in their ceaseless pursuit of new information, lost sight of the meaning of what they had already found. Nonetheless, as simple collectors of information, journalists are the detective's best friend—a proposition which is demonstrated by a small paragraph I found this morning in the *Clarion*. Here, take a look."

Holmes handed me the newspaper, where he had circled a sentence near the end of a story concerning funeral arrangements for Olaf Wahlgren. The sentence read as follows: "The Rev. Einar Blegen of Holandberg, a long-time friend of the deceased, will deliver the funeral oration during the services, to be held at ten o'clock this morning at the First Swedish M.E. Church in Holandberg."

"I fail to see what is so significant about this item of information," I said to Holmes as I handed the paper back to him. "Is it not commonly known that Mr. Wahlgren and Mr. Blegen were well acquainted?"

"It was not known to me until I read this article," said Holmes. "As you may recall, Watson, Mr. Kensington merely told us that Mr. Blegen had come over to Olaf Wahlgren's farm after the discovery of the stone and made a quick translation of it. We also know that Mr. Blegen in his capacity as a notary public signed the agreement between Mr. Wahlgren and Magnus Larson. But to deliver a man's funeral oration—that is irrefutable evidence of more than just a passing acquaintance. I must find a way to talk to Einar Blegen as soon as possible."

Holmes returned to his room after breakfast to ponder what he would only describe as "several troubling questions," while I was instructed to wait in the hotel lobby for Rafferty to put in an appearance.

The Irishman did so just after eleven o'clock, and the two of us then went up to Holmes's room, where we found the air almost unbreathable amid thick blue clouds of pipe smoke. This was a sure sign that Holmes had indeed undertaken a bout of serious thinking, for he had always found tobacco an aid to concentration.

"What say we go out for a stroll," suggested Rafferty, "since I am of the opinion, Mr. Holmes, that your lungs might benefit from the application of some fresh air. It is about time to be on the move anyway."

"A capital idea," said Holmes.

As it was another pleasant day, with bright sunshine and a temperature approaching fifty degrees, our stroll proved to be a welcome tonic. We headed along Broadway, past the wooden and, occasionally, brick storefronts which lined the wide, muddy street. I was not used to seeing much traffic along this thoroughfare, but I now noted numerous wagons and carriages parked in front of the shops, as well as many people on the sidewalks.

"Saturday's the big shoppin' day," said Rafferty. "All the farm families from around town come in to do their business. And, of course, it doesn't hurt that it's such a fine day."

After we had gone a short way, Rafferty told us how he had spent his morning, beginning with a visit to the office of Dr. William Barton, who was the county coroner.

"Got to know Dr. Barton on a fishin' trip up this way a few years back," Rafferty began. "He's a capable enough fellow. I also know his cousin, who runs a shoe store in St. Paul, so we had a nice little chat before gettin' down to brass tacks."

"And what did the good doctor have to tell you about Olaf Wahlgren's death?" Holmes asked with a hint of impatience in his voice.

"I was gettin' to that, Mr. Holmes. There were no particular surprises, I can tell you that. Dr. Barton performed the autopsy late yesterday and determined the time of death to be somewhere between about midnight and two in the mornin', give or take a few minutes."

"What was the basis for his judgment?" I asked.

"The usual things: degree of rigor mortis, postmortem lividity, body temperature, air temperature, stomach contents. The doc didn't arrive at the barn until after nine in the mornin', so he didn't have a warm corpse to work with. He let me examine the body and I saw nothin' unusual beyond that fact that Mr. Wahlgren's skull was just about split in two. I hadn't seen such a sight since shot and shell did their awful work at Gettysburg.[3] 'Tis obvious that whoever wielded the ax has got some strength, for you do not cleave a man's skull with a delicate blow."

"Were there any signs that Mr. Wahlgren had struggled with his killer?"

"No. In fact, the doc says the killer caught Mr. Wahlgren from behind, just as we thought. The poor man never saw what hit him."

"One more question, Mr. Rafferty," said Holmes. "Are you completely satisfied as to the competence of this Dr. Barton?"

"Oh yes, he knows what he's about. I think we are safe in assumin' that the time and manner of death are stated correctly in the doc's report, which has already gone to the sheriff and the county prosecutin' attorney."

We were now approaching the railroad depot, where we intended to catch an eastbound train a few minutes after noon. Holmes said: "Now then, Mr. Rafferty, I assume you have also been making inquiries about Magnus Larson? Have you succeeded in establishing his whereabouts at the time of Mr. Wahlgren's death?"

"Ah now, that's a bit of a puzzle, I'm afraid," said Rafferty. "I did learn that he was at the Majestic, and not some other waterin' hole, on Thursday night. Found that out from a couple of the regulars, who are prepared to swear that Mr. Larson was at the tavern till at least half past midnight."

"Midnight? But I recall you telling us, Mr. Rafferty, that the taverns in Alexandria close at eleven o'clock on weeknights."

Rafferty flashed a sly smile and said: "Well now, havin' more than a little experience in the saloon keepin' business, I can tell that closin' time is not always strictly honored. You see, the laws regulatin' such matters usually state only that liquor cannot be served past a particular hour. But if a man's got a powerful thirst and is on good terms with the barkeep, he can order up three or four drinks right before the appointed hour and then drink them at his leisure, providin' the establishment remains open, of course. Such was the case at the Majestic Friday night and, I suspect, every night."

"I see," said Holmes, adding: "Such a practice would never be tolerated in London. Very well then, what else did these 'regulars' tell you?"

"Well, they'll swear for starters that Mr. Larson was in his usual state of inebriation when he toddled out of the place. Now, if these witnesses are right, then it seems unlikely that Mr. Larson, as drunk as he was, could have raced all the way down to Mr. Wahlgren's farm in the dark of night and planted an ax in his skull within, say, an hour and a half. Unfortunately, the two fellows I chatted up are none too reliable and were probably well in their cups themselves."

Holmes said: "So it appears Mr. Larson may have an alibi and he may not. What about the bartender? Have you talked with him?"

"Oh yes, I spoke with Mr. Ericson, who informed me in no uncertain terms that he does not make a habit of discussin' the activities of his patrons with anyone unless, as he put it, 'the subpoena is in my hand, ja.' 'Tis not surprisin', Mr. Holmes, for any good saloon keeper knows that the second law of the business, after providin' an honest drink, is to keep your trap shut about what you've heard or seen."

"Have you found anyone who may have seen Mr. Larson after he left the Majestic?" I asked Rafferty.

"No such luck, I'm afraid. Mr. Larson is stayin' at the other hotel in town—the Lakeside Inn—so naturally I thought the night clerk there might have seen him. But when I woke up the clerk this morning—he was not exactly overjoyed about this, I might add—he told me that Mr. Larson, bein' a longtime guest, has a key to the hotel's rear entrance and often leaves and returns that way, since it puts him closer to his favorite waterin' hole. So unless we can find someone who saw Mr. Larson careenin' down the street after he left the Majestic, or, better yet, saw him hitchin' up a horse and buggy, we may never know for sure if he has an alibi."

"Did you ask whether—" Holmes began.

"Ah, you want to know if Mr. Larson owns a horse or buggy, don't you, Mr. Holmes?"

"I do," replied Holmes, who signified by a slight smile that he took no offense at Rafferty's interruption.

"The answer is no. And the only livery in town—run by your acquaintance Mr. Kensington—closes at six o'clock at night unless there's a special request for service. Mr. Kensington told me there was no such request on Wednesday night, which means Mr. Larson would either have had to borrow or steal a horse in order to reach the Wahlgren farm. So, the way it looks to me, we've got some real problems tryin' to pin this business on Mr. Larson, though it's certainly possible he was involved, especially if he had an accomplice who owns a horse and buggy."

"Which could well be the case," said Holmes as we reached the depot. "Unfortunately, we as yet have no firm evidence suggesting who that accomplice might have been."

Our plan was to take a train to the community of Sauk Centre, located about twenty-five miles east of Alexandria. Once in Sauk Centre, we intended to reverse course and catch the westbound train from St. Paul–Minneapolis on which Mr. Fogelblad would be aboard, if Rafferty's information was correct. We would then have an opportunity to interview the farmer before his arrival in Alexandria.

The success of this enterprise depended, of course, on both trains being on time, as Holmes was well aware.

"Mr. Hill has done us many favors in the past," Holmes remarked as we waited at the depot. "Now we can only hope that he will do us another one by living up to his reputation as the man who has made the Great Northern the most efficient and reliable railroad in the Northwest."

James J. Hill did not disappoint, for at five minutes past noon, precisely on schedule, our train arrived and we boarded it for the brief trip to Sauk Centre.

As we rode past the low wooded hills and rolling fields of central Minnesota, our discussion naturally centered on the rune stone case. Holmes and Rafferty exchanged numerous ideas and theories, and I was struck by how similarly the two of them thought despite their obvious differences in style and temperament. But it was Rafferty's knowledge of the local terrain, as it were, which proved most interesting to me, for he was able to answer a question that to a certain extent had baffled even Holmes.

The question had to do with why anyone would go to the trouble of carving such an elaborate fake (if indeed it was) as the stone, given the skepticism it would inevitably engender in many quarters.

As I put it to Rafferty: "Assuming that the stone is the work of a forger, did that person really believe he could make a fortune from his handiwork? Surely he must have known that the stone would be greeted with much skepticism and controversy?"

"Ah, Doctor, you've asked the very question that has been gnawin' at me like a mouse chewin' on a piece of cheddar cheese," said Rafferty. "But I just may have an answer for you. You see, over the years, I've gotten to know a few of the Swede farmers hereabouts. Now, when you first look at them with their long stoic faces and silent ways, why, you'd think they must be the most grim, humorless people on God's green earth. But once you get to know them, you find out that they're not. It's just that their sense of humor is mighty peculiar, dry as dust and quiet as a graveyard. That's why the rune stone is just the kind of joke one of these Swedes might decide to pull off."

"Can you be more specific, Mr. Rafferty?" asked Holmes, who had listened closely to our friend's remarks.

"I will do my best," said Rafferty, "though it is a hard thing to explain to somebody who doesn't know these Swedes. What you've got to understand is that if there's one thing they hate, it's big shots putting on airs. 'Tis the worst sin of all in their book, to be boastful or to put yourself up on a pedestal. That's why somethin' like the rune stone would appeal to them. Fact is, the good Swedes here would find nothin' funnier than springin' a sly joke on the professors and the nabobs and all the other highfalutin types who think they're smarter than everybody else."

Rafferty paused, glanced out the window, and said: "There's somethin' else the two of you should know. If there are folks around here who know the stone's a prank, they'll never admit it to you or me or anybody else. 'Tis not their way. No, they'll sit around their stoves in the darkness and cold and they'll laugh to themselves like crazy, only nobody will ever hear them. That's the kind of people these Swedes are. They'll laugh in silence, until the day they die, and then they'll take their secret to the grave. You can count on it."

Holmes now looked at Rafferty and said: "I pray you are wrong, sir, but I fear you may be right. In either case, let us see if we can learn something useful from Mr. Fogelblad, for unless I am mistaken Sauk Centre is but five minutes ahead."

Sauk Centre, with its wide, straight streets and undistinguished collection of buildings, looked little different from Alexandria or any other of the prairie towns we had seen. While waiting at the depot for Fogelblad's train, which was supposed to arrive at half past one, we were approached by a slender, red-headed lad who had overheard our conversation and asked Holmes whether we were English. Informed that we were, the young man, who told us his name was Harry Lewis, said he intended to become a famous writer who would travel all around the world one day.[4] Of more importance to us, the lad said the train we intended to catch was "always late on Saturdays" (the ticket agent had failed to mention this) and that we could anticipate a wait of an hour or more. The lad, unfortunately, proved to be correct, and it was not until a few minutes after two o'clock that we at last heard the whistle of the approaching train.

"I shall make a point of mentioning this to Mr. Hill," said Holmes, who had grown more impatient by the minute as we waited. Rafferty, on the other hand, was perfectly at ease, and chatted amiably with young Harry until the train arrived.

We boarded the front passenger coach at once and began looking for Fogelblad. None of us had ever seen him before, but Rafferty had obtained a complete description of the Swede from his "birdie," and when we reached the second-to-last coach of the train we saw him at once. He was sitting by himself near the front of the half-empty coach, and he averted his gaze when I caught his eye.

I was so used to seeing tall, blond, blue-eyed men on the streets of Alexandria that Fogelblad's appearance came as a surprise. He was a small, dark man, almost of the Mediterranean type, with a prominent nose, a rather pinched mouth, and close-set brown eyes. The most notable features of these eyes was that they appeared to be without any sparkle of hope, suggesting that Fogelblad possessed none of the bright, willful optimism so characteristic of most Americans. He was dressed in an ill-fitting blue suit and a starched white shirt, an outfit in which he looked quite uncomfortable.

Rafferty and Holmes had agreed beforehand on what might be called a strategy of interrogation, since both anticipated that the Swede, if he was as taciturn as most of his kind were reputed to be, would not give up information easily. By a stroke of luck, Fogelblad was the sole occupant of a pair of double seats which faced each other, so it was a simple matter for Rafferty and Holmes to take the seat across from Fogelblad while I slipped into the seat next to him.

"Good afternoon," said Rafferty in his typically inviting way. "You are Nels Fogelblad, who lives near Holandberg, are you not?"

The Swede looked at us suspiciously, his dark eyes darting back and forth as though he feared a bird of prey might at any moment swoop down and carry him away. "*Ja*," he finally said. "Who are you?"

"Rafferty," our friend said, and then to my surprise flashed a silver badge he had pulled out of one of his pockets. As he did so, his outercoat came open and I noticed he was carrying a large pistol—not "Mr. Stevens," to be sure, but a hefty weapon nonetheless. Fogelblad, I was sure, had also seen it. "Special investigator out of St. Paul," Rafferty continued. "These gentlemen are Mr. Baker and, next to you, Mr. Smith. They are my assistants."

Fogelblad took in this information without comment, but I could see his body stiffen with fear. After a moment, he said, "I must leave," and started to rise from his seat.

Rafferty, who was not only enormously strong but also uncommonly quick for so large a man, fairly leapt from his chair, put his arms on Fogelblad's shoulders, and pushed the startled Swede back down.

"You'll leave when I tell you to and not a second before," Rafferty growled. "Otherwise, I'll have to turn you over to Mr. Baker here"—he now glanced at Holmes, whose face had contorted into a menacing scowl—"and you would not like that. Mr. Baker, I am afraid, can be a very cruel man. Why, 'tis said he once threw a suspect off a movin' train. Happened somewhere near Duluth, as I recall. Poor fellow was horribly injured. Died in agony three days later. 'Twas very, very sad. As for Mr. Smith, who is sittin' beside you, well, you would not want to know the terrible things he's done."

I tried to appear suitably "terrible" as Rafferty uttered these words, though I fear I was unable to match the look of studied malevolence which gleamed from Holmes's eyes or the rough ferocity of Rafferty's manner.

"All right then," Rafferty continued, "the three of us are goin' to have a very pleasant conversation, Mr. Fogelblad, providin' you answer a few questions. We are charged with investigatin' Olaf Wahlgren's murder, and we intend to do so till we find the guilty party. Do we understand each other, sir?"

As Rafferty spoke, the conductor came through the door from the next coach. Fogelblad, perhaps thinking rescue was at hand, looked up hopefully in his direction. But such was the overwhelming sense of intimidation which Holmes and Rafferty conveyed that Fogelblad cast down his eyes and said nothing as the conductor passed down the aisle.

"A wise choice, Mr. Fogelblad," said Rafferty. "Now, we have but a few pertinent questions. I would begin by askin' for the name of your accomplice in the death of Olaf Wahlgren."

Such a provocative and accusatory question would have jolted most men into an instant and loquacious denial, but Fogelblad's reserve was not so easily penetrated. Betraying no obvious emotion, he said in his heavily accented baritone: "I do not know what you are saying."

"Oh, I think you do, Mr. Fogelblad," Rafferty shot back angrily. "Allow me to go through the logic of it for you. Your neighbor, Mr. Wahlgren, was murdered by someone who wanted that rune stone he found. We've learned that you are prepared to tell the authorities in Alexandria that you have the stone. Therefore, you must have killed Mr. Wahlgren. Seems obvious to me, for how could it be otherwise?"

"I killed no one," the Swede said.

"Liar!" Holmes said, spitting out the word with a sharp, savage intensity which sent goosebumps down my spine and must have inspired a similar reaction in poor Fogelblad.

"Now, now, Mr. Baker, let us give the man the benefit of the doubt," Rafferty said, a note of gentleness seeping into his voice for the first time. " 'Tis possible we're jumpin' to conclusions here. Maybe there's some other explanation. In fact, lookin' at Mr. Fogelblad, who seems a decent enough man, I'm thinkin' he may not be the murderin' kind after all. Maybe he just got caught up in this business through no fault of his own. So why don't you just tell us now, Mr. Fogelblad, how you ended up with the rune stone?"

Fogelblad let out a small sigh, no doubt of relief, and I could see that Rafferty's unexpected change of tone had achieved its desired result. Taking out a handkerchief and mopping his brow, where beads of sweat had formed, Fogelblad then delivered an answer to Rafferty's question which came as a revelation to all of us: "You must believe me. I never took the stone. Olaf was my friend. The stone, I have it because Olaf gave it to me."

Chapter Ten

"FOOLED YOU ALL"

F ogelblad's revelation must have made Holmes and Rafferty feel
like miners who, after pounding at hard rock, had suddenly
burst through to the mother lode. Neither man, however, gave
any evidence of excitement as the interrogation continued.

"So you are telling us Mr. Wahlgren gave you the stone," Rafferty
said with a trace of disbelief, though I knew perfectly well he did not
doubt Fogelblad's story for a moment. "When did this happen?"

"Monday."

"This past Monday?"

"*Ja.*"

"Why did he ask you to hide the rune stone for him?"

"He was afraid."

"Of what?"

"Thieves."

"Did he say who these 'thieves' might be?"

"No."

Rafferty tugged at his beard, setting off a small shower of food
crumbs which fell into his lap, and then asked: "Did Mr. Wahlgren

say why he had become so suddenly afraid? After all, the rune stone
had been in his possession for months, had it not?"

"He did not say."

"And you did not ask?"

"No."

The Swede—as Rafferty had led us to expect—seemed to parcel
out words the way a man lost in the desert might ration water.

"So let me see if I have this straight," Rafferty said while Holmes
stared venomously at Fogelblad. "On Monday your neighbor, Olaf
Wahlgren, approached you, announced that he had an item of enormous potential value that he wanted to hide on your property, and
you asked him no questions? 'Tis passin' strange if you ask me, Mr.
Fogelblad, but I'm willin' to hear your explanation."

"Olaf was a friend," Fogelblad said, as though this would indeed
account for everything.

"And?" prodded Rafferty.

"I help a friend if he asks," Fogelblad replied.

"How kind of you," said Rafferty, adding casually: "I suppose it
must have been an unpleasant job to pull that heavy stone out of the
manure pit."

This offhanded remark finally succeeded in eliciting a visible response from Fogelblad, whose mouth opened in astonishment, as
though Rafferty had just materialized a genie out of thin air.

Quick to exploit his advantage, Rafferty said: "You see, Mr. Fogelblad, you can't fool me. Now, I will ask you for the last time, what
made your neighbor so frightened that he decided to move the rune
stone to your property?"

Fogelblad paused, obviously uncertain of how to respond, before
telling Rafferty: "Olaf said there was big trouble, *ja*, and he had to be
careful."

"What kind of trouble?"

The Swede, however, was not easily drawn out of his natural reserve. "Big trouble, that is what Olaf said. The big men were after
him. I do not know more." This answer was exceptionally long by
Fogelblad's laconic standards, and he slumped down in his seat as
though exhausted by the effort.

"I think you do know more," Rafferty shot back. "Fact is, I think you know exactly what kind of trouble Mr. Wahlgren was in. Who were these 'big men' he spoke of? Was he being pressured in some way by Mr. Larson? Or was it someone else? Had he gone back on an agreement to sell the stone?"

So many questions asked at once seemed to confuse Fogelblad, who stared down at the floor and said quietly: "I do not know. That is the truth."

Rafferty now moved abruptly to another line of questioning, a technique which Holmes himself often used to great effect during interrogations.

"Was it your deep friendship with Mr. Wahlgren that also led you to help him carve the rune stone? Why, I bet the two of you had a gay old time pullin' off such a prank, didn't you."

For the first time, a flash of anger became visible in the Swede's sad, inscrutable eyes. "Oh no," he said with unusual force. "It was just as Olaf said. I saw it in the tree."

"Tangled in the roots, was it?"

"*Ja*, in the roots."

"And you and Olaf and perhaps another friend or two had nothin' to do with forgin' the stone?"

"I made nothing," Fogelblad insisted. "I do not know about anybody else."

Shifting subjects again, Rafferty asked: "Did you know that Mr. Wahlgren was hopin' to sell the rune stone for a lot of money?"

"Not my business," came the reply.

"So you knew nothin' at all in that regard, is that what you're sayin'?"

"No. I heard—" here Fogelblad appeared to be searching for a word before finally blurting out in Swedish—"*skvallerhistorier.*"

"Stories, gossip," Holmes instantly translated.

"Did any of these stories suggest who might be interested in buyin' the stone?" Rafferty asked.

"I do not listen much," Fogelblad said before repeating his earlier response: "Not my business."

"Of course not," said Rafferty with a sigh. "You see nothin', you hear nothin', you ask nothin', Mr. Fogelblad. I know some defense lawyers in St. Paul who'd love to put you on the witness stand."

Now came the question we had all been waiting for. Fixing his eyes on the Swede, who began to fidget in his seat, Rafferty asked: "Exactly where did you hide the rune stone, Mr. Fogelblad?"

"The sheriff, he told me—"

"Damn the sheriff!" Rafferty thundered before Fogelblad could finish. "I am the only man you must answer to at the moment. There is no one else—except, of course, for Mr. Baker and Mr. Smith. And they are, I assure you, most impatient men. Isn't that true, Mr. Baker?"

"Give me five minutes with this worm," Holmes snarled as he removed a small knife from his pocket and began to clean his fingernails with it. "I would have the truth from him."

Fogelblad took a deep gulp of air and shuddered slightly. At the same time, his eyes began to wander, as if they might somehow find a way out of his predicament. For a moment, I feared he might bolt, in which case our carefully contrived scenario would instantly fall to pieces, since the truth was that we could not—and would not—resort to extreme physical force to keep him in our presence.

Fortunately for us, the Swede lost his nerve, no doubt fearing what Holmes in particular might do to him if he failed to answer Rafferty's question. He said: "The stone, it is in the woodlot behind my house. I will go with the sheriff to dig it up. That is what he told me to do."

"And just when are you plannin' to do this diggin'?" Rafferty inquired.

"Today, after I get back to Alexandria. The sheriff, he will be at the station."

Rafferty sat back in his seat, flashed a quick smile, and said: "Well now, you have been most helpful, Mr. Fogelblad, most helpful. I appreciate your assistance very much. I am sure Mr. Baker and Mr. Smith share that sentiment."

Then he paused, his eyes once again boring in on the farmer, and said: "There is just one more thing you must do for us, Mr. Fogelblad. You must tell no one — absolutely no one — about our conversation this afternoon. Is that clear?"

"*Ja*, sure."

"For your sake, I hope so. Because if we do find out you've been blabbin', Mr. Baker in particular will be very upset and you don't want that to happen. I saw the last poor fellow who did such a thing. 'Twas an awful sight. Why, they still haven't found all the body parts, or so I'm told."

Having delivered this final absurd threat, Rafferty stood up. Holmes and I immediately followed suit.

"Good day to you, sir," said Rafferty as the three of us filed out into the aisle. "And don't forget that last piece of advice I gave you."

Once we had passed into the next coach and found seats, I said: "It may sound odd to ask, but do we know for certain that Mr. Fogelblad was in Minneapolis on the night his neighbor was murdered? The man struck me as somehow suspicious, and I cannot help but wonder whether his reticence is merely an act."

"Ah, 'tis a very good question you pose, Doctor," said Rafferty. "Mr. Holmes and I wondered the same thing, so I did some checkin' early this mornin' and discovered that the Swede's alibi is as ironclad as a ship of the line. You see, I took the liberty of telephonin' his mother in Minneapolis. Now, unless the dear old lady is a schemer in the class of Lucrezia Borgia and a brazen liar to boot, 'tis safe to say her son was with her in Minneapolis at the time of Mr. Wahlgren's death."

Rafferty then got out a cigar, clipped off the end, applied a match to it, and said: " 'Tis also safe to say that, in my humble opinion, we pulled off an excellent little charade with Mr. Fogelblad. You were especially fine, Mr. Holmes, for you make a most convincin' and steely-eyed terrorist. Why, I believe you scared the Swede half to death."

"That was my intention," replied Holmes. "You were quite believable yourself, Mr. Rafferty. Incidentally, where did you find that badge you flashed with such authority?"

Rafferty chuckled and said: "Why, I thought you knew, Mr.

Holmes. You see, I'm a special officer of the law, I am, duly deputized by Mr. Frank Woolworth himself. 'Twas worth every cent of the nickel I paid for it."[1]

We arrived back in Alexandria at shortly before three o'clock and watched from our coach window as Fogelblad alighted from the train into the custody of Sheriff Boehm. The two of them left the depot at once, after which we stepped out onto the platform ourselves.

"Do you think the sheriff will go at once to Mr. Fogelblad's farm?" I asked Holmes.

"I doubt it, Watson. I imagine Mr. Boehm will want to talk a bit with our Swedish friend before setting out to reclaim the stone. Do you agree, Mr. Rafferty?"

Rafferty nodded and said: "Seems likely enough. They'll probably talk in the sheriff's office over at the courthouse. But maybe I should follow them just in case. Besides, we'll need to hire out a carriage if they're goin' out to the farm later. I can take care of that."

"An excellent idea," said Holmes. "Dr. Watson and I will come along shortly. First, I wish to see if there is any message from Mr. Wooldridge in Chicago."

Much to Holmes's pleasure, there was. Knowing that we could be difficult to reach by telephone for much of the day, Holmes had asked the Chicago detective to send along any additional information — especially if it involved Mrs. Comstock — via telegram. The message from Wooldridge was ten pages long, and Holmes read it with his usual rapidity, pausing now and then to pronounce a loud "Ha!" This was a sure sign that it contained valuable information. After finishing with it, Holmes handed the message to me, and I could see upon reading it why it had provoked such a demonstrative response from my friend.

Wooldridge's telegram dealt almost entirely with the late Frank Comstock. We learned that Comstock was, as James J. Hill had suggested to us earlier, an inveterate speculator on the Chicago commodities exchange, buying and selling wheat, corn, and other crops with reckless abandon. He had for a time became quite rich in this enterprise. In the months before his death, however, Comstock had piled up enormous losses, with the consequence that he had died many thousands of dollars in debt, according to Wooldridge.

The detective also informed us that Comstock had made a habit of visiting Chicago at least once a month and that he was known to have a taste for enjoying the pleasures offered by that city's most expensive ladies of the night. One of those prostitutes, Wooldridge went on to say, was assuredly the woman who later became his wife. The detective even located the couple's marriage license, which revealed that they had been wed in July of 1898 by a justice of the peace in Chicago.

"Well," said Holmes as he tucked the telegram into his coat pocket, "it would appear that we have answered at least one troublesome question, for if Frank Comstock did indeed die with numerous debts outstanding, then we know why his late wife has been scheming to obtain and sell the rune stone: she needs the money. Indeed, her late husband's debts must be so large that not even selling off all the farm land she now owns will be sufficient to clear the balance."

"Given her past behavior, I fail to see why she simply didn't vanish after her husband's death," I said. "She is perfectly capable of starting a new life somewhere else."

Holmes nodded and said: "An excellent observation, my dear Watson. It is a point I shall have to consider. In the meantime, let us see if we can find Mr. Rafferty."

The Douglas County Courthouse—located in the midst of a square planted with small, gaunt trees—was a gloomy pile of gray granite dominated by a gawky tower punctured at the base by a pair of deep-set arches. The entire structure conveyed a sense of imperial heft, as though its builders believed the rule of law could be enforced in these sprawling hinterlands only by a form of architectural conquest. But when Holmes and I arrived at this rather daunting edifice, we were surprised to encounter a crowd of perhaps a hundred people, some milling about the square itself, others sitting in wagons and carriages parked along the surrounding streets.

I could see no speakers, musicians, or other performers in the square, and so the purpose of this unexpected gathering was a mystery. Holmes, too, seemed perplexed, but his face brightened when he spotted Rafferty, who was just pulling up in a carriage driven by our faithful helper George Kensington.

"Welcome, gentlemen, to the great rune stone festival," he said as we came over to talk. " 'Tis the social event of the season, or so it would appear."

"I am afraid you will have to be more specific, Mr. Rafferty," replied Holmes after he had greeted Kensington with a friendly nod. "What exactly is the occasion for this festival of which you speak?"

"Why, 'tis the recovery of the rune stone, Mr. Holmes. That is what everyone is waiting for. Word travels like wildfire in a small town like this. Everybody wants to be on hand when the great artifact is finally unearthed."

"How wonderful," Holmes said, disgust dripping from his voice like hot wax from a candle. "Really, Mr. Rafferty, don't these people have something more useful to occupy their time, such as planting corn, or doing whatever it is they do at this time of year?"

"Come now, Mr. Holmes, you must understand that many of these folks have come halfway around the world to eke a livin' out of a hard land. There's little to their lives but work and pain, and such pleasures as they have are of the simplest sort. But an event such as this, which is full of mystery and excitement, well, 'tis like a powerful stimulant for their weary souls."

"I do not quite follow you," I said.

"What I mean is that there's nothin' like somebody else's troubles to make a man forget his own. That is why people love to read the tales of crime and mayhem penned by you and your fellow scribblers, Doctor. 'Tis not mere morbid curiosity that keeps your readers turnin' the pages; no, I contend 'tis relief that makes them do it, relief that these terrible things are happenin' to some other poor fellow. You see, pain is a great anodyne so long as it is somebody else's."

Holmes responded to this curious speech by noting with a smile: "I am grateful you did not become a physician, Mr. Rafferty, for I fear the entire world would have been required to suffer in order to make your patients well."

It was, I thought, a clever rejoinder, as did Rafferty, who promptly gave a mock salute to Holmes. Kensington now joined the conversation by pointing us toward a handsome landau, pulled by two spirited black horses, which had just come up to join the collection of vehicles parked around the courthouse.

"That looks like Mrs. Comstock's carriage," he said. "Don't recognize the driver, though."

"Ah, that would be Mr. Billy Swift," said Holmes, peering at the carriage, which had parked on the opposite side of the square. "You might describe him as the lady's all-purpose servant. I cannot see Mrs. Comstock herself, but she must be in the carriage, for I do not think she would miss this event under any circumstances."

Intrigued by Mrs. Comstock's apparent arrival, Holmes began to make a thorough survey of the crowd, and before long he spotted Magnus Larson, who was sitting in a rather battered-looking chaise with another man.

"Who might that gentleman with Mr. Larson be?" Holmes asked Kensington.

"Oh, that's Einar Blegen. Haven't you met him yet?"

"No, I have not," said Holmes, staring intently at the paunchy, white-haired man seated next to Larson, "but I intend to make his acquaintance very soon. In fact, now might be as good a time as any."

But as Holmes turned to walk toward the chaise, Sheriff Gustavus Boehm and Nels Fogelblad suddenly emerged from one of the tunnellike arches at the base of the courthouse and walked briskly toward a waiting carriage. The crowd reacted to this development with a loud, steady buzz, but no one tried to approach the two men as they crossed the square and stepped up into their carriage. Paying no heed to the crowd, the sheriff took over the reins and immediately set his team in motion.

This was a signal for the drivers of the other waiting carriages to spring into action. So it was that within a matter of minutes a kind of impromptu procession formed behind the carriage bearing Boehm and Fogelblad. Naturally, Holmes saw no choice but to go along with the crowd, and so we joined Rafferty in Kensington's big four-seater, falling in somewhere near the center of the parade of perhaps fifteen vehicles.

"It beggars belief that the sheriff would permit this kind of unseemly spectacle," said Holmes, who had apparently assumed that only we would be privy (along with the sheriff and Fogelblad, of course) to the unearthing of the rune stone. How Holmes might have gone about arranging such a private viewing, as it were, was beyond me, but it hardly mattered now.

Kensington, as it turned out, had an answer of sorts to Holmes's complaint. "Gus didn't have any choice in this business," he told us. "When word leaked out that Nels was coming back to dig up the rune stone, all the big shots in town wanted to see it for themselves. The county commissioners are in the first two carriages, and they're the ones who sign Gus's paycheck."

"And why shouldn't they be on hand?" added Rafferty, who seemed to be enjoying himself immensely. " 'Tis a beautiful afternoon, with not a cloud violatin' the sky. What could be more pleasin' on such a fine day than to go out for a ride in the country?"

"Bah," replied Holmes, who slumped down in his seat, put his hat over his eyes, and said: "Wake me when we arrive."

Once we reached the edge of town, we turned south into the countryside, following the same road Holmes and I had taken to Olaf Wahlgren's farm after our arrival in Alexandria. The day was indeed most pleasant, and the miles seemed to roll by effortlessly as we made our way through the quiet brown countryside.

With Holmes in no mood for conversation, Rafferty was more than willing to fill in the slack, and he regaled me with further tales of his days in the Wild West. It was always difficult to tell whether Rafferty's stories had any basis in fact or whether they represented no more than lush examples of embroidery. His account of spending an afternoon "shootin' rattlesnakes with Calamity Jane" did not strike me as entirely improbable, but I was not prepared to believe that he had "stared down Wild Bill Hickok in a Deadwood saloon" only a week before that notorious gunman's death.[2] Still, the stories were invariably entertaining, and in what seemed hardly any time at all we arrived at Fogelblad's farmstead.

The farm looked no more prosperous than Wahlgren's, though it was at least a little better kept. The house itself was a makeshift affair, with lean-to additions jutting out here and there, some of them clad in nothing more substantial than tarpaper. The red-painted barn, however, looked in passable shape, as did several other small buildings around it, and what equipment could be seen appeared to be in working order.

I awakened Holmes as we pulled up into the yard. The carriage carrying the sheriff and Fogelblad had already stopped in front of the barn. Fogelblad went inside and returned moments later with a long spade. By this time, the other carriages and wagons had parked wherever they could and disgorged their eager riders.

After everyone had gathered in the yard, Boehm made a brief and decidedly chilly statement: "I will say this only once, so all of you had better listen. You are to keep out of the way and be quiet while Mr. Fogelblad digs up the stone. After that, you are to do whatever I tell you—nothing more and nothing less. If it was up to me, all of you would be home minding your own business, but certain people"—here he glared at a tall, portly, bearded man who I assumed was one of the county commissioners—"had other ideas. Now, does everybody understand?"

There must have been thirty or more people in the group, and they all nodded solemnly, as though about to witness a sacred rite.

Boehm then turned to Fogelblad and said: "All right, show us where the stone is, and make it quick."

"This way," said Fogelblad, leading us around past the back of the house and into a large grove of hardwood trees planted to provide shelter from the howling winter winds. A narrow path led through the grove, and we followed in single file until we reached a small tree with a mark emblazoned on its trunk.

"Now we turn," I heard Fogelblad say, and we all followed hir into the underbrush, which was not difficult to negotiate, since the was as yet no seasonal foliage. Only twenty or so yards from t path, Fogelblad stopped and pointed to an unusual oak tree distinguished by two main branches which extended almost horizontally from the trunk before turning upward at ninety-degree angles. The effect was that of a signalman standing with his arms raised.

"A rather appropriate way to mark buried treasure," Holmes noted as we and the rest of the crowd formed an irregular circle around the tree.

Fogelblad now went to a spot directly beneath one of the branches where it shot skyward. A thick, damp carpet of leaves left over from previous autumns covered the ground beneath the tree. Fogelblad quickly pushed the leaves aside with his spade, exposing a large patch of loose dirt. I had never been on such a treasure hunt before, and I could feel the air of excitement and anticipation among the crowd members, who looked on eagerly as Fogelblad removed each spadeful of soil.

I expected to hear at any minute the clank of metal on stone and to see at last the mysterious object which had drawn Holmes and me from so far away. As Fogelblad continued to excavate the loose dirt, everyone in the crowd instinctively leaned forward, anxious to get the first look at the famous stone.

Then I began to sense that something was wrong, for with each new spadeful of earth, Fogelblad's face seemed to grow more pale. He began to dig frantically, like a man trying to rescue someone buried alive. Finally, he struck something, but it did not sound like stone. He threw the spade aside, reached into the hole, and pulled out a piece of wooden planking, no more than a foot square and covered with moist dirt. With a look of bafflement and disbelief, he wiped off the dirt to reveal a series of angular symbols — runes — which had been carved into the wood.

Fogelblad studied this curious artifact for a moment and then said: "My God, the stone is gone!"

An excited babble arose from the crowd as Holmes stepped forward to look at the inscription, which Fogelblad held in trembling hands.

"Can you read it?" I asked.

"Oh yes," said Holmes. "Unless I am mistaken, the message is quite simple. It says: 'Fooled you all.' "

Chapter Eleven

We hardly had time to absorb this latest surprise before Magnus Larson, who had come next to Holmes, snatched the piece of wood from Fogelblad's hands. He scanned the inscription, his face contorting into a dark scowl, after which he broke the wood in half and threw it violently to the ground. Looking for all the world like some ancient Viking warrior about to commence a round of looting and pillaging, he uttered a series of curses and then confronted Holmes.

"Is this your work?" he bellowed at Holmes, who stood his ground without flinching. Sheriff Boehm, who was but a few feet away, made no effort to head off Larson, but instead seemed content to watch the drama which was now about to unfold. Although I could smell alcohol on Larson's breath, his steadiness afoot and unslurred speech suggested that he was not nearly as intoxicated as he had been the night before at the Majestic Tavern.

"Why would you think that, sir?" Holmes replied coolly while Rafferty moved up behind Larson, just in case — as the Irishman told me later — "the gentleman was of a mind to engage in fisticuffs."

Standing close enough to Holmes to literally breathe in his face, Larson now spoke so loudly that the entire crowd could hear every word: "What I think is that you're a filthy liar, that's what I think! And don't you for a minute believe I'll forget your trick last night. I know your game now, and I'll be ready for you the next time you try something. So you just watch yourself."

"Are you threatening me, sir?" said Holmes. "If so, I suggest it is you who should watch yourself."

"I will threaten you any time I damn well please," Larson shouted. "That stone is mine and I will have it back!"

Still a picture of calm, Holmes said: "I am curious why you seem to think the stone is yours, Mr. Larson, when in fact everyone here knows that it belonged to the late Olaf Wahlgren."

"It is mine!" Larson repeated even more loudly. "I bought it fair and square from that cheat, and if you and this moron Fogelblad think—"

For some reason, Sheriff Boehm now stepped in to break up the confrontation, grabbing Larson by one arm and starting to pull him away from Holmes.

"Let me go!" Larson said, slipping from the sheriff's grip and turning to face the crowd. He then said: "I don't know which one of you lying thieves has got the stone, but I will find it! Do you hear?"

"That will be enough," said Boehm, who now came around in front of Larson. "You'd best go home, Magnus."

"Out of my way. I'm not through—" Larson began, but his words were cut off by a stinging slap to the face, which the sheriff delivered so quickly that none of us saw it coming.

"I will not tell you again," Boehm said, in the quiet but unmistakable voice of a man prepared to back his words to the limit.

Larson must have understood this, for he suddenly backed away from Holmes, like a dog brought to heel by a sharp yank on his chain. He then walked off through the startled crowd without saying another word.

"All right, the show is over," Boehm announced. "Everybody can go home now. There's nothing more to see here." He then motioned toward Fogelblad and said: "You, come with me. Right now."

As the crowd began to disperse, I caught a glimpse of Mary Comstock and her young "companion," who must have been standing at the far rear of the crowd. They turned onto the path leading back to the farmyard and vanished from sight before I could alert Holmes.

"We will talk again with Mrs. Comstock in due time," he said. "For the moment, I am more interested in speaking with Einar Blegen. Let us see if we can find him before he leaves."

"Well now, since he came here with Magnus Larson, he probably won't be too anxious to talk with you," Rafferty noted.

"I agree, Mr. Rafferty. That is why I am wondering if you might do me a little favor."

It took but a few seconds for Holmes to explain his plan, which Rafferty readily agreed to.

We then walked quickly out of the woodlot and into the farmyard, where all the carriages and wagons were parked. The chaise carrying Larson and Blegen had been one of the last in the parade of vehicles going out to Fogelblad's farm, and so it was now in a position to be among the first to leave.

Blegen, in fact, was just climbing up into the chaise, with Larson not far behind him, when Rafferty, who had gone ahead of us, intercepted them. Although we could not hear what was said, Holmes had instructed Rafferty to tell Larson that the sheriff wished to speak to him at once, alone.

Rafferty was, as we well knew, the kind of man who could be magnificently persuasive, especially when, as he liked to describe it, "shadin' the truth a bit."

However he managed to do it, Rafferty soon convinced Larson that he must go back and find the sheriff. On his way back to the woodlot, he walked right past us, glaring fiercely at Holmes. Once he was out of sight, we approached Blegen, with whom Rafferty had already struck up a conversation.

Blegen was a rather rotund man, about fifty-five years of age, with a big round head marked by doughy cheeks, owlish hazel eyes, a weak, receding chin, and thin gray hair combed back in a futile attempt to cover a large bald spot. He wore a shabby dark-gray topcoat, well-worn boots, and wool gloves in which he held the reins.

His appearance overall conveyed a sense of dishevelment—evident by holes in his gloves and a torn sleeve on his coat—and he rather reminded me of a proud old building which had fallen on hard times. Still, he sat perfectly erect in his chaise, as though faultless posture might somehow protect him against the encroaching decay of his life. He gave us a nervous glance as we approached.

"Ah, Mr. Blegen, I have been waiting for a chance to meet you," said Holmes, who identified us in the usual fashion, as experts from the British Museum investigating the authenticity of the rune stone. "It is a pleasure to make your acquaintance. I see you have already been introduced to our friend Mr. Rafferty."

"Yes, I have. It is nice to meet you, too, I'm sure," said Blegen in a high, reedy voice as he fiddled with the reins.

Wasting no time, Holmes said: "I understand you are the local expert in runic writing."

"Oh no, not really," came the reply. "It is just a hobby of mine, that's all."

"Ah, but it must be more than a hobby, sir, for I understand you provided a very accurate first translation of the rune stone."

"Well, it was nothing, you know. I just did the best I could. I'm sure there are much better translations to be made." As Blegen spoke, he never once looked directly at Holmes, Rafferty, or me, and there was distinct nervous hesitation in his voice. "I really must be going," he suddenly said.

"But aren't you forgetting something?" Holmes asked.

"No, I don't think so."

"But wasn't Mr. Larson with you?"

"Oh yes, yes, how could I forget," Blegen replied with a weak smile. "Yes, I must wait for him."

"While we're waiting," said Holmes smoothly, "perhaps you could tell us a little about poor Olaf Wahlgren. Did you know him well before you became involved with the rune stone?"

"Yes, I knew him. But we were just acquaintances, you understand. Certainly we were not close friends. I would not want you to think that."

"Of course not," said Holmes amiably. "Still, I recall someone telling me that you delivered Mr. Wahlgren's funeral oration. Naturally, I concluded from this that the two of you were more than merely casual friends."

Blegen, looking more tense and uncomfortable by the minute, could barely make a coherent reply. "Well, yes, we were friends, as I said . . . friends . . . and so . . . well, I was asked to say a few words, that's all . . . to say a few words . . . and of course — "

"You did so," said Holmes, interrupting with a smile. "I understand. So what you are saying, if I follow you, is that it was your reputation as a runic scholar that drew you into this affair, more than any particular friendship with Mr. Wahlgren. Is that correct?"

"Yes, that's it. As I said, we were not really good friends."

"I see," said Holmes in a skeptical tone which conveyed the exact opposite. "Very well, then, tell me, sir, do you think the stone is genuine? Or do you suppose that someone highly skilled in the runic alphabet — a person much like yourself, in other words — forged it?"

This indirect accusation caused a distinct reaction in Blegen. His hands began to tremble slightly, and I also noted a rapid blinking of his eyes. "Oh, I couldn't say one way or another," he finally responded. "That's a matter for experts such as yourselves to decide. I would know nothing about it."

"But don't you agree, sir, that it would have taken someone with considerable knowledge to have forged the stone?"

There was more trembling and blinking before Blegen said: "Well, again, I really couldn't give you an answer. I don't know about such things."

"Uh-oh," Rafferty said, joining the conversation for the first time. "Trouble is headin' our way."

I turned around to see Boehm, with Larson a step behind, striding toward us. As the sheriff drew up to us, he said to Blegen: "All right, Einar, move along now, and take Magnus with you. And I don't want to see either of you talking with these characters" — by which he obviously meant Holmes, Rafferty, and me — "again. Understand?"

"Certainly," said Blegen. "Certainly."

"Well, I've got—" Larson began.

"You've got nothing to say," Boehm broke in, giving Larson a rough shove toward the chaise. "Just get in and shut up."

Larson glared at the sheriff but kept his tongue as he climbed in next to Blegen, who gave a hard shake to the reins and left at once without so much as looking at any of us.

Boehm now stepped back, put his hands on his hips, and looked over the three of us as though he were eying an especially dubious herd of livestock. Then he focused in on Holmes and said:

"You look a lot better today than Magnus Larson. Why is that?"

It was such an odd question that even Holmes was caught off guard and could only reply: "I fear I do not understand your question, Sheriff."

"Then let me explain. I heard about your little performance at the Majestic. It was the talk of the town. All I'm saying is that you look mighty fine for a fellow who supposedly drank himself halfway to death's door last night."

"I have always had remarkable powers of recuperation," Holmes said.

"Must be. The clerk over at the Douglas House told me you looked perfectly normal when you came back last night. Amazing, isn't it?"

"Life is indeed full of mysteries," said Holmes.

"I'd agree with you there. For instance, there's the mystery of just who you really are. I've been wondering about that, but you know what, I'm not really worried about it. Do you want to know why I'm not worried?"

"I would be delighted to know that, Sheriff."

"I thought you would. I'm not worried because the three of you"—here he now expanded his gaze to include Rafferty and myself—"are no longer a factor. You're out of the game. Finished. What that means is this: from now on, all of you are to stay out of my business. You're not to question people around town. You're not to go to Olaf Wahlgren's farm or any other crime scene. You are not, in short, to cause me any kind of trouble or interfere in any way with my investigation. If you do, you will find yourself behind bars — or worse. Now, have I made myself clear?"

"Abundantly," said Holmes. "But may I ask why you appear to be so fearful of our presence here? After all, we are merely working toward the same end which, I presume, you are."

Bochm took a step toward Holmes, looking at him from head to toe the way a drill sergeant might examine a raw recruit, and said: "Listen, whoever you are, and listen carefully. I know an impostor when I see one, and I know I'm looking at one right now. I haven't exactly figured out what your game is here, but I will. And when I do, you'd better not be around if you know what's good for you. That's all I've got to say — " he paused momentarily, before adding — "to you."

He then abruptly turned toward Rafferty, who was standing next to Holmes, and said: "I see by that bulge in your coat that you're carrying a pistol. I don't like people carrying concealed weapons in my county. So you'll want to give it to me now, won't you."

I instantly feared for the worst. Rafferty, as both Holmes and I well knew, possessed a ferocious temper and was absolutely fearless, a combination of character traits that could all too easily invite violent confrontations.

Holmes saw the danger at once and said: "I do not think that will be necessary, Sheriff. Mr. Rafferty — "

"Can speak for himself," our friend said in a booming voice. "I will ask you to be quiet, Mr. Baker, for this is now my business and mine alone."

Staring contemptuously at the sheriff, Rafferty continued: "All right, Mr. Boehm, what say the two of us have a nice little talk. You're right, sir, in notin' that I carry a pistol. You would also be right in thinkin' that it's loaded, for what good is a pistol that isn't? You would, however, be wrong in thinkin' that I'm goin' to give it to you. Dead wrong."

I realized now that, short of an attempt to physically subdue Rafferty, Holmes and I were powerless to defuse the situation if the sheriff continued to press his demand. Once Rafferty's blood was up — and I could tell by the way he had spoken to Boehm that it was very much up now—he was a runaway freight train of a man, and God help anyone in his path. My only hope was that the sheriff might have enough common sense to back away.

Unfortunately, this did not seem to be the case, for Boehm— whose temperament seemed as explosive as Rafferty's—gave him a malevolent look and said: "Give me the gun, you fat mick, or I will take it from you."

"You can try, you dirty little kraut," Rafferty replied.

I now expected gunshots to ring out at any second (and having seen Rafferty's handy way with the derringer he usually kept up his sleeve, I did not like the sheriff's chances). But instead of the crack of pistols, I heard the mellifluous voice of a woman.

"Am I interrupting something, gentlemen?" said Mary Comstock, who had come up behind us, from where I did not know.

Whether it was because of the calming quality of Mrs. Comstock's voice or the mere presence of a woman on the scene, Boehm seemed to lose his taste for combat. Slowly backing away from Rafferty, he doffed his hat at the lady and said: "We were merely having a discussion, Mrs. Comstock. But it is over—for the time being."

"Yes, it is over," said Holmes, glaring at Rafferty. He added: "As always, it is a pleasure to see you, Mrs. Comstock."

"As it is to see you, Mr. Baker," she said, putting a peculiar emphasis upon his assumed name. "In any case, I was wondering if I might have a few minutes with the sheriff. As you might imagine, I am concerned about the disappearance of the rune stone. I am hoping, Mr. Boehm, that you might be able to tell me how you hope to proceed in your investigation. As you know, my dear husband wanted so much to purchase the stone. Now, however, I fear I shall never be able to complete what he set out to do."

Boehm, who seemed no more immune to the lady's charm than any other man, said he would be happy to talk to her, quickly adding that he could not, of course, reveal any details which might compromise his investigation.

"I understand," she said sweetly. "I merely wish to find out if there is any hope left for me. Now, if you will excuse us, gentlemen, I will spirit the sheriff away so we can have our talk."

Once Mrs. Comstock had left with the sheriff in tow, Holmes said to Rafferty: "Well, sir, I see your talent for mayhem has not diminished one iota since our days together in St. Paul. But I do wish you would exercise a little more discretion. A shootout with the sheriff would hardly have profited our investigation."

"Guilty as charged," said Rafferty with a sheepish grin. "But it is a point of honor with me, Mr. Holmes, that I do not give up my guns — not to that little weasel Boehm or to any other man. 'Twas the rule of the First Minnesota and 'tis my rule as well."[1]

"Well, said Holmes dryly, "I think you succeeded in making your point. As for the sheriff, there is at least one useful conclusion we can draw from our confrontation with him. You see, it is quite obvious that he knows who I am, and I should be very interested to learn how he came upon that knowledge."

Dusk was now approaching, and I expected — given all that had already happened this day — that we would return to Alexandria at once. Holmes, however, was not ready to leave. Even though the light was failing, he insisted that we return to the woodlot, and the area of the farmyard around it, to search for clues that might help explain the stone's disappearance from its supposed burial place.

"Then you must believe Mr. Fogelblad was tellin' the truth," Rafferty said.

"I do," Holmes acknowledged, without offering any further explanation.

"What will we be looking for?" I asked.

"Why, we'll be lookin' for a clue," said Rafferty, whose jovial manner had returned. "Of course, not havin' any idea as to what this clue might be could slow us down a bit, but not much. Isn't that right, Mr. Holmes?"

"If you say so, Mr. Rafferty. Now, come along, the two of you, before it's dark."

Like most extraordinary men, Sherlock Holmes had come to believe in his own luck, and so for him no discovery was ever a matter of pure chance but rather a kind of vindication, concrete evidence that the endless roil of the world had once again succumbed to his superior intellect and will. And so it was, as darkness fell and a stiff wind roared in from the north, crashing through the branches of the trees in Nels Fogelblad's woodlot, that Holmes came across the unknown clue he had been looking for.

It was a fragment of curved glass with raised lettering which Holmes picked up near the entrance to the path leading into the woodlot. In the dying light, Holmes showed the piece of glass to Rafferty and me and asked what we made of it.

Rafferty, who like Holmes seemed to be blessed with unusually acute eyesight, studied the glass and said: "Well, I can make out the letters *S* and *G* and what looks like the start of another letter. I can't say for a fact, but my guess would be that this glass is from a lantern."

"My thoughts exactly," said Holmes. "If so, it might be useful to see what sort of lantern it came from."

" 'Twould be a long shot, Mr. Holmes," said Rafferty. "Just about everybody owns a lantern."

"Then we must hope that this glass comes from a lantern that is unique," said Holmes, putting the fragment into his coat pocket, "for it is the best clue we have at the moment. It is also a curious clue, for one would not normally expect to find a broken bit of lantern glass at the edge of a woodlot, which is hardly the sort of place where nighttime visitors are a regular occurrence."

"Speaking of nighttime, we had best be on our way," said Rafferty, "or Mr. Kensington will begin to wonder if we got swallowed up by the dark."

On our way back to Alexandria, we were forced to bundle up, for the temperature dropped rapidly as darkness settled in and the stars emerged in all their grand profusion. Although I would have been content to nap in silence, Holmes—who had taken the front seat next to Kensington—was soon asking him to relate everything he knew about Einar Blegen.

Kensington, who was not only a remarkably patient man but also extremely well informed about virtually everyone in the area, gladly acceded to Holmes's request.

"I first met Einar not long after he came to town," Kensington told us. "That was about ten years ago, I guess, when he was appointed minister of the First Swedish Church in Holandberg. I liked him right off the bat. He was a smart fellow, and interesting to talk to, which is more than you can say about a lot of people around here. He also was funny in a wry sort of way. But then the rumors started that he was a drinker, and before long the congregation booted him out."

"Because of his drinking?" Holmes asked.

"No, I think it was because, well, from what I heard, they thought he had turned into a pagan. He told me once, in fact, that he'd quit believing in God years ago."

"That is not the sort of résumé which would seem to highly recommend him as a man of the cloth," Holmes observed.

"Not around here, that's for sure," said Kensington with a chuckle.

"What did he do after he lost his ministry?" I asked.

"He just sort of hung around," Kensington said. "Rumor has it that he got a big settlement after his parents died back in Sweden and he's living off that. He's got enough money to own that horse and buggy of his, so he ain't exactly dirt poor."

"I see," said Holmes. "Tell me, did you ever discuss the subject of runes with Mr. Blegen?"

"Once or twice. Like I said, he's a sharp fellow. I don't know if you could call him an expert on the subject, but I do know he was mighty interested in that stone of Olaf's."

"In fact, he made the first translation of the stone," Holmes noted.

"He sure did. The story I heard is that on the day after the discovery, Einar marched right over to Olaf's farm, sat down in front of the stone, and produced a translation lickety-split. I talked to a farmer who saw the whole thing, and he said Einar translated the inscription 'just as easy as you'd read your Sunday prayer book.' "

"Most interesting," murmured Holmes. "Were Mr. Blegen and Mr. Wahlgren good friends?"

"I think so, but I couldn't say for sure. I do know they'd met long before the stone was found. Of course, just about everybody around here knows everybody else."

"Of course. Incidentally, do you happen to know when Mr. Larson and Mr. Blegen became acquainted?"

"That I can't help you with. I was kind of surprised to see them together today, if you want to know the truth. But I guess that since they both know a lot about runes, they've got something in common."

"Oh, I have no doubt that they do," Holmes said. "No doubt at all."

Holmes was silent for a time, but as we drew nearer to Alexandria, he asked about Moony Wahlgren.

"I trust the child is doing well," he said. "I am surprised, Mr. Kensington, that she did not come along with you this afternoon, given her intense interest in the rune stone."

"I decided against it," Kensington replied. "To tell you the truth, Mr. Baker, I'm a little worried about her."

"She is not ill, is she?"

"Nothing like that. It's just that, well, somebody got into our house last night while we were away. And the funny thing is, it was Moony's room that the burglar seemed most interested in."

Chapter Twelve

"THERE WAS SOMETHING VERY WRONG ON THAT FARM"

Kensington's revelation disturbed Holmes greatly, and he immediately insisted upon hearing further details. First, however, he
wished to know why Kensington had waited nearly twenty-
four hours to tell us of the burglary.

"Well, I wasn't sure if it was really all that important," Kensington
explained. "Break-ins do happen around here, although not that
often. But the more I've thought about it, the more it looks like
Moony's room was the burglar's target, and I guess that's kind of
scary to me."

"As it should be," said Holmes gravely. "All right, sir, let us have
all the details. Overlook nothing!"

Kensington took a deep breath and began his story, while Rafferty and I moved up as closely behind the driver's seat as we could
so as not to miss a word. With occasional prodding from Holmes,
Kensington told us how he, his wife, and the Wahlgren girl had gone
to a church social the previous night at about seven o'clock. As the
event included a quilting bee ("Moony loves to sew, and we had to
practically drag her away," Kensington said), the three of them did

not return home until about ten. They saw nothing wrong as they approached their house. They had locked the front door but left the back door open, as was their custom, since the forgetful old woman who lived next door often came over to borrow sugar, flour, or some other baking item and thought nothing of helping herself.

When they got inside, however, the Kensingtons could tell at once that something was amiss. "The sideboard in the dining room was open, and it looked like some silverware might have been taken," he said. "We also found a couple of open drawers in the kitchen, but whoever got in didn't do a very good job of searching, because we had twenty dollars in coins in a jar on one of the kitchen shelves and it wasn't touched. But Moony's room was a different story."

"Describe to me as exactly as you can the conditions you found in her room," Holmes instructed, a note of urgency in his voice.

"Well, it was one big mess," Kensington said. "Whoever was in there ransacked all the drawers in her desk and clothes chest and threw everything out on the floor. He also went through the closet and opened up a big trunk where Moony keeps a lot of her personal things. There was even a floorboard that got pried up. I guess you could say it pretty much looked like every inch of the room had been searched. But as far as we could tell, not a thing was missing."

"And yet at first you thought all of this was the work of a common burglar?" Holmes asked skeptically.

"Well, I don't know about that, Mr. Baker. I guess I just figured that whoever broke in might have thought for some reason that we had a big stash of money upstairs. But now, I'm not so sure. Do you think he was looking for something of Moony's?"

"There can be no other possibility," said Holmes. "The opened cabinets and drawers downstairs were merely a poor attempt at covering up the burglar's real purpose. Do you have any idea, Mr. Kensington, what the burglar—for whom you so conveniently left open the back door—may have been looking for."

"None. The poor child has few worldly possessions and certainly to my knowledge owns nothing of significant value."

"I see. Did you report this break-in to the authorities?"

"Yes. I told the sheriff this morning what had happened and he said he would send over his deputy to take a look. Haven't seen anybody yet, though."

"The sheriff obviously has other matters on his mind at the moment," said Holmes. "By the way, did any of your neighbors hear or see anything unusual last night?"

"I asked, but nobody seems to have noticed anything out of the ordinary."

Holmes thought for a moment and said: "Tell me, how did Moony react to all of this?"

"She was very upset, as you might imagine," Kensington said. "But once she saw that nothing was gone in her room, she seemed to be all right. Elsie, on the other hand, was terribly upset. That's why I arranged to have a neighbor keep a watch on the house while I was gone today, just in case."

"A wise idea, Mr. Kensington. Indeed, I would suggest that you keep a very close watch on Moony from now on. She may be in danger."

"Danger?" echoed Kensington, suddenly sounding very alarmed. "I don't understand. Why would anyone want to harm Moony?"

"I am not sure," Holmes admitted. "But I greatly fear the girl knows something which could put her in jeopardy. I must talk to her again, Mr. Kensington, tonight if at all possible."

"Yes, of course. Tonight would be all right. Come over any time after eight. But you know Moony. I'm not sure what you'll learn by talking to her again."

"Nor am I," Holmes said. "But there is always hope."

It was nearly seven o'clock by the time we arrived back in Alexandria. Although Holmes would have been happy to retire to his room to prepare for his second interview with the elusive Moony Wahlgren, Rafferty and I—who had not eaten since morning—insisted upon having supper in the hotel's restaurant and finally prevailed upon Holmes to join us. As we ate our dinner of cream of broccoli soup, roast beef, baked potatoes, rolls, and cheesecake, the conversation turned at once to the day's events and how we should proceed next.

Holmes began by apprising Rafferty of his telegram from Wooldridge, since he had neglected to mention the message earlier.

Rafferty's reaction to the Chicago detective's findings was amusing, for he said: "Mr. Comstock was not the first man to marry a whore, nor will he be the last, though I have always found that such relationships generally do not end as pleasurably as they began."

"In Mr. Comstock's case, it also ended quite quickly," Holmes said. "Indeed, I am very curious about the gentleman's fatal accident. Do you suppose you could make a few inquiries about the matter tomorrow, Mr. Rafferty? I have no doubt that you know someone with connections to the case, which must have prompted at least a cursory investigation by the authorities."

"I'll see what I can do," Rafferty promised as he dug into his baked potato. "It happened not far from here, is that right?"

"Yes, that is what Mr. Hill told Watson and me. Otherwise, I fear I have few details regarding the accident."

"Don't worry," said Rafferty, "I'll get the lowdown."

"I have no doubt that you will," said Holmes with a smile. "Now then, let us consider the more pressing issue of what happened to the rune stone."

"That business in the woodlot was a perfect April Fools' Day surprise, was it not?" said Rafferty. "It made all of us look like the biggest gatherin' of fools on the continent! 'Twas as if we found ourselves in a regular old-fashioned shell game, Mr. Holmes, the only problem bein' that the pea weighs two hundred pounds."

"I cannot argue your point, Mr. Rafferty," Holmes remarked. "Indeed, I am beginning to think that every aspect of this case is quite fantastic. The stone itself—whether an elaborate hoax or an object which will rewrite the history of this continent—defies logic and common sense. Then there are the coincidences which seem to haunt us at every turn. No self-respecting dramatist, even in his most dark and feverish imaginings, could invent a more improbable deus ex machina than the appearance of our old adversary from Hinckley, the woman we must now call Mary Comstock. What were the odds that she of all people should turn out to be a key player in this affair? And now we have added to all of this the mystery of the traveling rune stone. I must tell you, Mr. Rafferty, that if one of those famous midwestern cyclones were to swirl out of the sky this afternoon and deposit the rune stone at my doorstep, I should not be in the least surprised!"

" 'Tis too early for twisters in these parts," said Rafferty, "so I think you are safe on that account, Mr. Holmes.[1] But I do not dispute that this has become a surpassingly strange business."

"Be that as it may, we have no choice but to move forward despite the difficulties before us," Holmes said. "As I see it, there are two possibilities we must now consider, neither of which is without problems. The first is that Mr. Fogelblad lied to us all along about the stone and that this afternoon's adventure was nothing more than an elaborate charade. But for the life of me, I cannot see what the point of it would be."

"I can't either," said Rafferty. " 'Tis hard to see how Mr. Fogelblad could benefit himself, or anyone else, by pretendin' to know where the stone was hidden and then leadin' us all on a wild goose chase. Then again, maybe he's just a fun-lovin' jokester beneath that dark, dour face of his and likes the idea of tweakin' all us city folks. That's the thing with these Swedes, Mr. Holmes. They like to do their laughin' in a real strange sort of way."

Holmes tapped his long fingers on the table and said: "You have already made that point, Mr. Rafferty, and I do not discount the possibility that this was some strange sort of private joke. Nonetheless, as I indicated before we searched the woodlot, I am inclined to think that Mr. Fogelblad is telling the truth. He was, it seems to me, genuinely shocked when he failed to find the stone."

"I'll go along with that," Rafferty said. "If the Swede was pullin' our legs, then I'd have to rate him as the best fibber since Brutus sidled up to Caesar to wish him a good afternoon. And that leaves the second possibility you were gettin' at, Mr. Holmes, which is that somebody went out one night, dug up the stone, moved it to someplace unknown, and then left behind that little message to taunt us with his handiwork. What I'm wonderin', of course, is who would do such a thing and why they would do it. I'm hopin' you will have some answers for me."

Holmes rubbed his eyes, cupped his chin in his hands, and said: "I have none at present, Mr. Rafferty. I should be happy to hear your thoughts on the matter, however."

"Well, I confess I've been workin' on a little theory," Rafferty said. "You see, I'm beginnin' to think there's a regular elf in the vicinity who's up to all manner of trickery. It could even be this elf who left behind the fragment of glass Mr. Holmes found today."

I could not imagine what Rafferty meant by his talk of an "elf," but Holmes seemed to have no trouble grasping the idea. He said: "You have an interesting way of putting things, Mr. Rafferty. I take it you believe there is a mischievous quality to today's events."

"Exactly, Mr. Holmes. You see, the way I look at it, there's a wild card operatin' in the middle of this whole business, somebody who isn't playin' the game accordin' to everybody else's rules. He's sly and sneaky, this fellow is, and he seems to know everything that's goin' on with the rune stone. But he doesn't seem to have the same kind of stake in the game that the other players have."

"What do you mean?" I asked.

"Just this, Doctor. From all we know at the moment, money is at the bottom of this business. We know, for example, that any number of people — Mr. Larson, Mrs. Comstock, that fellow Lund in Chicago, and the Lord knows who else — are tryin' to get their paws on the stone because they're convinced it's worth a fortune. But for some reason, I don't think our naughty elf is interested in money. Somethin' else is drivin' him to play his game of hide-and-seek. Now, I don't pretend to know who this person is or why he's doin' what he's doin', but I'd bet my last dollar that he won't make it easy for us to find the rune stone, and that's a fact!"

"A most intriguing hypothesis, Mr. Rafferty," said Holmes. "Most intriguing. And if it's true, then this elf of yours must be someone who was very well acquainted with the late Mr. Wahlgren."

"Why do you conclude that?" I asked.

"It is simple, Watson, for how could Mr. Rafferty's elf have found the stone unless Mr. Wahlgren told him where it was hidden? This assumes, of course, that Mr. Fogelblad is telling the truth."

"But is it not possible that Mr. Wahlgren might have told others of the hiding place and that the thief learned it from one of those people?" I objected.

"Oh, 'tis possible," Rafferty admitted, "but not likely. From all we know of Mr. Wahlgren, he wasn't the type to go tellin' his secrets. No, I think that Mr. Holmes is right. Still, it might be worth our time to see if there was anybody close enough to Mr. Wahlgren to have learned the secret of the stone's hidin' place. Maybe there's another farmer hereabouts he was close to or maybe he had a good friend here in town. Or maybe it was Mr. Blegen down in Holandberg."

"Speaking of Mr. Blegen, what were your impressions of him?" I asked Holmes and Rafferty. "He struck me as a very nervous sort of man."

" 'Twas more than nervousness, if you ask me," said Rafferty. "He had the look of a man with somethin' to hide. "I'm thinkin' he's in-volved in this rune stone business up to his shifty little eyeballs."

"I cannot disagree with you," said Holmes. "I should like to know a great deal more about him. I would be especially interested to find out how he was able to translate the stone so quickly. I should also like to read his translation."

"You mean, to see how accurate it is?" I asked.

"Yes, but for another reason as well," Holmes said. "In any event, we shall have to have a longer conversation with Mr. Blegen, per-haps tomorrow."

"The sheriff will not be happy about that," I pointed out.

"Ah, the sheriff. I am glad you brought him up, Watson. He is a most intriguing figure, though Mr. Rafferty may have a different opinion."

Rafferty grinned and said: "My only opinion, Mr. Holmes, is that I'm ready to take on the sheriff any time he chooses. I am not fond of the man, and the more I see him, the less I like him."

"We have noticed," said Holmes dryly. "But Mr. Boehm's conduct today nonetheless raised several interesting questions. What is his relationship to Magnus Larson, with whom he seems almost inti-mately acquainted? Why does he want us out of the investigation?

Who, if anyone, is he working for? Does he have a personal stake in the discovery of the stone? Or is he merely one of those irritating, officious men who, as the largest fish in a very small pond, will brook no outside interference?"

"And just how might you answer those questions, Mr. Holmes?" Rafferty inquired.

"I have no answers at present — only theories. Still, I was struck by his conduct toward Mr. Larson. The way he slapped Larson — almost in the manner of an angry man disciplining an especially fractious and sassy child — was quite revealing."

"So you're thinkin' the two of them might be in cahoots," said Rafferty.

" 'Cahoots,' Mr. Rafferty, is not quite the word I would use, but yes, I do think it possible that the two of them may have more intimate connections than we know about. Then again, we may be reading far more into the situation than we should. The sheriff may simply be doing his job as he sees it."

"Perhaps that is how he found out your identity, Holmes, if in fact he did," I said. "He strikes me as a highly intelligent man. He may simply have wired the British Museum to verify our identities."

"That thought has occurred to me," Holmes replied. "So has another, more troubling one, which I will not go into at the moment. In any event, I suggest that you two trenchermen finish your supper as quickly as possible, for I am anxious to talk to Moony Wahlgren again."

We reached Kensington's doorstep at quarter past eight and rang the bell. Rafferty had come along with us this time, for Holmes was curious to see how he would respond to the mysterious young girl who increasingly seemed to be at the center of the rune stone affair.

Kensington answered at once and escorted us inside, where we once again took seats in the cozy parlor amid its gallery of family photographs. Rafferty was then introduced to "the missus," as Kensington generally referred to his wife, Elsie. The good woman was waiting for us with a plate piled high with cookies, cupcakes, and other delectables fresh from her oven. Holmes and I ate sparingly of

these riches, but Rafferty sampled everything on the plate and so en-
chanted Mrs. Kensington with his paeans to her virtuosity as a
baker that within minutes he had made another friend.

After the exchange of further pleasantries, Mrs. Kensington re-
treated to the kitchen to bake up an additional batch of cookies for
Rafferty. Holmes then asked George Kensington if we might, as he
put it, "speak frankly" about Moony Wahlgren.

"I do not see why not," Kensington said. "What is it you wish to
know?"

"First, I would like to know more about the circumstances under
which the girl came to live with you and your wife. You mentioned
earlier that her father had not treated her well. What exactly did you
mean by that?"

Kensington slowly nodded and said: "I guess you should hear the
full story. It was in early November, no more than a week or two before Olaf found the rune stone, that she showed up at our door one
night, carrying a bag and a knapsack. She also had something else—
a big black eye."

"May I ask why she came to your house?" Holmes said.

"Well, we had gotten to know her pretty well over the years
through the church we belong to. As the missus and I were never
blessed with children of our own, well, we took a shine to her right
away. She'd even stay at our house on weekends now and then.
We'd take her out to picnics or for short train trips—oh, how that
child loves to ride the train!—so I guess she started to think of us as
her second parents."

"I see. Please go on."

"Sure. As I was saying, she showed up at our door with that big
black eye, carrying all her things, and we naturally asked her what
had happened. All she would say at first was that 'bad things happened.' But we talked for a while and she finally told me who had
done those 'bad things.'"

"Her father," I said, wondering how any man could be so cruel to
his own daughter.

"Yes, it was Olaf who hit her, of that I am sure," said Kensington.
"I greatly fear he did other things as well."

"What kind of things?" Holmes asked.

Kensington now leaned forward toward us and said softly: "Unspeakable things."

"Oh dear," said Rafferty. "You mean he molested the poor child?"

"It is possible," Kensington acknowledged with a slow, sad shake of his head. "There was something very wrong on that farm."

We all sat in silence for a while, as though words were insufficient to deal with the horrible possibility Kensington had laid before us.

It was Holmes who spoke up at last. "I pray you are wrong, Mr. Kensington, but I also know that you may be right. Such a terrible violation could account for the girl's apparent withdrawal from the world as we know it. Now, if you would, please tell us this: did Mr. Wahlgren try to reclaim custody of his daughter from you?"

"He did, but I would not let him," said Kensington. "No sir, I would not let that happen."

"Good for you," said Rafferty. "Still, I'm wonderin', Mr. Kensington, just how you did that. The courts are usually not inclined to take a child from his or her parents, no matter what terrible thing they might have done."

"You're right about that. But I made it clear to Olaf that if he did go to court and try to get the girl back, I would make sure the world knew about what he had done to her. That stopped him in his tracks. Besides, I'm not so sure he even wanted her around anymore. It was obvious she had done something to make him mad enough to hit her, but I was never able to figure out exactly what happened."

"And I suppose Moony never told you," Holmes said.

"That's right. It's not her way to be direct with anything. I told the missus once that trying to get information out of Moony is like sitting under a very tall and very strong apple tree. You can't reach the fruit and you can't shake it down, so all you can do is wait for the apples to fall."

"Let us hope that is the case tonight," said Holmes, "for we are much in need of fruitful information."

❊   ❊   ❊

"Hello, Moony," said Holmes after we had climbed up the steep steps to her room and quietly walked over to where she was sitting.

She glanced up at us but otherwise gave no greeting. As had been the case during our first visit, she was seated at her desk, hard at work upon a drawing, her face as smooth as porcelain in the flickering light of her lamp. We took seats around her, after which Kensington asked if she would be willing to talk to "a few gentlemen" again.

"I am making something," she announced, holding up her drawing. "I think it is very pretty."

The drawing, which could hardly be described as "pretty," was in fact one of the eeriest pictures I had ever seen. Done in colored inks, it centered on the image of a man — Olaf Wahlgren perhaps? — lying face up in a shallow grave. The man, who wore a black funeral suit, had no eyes, only empty sockets. Above his body was something like a tombstone, but it had no name carved into it. Instead, it was clearly meant to be the rune stone, its inscription only half completed in the manner of the drawing Holmes and I had seen previously. Perched atop the stone was a huge vulture, looking down hungrily at the corpse. In the distance, peeking out from a line of trees, could be seen the figure of a girl — Moony? — holding something in her hands which looked like a small box.

"I have not seen this before," Kensington whispered to us.

Holmes now said: "You are a wonderful artist, Moony. Tell us about your drawing."

"I remember you," she said, her huge blue eyes focused on Holmes, though I had the impression she was not looking at him but through him, at something only she could see. "You're the question man. I have a question for you."

"Is it a hard question?"

"Maybe. Where did Papa go when he died?"

Holmes, for once, seemed stumped by a question, but before he could formulate an answer Rafferty said: "I can answer that."

The girl turned her gaze on Rafferty and said: "You're fat."

" 'Tis true, child," Rafferty admitted with a chuckle. "Why, just today, somebody else told me the same thing. But I know a lot of things for a fat man. I even know where your papa went."

"Do you really?"

"Oh yes."

"Do you think he went to heaven?"

"No. Do you?"

"No. Heaven is too far away. Nobody lives there. Papa will get eaten, that is what I think. Everything gets eaten."

"By the vultures," said Rafferty. "The vultures will eat your papa."

"But first they must poke out his eyes."

"Yes, they will do that."

I was astonished by this gruesome conversation, yet at the same time I sensed that Rafferty had somehow begun to open up a small, tenuous path into the girl's mind.

"I have seen them," she now said.

Rafferty thought for a moment, trying to figure out the girl's strange way of thinking, then asked: "Where did you see the vultures?"

"In the box. Everything is in the box."

"Can I see the box?" Rafferty asked.

"No, the box is gone. Rochester has it."

"Of course. I almost forgot about Rochester. Will he keep the box, do you suppose?"

"I will get it," she said. "I will get the box."

"Good. You would not want to lose the box."

"No. The box is mine. They were looking for it."

"Yes, I know that. But they didn't find it, did they. You saw to that."

"They won't find it," she agreed.

"Why do you suppose they want the box?"

"Can I touch your beard?" the girl suddenly asked.

"Of course," said Rafferty, leaning toward her so that she could run her fingers through his long, shaggy growth.

"It feels like a brush," she said. "A big brush."

"You're right," said Rafferty. "Tell me, does your friend Rochester have a beard?"

The girl now surprised us by breaking out in a giggle. It was the first time Holmes and I had seen her laugh. "I like you," she said to Rafferty. "You're funny."

"I like you, too, Moony. I like you so much that I'll tell you a secret if you'll tell one to me."

"All right. You first."

Rafferty leaned over and whispered into the girl's ear. Her response was another giggle.

"Your turn," said Rafferty.

The girl complied, still giggling as she put her arms around Rafferty's neck and then whispered something to him. It must have been quite a secret, because she whispered for some time before settling back into her chair.

"Why, that's a very fine secret, Moony," said Rafferty. "But I'm wonderin' if you could tell me a little more?"

Ignoring Rafferty's question, the girl stood up and announced, just as she had on our earlier visit, that she was tired and wished to go to bed. Knowing from experience that our presence would not deter her from changing into her sleeping clothes, Holmes arose from his chair and we all quickly bade her good night.

Once we were back downstairs, Holmes again advised Kensington in the strongest possible words to keep a close watch on his adoptive daughter for fear that someone might try to do her harm. Kensington promised he would do so, after which we bade our farewells and went out in the crisp night air.

"Well, we are waiting, Mr. Rafferty," said Holmes as we went through Kensington's front gate and out onto the sidewalk. "What little secrets did you and Moony exchange?"

"I told her that she was the cutest girl I'd ever seen and I asked her to marry me," Rafferty said. "She thought that was pretty funny, as you noticed. As for what she told me, I'm afraid you won't believe it, Mr. Holmes. You see, she said she knows where the rune stone is. Trouble is, she wouldn't tell me where it's hidden."

Chapter Thirteen

"I FELT THE PRESENCE OF A HORRIBLE CHILL"

The next day, a cold and rainy Sunday, Holmes stayed in his room until late afternoon, refusing breakfast or lunch, and obsessed by what he had come to call "the Rochester problem." He was convinced that Moony Wahlgren held the key to the rune stone mystery, but as he told me that morning, "I do not yet know how to open the lock. Only if I find Rochester will I gain that knowledge."

Holmes's fascination with the girl had, not surprisingly, intensified after Rafferty revealed the "secret" she had shared with him. "We must assume she is telling the truth," Holmes had told us as we walked back to the Douglas House. "But how did she discover the stone's hiding place? That is the most tantalizing question of all."

With Holmes locked in one of his bouts of cerebration, it was left to Rafferty and me to push the investigation forward "in the field," as Rafferty liked to say. "Your friend Mr. Holmes is a brilliant man," he told me as we ate breakfast in a little cafe he had found about two blocks from the hotel. "But sometimes I think he works his mind too hard, if you know what I mean. You can only think through a thing for so long before you become just like a dog chasin' its tail. You just turn and turn and turn until there's nothin' left to chew on but the painful stub of an idea. When that starts to happen, it's time to get up off your hinder and go out and do somethin' useful. And that's what I propose to do today, Doctor. Would you care to join me?"

"I do not see why not. What do you have in mind, Mr. Rafferty?"

"I'm thinkin' it might be interestin' to have another talk with that little birdie of mine."

"And just who is this informant?"

"Come along after you finish up that sausage you're workin' on, Doctor, and you'll find out soon enough."

Once we left the cafe, Rafferty began walking at a brisk pace toward the direction of the railroad depot. The town felt especially drab and gloomy in the rain, which seemed to wash away what little color there was in the small wooden and brick buildings along Broadway. The stores were all closed—for there was no business to be done on Sunday—and the street itself had turned into a long, wide mud pit. We saw a single horse and carriage parked in front of the local apothecary shop—or drug store, as the Americans prefer to call it— but there was no light inside. We stopped beneath a large canopy sheltering the store's entrance so that Rafferty could light a cigar.

" 'Tis a real soaker," he remarked once he had accomplished his task. "The farmers will be happy, for this is just the kind of rain they like before plantin' season."

"It reminds me of London in January," I said as I stared idly at the array of merchandise—creams and lotions of all kinds, bottles of various "miracle" tonics, pocket watches, cameras, stationery— displayed in the store's large plate-glass window. Also on display was a large porcelain doll, which at once brought to mind Moony Wahlgren.

"What do you think about the girl's references to 'Rochester'?" I asked Rafferty, who appeared to be in no hurry to go back out into the rain.

"I've given it some thought, Doctor, and I'm wonderin' whether

'Rochester' has to be the name of a person, as we've been assumin' all along. 'Tis possible it could refer to somethin' else."

"Such as?"

Rafferty shrugged and said: "A town, maybe. There's a Rochester here in Minnesota that's gotten pretty famous because of a couple of sawbones — no offense, doctor — who set up shop there.[1] Then, of course, there's Rochester, New York. Never been there, but it's a good-sized city. Or it could be that 'Rochester' refers to a street or a park or a buildin' somewhere. There's just no tellin' what the girl means. 'Tis a regular conundrum. But I'm sure Mr. Holmes will figure it out soon enough."

"Let us hope that for his sake, he does," I said as Rafferty stubbed out his cigar and we headed out once again into the rain. "Can you tell me where we're going?"

"You'll see," said Rafferty.

Our destination turned out to be the Great Northern depot. This should have been obvious to me, since the railroad was the one business in town which operated twenty-four hours a day, even on Sundays. I also should have guessed the identity of Rafferty's informant, who turned out to be the depot's stationmaster. As such he was in a perfect position to know almost everything that happened in town. The stationmaster's name was Jack Christianson, and he had known Rafferty since the latter's days selling Bibles throughout the territory.

We found Christianson in his small office, sitting in a swivel chair before a large wooden desk with cubbyholes designed for the numerous manifests, reports, statements, receipts, and letters generated by an enterprise as large and far-flung as the Great Northern Railway. Christianson was a slender man in his fifties, with thick, carefully combed hair the color of light sand, a long and rather morose face, and close-set gray eyes which looked up at us from beneath wire-rim spectacles. His perfectly pressed blue uniform and ramrod-straight bearing as he stood to greet us all suggested a man of military precision. Yet there was nothing prim or formal about the way he addressed Rafferty.

"Shad, it's good to see you," he said with a warm smile, rising from his chair. "Come on in and sit down a spell."

"Be my pleasure," said Rafferty as we took the only other chairs in the office. "Jack, I would like you to meet a friend of mine. This is Peter Smith of London. He's helpin' me with this queer rune stone business."

"Well, if you're a friend of Shad's then you're a friend of mine," said Christianson, giving me a firm handshake. "You're with that other British fellow, aren't you?"

"Yes, I'm Mr. Baker's assistant. He is occupied with other matters at the moment."

After this brief introduction was completed, I watched with a mixture of amusement and admiration as Rafferty worked his peculiar verbal magic on Christianson. Whereas Holmes could be extremely blunt at times, going directly to the business at hand like a lion in full stride, Rafferty reminded me more of a subtle and infinitely patient hunter circling his prey for just the right moment to strike.

Rafferty therefore spent the better part of half an hour exchanging reminiscences with Christianson, inquiring as to the health and progress of his family, discussing the onerous duties of a stationmaster, and even talking about the weather—a topic which seemed to be a source of endless conversation among Minnesotans. It was only after these lengthy preliminaries that Rafferty posed the question he had come to ask all along:

"By the way, Jack, did you dig up that report I was lookin' for?"

"I've got it," said Christianson, "but you understand this all must be on the QT. I could get in trouble with James J. Hill himself if anybody was to find out I was passing around company documents."

"My lips are sealed," Rafferty assured him. "I can also vouch for Mr. Smith. He is a man in whom you can have complete confidence."

"All right, Shad, I know your word is good as gold. Here it is—" he gave Rafferty a small document of perhaps fifteen pages, bound in a loose-leaf notebook—"but I must have it back as soon as possible."

"It will be in your hands again tomorrow," Rafferty promised, "with no one the wiser. And you can be sure, Jack, that I won't forget this favor."

It was only after we had returned to the hotel, shed our wet coats, and secured steaming hot cups of coffee that Rafferty described the documents he had obtained from Christianson.

" 'Tis the report on Mr. Comstock's death prepared by the Great Northern's own dicks," he said as we took seats in the lobby. "Whenever there's a accident—especially a fatal one—anywhere on the line, the railroad sends in its private coppers to do an investigation."

"But don't the authorities also investigate?"

"Sure, but the railroad doesn't trust the locals, here or anywhere else, to do the job. So it sends in its own boys, who—and this will be no surprise to you, Doctor—invariably discover that the deceased was at fault for the accident. But even if they're more than a little biased, the railroad dicks are very thorough, and that's why the Great Northern doesn't lose a lot of cases in court. Now then, let's just see what the railroad's investigators had to say about Mr. Comstock."

Like Holmes, Rafferty was a swift and insightful reader, and it took him but a few minutes to work his way through the entire report.

Putting it down on the small table between our chairs, he said: "Well, Doctor, you can read it yourself or I can give you the gist of it."

"The gist would be fine for the moment," I said. "Holmes, I am sure, will want to read it later, as will I."

"All right, here's the story," said Rafferty, settling into his chair and taking a swig of coffee. "On the afternoon of December 14, 1898, Mr. Frank Comstock and his lovely bride were aboard an eastbound Great Northern train that originated in Seattle and was headin' to Minneapolis–St. Paul. The train carried several Pullman cars, and it was in one of these that the couple, who boarded the train in Fargo-Moorhead, had a compartment.[2] They had tickets to St. Paul, where they were to switch trains and continue on to Chicago. This is all accordin' to another passenger who spoke briefly with the Comstocks in the dinin' car. Now, this same witness said Mr. Comstock drank at least two glasses of whisky in his presence and appeared, if not fallin'-down drunk, well lubricated."

"I am curious. What time of day was this?"

"A good question, Doctor. 'Twas about six o'clock at night. Of course, at that time of year, it was already pitch black outside, which is always a convenient circumstance if you happen to have murder on your mind. Now, again accordin' to this witness, the couple left the dinin' car around seven, presumably to return to their compartment. What's interestin' is that from this point forward, there's only one person who remembers seein' Mr. Comstock on the train."

"His wife," I said.

"Sad but true, Doctor. The lady's account, as it turns out, is very simple. She says she and her husband went back to their compartment, where they no doubt chatted about wheat farmin' or some other stimulatin' subject. At about eight o'clock, she says, Mr. Comstock decided to go out and smoke a cigar, since the lady did not like the smell of tobacco in the compartment. And that, she told the railroad dicks, is the last she saw of her husband. When he did not return after half an hour or so, she became alarmed and went out to look for him. Of course, she couldn't find him. The conductor was then summoned, inquiries were made, et cetera, et cetera. The upshot is that Frank Comstock's body was found later that night, lyin' beside the tracks about five miles east of Alexandria."

"Was he dead when they found him?"

"He was. When he took his swan dive off the train, he hit a telegraph post head first. 'Twas not a pretty sight, I imagine. The official theory is that instead of goin' to the lounge car, where most gentlemen do their smokin' on a train, he stood in one of the vestibules between the cars, or perhaps on the platform behind the last car, and somehow fell to his death."

"Was there any evidence that he might have been pushed from the train?"

"Ah, that's where it gets interestin'. Accordin' to the report, two points intrigued the local investigator, who was none other than our friend Sheriff Gustavus Boehm. The first item of interest was that neither cigars nor matches were found on or near the victim's body. Mrs. Comstock's only explanation for this was that the cigars and matches might have dropped from her poor husband's hand and lodged themselves somewhere on the vestibule steps before he went tumblin' from the train. If that happened, she said, then these two pieces of evidence could easily have been blown off the train somewhere down the line."

"That does not sound very convincing to me," I said.

"No, but it's possible, and that's all the lady needed to demonstrate."

"Very well. What was the second point of interest?"

Rafferty took another big gulp of coffee and said: "The second point is that a woman aboard the train saw Mrs. Comstock in the aisle of the Pullman car, walking back toward her compartment, at about quarter past eight."

"What was her explanation for this?"

"Again, the lady offered no elaborate story. She simply said she was feelin' a bit cramped in her compartment and went out to stretch her legs."

"And the sheriff believed her?"

"Who knows? But it doesn't really matter, because the fact is, there wasn't nearly enough evidence to charge her, or anybody else, with a crime. I will say this, though: Sheriff Boehm did a thorough job. Accordin' to the railroad dicks' report, he even checked to see what sort of life insurance policy Frank Comstock had. You'd think a fellow like that would have a big policy, but the sheriff discovered that he didn't have a dime's worth of insurance. As Mr. Holmes's copper friend down in Chicago has already told us, Frank Comstock seems to have passed penniless from this vale of tears, which must have come as quite a shock to the grievin' widow."

"So I take it no charges were ever filed in connection with his death?"

"That's right. The coroner, havin' no good evidence to the contrary, ruled the death accidental and said it was probably related to excessive consumption of alcohol."

"And what do you think, Mr. Rafferty?"

"I think I'd be wary of marryin' his widow," said Rafferty with a grin.

When Holmes finally emerged from his room at about three o'clock and met us in the lobby, Rafferty gave him the report to read. After perusing it with his usual dispatch, Holmes told us he found the report "most suggestive," but would not elaborate on that statement. As he spoke, he drummed his fingers on the armrest of his chair, looking as impatient as a schoolboy awaiting recess.

"You appear terribly anxious, Holmes," I remarked. "Is the Rochester problem still bothering you?"

"It is, but I am bothered even more by the emptiness at the center of this case," he replied, his nervous fingers still tapping out an incessant beat.

"What do you mean?"

"I mean the rune stone, Watson. It has generated all that has happened here, brought covetous men to murder, and yet it remains hidden, a tantalizing artifact known to us only through the testimony of others. How I would like to see that stone!"

" 'Twould indeed be wonderful to find the thing," Rafferty agreed. "Sometimes I think we're chasin' a ghost."

I now had an inspiration. "Perhaps someone took a photograph of the stone shortly after it was found," I said. "Such a picture could prove very useful."

" 'Twas a thought that occurred to me, too," said Rafferty. "A photograph from the scene could answer a good many of the questions that bedevil us. Maybe we should start nosin' around to see if any of the farmers hereabouts, or anybody in town for that matter, might have taken a picture of the stone at Wahlgren's farm."

"An excellent idea," said Holmes. "In the meantime, I would be most interested in having another talk with Einar Blegen. I am sure he knows more than he is saying about the stone."

"Too bad the sheriff came along when he did yesterday," Rafferty noted. "Mr. Blegen struck me as a tree that you'd have no trouble shakin' the fruit from."

Holmes smiled and said: "The sheriff is not the only one who made a timely appearance yesterday, Mr. Rafferty. Had not Mrs. Comstock arrived on the scene when she did, I fear you and the sheriff could have ended up in a gunfight."

"Not a chance of it," Rafferty said. "The two of us were just doin' a little jig, seein' how far the other fellow might be willin' to go. 'Twas nothin' to worry about."

"Speaking of Mrs. Comstock, do you intend to talk with her again?" I asked Holmes.

"I do. First, however, I would like to have a discussion with Mr. Billy Swift. Indeed, if we can get him alone, he may be far more useful to us than his mistress."

"Why do you say that?"

The answer came from Rafferty: "I think what Mr. Holmes is sayin' is that young Billy boy doesn't shine quite as brightly in the intellectual department as Mrs. Comstock. The lad struck me as the rough-and-tumble sort who likes to ride horses and shoot guns but who doesn't spend much time in the company of deep thoughts."

"Well put, Mr. Rafferty," said Holmes. "Mr. Swift is an example of what the Americans like to call a 'henchman.' He is, I suspect, a man who will boldly carry out orders so long as he has someone to think for him. It is quite apparent that Mrs. Comstock has the young man wrapped completely around her finger and he will do whatever she tells him. There can also be no doubt that she has taken him as a lover."

"But he is half her age," I protested.

"Ah now, Doctor, don't sound so shocked," Rafferty said. " 'Twas Ben Franklin who said, if I recall, that a man should always take an older woman as a mistress because she'll be so grateful."

"Somehow I do not think that describes Mrs. Comstock's situation," said Holmes, "for she —"

He suddenly stopped, his eyes locking on something behind me. I swung around and caught sight of Billy Swift. He was just coming in the front door of the hotel, and he was alone, as though delivered to us on cue by one of those mysterious coincidences with which the entire rune stone affair was so rife.

"Ah, Mr. Swift," said Holmes in a voice loud enough to be heard throughout the lobby. "How nice to see you. Why don't you come over and join us?"

The young man, dressed in his usual cowboy attire, looked over at Holmes and seemed to recoil, as though he had just found a scorpion in his boot. "I got nothing to say," he stated, walking past us toward the main stairs.

"How unfortunate, for there is some very interesting news about the rune stone," Holmes said, adding: "I am sure Mrs. Comstock would be most intrigued by what we have discovered."

This was enough to give the young man second thoughts, for he slowly turned around, walked a few steps back toward us, and said: "And just what is that?"

"Why don't you sit down and we'll talk about it," said Holmes, maintaining an amiable air. "Would you care for some coffee?"

"I'll stand," Swift replied, leaning up against a pillar next to our chairs. As he did so, his buckskin jacket swung slightly open to reveal the butt of a pistol in his belt. Ignoring Holmes's offer of a drink, he said in his surly way: "If you've got something to say, say it."

"I see you are a very direct young man," said Holmes. "Then I shall be direct, too. We have uncovered significant new evidence which could lead shortly to the recovery of the rune stone. I wish you to inform your mistress of this fact and to tell her that—"

"She ain't my mistress," the young man spat out contemptuously, "and I ain't no errand boy." As he spoke these words, he rested his right hand on the butt of his pistol.

"My apologies," said Holmes coolly, "for when we met the other day, you certainly looked and acted very much like an errand boy."

Holmes's scalding insult caused Swift's face to redden and his mouth to open in the way a predator might bare its teeth. For a split second I even thought he might reach for his weapon.

Fortunately, Rafferty stepped in at once to apply a little balm to the young man's wounded pride while at the same time suggesting that any rash action on his part would be unwise.

" 'Tis a nice piece you're carrying under that jacket," Rafferty observed. "Looks like a Colt Frontier.[3] I've always found that small men such as yourself prefer big guns, so I'm guessin' it's a .44. That's a mighty fine weapon, mighty fine indeed, but a bit slow and heavy for my tastes. No sir, a derringer, that's the thing for close-in fightin' if you ask me. You'd be surprised how fast a man can get a derringer out of his sleeve if he needs to. There's nothin' faster, don't you agree, young Billy?"

Swift's sharp, feral eyes honed in on Rafferty, who sat easily in his chair, his arms resting in his lap. I knew for a fact that Rafferty often carried a derringer, for I had seen him display just such a weapon in his encounter with "Bull" O'Connor during the ice palace case.[4] I watched Swift now, and I saw a hint of indecision in his eyes as he tried to decipher the meaning of Rafferty's comments. The young man finally arrived at the right conclusion and slowly withdrew his hand from his pistol.

"By the way, a word of warnin' to you, lad," Rafferty continued. "Sheriff Boehm doesn't like people packin' weaponry in his jurisdiction, so I'd be discreet with that six-shooter of yours."

"I ain't afraid of him," Swift said.

"Your courage is commendable, Mr. Swift, if perhaps not well considered," said Holmes, who added: "Now then, as I was saying, I hope you will tell Mrs. Comstock what I have told you. Please tell her as well that I would like to discuss the matter further with her tomorrow."

The young man's only response to this request, however, was to hurl a crude epithet at Holmes, after which he turned around and walked away without another word.

"Well," said Rafferty as we watched Swift reach the top of the stairs and turn in the direction of Mrs. Comstock's room, "I'd be interested to know what that was all about."

Holmes replied: "I have always found, Mr. Rafferty, that a good detective must not only harvest clues but also, on occasion, sow them. I have merely planted a small seed of doubt. Whether it will grow into anything useful remains to be seen."

Mrs. Comstock's response to Holmes's attempt at provocation was not long in coming, for less than half an hour after our encounter with Swift, a bellboy delivered a message from the lady. It was addressed to "Mr. Baker and his friends" and read: "Never bluff with an empty hand. M. Comstock."

"Well, you don't seem to have stricken fear into the lady's heart," said Rafferty with a soft chuckle. "She'd be a good one at five-card stud, and that's a fact!"

Holmes sighed and said: "It was a long shot at best, Mr. Rafferty. Still, if nothing else, we have learned that Mrs. Comstock and her youthful companion do not seem to be on the best of terms at the moment."

"Maybe they just had a lover's quarrel," Rafferty suggested.

"I doubt that," said Holmes, "for I do not think the lady wastes her time quarreling over love. Indeed, as far as I can tell she is that rarest of women — one who has no need of men. She does, however, have uses for them. You see, I am convinced that the only thing she craves is not love but rather constant stimulation. She thrives on a challenge, whether it be operating a whorehouse or marrying a rich man and sucking him dry of his money, as I'm sure she intended to do with her late husband. Now, we are her challenge, the focus of her attention, and that is why she must be regarded as extremely dangerous."

"You make her sound like one of the Borgias," said Rafferty, who of course did not know the lady as well as Holmes and I.

Holmes looked at Rafferty with his piercing gaze and said: "There is one thing you must understand, my friend. Mary Comstock is no ordinary criminal. Crime for her is not merely a way of life but a means of artistic expression. So it was with Professor Moriarty. What made the professor so effective as a criminal mastermind was not just his intellect but the deep and abiding pleasure he took from his misdeeds. Crime was in his blood, coursing through his veins like a dark toxin, and was therefore as natural to him as breathing. He lived for crime, Mr. Rafferty, and I believe Mrs. Comstock is cut from the same cloth. She will be more dangerous than ever now that we have found our way into her arena again, and we must be extremely careful, for she will strike like a cobra if we make the slightest misstep."

I thought this a most extraordinary speech, since Holmes had never before compared any criminal, however skilled and ruthless, to Moriarty, whom he regarded as a kind of malignant touchstone against which all other wrongdoers must be measured. That Holmes would now put Mrs. Comstock in such elite company, if it could be called that, struck me as an overreaction on his part.

"I am surprised that you consider Mrs. Comstock such a formidable criminal," I said. "She is certainly a clever and deceitful woman, but to compare her to Professor Moriarty seems—"

"A bit much?" Holmes volunteered. "Perhaps you are right, Watson. But I must tell you that when I bent over to kiss her hand two days ago, I felt the presence of a horrible chill of the kind I have not experienced since I confronted Professor Moriarty at the brink of the Reichenbach Falls. You see, I believe that evil is not merely a character trait but a thing in itself, which gusts through the affairs of mankind like a relentless wind. Some stand firmly against it, others bend with it, but a dangerous few inhale it greedily so that they might breathe out its cold, concentrated poison upon the world. Moriarty was such a person, and Mrs. Comstock, I fear, may be his soul mate. Had they ever met and married, I do not doubt they might have ruled the world!"

By supper time, the rain had stopped and the sun made a late appearance, just in time to set over the western horizon. Holmes, Rafferty, and I went for a walk up and down Broadway, then ate a leisurely meal, during which we reviewed every aspect of the case. By nine o'clock we had all retired to our respective rooms. I was looking forward to a long night's sleep, for the pace of events since our arrival in Alexandria had been unrelenting.

But there was to be one more development on this rainy Sunday. Just after ten o'clock, as I was preparing to retire for the night, Holmes knocked on my door.

"Look what has arrived," he said, handing me a brief handwritten note which said: "Mr. Baker: Come see me tomorrow in Holandberg. I have something important to tell you. Einar Blegen."

"Where did you get this, Holmes?"

"Mr. Blegen telephoned the front desk and dictated the message."

"That is rather strange," I noted. "Why didn't he simply ask to speak with you?"

"I have no idea," said Holmes. "But I do know that we must see Mr. Blegen as soon as possible in the morning."

Chapter Fourteen

"MURDER IS ALWAYS HARD TO BELIEVE"

olmes and I left for Holandberg at eight o'clock the next morning after eating breakfast with Rafferty at the hotel. Although I knew that Rafferty would have liked to come along with us, Holmes asked him to stay in Alexandria to undertake much-needed work there. Among other things, Rafferty was to canvass local hardware stores (to see if he could identify the type of lantern glass Holmes had found at Fogelblad's farm) and to scout for any photographs that might have been taken of the rune stone. Holmes also wanted Rafferty to keep an eye on George Kensington's house, since he would be driving us to Holandberg.

Even though a neighbor had already agreed to watch over the house, Holmes told Rafferty: "It would be useful if you could stroll by the property every so often, just to make sure no one is loitering in the vicinity. I am still worried about the Wahlgren girl."

"I'll keep an eye peeled," Rafferty promised, "and if there's any trouble, I'll handle it pronto."

"I have no doubt you will," said Holmes, adding that he thought he would be back in town not long after noon.

The day had dawned crisp, clear, and windy, with only a few light clouds racing across the sky. Our trip to Holandberg, with the ever able Kensington at the reins, turned out to be a pleasant drive in the country. I was surprised to see how quickly the roads had dried after the rain of the previous day—a phenomenon Kensington attributed to the constant wind.

"That's the nice thing about the prairies," he said. "Once the wind starts blowing, and it almost always does, everything dries out in a hurry."

We followed the same route we had taken just four days earlier to Olaf Wahlgren's farm, winding past frozen ponds, brown stubbled fields, and small wooded hillocks scattered like tiny archipelagos across the landscape. Small farmsteads—the houses usually white, the barns red—could be seen here and there, invariably set well back from the road, for the Americans liked their space and did not live in farming villages in the English manner. This pastoral scene possessed a certain raw beauty, yet it also conveyed an unmistakable sense of melancholy. I felt—as I did almost every time we ventured into this thinly settled countryside—the urge to return as quickly as possible to the close and busy world of London.

Such were my thoughts when at half past nine we reached the village after which the rune stone was named. Holandberg, we discovered, was so tiny that it made Alexandria seem by comparison a vast and teeming metropolis. Despite its minuscule size, the village was platted around a main thoroughfare which was broader than all but a few of London's major arteries. This absurdly wide street seemed so out of scale with its modest surroundings that I could not but wonder how it had come about.

Holmes was thinking along similar lines, for he observed: "Have you noticed, Watson, how every American town seems to be a hopeful hallelujah awaiting its chorus? Look at this ridiculous street. What dreams of civic grandeur must have inspired it! And yet I sense nothing permanent here. The town looks as though it was nailed together in a day and might well be taken apart with equal speed, should its occupants decide to move on. Perhaps they have already done so, for it appears we have the street to ourselves."

The street was indeed deserted save for a couple of wagons parked along one side. I doubted, however, that the street would offer much excitement even on the busiest of days, for only a dozen or so small buildings stood along its brief course. Mostly built of wood and all of nondescript character, these structures provided what little there was of the town's commercial district. We passed a hardware store, a dry goods establishment, a bank, a harness shop, and an implement dealer before reaching our destination — the two-story building where Einar Blegen lived above a tavern which identified itself, by means of a large painted sign, as HONEST ED'S SALOON.

"We will be an hour at least," Holmes told Kensington as we stepped down from the carriage.

"That's fine," Kensington replied. "If you don't find me here when you're done, I'll be at the harness shop just up the street. I know the fellow there."

An alley of sorts ran along one side of the saloon and it was there that we found the entrance to the apartments above, which were reached by an open stairway. We climbed the stairs until we arrived at a small landing with two doors. The name "Blegen" was handwritten on a small card beside the left-hand door. Holmes knocked several times but received no answer. He then tried the other door, with the same result.

"Perhaps Mr. Blegen is downstairs," I said.

"You forget it is not yet ten in the morning," said Holmes. "I doubt the saloon is open."

We went back down to the saloon, which was indeed closed. However, we could see through the only window that a man was working inside. We knocked on the door until we got his attention.

"Something you fellows want?" he asked, unlocking the door. "We don't open until eleven."

Holmes explained that we were looking for Einar Blegen but had received no answer when we knocked on his door. The man, who I assumed to be "Honest Ed," was tall and heavy, with a puffy, blotched face which bespoke too many years spent indoors. He told us that he had not seen Blegen since Saturday.

"Einar's probably in Alexandria visiting one of his friends," the man added. "Otherwise, he'd be upstairs working on his project, as he does most every day. He's writing a history of the town, you know."

"I am sure that will be a most thrilling narrative," said Holmes.

Hoping to gather more information, Holmes continued to chat with the bartender, whose name we soon learned was Edvard Olson and who was in fact the establishment's owner. After a few more minutes of idle conversation, Holmes thanked Olson and we left.

I assumed we would now return to Alexandria, but Holmes had other ideas. "Come along, Watson," he said. "I should like to take a look at Mr. Blegen's apartment."

I knew there was no use arguing with Holmes. He had a propensity for breaking and entering in the pursuit of knowledge, and all I could do was try to keep him from being caught. Kensington was nowhere to be seen — he presumably had gone to the harness shop — and the street remained deserted. We went back around to the side of the building and climbed up the steps. Holmes once again knocked firmly on Blegen's door. He then tried the door of the adjoining apartment. Again, there was no response.

"Keep a sharp eye out," Holmes said as he removed a small leather case from his coat pocket. The case contained an array of lock picks, in the use of which Holmes was thoroughly expert. He quickly selected the right tool, inserted it into the lock, and within a matter of seconds opened the door, where a grim and surprising scene awaited us.

The body of a man, dressed in a long wool coat, lay facedown near a desk in one corner of the room. Beside him was a pool of congealed blood which had flowed out from a huge wound to the back of the skull. The room itself was a shambles, with paper and other items strewn across the floor. But the real surprise was the identity of the victim, for it was hard to mistake a man of Magnus Larson's height and bulk.

"Close the door," said Holmes as I looked upon this ghastly scene. "We have much work to do and little time to do it."

❖   ❖   ❖

I went over at once to examine the corpse, but Holmes took only a glance at the body before beginning a careful search of the room, which appeared to be the apartment's parlor. A doorway led to another room, presumably the bedchamber. The parlor was furnished with a decrepit sofa, a lounging chair, two end tables with lamps, a large bookcase, and the desk. Both the desk and the bookcase had been thoroughly ransacked, and even part of the room's carpeting had been pulled up.

The room also contained a small fireplace, which Holmes went over to inspect immediately. "Well, at least we know that the murderer is not an entirely untidy individual," he said, holding up a heavy iron poker, one end of which was stained with blood. "He went to the trouble of putting the poker back on its stand after he searched the room. Incidentally, can you estimate the time of death, Watson?"

I examined the wound and the general condition of the corpse. The back of Larson's head was utterly smashed in, suggesting that he had been struck more than once with the poker and had probably died almost instantly. I noted that rigor mortis had begun in the face, that some lividity was still evident, and that the body was not yet cold.

"I would guess he has been dead about six to eight hours," I told Holmes, "but I cannot be entirely certain."

"Then death must have occurred after Mr. Blegen sent us the message last night," said Holmes, who had moved over by the bookcase to examine the volumes scattered on the floor in front of it. He found several books of interest and paged through them. "Mr. Blegen's library is well stocked with works of Scandinavian history," he remarked. "The latest works of Jorgensen, Steenstrup, and Keary are here, as is Mr. Rosander's excellent volume.[1] Mr. Blegen is more of a scholar than he let on to us."

After I had completed my examination of the corpse, Holmes knelt down and began rooting through the papers on the floor. But he apparently found nothing of interest, for he soon went over to the desk to search its drawers and compartments. This required him to straddle Larson's body, which lay directly in front of the desk. As Holmes eagerly rummaged through the desk, I could only guess what he might be looking for. Whatever it was, he did not find it at once.

"Can I help you?" I said.

"I think not, my dear Watson. The problem, you see, is that even I do not know what I am looking for. In any case, why don't you go through Mr. Larson's pockets to see what you can find while I have a look at the rest of the apartment, which is no doubt in a similar state of disarray."

It was not a pleasant task, but I did as I was told. Larson's pockets—he was wearing black trousers beneath his usual Viking tunic—at first yielded nothing out of the ordinary. I found a watch, a few coins, a jackknife, and a handkerchief. Then I came upon something curious—a piece of plain paper which, when I unfolded it, appeared to be a crudely drawn map of some kind.

When Holmes came back into the parlor, having found nothing of value in the bedchamber, I showed him the map. His eyes shone with excitement as he studied it.

"Well, Watson, it appears we are about to embark on a treasure hunt," he said before folding up the map and putting it in his coat pocket. "Now let us see if there are any other prizes to be found here."

Holmes returned to the bedroom, where I could hear him tapping softly on the walls. Soon, he was back again in the parlor, where he continued sounding out the walls and floorboards. Holmes was expert at this kind of investigation—he once told me that he had a "special instinct" for locating hidden safes and compartments—and his skill was soon rewarded.[2] As he tested the floor beneath the desk, kneeling over Larson's body as he did so, he found a loose board. Using a letter opener from the desk, he pried open the board and found a compartment containing a small bag of gold coins and, more importantly, an envelope stamped with the name MERCHANTS NATIONAL BANK OF ALEXANDRIA. Inside was the key to a safety deposit box.

"Whatever the box contains, it must be quite valuable — or perhaps quite revealing — for Mr. Blegen seems to have required a special hiding place for it," said Holmes, who slipped the envelope and key into his coat pocket.

He then stood up and went over to the front door, which was the only entrance to the apartment, and scrutinized its lock.

"It is just as I suspected," he said. "There is no evidence of a break-in. Now then, let me have a look at the body."

He bent down and undertook a detailed examination of the corpse, paying special attention to the head wound, the hands, and the overall placement of the body. He also carefully examined the desk, the top of which was splattered with bloodstains.

Then he turned to me and said: "It would appear that Mr. Larson was walking toward the desk when he was struck from behind. I would also point out that Mr. Larson's notebook — the one he showed us at the Majestic Tavern and which I suspect he always carried on his person — appears to be gone."

"Do you suppose he was killed by Mr. Blegen, who then fled?"

"I have no evidence to that effect one way or the other," Holmes replied. "But I would most certainly like to speak with Einar Blegen, wherever he may be. In the meantime, I think it best we leave, as discreetly as possible."

"But aren't we going to notify the authorities?" I protested.

"I think not, Watson. Sheriff Boehm would be extremely difficult to deal with in a situation like this and might well be tempted to toss us in the local jail. Therefore, I am hoping we can slip away unnoticed. In fact, why don't you check the stairs to see if anyone is about?"

I cracked open the door and peered outside. I could see no one on the street immediately in front of the saloon. "It looks all clear," I reported.

"Very well then, let us be on our way. There is nothing more we can accomplish here."

❊   ❊   ❊

Holmes's comments in the apartment had led me to believe we would now return to Alexandria. Instead, at the bottom of the stairs he turned and knocked once again on the door of the saloon.

When Olson answered, Holmes said: "My apologies for bothering you again, sir. We had intended to leave town earlier, but our driver was so busy talking to his friend over at the harness shop that we decided to stay a while longer and enjoy—" Holmes paused to find the right word—"the scenery. Holandberg is a most attractive village, as you well know. In any event, I am wondering if Mr. Blegen might have returned by now."

"Haven't seen him," the saloon keeper replied. "But you could always check his apartment again."

"That will not be necessary. Still, I am a bit concerned. He was supposed to meet us here this morning, and I imagine it is not like him to miss an appointment."

"No, Einar's pretty reliable," Olson agreed.

"I see. May I ask if you by chance live above your tavern, in the apartment adjoining Mr. Blegen's?"

Olson said he did, adding: "But I didn't hear him go out, if that's what you're asking."

"But he was here last night, I presume."

"Couldn't say. We're closed on Sundays, of course, and I was out of town myself, visiting a lady friend"—here Olson favored us with a lecherous wink—"up in Alexandria."

Holmes, to my surprise, nudged the saloon keeper in the ribs and said: "Ah, so you're a lady's man, are you? I thought as much. You have that look in your eyes, sir. Now, promise me you didn't stay out too late last night."

Olson, who clearly enjoyed talking about his prowess with the fair sex, gave Holmes a crooked little smile and said: "Well now, sir, a lady's man can't spend too much time watching the clock, if you know what I mean. Truth is, I didn't get back here until the wee hours of the morning. But it was worth losing a little sleep over, if you catch my drift."

"I catch it perfectly, you old dog," said Holmes with a grin. "Well, sir, we will bother you no further. Have a good day."

We started to leave, but after taking a few steps, Holmes wheeled around and said: "I almost forgot to ask, Mr. Olson. Do you have a telephone I could use. I need to talk to a friend in Alexandria."

"No, sir, I don't. The way I look at it, these telephones are just a passing fad. I see no need of one."

"You may be right, Mr. Olson. Is there a telephone anywhere else in town I could use?"

"Oh sure, there's one down at the depot. They've got one over at the village hall, too."

"Thank you."

As we walked down to the harness shop to find Kensington, Holmes said: "Well, Watson, it looks as though we will find no witnesses to what happened in Mr. Blegen's apartment last night. I suspect Mr. Olson was our best hope."

"Perhaps someone else in town saw something," I suggested.

"Do you really think so, Watson?" asked Holmes, gesturing toward the wide expanse of the street, which even at this hour had attracted only a handful of people—two old women in bonnets, a man driving a hay wagon, and a small boy playing in the dirt. "It is broad daylight and the town looks nearly dead, Watson. At one o'clock on a Sunday morning, I suspect you would find more activity in a London cemetery than you would here."

Not long after Holmes spoke these words, I saw Kensington walk out from the harness shop.

"You gents ready to go back to Alexandria?" he said as we approached.

"Soon," said Holmes. "First, however, I must pass on some distressing news and then ask of you a big favor."

It was a measure of our trust in Kensington that Holmes now told him what we had found in Blegen's apartment.

Kensington let out a small gasp and fell silent for a moment. "Oh dear," he finally said. "Now I will have another body to haul to Alexandria. When did this happen?"

"Some time early this morning," said Holmes.

"Do you think Einar killed Mr. Larson?" Kensington suddenly asked. "I'd find that hard to believe."

"Murder is always hard to believe," said Holmes. "My chief concern at the moment is to locate Mr. Blegen, who naturally must be considered a suspect. I know you were acquainted with him, Mr. Kensington. May I ask if the two of you were good friends?"

"I guess that depends on your definition of 'good friends,' Mr. Baker. Einar comes up to Alexandria once or twice a week and he usually stops in at the livery stable for a chat. He liked to talk and I don't mind listening."

"Did he ever talk about his relationship with Olaf Wahlgren? They were close friends, as I understand."

"They were," Kensington acknowledged. "But something happened between them a few months back. I know that because Einar told me one day out of the blue that he couldn't trust Olaf anymore."

"Did Mr. Blegen say why he couldn't trust his friend?"

"No. You know how these Scandinavians are, Mr. Baker. They don't talk a lot."

"So everyone tells us," said Holmes with a slight note of irritation. "Incidentally, do you know exactly when this rift developed between the two men?"

"Einar wasn't specific, but I gathered that it was sometime after the rune stone was found."

"Most interesting," said Holmes. "Tell me, when did you last see Mr. Blegen?"

"On Saturday, at the Fogelblad farm, with you and Mr. Smith. Don't you remember?"

I could not but smile at this response, but Holmes was not amused.

"My memory is quite good, Mr. Kensington," he said stiffly. "Now, sir, can you tell me how many relatives or close friends Mr. Blegen has in this area?"

"No relatives," said Kensington. "Einar never married. But he's got quite a few friends, here and in Alexandria."

"Good. Then I would appreciate it, Mr. Kensington, if you could jot down the names of those friends when we get to Alexandria. You can also do us a much larger favor."

Holmes now explained our desire not to be connected with the discovery of Magnus Larson's body. He also asked if Kensington would agree to "cover" for us if questions arose as to our whereabouts during the half hour or so we had spent in Blegen's apartment.

To his credit, Kensington did not hesitate. "I like the two of you," he said. "You strike me as righteous fellows. Sure, I'll go along. If the sheriff or anybody else asks, I'll just fudge a little on the time or say I happened to see you walking out in the street. Would that do?"

"It would do very nicely," said Holmes, shaking Kensington's hand. "Now then, before we leave, I have but one other question. Did Mr. Blegen keep his horse and buggy here in town?"

"Sure, over at the stable behind the harness shop."

"And is his rig there now?"

"To tell you the truth, I didn't notice."

"Then perhaps we should have a look for ourselves before we leave," said Holmes.

We walked back around to the stable and introduced ourselves to its proprietor, a stout fellow by the name of John Anderson. He told us that he had last seen Blegen, and his rig, early Saturday evening.

"I guess he was with that crowd of fools over at Nels's farm looking for the rune stone," said Anderson. "A waste of time, if you ask me."

"You may be right, sir," said Holmes with a thin smile. "Did Mr. Blegen say anything when you saw him on Saturday evening?"

"No, just the usual talk about this and that. But he did say he was thinkin' about taking a 'little trip'—that's what he called it—on Sunday. I guess he did, because I haven't seen him or his rig since."

"Did he tell you where he might be going?"

"He didn't say and I didn't ask. Mr. Blegen pays by the month, which means he comes and goes as he pleases as far as I'm concerned. There's been other times when he's taken off for a couple of days, so I didn't worry about him being gone."

"Perhaps you should," said Holmes as we left.

After we had stepped into our carriage, Holmes directed Kensington to take us to Holandberg's railroad depot, which was at the south end of town.

"By the way, which railroad runs through here?" he asked Kensington.

"That would be the Minneapolis, St. Paul and Sault Ste. Marie."[3]

"And where does it go?"

"Well, to St. Paul and Minneapolis, of course, and then over to Fargo-Moorhead and points west."

Holmes sighed and said: "In other words, Mr. Blegen could be almost anywhere by now if he took a train."

"Afraid so," said Kensington.

Holandberg's depot turned out to be little more than a shack standing beside the tracks. Inside, we found the agent on duty and asked if he knew Blegen. He indicated that he did. Holmes then asked if Blegen had boarded any train since midnight Sunday. The agent proved reluctant to answer this question, but the liberal application of gold coins to his grasping palms quickly overcame any objections. He checked his records and told us that of the eight passenger trains which had gone through Holandberg since the hour in question, only two had been flagged down to pick up passengers. The agent further informed us that he had been on duty on both occasions, and that in neither instance had Blegen been among those boarding the train.

Holmes now described another person—Billy Swift—to the agent, but the answer was the same. No one matching Swift's description had taken a train from Holandberg since midnight Sunday.

"Well, it looks as though we've drawn a blank," I said to Holmes as we climbed back into our carriage.

"Not entirely," he replied, "for we have ruled out at least two possibilities, and that is always a useful thing to do. I think we must now look to Alexandria for answers."

But as we were to learn shortly, the final episode in the rune stone mystery was to occur a hundred miles away, in the daunting emptiness of a place unlike any other in the world.

Chapter Fifteen

"I HAVE FORMULATED A LITTLE PLAN"

Once we reached Alexandria, shortly after noon, we waited in the lobby of the Douglas House for Rafferty, who soon put in an appearance. Holmes told him at once about Larson's murder and the circumstances surrounding it, including Einar Blegen's disappearance. He also informed Rafferty of his decision not to report the crime to the local authorities.

Settling his bulk into one of the lobby's overstuffed chairs, Rafferty slowly shook his head and said: "You're walkin' a fine line, Mr. Holmes, a very fine line. Sheriff Boehm will be as angry as a nest of disturbed hornets if he finds out what you did. And my guess is he will. He's a sharp fellow, from what I've seen of him."

"I understand your concerns," Holmes replied, "but I saw no other choice. Had we called in the sheriff, we would have spent the rest of the day in Holandberg, and probably half of tonight behind bars."

"Well, I guess you know what you're doin', so I'll say no more on the subject. But I will tell you it's quite a shock to learn that the big Swede is dead, though I'm of the opinion that drink would have killed him soon enough anyway. Still, I didn't figure him as the next victim in this business. Truth be told, I thought he was probably the one who buried that ax in Farmer Wahlgren's skull. Now I just may have to reconsider my thinkin' in that regard. By the way, did you find anythin' useful in Mr. Blegen's apartment?"

"Indeed we did," said Holmes, taking out the map I had found and placing it on a small table in front of us. "It was folded up in one of Mr. Larson's pockets."

I looked once again at the map, trying to divine its meaning. The paper appeared to be of the ordinary sort used for notebooks and tablets, while the map itself obviously was not the work of a skilled cartographer. The rudely drawn lines indicated what I assumed to be roads, buildings, and various natural features. There were, however, no words on the map to indicate what it depicted. Instead, various abbreviations, mostly in capital letters, were used. In one corner were the letters "FF"; in another, "GE." Other abbreviations included "TR" (several times) and "GNR." But the map's dominant letter was a large letter "X," written in red ink over the notation "GE." Beneath the "X," scrawled in handwriting, was the notation: "b#4, bnth ch."

After we had all stared at the map for a while, Holmes said: "My presumption is that this map points to the location of the rune stone. I can see no other reason for it being in Mr. Larson's possession."

Rafferty concurred: "Sounds like you're on the right track to me, Mr. Holmes."

I must confess that I felt mixed emotions now that Holmes had apparently located the stone at last. The reason, I suppose, is that by this time I had begun to doubt, in some peculiar way, the stone's very existence. This was, of course, a perfectly irrational belief, for the evidence to the contrary was as plain as could be. Scores, if not hundreds, of people had seen the stone and all could attest to its adamantine reality. Nonetheless, the stone's unlikely provenance, its fantastic message, and its curious ability to elude Holmes's grasp had come to endow it with a fabulous quality in my mind. Or, to put it another way, I had begun to think of it as a thing too strange and incredible for the real world, like one of those mythical creatures

adorning medieval maps. And that is perhaps why I now felt something akin to a twinge of regret, for I knew that once the stone was
found, its magic would be forever gone.

As these thoughts went through my mind, Rafferty continued to
study the map. When he finally looked up at Holmes again, he said:
"There's one thing I'm wonderin' about."

"Let me guess," said Holmes. "You are wondering why, if Mr.
Larson hid the stone, he would be so careless as to keep a map of its
location in his pocket."

"You're right, Mr. Holmes. It doesn't make a lot of sense. He'd be
askin' for trouble walkin' around with that map."

"Your objection is well taken, Mr. Rafferty, but consider this possibility: what if Mr. Larson had only recently obtained the map from
someone else before he was murdered? In fact, it could have been
Blegen himself who gave him the map. Or what if Mr. Larson found
it in the apartment just before his demise? That might explain why
the apartment had been ransacked. Or what if—"

Rafferty held up his arms in mock surrender and said: "You've
made your point, Mr. Holmes. We don't know enough at the moment to understand why the map was where it was. But I'm thinkin'
you do have a pretty good idea as to what it depicts."

"I do," Holmes acknowledged, leaning over the table to point out
various features. "Note, if you would, the letters "FF." Do these
sound at all familiar to either of you?"

The sly grin on Rafferty's face told me that he knew the answer
but wanted to see if I did as well. I thought for a moment, trying to
associate the letters with names or places which had become familiar
to us during our investigation. Soon the answer became obvious.
"Fairview Farms," I said.

"Excellent, my dear Watson!" said Holmes. "The letters could
mean nothing else."

"Well, Mr. Holmes, at least we know now why your lady friend
wasn't taken in by that little ruse you pulled regardin' new information about the stone's location," Rafferty noted. " 'Twould seem she
knew where it was all along."

"So it would appear," Holmes admitted.

"What about the other notations on the map?" I asked. "Have they helped you pinpoint precisely where the stone is hidden?"

"Not yet, Watson. The various abbreviations and figures will require some study, but I do not think it will take long to decipher them."

"I can guess at one right off the bat," said Rafferty. " 'GNR' probably refers to the Great Northern Railway. I've never been to Fairview Farms, but most of the big spreads up in the Red River country adjoin railroad tracks."

"An excellent deduction, Mr. Rafferty," said Holmes.

Rafferty shifted in his chair, took out a small cigar, and said: "Another point worth considerin' is just how the stone got taken to Mrs. Comstock's farm. She's up near Moorhead, as I understand it, and that's a hundred miles or so away. 'Twould be an awfully long wagon ride, so I'm guessin' the stone must have gone by rail."

"I am inclined to agree," said Holmes. "What still remains to be discovered, however, is exactly who sent the stone to Fairview Farms."

"Surely it must have been Mrs. Comstock," I said.

"Oh, I am certain she is behind it," Holmes said. "What I am not so certain about is how many accomplices she may have had in addition to Mr. Swift. Nor, of course, do we know who murdered Mr. Larson, or, for that matter, why he was killed. It cannot have been for the map, since that was left in his pocket."

"Maybe he was murdered because he knew too much," Rafferty offered. "If he was in on Mr. Wahlgren's murder, for example, his accomplice might have decided to eliminate the only other witness."

Said Holmes: "That is one possibility, among many, Mr. Rafferty, although it does not explain why the murderer chose to do his work in Mr. Blegen's apartment. Nor does it tell us why we were invited to find the body."

"Ah, so you've been puzzling, too, over that message we got last night," said Rafferty. "I thought it was mighty queer that the caller left a message over the telephone rather than tryin' to speak directly to one of us. There's at least one good reason why he might have done so, of course."

"And what would that be?" I asked.

Rafferty clipped off the end of his cigar, put a match to it, and said: "Maybe, just maybe, the caller wasn't Einar Blegen."

"But why—" I began.

"—were we lured to the murder scene?" said Holmes, finishing my question. "I do not know, Watson. What about you, Mr. Rafferty? Do you have any ideas?"

"Nothin' worth the contents of a spittoon," Rafferty admitted, scratching the back of his head. "All I can tell you, Mr. Holmes, is that this whole business is gettin' stranger by the day."

"I could not agree with you more," said Holmes. "Indeed, this case has come to resemble nothing so much as the fevered imaginings of some blood-and-thunder playwright with a taste for sordid melodrama. The plot is riddled with strange coincidences and unlikely reappearances, not the least of which involves our old adversary from Hinckley, Mrs. Comstock. Meanwhile, the drama's chief prop—the rune stone—is a traveling ghost, invisible and yet at the same time crucial to all the action. As for the characters, they are, it would seem, either dead or plotting to do one another in. And, of course, at the center of all this dramatic confusion is the Wahlgren girl and the incomprehensible clue she has hurled at us. Who or what is Rochester? I still believe the answer lies with her."

"Well, if it does, you'll be pleased to know that the girl is doin' fine," said Rafferty. "I wandered past the Kensingtons' house a couple of times this mornin' and talked to the neighbor keepin' watch. He assured me that all was quiet at the house."

"Good. We must make sure that there is not another burglary attempt—or worse," said Holmes, who did not explain what he meant by that final word of warning. "In any event, I suggest we move on to other matters. There is one other development you should know about, Mr. Rafferty."

Holmes now showed our friend the safety deposit key we had found in Blegen's apartment.

Rafferty examined the key and said: " 'Twould be nice to know what's in that strongbox. I'm sure the sheriff would like to know too, but I'm assumin', Mr. Holmes, that you don't intend to tell him about your little find."

"Not for a while," Holmes said. "I do not wish to complicate his life."

"Why, that's very thoughtful of you," said Rafferty with a sly grin. "I take it, then, that you plan on tryin' to look into that box yourself."

"I do."

Rafferty directed a skeptical eye at Holmes and said: "And just how do you propose to pull off that little trick? It will take two keys to open the box, and I don't think anyone at the bank will mistake you for Einar Blegen. For one thing, you're much better-lookin'."

I found Rafferty's comment amusing, and even Holmes broke out into a smile. "I am well aware of the need for two keys," he said, glancing over at me, "and that is why I intend to call upon Dr. Watson for assistance. I would note, however, that you are looking a bit peaked, my dear friend."

"Whatever do you mean?" I replied. "I have never felt better."

"No, I think not. You look bilious, Watson, exceedingly bilious," Holmes insisted, leaning back and looking me over the way he might study a portrait at the National Gallery. "Perhaps you have caught a touch of something. You are not a well man, I fear."

"Really, Holmes, I—"

With an airy wave of the hand, Holmes interrupted me: "I shall be the judge of your health, Watson, but let us not argue over the matter. You will understand soon enough. You see, I have a formulated a little plan."

Over the course of my long friendship with Holmes, I had frequently been caught up in his "little plans," which generally required me to play a role of some kind. Holmes, of course, was a consummate actor, a man who delighted in the infinite varieties of masquerade. I, on the other hand, did not take readily to the thespian arts, preferring at all times to be myself, and so it usually required vigorous coaching on Holmes's part before I could perform my assigned role to his satisfaction. Nonetheless, I gradually improved my acting skills, and even Holmes paid me the supreme compliment that I was "quite the ham" when I took on the role of a dissolute country squire in the infamous murder case involving Lord Claverton.[1] Still, none of my experiences prepared me for what Holmes now had in mind.

"It is an insane idea," I told Holmes after he had explained his "little plan." He would not be dissuaded, however. Nor was Rafferty any help.

" 'Tis a marvelous scheme," he said, patting me on the shoulder. "I only wish I could be there to see your performance."

"Do not worry," said Holmes as I glared at him. "I shall give you a full report. The good doctor, I am sure, will be quite memorable in his role. Now, Mr. Rafferty, I should like to hear what you have learned today."

"I've not had much success, I fear," he said. "After you and Dr. Watson left for Holandberg, I went over to the local grain elevator, where a lot of the local farmers like to gather and shoot the breeze. Sure enough, a bunch of them were there chattin' about wheat prices and such things, and pretty soon we got to talkin' about the rune stone. They'd all seen it, of course, and thought it was the genuine article, *ja*, sure"—here Rafferty fell briefly into an awful imitation of a Swedish accent—"and by yeorge vasn't it strange how it vas wrapped around dose roots yust as neat as could be."

"You have no future as a mimic," I told Rafferty, who responded with a mock look of injured pride.

Then he said: "I did ask them if they knew of anyone who'd taken a picture of the stone up on the hill where it was found. But they all said they'd never seen a photograph of any kind, which is surprisin' in view of what a tourist attraction Mr. Wahlgren's hilltop became. Seems like everybody for miles around went up to see the site of the miraculous discovery. Unfortunately, none of them got a gander at the stone until after it'd been pulled out of the tree roots and set on the ground. But Mr. Wahlgren did leave the tree itself by the stone for a few days. The fellows I talked to said they could tell by lookin' at how the roots were bent that somethin' had been lodged between them."

"Could any of the farmers who saw the tree estimate its age?" Holmes asked.

"Opinion was wildly divided on that question," Rafferty reported. "One bearded codger told me the tree looked like it was 'real old,' but another farmer said he thought it was probably no more than 'ten or twenty' years old. I doubt we'll ever get agreement on the point."

"Why does the age of the tree matter so much?" I asked.

Rafferty said: "It matters because if the tree wasn't all that old, somebody could have slipped the rune stone between the roots when the tree was small—say, four or five years ago. That way, the roots could have grown around the stone, making it look like it had been in the ground for a long time."

"That would seem like an enormous amount of trouble," I noted.

Rafferty acknowledged that this was so, but added: "Then again, tryin' to slip a stone inside a big tree's roots would be even more trouble. I've done a little stump pullin' in my time, and I can tell you that roots grow as hard as iron. 'Twould take somethin' mighty strong to pull them apart."

"It's obvious that the age of the tree in question will remain a mystery for the time being," said Holmes. "Therefore, let me ask you, Mr. Rafferty, if you made any progress this morning identifying the piece of lantern glass from the Fogelblad farm?"

"There's little to report on that front, Mr. Holmes. I did manage to get over to one store—Peck's Hardware—which is right across the street. Unfortunately, Mr. Peck doesn't know much about lanterns and couldn't help me. But there are two other hardware dealers in town, I'm told."

Holmes nodded and said: "Since Dr. Watson and I will be strolling over to the bank after lunch, we'll check at those stores. In the meantime, Mr. Rafferty, I would like you to take a look at Mr. Larson's hotel room, if you can do so discreetly. I am particularly interested in finding the notebook he carried. I would also like you to—"

"Say no more," said Rafferty. "You want me to find out if somethin' like the rune stone was shipped recently to Fairview Farms. I'll have a chat with Mr. Christianson over at the Great Northern depot after lunch. Speakin' of which, I see that roast beef sandwiches, mashed potatoes, and gravy are on the menu in the dining room. I'm not sure about many things in life, Mr. Holmes, but one thing I do know is that a man should never investigate on an empty stomach. It's time to eat."

After our lunch with Rafferty, Holmes and I walked quickly down Broadway to the offices of the Merchants National Bank. Unlike its plain neighbors, the bank strove to make at least something of architectural statement, for it was built solidly of brick and faced in smooth gray stone. A pair of squat Doric columns flanked the main entrance, as did two small terra-cotta griffins whose fierce pose suggested that the institution within would not easily yield its treasures to robbery or other forms of mayhem. Above these twin guardians, carved into a stone panel above the doors, were three words: THRIFT SECURITY PROSPERITY.

Holmes stopped to gaze up at the panel and said: "We shall soon see just how well the bank lives up to its motto."

Once inside, we indicated that we wished to rent a safety deposit box. We were sent down to the basement, where we found the boxes in charge of an elderly guard who identified himself as Thomas Amdahl. After accepting our payment and taking samples of our signatures—for Holmes and I wished to jointly sign for the box— Amdahl gave us the key to box number 148.

"I am a superstitious man," Holmes suddenly announced, handing the key back to Amdahl. "I like a nice round number. What about 200? Is that box available?"

Amdahl pulled a chart from his desk drawer, studied it for a moment, and said: "Yes, you can have number 200."

"Splendid!" said Holmes as Amdahl gave him the key.

"Now, don't lose it," the old guard cautioned in a voice so thin and raspy it might have been the last exhalation of a dying man, "or there will be a fifty-cent replacement charge."

"Have no fear, we shall guard it with our lives," Holmes replied, carefully secreting the key in his coat pocket. Then he added: "Mr. Smith and I have several items arriving later today or possibly tomorrow which must be put in our box at once. I trust, sir, that you will still be here then to take care of our needs."

"I'm always here," Amdahl said. "Haven't missed a day in twenty years."

"Admirable!" said Holmes, after which we bid the guard goodbye and walked back upstairs.

"Well," said Holmes once we reached the street, "all is ready for your grand performance, Watson. Now, let us see what we can find out about that piece of lantern globe."

We got directions from a man on the street to the various hardware stores in town and found out that there were indeed three. The two not visited by Rafferty were on opposite ends of Broadway. Visiting these establishments proved to be less than an hour's work, with mixed results.

At each store, Holmes explained to the proprietor that he wished to replace a lantern which had somehow been lost. Holmes went on to say that while the mislaid lantern had provided "most excellent service," he could not remember what type it was, other than that he seemed to recall the letters *S* and *G* on its globe. The owner of the first store we visited could offer no help, since he carried only one brand of lantern, made by the Dietz Company, and the initials *S* and *G* meant nothing to him. At the second store, however, we received a more encouraging response to our inquiries.

"You must have had an SG&L lantern," the proprietor, a friendly man with a broad, ruddy face, told us. "Used to be made by the Steam Gauge and Lantern Company out east somewhere.[2] Syracuse, I think."

"Ah, so I take it they are no longer manufactured," said Holmes, sounding utterly crestfallen.

"That's right. I heard somewhere that Dietz bought them out a year or two ago."

"And did you carry these lanterns at one time?"

"Had some a few years ago, but didn't sell many. Most folks prefer the Dietz lanterns. That's all I carry now."

"I see. You wouldn't by chance happen to know of anyone in town who has an SG&L lantern, would you? I'd be happy to buy the lantern from them for a good price."

The proprietor gave Holmes a sharp look and said: "You must have been awfully fond of that lantern."

"I was," said Holmes. "I frequently work at night."

"Well, I'm afraid I can't help you. Like I said, I didn't sell many of them. But if you're all that desperate, you might write to Farwell, Ozmun and Kirk down in St. Paul.[3] They're the biggest hardware wholesalers in the Northwest. If anybody would still have one of those lanterns in stock, it would be FOK."

"Thank you," said Holmes. "I shall have to do that. Incidentally, was there a type of lantern SG&L specialized in before the company was sold? I only ask because I am curious why the maker of such a superb lantern failed to flourish. Perhaps they simply failed to keep up with changing demand. I am told such things happen all the time."

"Sure do," replied the proprietor, "especially in this business. But I don't think SG&L had a problem like that. They made a real good carriage lantern, for instance. All I can figure is that the competition just got too hot for them."

"Too bad," said Holmes, still sounding as though he was pining over his lost lantern. "Well, sir, we thank you again. Have a pleasant day."

After we left the store, Holmes said: "It appears the lantern will not be as easy to trace as I had hoped. Still, we now know who manufactured the lantern, which is a step forward. Come along, Watson, I wish to send a telegram."

At the railroad depot, we ran into Rafferty, who was just leaving after a long conversation with his friend the stationmaster.

"I've got some interesting news," he announced.

"Wait a moment while I send off a telegram and then we shall hear it," said Holmes.

The telegram went to our friend Joseph Pyle in St. Paul. Holmes asked Pyle, who had excellent connections throughout the city, to find out whether Farwell, Ozmun and Kirk, or any other hardware jobbing house in the city, had shipped SG&L lanterns to Alexandria in recent years. Pyle was also instructed to find out, if possible, the names of any customers to whom the lanterns had been sent.

"It is the longest of long shots," Holmes remarked as he handed over his message to the telegraph clerk, "but luck never comes to those who do nothing."

We found Rafferty outside, smoking a cigar on the train platform.

"All right, let us hear your news," said Holmes.

Rafferty said: "Well now, as you requested, I took a gander at Mr. Larson's room — 'twas an easy lock to pick — but found no sign of his notebook. In fact, I didn't find anythin' of interest. So then I came over here to make some inquiries regardin' any shipments to Moorhead in recent days. You'll be interested to learn that late on Friday night a large wooden crate measurin' three feet long, twenty-one inches wide, and nine inches thick, and weighin' 210 pounds, was shipped out from here to Moorhead. The bill of ladin' said it was a tombstone. I'd have found out about it earlier except that Mr. Christianson, the stationmaster, was ill that evening and a new man was on duty. For some reason, this new fellow hadn't heard about the reward I'd offered for identifying any shipment of a certain size and weight."

"I see," said Holmes, a hint of excitement creeping into his voice. "And who, may I ask, was the person who shipped this supposed tombstone?"

"That will come as no surprise," said Rafferty. "The stone was shipped by a certain Mr. William Swift of Fairview Farms."

Chapter Sixteen
"YOU WILL HAVE TO PLAY ALONG"

T he news that the rune stone had, as it were, been spirited away before our very eyes, left Holmes in an eager and anxious mood.

"Events are beginning to gallop," he said as we walked with Rafferty back to the hotel, "and we must be certain that it is we who are in the saddle. We must go to Moorhead, and from there to Fairview Farms, as soon as possible."

"There's a train out this evenin', if I read the schedule right," said Rafferty. "We could be there in three hours."

"I do not think we should go quite yet, Mr. Rafferty," said Holmes, who paused to consult his watch. "There is still one important piece of business to be accomplished here. It is just before four o'clock at present. Do you suppose the Merchants Bank is still open?"

"I doubt it, for in my experience bankers' hours are always short and sweet," Rafferty observed. "Mine would be too if I had their money."

Rafferty's assessment proved correct, for as we passed the bank, we noted that it had closed at three o'clock and would not reopen until nine the next morning.

Holmes received this information with a frown and then fell deep into thought, a condition signaled by the curiously distant and detached look in his eyes, which under all other circumstances were sharply observant. We then walked in silence until we reached the hotel's front porch, where Holmes said:

"I fear we are awash in loose ends and unanswered questions, and I am by no means certain how best to proceed. Still, I am of a mind that I must inspect the contents of Mr. Blegen's safety deposit box before we go to Moorhead."

"You must be countin' on more treasure in there," Rafferty said.

"I am. The care with which Mr. Blegen hid the key to the box suggests that its contents must be of the greatest importance. Therefore, I think it best if Dr. Watson and I go to the bank immediately in the morning and try to get into that box. We shall then take the first available train to Moorhead."

We stopped at the hotel's front desk, where there was a message waiting from Kensington, who had promised to draw up a list identifying Einar Blegen's friends in the area. To Holmes's dismay, however, the list consisted of more than twenty names, in six different towns, including Alexandria.

Holmes took a deep sigh, crumpled up the list, and put it in his coat pocket. "Too many names," he said simply. "We could not begin to check them all. We will have to look for Mr. Blegen another time, if in fact he is to be found alive."

This was the first time Holmes had mentioned the possibility that Blegen might be dead, but the remark did not appear to surprise Rafferty in the least. "I've been thinkin' all along that old Einar might be dead and buried someplace," he said. "If he is, we may never find him. There's plenty of good places to hide a body hereabouts."

As we stood in the lobby, I found myself wondering what Holmes intended to do next, for I could sense that we had reached a crucial intersection in the case—that point at which many different avenues of inquiry presented themselves to us. Holmes himself liked to say that a detective in any complicated criminal case was much like a man trying to get from one end of London to the other. With enough time, skill, and luck, almost anyone could reach the proper destination, Holmes contended. But the genius of a great detective, he said, was in finding the shortest, fastest, and most direct route. That route, I now discovered, would once again take us into the devious world of Mary Comstock.

It was just after five o'clock when we knocked on the door of Mrs. Comstock's room. Holmes had not indicated to us what he wished to ask the lady, but Rafferty clearly relished the opportunity to talk with the "famous vixen," as he had taken to calling her.

The lady herself soon answered the door. As always, she was dressed elegantly, in a lacy white blouse, a high collar secured with a bow tie, a dark blue coat with billowed sleeves, and a long, wasp-waisted skirt which showed off her pleasing proportions.

"How good to see you again," she said, inviting us in with an enigmatic smile. "Please, sit down."

As we all took seats around the couch where Mrs. Comstock liked to sit, Holmes noticed that a journal of some kind lay open on a desk nearby. Also atop the desk were a pen and an open ink bottle.

Observing these items with his usual efficiency, Holmes said: "I see you have been writing this afternoon, madam. Your memoirs, perhaps? What an interesting book that would make!"

"Do you think so, Mr. Holmes?" the lady replied as she went over to the desk and carefully closed the journal. "In fact, I have merely been making a few notes. Besides, I can hardly imagine any aspect of my life that would be more exciting than the rather lurid tales penned by Dr. Watson."

Having delivered herself of this backhanded compliment, the lady took her place on the sofa and looked up at us with a kind of confident expectation, suggesting that she was fully prepared for whatever question Holmes might direct at her.

Holmes, however, began instead with an introduction. "I do not know, madam, if you have had an opportunity to meet our friend, Mr. Shadwell Rafferty of St. Paul."

"I saw the gentleman out at the Fogelblad farm," she said, inspecting Rafferty as she might study some object in a store window. "Of course, I have already heard much about him."

"Have you now?" said Rafferty. "Well, I'm hopin' that what you've heard has been favorable."

"Generally," she replied, a succinct response which Holmes seemed to find quite amusing.

He said: "I am surprised to see that Mr. Swift is not with you, madam. I had expected him to answer the door."

"Billy is elsewhere on business," she said, offering no further explanation. "But I imagine it is not he whom you wish to talk to."

"You are correct, Mrs. Comstock. There are a few questions we would like to ask, if it would not trouble you greatly."

"I am used to trouble, Mr. Holmes," she said, "as, of course, are you."

"Of course. And that is why I am wondering if you have seen Magnus Larson today. We had hoped to talk with him about a matter involving the rune stone, but he does not seem to be anywhere in town."

If Mrs. Comstock knew anything of Larson's death, that knowledge was not reflected in either her voice or her manner. Indeed, her beautiful face remained as smooth and unyielding as marble.

She said: "Mr. Larson has never been in the habit of keeping me informed as to his whereabouts. Have you checked the local taverns? He seems to spend most of his time drinking, from what I have heard."

"An unfortunate affliction," Holmes agreed. "A man who drinks is not a man who can be relied upon, and I would think that you place a high value on reliable men, Mrs. Comstock."

"It would be unwise to do otherwise, Mr. Holmes."

"Indeed. Was your late husband a reliable man?"

Mrs. Comstock took this odd question in stride—she seemed, in fact, to have become inured to all of Holmes's interrogatory tricks—and said: "Frank was as reliable as he could manage to be, Mr. Holmes. You see, I have found that men are always a disappointment. Perhaps that is why I find them so interesting."

"And have we disappointed you, Mrs. Comstock?"

"Time will tell," she said.

Holmes flashed his own cryptic smile and said: "I have no doubt that it will. Speaking of time, now that your husband has gone to his eternal rest, I assume you visit his grave site regularly, to pay your respects."

To my surprise, the lady turned to Rafferty and said in a mocking way: "However do you put up with Mr. Holmes, sir? His cleverness must become wearying after a while. I only pray he does not try to entrap you as he does so often with me."

For once, Rafferty was left temporarily speechless, and it was Holmes who now said in a stern voice: "You have not answered the question, madam."

Mrs. Comstock turned toward Holmes and said with a kind of icy passion: "Do not think that because I am a woman I am a fool, Mr. Holmes. It is apparent that, for reasons which I cannot fathom, you continue to believe that I am somehow involved in Mr. Wahlgren's murder and the theft of the rune stone. Presumably, that is why you went to the bother of checking on the shipment Billy sent out Friday night. It is a gravestone, Mr. Holmes, one that will honor my late husband. Why can you not let poor Frank rest in peace?"

Sensing that he had finally penetrated the lady's haughty veneer, Holmes pressed forward: "I should like to see that gravestone and its inscription, Mrs. Comstock. Would you perhaps be willing to show it to me one day?"

"I do not see that it is any of your business, Mr. Holmes."

"Then I shall have to make it my business," said Holmes, who now confronted the lady with a direct and terrible accusation. "You pushed your husband from that train, didn't you?"

The lady reacted to this question with open hostility. Rising from her seat, she said: "You and your impertinent questions are becoming tiresome, Mr. Holmes. I must ask all of you to leave — at once. And please do not disturb me again."

Holmes, however, stayed in his chair. "Once again, you have not answered my question, Mrs. Comstock. I must say I am baffled by your evasiveness. I can only believe you have something to hide."

"Believe what you will," said the lady, casting a poisonous glance at Holmes. "But believe it elsewhere. Now, must I call the front desk and have you evicted, or will you behave like a gentleman and leave?"

Holmes stared into the lady's lustrous eyes, as though trying to fathom the depths of evil which lay behind them, and then slowly rose from his chair. Rafferty and I, who had followed the encounter with rapt attention, did likewise.

"We will leave now," Holmes said, "but do not think that we are gone from your life, Mrs. Comstock. You will not escape this time, as you did in Hinckley."

"Get out," she said. "Now."

"As you wish," Holmes replied. "But do not forget what I have said. You are finished, Mrs. Comstock."

Once we were in the hall and Mrs. Comstock had slammed the door behind us, Rafferty wiped beads of perspiration off his brow and said: "Well now, that was quite a scene, Mr. Holmes, quite a scene. If looks could kill, you'd soon be six feet under, and that's a fact!"

"Then it is a good thing looks cannot kill, Mr. Rafferty," said Holmes, who appeared exultant. "Do you not see what has happened? She now knows that we are closing in on her, that her careful plans are beginning to unravel. That was evident by her unprecedented display of temper. We at last have her in our grasp, and we must not let go until justice is done!"

"I'll take your word for it," said Rafferty, who did not appear quite as enthusiastic as Holmes. "But if she's as dangerous as you say she is, then we'd all better watch our backs from now on."

After finding chairs in the lobby, we ordered coffee and discussed our plans for the rest of the evening. Holmes was certain that Mrs. Comstock would leave town soon, presumably to return to Fairview Farms.

"I think she will take the last train out tonight," he said. "I am wondering, Mr. Rafferty, if—"

"—I could be on it," our friend said matter-of-factly. "I was thinkin' the very same thing myself, Mr. Holmes. 'Twould seem we need to keep an eye on the lady, for who knows what she might do next? I'll have my bags packed right away and sent ahead to the depot. Then I'll plan on hangin' around there to see if she takes the evenin' train. If that does happen, I assume the two of you'll come up to Moorhead tomorrow as soon as you can."

"I knew I could rely on you, Mr. Rafferty," said Holmes. "If all goes well, we may be able to bring this affair to an end by tomorrow."

We ate supper again at the hotel, and Holmes was in an ebullient mood until George Kensington arrived with a sobering message. He told us that Magnus Larson's body had finally been discovered, about half an hour earlier, by Edvard Olson, the saloon keeper.

"I guess Ed finally started to wonder where Einar might be, so he looked in his apartment," Kensington said. "Must have been an awful surprise."

"I am sorry it had to happen that way," said Holmes, "but I saw no alternative. Will you be going to Holandberg pick up the body?"

Kensington nodded and said: "I'm going with the sheriff. I'm guessing he'll want to talk to you after he gets back."

"No doubt he will," said Holmes. "Thank you for the information, Mr. Kensington. And how is Moony?"

"Oh, she's just fine. But the missus is still keeping a sharp eye out after that break-in."

"A wise idea," said Holmes. "Well, good luck to you, Mr. Kensington. I should tell you that Dr. Watson and I may be going to Moorhead tomorrow. I am not sure when we will be returning."

"What's in Moorhead?" Kensington asked.

"Answers," said Holmes. "At least that is what we hope."

Shortly after our supper together, Rafferty left for the depot while Holmes and I, as a precaution, made plans to switch to another hotel in town. Holmes hoped the move would keep the sheriff off our scent until morning, when we could go to the bank and then join Rafferty in Moorhead, if indeed he had gone there.

As it turned out, we soon learned that Rafferty would indeed be traveling to Moorhead, for as we prepared to check out of the Douglas House we caught a glimpse of Mrs. Comstock leaving the hotel, a bellboy loaded down with luggage trailing behind her. She left at half past eight, giving her more than enough time to catch the day's final westbound train, which was scheduled to depart Alexandria at nine-twenty.

"She is on her way to Fairview Farms," Holmes said. "Let us hope Mr. Rafferty does not let her out of his sight."

Once we had arrived at the Lakeside Inn, our new hotel, I hoped to settle in at once for a good night's sleep. Holmes, however, had other plans, and it was to be well past midnight before I finally enjoyed some rest.

At precisely nine o'clock the next morning we appeared at the Merchants Bank just as the front doors opened. Inside, we went at once down to the safety deposit vault, where Amdahl—true to his word of the day before—could be found at his post. The vault was located behind a sort of anteroom fitted out with two chairs, a small table, and the desk where Amdahl maintained his eternal vigilance. Next to him was a heavy bronze gate providing the only entry to the vault.

"Ah, Mr. Amdahl, we are back as promised," said Holmes, who leaned over the desk to sign in. I did likewise. Even though he had seen us only the day before, Amdahl made a great show of studying our signatures, as if we might be confidence men come to trick him in his old age. Finally, he nodded slowly and said: "Yes, everything is in order."

Holmes handed him our key and he unlocked the bronze gate with a key of his own he kept at his desk. The vault proper contained three rows of gleaming security boxes on one side of a wide aisle. On the other side were a pair of small rooms where customers could examine the contents of their boxes in private.

Amdahl led us to our newly rented box, which was in the middle of the three rows. Holmes had selected box number 200 on our initial visit because Blegen's key was number 202. Since Holmes intended to work quickly, it was essential that the two boxes be as close together as possible. Amdahl now used the bank's pass key, which he had retrieved from the top drawer of his desk, and inserted it in one of the two locks securing the compartment holding our box. Holmes then handed him our key to open the second lock. Once both keys had been turned and the compartment door swung open, Amdahl used a small hook to remove the safety deposit box, which he then handed to Holmes.

"Thank you," said Holmes, lighting his pipe. "We will call you when we are finished."

"I'll be there," said the faithful guard.

We went into one of the private rooms and closed the door. The room's meager furnishings consisted of a desk equipped with a pen and a small stack of stationery, a straight-backed wooden chair, and a metal wastebasket. Holmes, who had carried a satchel into the bank, opened it, took out several sheets of paper torn from a ledger book he had purchased, and put them into the wastebasket. He also checked to be sure that a small hooklike device, which he had fashioned from a coat hanger at our hotel, was in his coat pocket. It was. Meanwhile, I removed from my shirt pocket two large capsules—prepared the night before by Holmes—and curled them in one hand. Holmes had refused to tell me what had gone into these capsules, but I had no doubt they contained something quite vile, since Holmes delighted in concocting substances well beyond the bounds of respectable chemistry.[1]

After these preparations were complete, Holmes said: "Well, Watson, are you ready?"

"I am," I said, though in truth I was already feeling rather mortified by what was about to occur. Still, I knew it had to be done. I took a deep breath and said: "All right, let us get this ridiculous business over with."

"Good man!" said Holmes. "You know what to do. Have you got the capsules?"

"In my hand. I assume they will not make me terribly sick."

"They are harmless," Holmes assured me. "You may even find them quite tasty."

"I am not counting on it," I said, steeling myself for what was to come.

My impending performance had been well rehearsed the night before. At Holmes's insistence, we had walked more than two miles out of Alexandria at around ten o'clock until we reached a deep gravel pit from which no farmhouses could be seen. Within this remote locale, Holmes had coached me for an hour until, as he put it, I looked and sounded "truly horrendous."

Such was my goal now, and I inhaled deeply one more time before Holmes tossed a match into the wastebasket, dropped in the ashes from his pipe to help the small blaze along, and then led the way out into the vault area. Hardly had I gone through the door than I emitted the most blood-curdling scream I could muster, began shaking my limbs violently, and fell headlong to the floor, where I did my utmost to twitch and writhe as though seized by Lucifer himself. At the same time, I slipped the capsules into my mouth and bit down on them. To my relief, the liquid inside tasted more like tomatoes than anything else. More importantly, it looked very much like blood as I let it spurt from my mouth.

"Mr. Amdahl!" Holmes shouted, bending over me. "Come at once! Hurry!"

The guard, looking entirely nonplused, rushed into the vault, and I can only imagine what he must have thought at the sight of me thrashing on the floor like some helpless cod pulled from the North Atlantic.

"Quick," said Holmes as the guard bent down beside him to help me, "run for a doctor! It is a seizure, I fear, and one of the worst kind. My friend's very life may depend on you."

"But, I can't—" Amdahl protested.

At this critical juncture, I caught my first smell of the fire burning in the wastebasket.

"My God!" Holmes shouted. "Fire! Fire!"

"Fire?" the guard repeated, confusion apparent in his startled eyes. Then he, too, caught a whiff of the smoke, and his confusion turned to panic.

"Fire!" Holmes repeated. "Can't you smell it? Hurry, man, hurry! You must go at once while I try to help my friend."

"All right, yes, I will go for help," Amdahl said.

"Hurry," Holmes repeated, "hurry!"

The instant Amdahl was gone, Holmes set to work. Grabbing the guard's key from the desk, he quickly used it and the one found in Blegen's apartment to open compartment number 202. With the aid of his makeshift hook, Holmes pulled out the box, opened it, removed several pieces of paper inside, and stuffed them into his jacket pocket. All the while I continued my absurd charade, moaning and howling with shameless abandon. It seemed as though Holmes was taking far too much time to do his work, but in truth it was probably a matter of no more than half a minute, perhaps less, before Holmes had closed up the box, slid it back into its compartment, locked it, and dropped Amdahl's key back on the desk.

Holmes's timing turned out to be superb, for only seconds after he knelt back down beside me, Amdahl and a teller from upstairs rushed back into the vault carrying small pails of water.

"In there," said Holmes, pointing to the room where we had taken our box, after which he gave me a wink. This was my sign to bring down the curtain on my little performance, and I did so gratefully, closing my eyes as though dropping off into a peaceful slumber.

"It was just some papers burning in the wastebasket," Amdahl reported when he came back to look at me. "You left some burning ashes in there. How's your friend? I've called for the doctor."

"Thank God, I think Mr. Smith is going to be all right," Holmes said. "He has had these seizures before, but never one of such violence. I do not mind telling you I was very worried. Mr. Smith . . . Mr. Smith! Can you hear me?"

After Holmes called my name several more times, I slowly opened my eyes and looked around, trying to appear as dazed as possible. Finally, I said: "What am I doing on the floor?"

"You had an attack," Holmes explained, cradling my head in his arms. "A very serious attack. But you are going to be all right."

"An attack? I don't remember any such thing."

"Well, you may trust us that it occurred, Mr. Smith. We were quite worried."

The conversation continued along these lines for several more minutes, until Holmes helped me to my feet and told Amdahl:

"There will be no need for a doctor now. Rest is the only treatment Mr. Smith requires. He will be fine."

"Are you sure?" asked the guard.

"I am sure," Holmes said. "However, I cannot thank you enough for your help, Mr. Amdahl. I also wish to apologize for the fire. I must have gotten careless with my pipe ashes."

"Well, there was no harm done."

"Perhaps not, but I still must insist that you receive something for your trouble," replied Holmes, pressing a twenty-dollar gold piece into the guard's palm and clasping his hands. "You truly saved the day."

"Well now, I really can't—" Amdahl said as he looked down at the gold piece, which must have been a princely sum for a man such as himself.

"As I said, I must insist," Holmes interrupted. "It is the least I can do. You were a hero, sir, a hero! Now, if you will be so kind as to help us put away our safety deposit box, Mr. Smith and I will be on our way. My friend will need all the rest he can get today."

"My dear Watson, you were quite magnificent," said Holmes after we left the bank and began walking down Broadway. "Your twitching was a thing to behold! And the way you moaned and screamed! Had I not known better, I might have thought you were in the midst of a grand mal seizure."

"I do not wish to talk about it," I replied, for I took no pleasure from behaving in such a ludicrous and undignified manner. "I would like to know, however, what you found inside Mr. Blegen's safety deposit box. I trust whatever you discovered was worth the cost of making me act like a blithering idiot."

"On the contrary, Watson, your performance, as I told you, was absolutely superb. Indeed, I am beginning to think you missed your calling in life and that your decision to pursue medicine rather than the dramatic arts was a tragic loss to the stage."

"Please, humor me no more," I said, irked by Holmes's teasing. "Now, what was in the box?"

"We shall see," said Holmes as we approached a dry goods store with a bench out front. Once we had sat down, Holmes began examining his "treasure" from Blegen's safety deposit box—five documents in all. The first three were, as Holmes put it, "exceedingly amorous letters from Mr. Blegen to a woman who is in the inconvenient position of being married to another man." But the last two documents turned out to be, in Holmes's words, "pure gold."

The first document which Holmes showed me consisted of four pieces of plain paper stapled together. The pages were covered with runic symbols, arranged line by line, with translations below in Swedish and English.

"Is this Mr. Blegen's original translation of the rune stone?" I asked.

"Perhaps, although another, more intriguing possibility comes to mind, especially in view of the fact that Mr. Blegen saw fit to keep this document in what he presumed to be an absolutely safe place."

"What are you getting at, Holmes?"

"There will be time for explanations later," he said, handing me a sheet of yellow, lined paper. "Now, take a look at our second piece of treasure."

This document was a copy of the legal agreement we had found at Olaf Wahlgren's house in which he agreed to sell the rune stone to Magnus Larson for two hundred dollars. At first glance, there seemed to be nothing remarkable about this copy, since Blegen had notarized the transaction. Attached to it, however, was a small sheet of stationery with a message scrawled in bold handwriting. It said: "I know the truth. You will have to play along if you want to make any money. M.L."

"What do you make of this?" I asked, realizing at once that the note must have been written by Magnus Larson.

Holmes did not reply immediately, for he was already lost in thought. Finally, he said: "Magnus Larson saw the truth, Watson, and now I think I have seen it, too."

Chapter Seventeen

"THIS CASE HAS BECOME A CONSPIRACY OF LIES"

T he next train to Moorhead was not due until half past twelve,
which left us ample time to eat breakfast. Holmes, who seemed
to be living on coffee and tobacco, had little appetite. I, however, did not propose to starve on his behalf, and therefore insisted
that we find a restaurant. Holmes finally agreed, but only after cau-
tioning that we must dine at an inconspicuous place, since he was
still worried that Sheriff Boehm might become unmanageable if he
found us. We walked for a time, stopping to pick up a copy of the local newspaper, before we found a small restaurant a few blocks behind the railroad depot.

Advertising itself as "Linda's Home-Cooked Food," the restaurant
was indeed inconspicuous, occupying what appeared to be the parlor of the owner's house. It was clearly a workingman's establishment, and we drew stares from the handful of other patrons as we
walked in and took a table near the window. After I had ordered a
breakfast of pancakes, sausages, and eggs—Holmes, who was busy
poring over the newspaper, took nothing except coffee—I asked him
whether the *Clarion* had reported on Larson's murder.

"At great length," Holmes replied. "But there is little of value to us. Sheriff Boehm is apparently keeping a tight lid on the situation, for the newspaper has only sketchy details, along with all the usual fragrant goulash of speculation. The article does say, however, that authorities in the surrounding area have been requested to be on the lookout for Mr. Blegen, who is considered 'a suspect in the case.' So perhaps someone will flush him out of hiding, if he is indeed alive. The *Clarion*'s account, I should add, makes no mention of our visit to Mr. Blegen's apartment before the official discovery of his body. Even so, I have no doubt that the sheriff knows we were in Holandberg knocking at Mr. Blegen's door."

The conversation now turned to other topics, beginning with the handwritten note—apparently from Magnus Larson—which Holmes had found in Blegen's safety deposit box.

"What do you make of the note?" I asked.

Holmes said: "No matter how hard I look at it, I can come to only one conclusion about what Mr. Larson meant when he wrote: 'I know the truth.' The truth in this case, Watson, was a lie."

"What do you mean?"

"I mean that Mr. Larson must have concluded that the stone was, in fact, a forgery."

"But that makes no sense, Holmes," I protested. "Mr. Larson was the stone's strongest supporter. I still recall how vigorously he defended the stone on the night when you and Rafferty got him so drunk."

"It was all part of the show, Watson. By that time, Mr. Larson was prepared to defend the stone in public no matter what the circumstances. He was simply repeating a memorized prayer, as it were."

I pondered the implications of Holmes's surprising conclusion and then asked: "So, are you saying that Mr. Larson set out from the very beginning to defraud King Oskar and everyone else?"

"No, not at all. I am of a mind that Mr. Larson truly believed at first that the stone was genuine. But at some point he learned otherwise—perhaps by closely examining the language and form of the inscription, or perhaps because of something he found out about

Wahlgren. In either case, he was forced to conclude that the stone was a fraud."

"Why are you so certain of this?"

"I am not certain," Holmes admitted. "But there are a number of circumstances, aside from the note in the safety deposit box, which all point toward the conclusion I've suggested. Ask yourself these questions, Watson: Why did Larson never carry out the authentication process he promised the king? Why, when Mr. Wahlgren apparently reneged on his agreement to sell the stone, did Mr. Larson not take the matter to court? Finally, why did Mr. Larson, during our little drinking adventure at the Majestic, specifically state that he was no longer interested in selling the stone to King Oskar but had instead pinned his hopes on Karl Lund, the Chicago Match King?"

I thought for a moment and said: "I take it you are saying that he was concerned that the stone might not pass scientific scrutiny, as it were."

"Exactly, Watson. Magnus Larson was not a stupid man. Once he himself began to have doubts about the stone, he knew that it would never be accepted by Swedish runologists, who are acknowledged to be the finest in the world. And that meant he could never hope to sell the stone to the king. Mr. Larson avoided legal action for the same reason, because he understood that the rigorous proof required in a court of law might well end up discrediting the stone. On the other hand, he must have learned from Mrs. Comstock that Lund would not demand such a high standard of evidence. I would dearly love to know how much Lund has agreed to pay for the stone, for I am sure that is what is now driving Mrs. Comstock and her accomplices."

"Then I presume Mr. Larson was murdered because of what he knew about the stone."

"I believe so. This case has become a conspiracy of lies, Watson, and the liars have turned on one another in murderous fashion in order to protect those lies."

"What about Mr. Wahlgren—was he murdered for the same reason?"

"I cannot be sure," Holmes said. "Clearly he was in the best position of all to know whether the stone was genuine or a fake. It may be that he was killed simply because he interrupted an effort to steal the stone, before Mr. Larson or anyone else had concluded that it was a forgery. Or he may have been murdered because he was no longer interested in continuing the great charade."

"Do you know who killed him and Mr. Larson?" I asked, knowing that I would be unlikely to receive an answer.

Holmes smiled, took a sip of coffee, and said: "Ah, that is a question which has yet to be resolved, my dear Watson. But as I said before, I believe we will find the answer in Moorhead."

Seeing that I could progress no further on this topic, I asked Holmes if he had been able to decipher the map found on Larson's body.

"It turned out to be a ridiculously simple matter," he told me. "There was really no code at all, which is rather surprising."

"Well, perhaps whoever drew the map did not envision it ending up in the pocket of a dead man, where someone such as ourselves might find it."

"True, but if I were to go to the trouble of drawing a map to some secret location, I would encode it in such a way that no outsider would be able to decipher it."

"Well, Holmes, I am sure not everyone thinks as you do."

"I have noticed that, Watson. In any event, I think I know exactly where the rune stone is hidden."

"And where might that be?"

"Patience, Watson, patience. With luck, you may even see the stone before the day is done."

My food now arrived, but hardly had I taken my first bite when there occurred yet another of those remarkable coincidences which had characterized the rune stone affair from the very beginning.

Sitting at a table across from us were two men, both blond and bearded and both wearing denim overalls, which instantly identified them as farmers. I had overheard them discussing Larson's murder, but as their comments showed no firsthand knowledge of the matter, I paid them little heed. But then the first of these worthies—who had the sort of voice which even a barrage of cannon fire could not have drowned out—suddenly asked his friend if he had heard the news about "Fogelblad's disappearance."

Holmes came to immediate attention when he heard this remark, as did I.

"*Ja*, it is a strange thing," said the second farmer. "I wonder what is going on with Nels."

"I don't know," said he of the stentorian voice. "But imagine him leaving just like that, and no water for the cattle and horses. It's just lucky somebody came by. I always figured Nels was a little queer. Don't you think so, Arne?"

Arne, who spoke in much quieter tones, allowed that "Fogelblad was always a strange one," and so expressed no surprise that he had "run off like that. If you ask me, he's got a woman up there in Moorhead he's courting."

"Oh, I don't think so," answered his friend. "Nels is too shy for anything like that. I bet it's got something to do with that rune stone. It's made him loony, from what I hear. Don't you remember how he got everybody out to his place? Claimed he'd buried the thing there. And what did they find? Nothing. That's what they found. Nothing. *Ja*, I think he just went off the deep end all right. But who would have thought it would come to this?"

"Nobody, I guess," said Arne. "So who's taking care of the livestock?"

"Vint Johnson. He's over on the next forty. But he can't do it forever."

I glanced over at the duo and saw Arne, who appeared to be the younger of the two, shake his head. Then he said: "And there's been no word from Nels yet?"

"Not a peep," replied the other farmer. "Oh, he's gone out of his mind all right. That's what I think."

"*Ja*, I guess so."

There was now a brief pause, after which the deep-voiced farmer said: "Anyway, Arne, I hear wheat is up two cents in Chicago. You going to sell those bushels you've got down at the elevator?"

This sudden shift in the topic of conversation was Holmes's signal to enter the discussion. He stood up, walked over to the table where the two farmers sat, and said in his most ingratiating manner: "Excuse me, gentlemen, but as I was dining with my friend"—here he glanced back at me—"I could not help but overhear one of you mention that something has apparently happened to Mr. Fogelblad. I hope it is nothing serious, for I have gotten to know him quite well over the past few days and would be most distraught to hear that some ill has befallen him."

I have always been amazed by Holmes's ability to elicit information from men of every rank and station. Although his natural manner could be haughty and disdainful, he possessed to an inordinate degree what is sometimes called "the common touch," and he easily entered into conversation with men of even the lowest classes. In this instance, it took him but a matter of minutes to win over the confidence of the two sons of the soil (an accomplishment much aided by his surprising familiarity with the perturbations of the Chicago grain market), and so we soon knew the full story of the "crazy thing" involving Nels Fogelblad.

Early the previous morning, they told us, a neighbor had stopped by Fogelblad's farmhouse to return a tool and found a note tacked to the front door. The note said only that Fogelblad had gone to Moorhead and asked that his livestock be watered and fed during his absence.

The two farmers, both of whom claimed to know Fogelblad quite well, went on to say that he had been acting "strangely" since his failed attempt to dig up the rune stone. "It's like he's hiding some secret. At least that's what people around here think," remarked Arne, who obviously was well connected to that intricate web of gossip common to all rural communities.

After asking a few additional questions which yielded no information of value, Holmes thanked the farmers. The news of Fogelblad's sudden leave-taking seemed to disturb him greatly, and when he returned to our table he sat for a time in pensive silence.

Seeing that Holmes would not volunteer his thoughts, I finally asked to hear them.

"I will not deceive you, Watson," he said. "This situation is growing more unpredictable and dangerous by the moment."

"Then you think Mr. Fogelblad might meet with foul play?"

"It is possible, I fear, but I cannot be certain. I do know, however, that I need to make a telephone call. Finish up your breakfast, Watson. We must move quickly."

I wolfed down the remainder of my food and then followed him outside. Using side streets, we walked back to the Lakeside Inn, where Holmes asked to use the telephone near the front desk.

After his call had been connected by the operator, Holmes began to speak in a strange, singsong manner which I took to be his version of a Swedish-American accent.

"*Ja*, this is Detective Alf Olson up in Moorhead . . . *Ja*, with the police there. I am investigating a matter and need some information. Did a Mr. Nels Fogelblad get on any of the trains yesterday? . . . *Ja*, to Moorhead." There was a pause before Holmes continued: "I see. But you are not sure? . . . *Ja*, all right then, thank you."

Holmes hung up the receiver and said: "Well, Watson, we now know that Mr. Fogelblad did not take a train to Moorhead yesterday, at least from Holandberg. But he could have taken one from here or somewhere else nearby."

"Why do you suppose Fogelblad might have gone to Moorhead?" I asked.

"I cannot say, Watson. But I do know that all of the principals in this affair appear to have converged on that city and that we must soon join them."

After leaving the hotel, we went for a stroll, for there was still an hour before our train left. At first, we kept to the back streets, but after a time Holmes grew tired of the scenery—one house and yard looked much the same as the next—and we turned back toward Broadway, despite Holmes's concern about running into the sheriff. The day was bright and pleasant, with a soft southern breeze, and quite by chance we found ourselves in front of the very same drug store where Rafferty and I had sought shelter from the rain two days previously. Just as Rafferty had paused beneath the store's awning to light his cigar, so Holmes now came to a halt to administer to his pipe. As he did so, he stared idly at the store window and its array of goods.

I shall never forget what happened next, for Holmes, in a jubilant voice, said: "My God, Watson, I have found Rochester!"

"What is it, Holmes?" I asked, turning around to look into the window, where I must confess I observed nothing other than the same collection of ordinary merchandise I had seen earlier. I noted, however, that Holmes's eyes were riveted on one of several cameras on display.

"Look at the name plate on that small box camera," Holmes instructed me. I peered through the glass, trying to make out the manufacturer's name on the camera, which was in the form of a black box with a lens at one end, a viewer, and a winding mechanism and button on top. I was able to read the name "Kodak" on the camera but could not make out a smaller group of words printed below.

"All I see is the word 'Kodak,'" I said.

"Then I fear you need spectacles," said Holmes, who had always been blessed with exceptionally acute eyesight. "The words below the name 'Kodak' are 'Rochester, New York.'"

Before I could absorb the full significance of this discovery, Holmes bolted away from the window and went directly into the drug store. I followed behind and caught up with him as he approached the store's proprietor, a man somewhere in his thirties with curly red hair, a thin mustache, and a bright, accommodating face. He was standing behind a counter at the rear of the store and caught Holmes's eye at once.

"What can I do for you, sir?" he asked.

"I am interested in a camera," Holmes said. "I have been thinking for some time that I ought to take up photography. My friend and I happened to be passing by your store and saw the cameras displayed in your window."

"Oh yes, we have a very nice selection. Which one were you interested in?"

Holmes now described the camera he had pointed out to me.

The proprietor, whose name we soon learned was Peterson, told Holmes politely that he might consider looking at a different camera.

"Why is that?" Holmes asked.

"Well, sir, that particular camera you mentioned is one of the early Kodaks. I guess you would have to say it is something of an antique now."

"Really? It looks quite new to me."

"I suppose it does. I don't think it's had much use. I took it in as a trade some time back. It's the first box camera that Kodak came out with, back in '88 or thereabouts.[1] You could take a real nice picture with it, sir, but I'm sure you would prefer one of the newer cameras with removable film. I could show you one of the latest models if you'd like."

"Not at the moment," said Holmes with a smile. "You see, for some reason that old camera struck my eye. I gather, however, that it does not have roll film like the newer cameras."

"Oh, it does, but the problem is that you can't remove it yourself," Peterson explained. "You have to send the camera itself in for developing."

"How odd," Holmes remarked. "And where would you send it?"

"Why, to Eastman Kodak in Rochester, New York. You see, that's the way they did it at first. You'd take a hundred exposures—that's how many were on the roll—and then you'd just bring the camera back here, or wherever you'd bought it, and we'd ship the whole thing to Rochester. Then they'd develop the film and send it back with the camera and a fresh roll of film all loaded up and ready to go. But as I was saying, with the new cameras now, you can just bring in the film for developing. It's easier that way, and cheaper, too."

"Of course, that would be a definite advantage," Holmes agreed. "But I imagine there are still a few people who use the old kind of camera."

"Oh sure, I've got customers who stay with the old Kodaks. Folks around here aren't the type to throw things away."

Holmes nodded and said: "That is a point well made, sir. In fact, now that you mention it, I recall meeting a gentleman here in town whose daughter had a camera very much like the one in your window. Perhaps you know the girl—Moony Wahlgren."

Peterson grinned and said: "Everybody knows Moony. She loves that camera of hers. Takes beautiful pictures, too, from what I've seen. You wouldn't expect that from her."

"What do you mean?"

"Well, sir, if you've met Moony, then you know she's . . . well, she's not quite right in the head."

"Ah, I see what you are saying. Yes, she is different, there is no doubt about that. Does she take a great many pictures with that camera of hers?"

"I'd guess she comes in two or three times a year, whenever she can scare up enough money to have her pictures developed. Costs ten dollars, you know. That's a lot of money for a girl like her. But she must have gotten a windfall, because when she came in yesterday to get her latest batch of pictures, she gave me a ten-dollar gold piece. Most times, she pays in small change."

"So Moony was in yesterday. What a coincidence!" said Holmes, who then launched an impromptu but impeccably crafted fabrication. "We just saw her yesterday over at Mr. Kensington's place. But she did not have any new pictures to show us then, as I recall."

"Well, she wasn't here until late in the afternoon. Came in about four."

"Ah, that explains it," said Holmes. "We were at Mr. Kensington's house in the morning. By the way, did Moony show you any of her new pictures? The last ones I saw were quite extraordinary. Don't you agree, Mr. Smith?"

"Oh yes," I said, adding my own little falsehood to the proceedings. "They were very nice indeed."

"No, she didn't take out any of her pictures for me to look at," said Peterson in response to Holmes's question. "Usually, she does. In fact, sometimes she'll try to show you all one hundred of them if you don't stop her. But she seemed in kind of a rush yesterday. It's kind of funny now that I think about it."

"How so?" Holmes asked.

"Well, Moony said before she left that she was going to see her brother. But he's long gone as far as I know. I heard he was out in California or some such place."

A bell now rang behind us, announcing the presence of a new customer.

"Be with you in a minute, Mrs. Moberg," said Peterson to the elderly woman who had entered the store. "Now, then, I guess I've been jawing long enough about this and that. Would you like to see some of our newer cameras?"

"Perhaps another day," said Holmes as he took out his pocket watch. "We have a train to catch. Good day, Mr. Peterson."

As we left the store and walked to the depot, Holmes could not hide his excitement over what we had just learned.

"We have found at last where to obtain what is quite literally a true picture of this case," he said.

"So you believe Moony took photographs of the rune stone," I said.

"She must have, Watson. There can be no other explanation. Moreover, I suspect her photographs will show conclusively that the stone is a fraud. I should have seen it earlier, for Moony showed me what she had done in one of her drawings. Do you remember it, Watson? It was the drawing of her father in the grave, with a young girl — Moony, of course — standing in the trees, holding a box in her hands. The box, of course, was her camera. She provided me with one clue after another, Watson, and I missed them all."

"There is no point in blaming yourself," I told Holmes. "Indeed, I think the deductions you have made today are quite brilliant."

"And quite late," Holmes added with disgust. "I also understand now why her father so brutally mistreated her. He must have found out that she had taken the pictures. Perhaps he beat her — or worse — in hopes of forcing her to turn over the camera. But she is a mysterious and secretive child, and also a very brave one. She would not give up her prized photographs to her father or anyone else. So she kept the camera until she had enough money to send it off to Rochester to have the film developed."

"What exactly do you think her pictures show, Holmes? Are they photographs of the stone as it was being pulled from the ground?"

"Perhaps. But the photographs could be even more revealing than that. You see, I think it entirely possible that she has pictures of the stone as it was being carved by her father and whoever may have assisted him. That would explain the other drawing of hers we saw — the one which shows the stone's inscription only half completed. The drawing was simply another version of one of her photographs."

"I take it, then, that you believe it was the rune stone photographs which she picked up yesterday at the drug store."

"That must be the case. If only we had more time! I would like to see those photographs at this instant, but we must go to Moorhead. I wish now that I had not sent Rafferty on ahead of us. I am sure he could persuade Moony to show him her photographs."

"Do you think Mr. Kensington has seen them?"

"I doubt it. But when we reach the depot, I will try to call him. It is of the utmost importance that both Moony and her photographs be protected. I am very worried about the child, Watson, very worried, for we may not be the only ones who know, or suspect, that she possesses incriminating photographs. I fear Mrs. Comstock and her agents may also be aware of the situation. How else explain the fact that Moony's room was burglarized? I should also like to know where she got that ten-dollar gold piece and why she believes she will see her brother soon."

"But how could Mrs. Comstock have known about the pictures?"

"I do not know," said Holmes. "But I do know that the lady's wickedness and guile know no bounds, Watson. I can only pray now that we are not too late to prevent a great catastrophe."

"My God, Holmes, you do not think Mrs. Comstock would harm the poor girl, do you?"

"Think the matter through, Watson," said Holmes as we approached the depot, where a dozen or so people were already waiting on the platform for the train. "Mrs. Comstock is the purest, and therefore potentially the deadliest, of realists. For her, there are only two kinds of people: those who can help and those who can harm. And I have no doubt that she will ruthlessly expunge the latter if she thinks it necessary for her own well-being. I can only hope now that we are not too late to prevent a great catastrophe."

These frightening words were still echoing in my ears when we reached the depot. I waited on the platform while Holmes went inside to purchase our tickets and make sure that our luggage, which we had already sent ahead from the hotel, would be placed aboard the train.

When Holmes returned, I was astonished to see George Kensington with him. The look on Kensington's face could only be described as wild and desolate, the look of a man staring at the end of his world.

Holmes had an arm around Kensington's shoulders, trying to console him. As they walked up to me, Holmes said quietly: "Moony is gone."

Chapter Eighteen
"I DO NOT HAVE TO TELL YOU WHAT THAT MAY MEAN"

Holmes had found Kensington at the depot's ticket counter, and the story he now told us was simple yet chilling. After returning from Holandberg the previous night with Magnus Larson's body, Kensington had performed his various undertaking duties before finally arriving home at ten o'clock. Moony had gone to bed, as was often her custom, about two hours earlier and had seemed perfectly normal to Mrs. Kensington.

When Kensington himself came home, he saw no reason to disturb the girl, since he assumed she was fast asleep in her upstairs bedroom. He and his wife then went to bed themselves. It was only in the morning, at about nine o'clock, that Mrs. Kensington—thinking the girl had slept unusually late—went upstairs to awaken her. But Moony was not in her room or anywhere else in the house.

Holmes took in all of this information, which the distraught Kensington related in a rather chaotic manner, and said: "Mr. Kensington, you must get hold of yourself if we are to help Moony. Now tell me, were there any signs of a break-in at your house?"

"Not that I could see. Everything looked just as it always does."

"You did not, for example, find blood or any other evidence that Moony might have been taken from your house against her will?"

"No, there was nothing like that. Everything was very neat and clean."

"And did you look to see whether any of Moony's clothes or luggage was missing?"

"I did not think to do that," said Kensington. "That was very stupid of me, wasn't it?"

"Do not worry yourself about that, Mr. Kensington. It is hard for a person to think clearly when he is as upset as you must have been. Now, were any windows in Moony's room open when your wife discovered her missing?"

Kensington thought briefly and said: "I'm not sure. But I think the back window was open when I came home after Elsie called."

"What does that window overlook?"

"Well, there's a small porch there, and of course, our yard goes back quite a ways."

"A two-story porch?"

"No, it's just a small open porch connected to the kitchen."

"So the window overlooks the porch's roof?"

"Yes."

"Would it have been possible for someone like Moony to go out that window onto the porch roof and then make it down to the ground without risking serious injury?"

Kensington thought again and said: "Yes, it wouldn't be too hard. There's a downspout back there. A person could shinny down it pretty easily from the porch roof."

Holmes's steady stream of questions seemed to calm Kensington, forcing him to concentrate on something other than the missing girl. Many more questions followed, by means of which Holmes was able to establish that Kensington had made a thorough search of town before coming to the depot as a last resort.

"Moony loves trains, so I thought maybe she just decided to go off somewhere," Kensington told us. "You know how she is. Something will pop into her head and she'll just go ahead and do it without always thinking about the consequences."

"Of course. And that is how you found out she took the eight o'clock train this morning to Moorhead."

"Yes. The agent here knows her, of course, and he even asked her why she was traveling by herself."

"What did she say to that?"

"She said she was making a 'special trip' but that she would be back soon. At least that's what the agent remembers her saying. That was the last thing the agent told me before I saw you come into the depot, Mr. Baker. Now, I must go to Moorhead to find her."

"And we shall go with you," said Holmes as I heard the whistle of our approaching train. "But first let me ask a few more questions. Did the agent say whether anyone was traveling with Moony?"

"No, he said she seemed to be alone. But there were quite a few people boarding the train, so he was too busy to pay much attention."

"I see. Now, let me ask you this: have you notified the authorities that Moony is missing?"

Kensington nodded and said: "I talked to the police chief here in town, but he didn't seem at all concerned about it. He said she'd probably turn up by afternoon, being the flighty child she is. But I know Moony. She's never run off like this before. It isn't like her. I know everybody thinks she's wrong in the head, but she isn't a foolish girl."

"Of course not," said Holmes. "Incidentally, did you also notify Sheriff Boehm of Moony's disappearance?"

"I tried to. But as I understand it, he intended to stay over in Holandberg last night because of the murder investigation. When I called down there this morning, nobody seemed to know where Gus was. He probably wouldn't have time to go chasing after Moony anyway."

"I am sure you are right. My next question may sound strange to you, Mr. Kensington, but please bear with me. How did Moony pay for her ticket to Moorhead?"

"I . . . I don't know," Kensington said. "I guess I should have asked."

"Did Moony typically have much spending money?"

"I'm not sure why you ask, but the answer is no. We do pay her a small weekly allowance for chores."

"Did she ever convert her savings into gold—a ten-dollar gold piece, for example?"

"You are losing me, Mr. Baker," Kensington said. "I don't see—"

"I assure you, sir," Holmes broke in, "that I have the very best of reasons for every question I ask. You must trust me. Moony's life may depend on it."

Such were the sincerity of Holmes's words and the power of his personality that Kensington said: "All right, sir, I will place my trust in you, for I believe you will help me. You asked if Moony ever had a ten-dollar gold piece. All I can tell you is that I never saw her with anything like that. Her allowance was paid in small coins, which she kept in a big jar in her room. She was very good about saving up her money."

"For that camera of hers?"

"Why, yes," said Kensington, looking curiously at Holmes. "But how did you know about that?"

"I will explain later. Where does Moony keep her camera and photographs?"

Although this question too must have struck Kensington as exceedingly odd, he answered without hesitation: "The truth is, I'm not sure where Moony keeps them. She's always been very secretive about her photography, although I know she loved to take pictures."

"Did she ever show you any pictures of her father or of the family's farm?"

"Yes, she had pictures like that. But the ones I've seen are from a few years ago. Mostly, they were photographs of her brother. She adored Olaf Jr."

"What other kind of pictures did she take?"

"Well, let's see. I saw some photographs of her father's draft horses. In fact, now that you mention it, she liked to take pictures in the barn. I saw quite a few that she must have taken from somewhere up in the hayloft, looking out over the house. As I said, she really loved that camera of hers."

"Did she ever show you any photographs of the rune stone?"

"No, I never saw anything like that. But she'd only have her film developed maybe twice a year because it was so expensive. It costs about ten dollars with that camera. We'd help out, but we also told her that she just couldn't go snapping pictures every day and expect us to pay for them. We don't have that kind of money."

Our train appeared around a bend just east of the station, brakes squealing as it began to slow to a stop.

"We will talk more on the train," Holmes told Kensington. "In the meantime, I promise you that Mr. Smith and I will do everything in our power to help you find Moony. I know how precious she is to you."

"Thank you," said Kensington, tears forming in his eyes. "Moony means everything to Elsie and me. Everything."

As we made our way toward Moorhead in a rattling, overheated coach which did not represent James J. Hill's Great Northern Railway at its finest, Holmes spent another half hour interrogating Kensington. There was little else to learn, however, other than that Kensington knew nothing of Moony's supposed plan to see her brother.

"We had a letter from Olaf Jr. about two weeks ago," Kensington said. "He told us that he had taken a new job driving wagons somewhere in California. Near San Francisco, I think."

"Did he give any indication that he would be coming back to Minnesota soon?" Holmes asked.

"No, he said nothing like that. I wrote back telling him of his father's death—I assumed he didn't know about it—but I've received no reply. The mail out there is very slow in any case."

"But if Moony thought her brother was coming home, I take it she would be very excited," Holmes said.

"Oh, 'excited' wouldn't be a strong enough word," Kensington told us. "She'd be beside herself. As I told you, she thought the world of Olaf Jr., who was always very sweet to her and would stick up for her when she got teased."

"All right, Mr. Kensington, you have been a great help," Holmes said. "I am certain we will find Moony once we get to Moorhead and that she will be all right. Why don't you go ahead and take a rest while Mr. Smith and I take a little walk. There are some business matters we must discuss."

Kensington thanked us profusely and let himself slide back into his seat. He appeared exhausted and I had little doubt that he would soon fall asleep. Holmes and I then moved up to another car, where we found a pair of unoccupied seats.

"You sounded very confident about finding Moony," I said to Holmes as we sat down. "Are you really that certain of success?"

Holmes sighed and said: "I am certain of nothing, Watson, but I wished to do my best to put Mr. Kensington at ease. He is much perturbed about Moony's disappearance, as well he should be. I have no doubt that Mrs. Comstock has her."

"But if Mrs. Comstock wanted the pictures, why would she kidnap the girl?"

"An excellent question, Watson. In the first place, I doubt it was a kidnapping in the usual sense. Mrs. Comstock is far too clever for that. No, I think she and her accomplices found a way to persuade Moony to go to Moorhead on her own accord. Someone told her, I imagine, that her brother would meet her there and that their reunion must be a secret. I also think she was given money by this same person to retrieve her pictures. As to why Moony was kidnapped, I cannot be certain, since it was presumably the photographs which Mrs. Comstock wanted above all else. Now that she has them, she presumably will destroy them. And now that she also has the girl, well, I do not have to tell you what that may mean."

"Good Lord, Holmes! Are you saying that the poor child may already be dead? I can scarcely imagine such monstrous villainy."

"It is possible, Watson. All too possible. Let us pray I am wrong. In the meantime, there is one piece of information I have to report to you. While I was at the depot in Alexandria, I picked up a telegram from Mr. Pyle. As I requested, he has begun checking all of the St. Paul and Minneapolis hardware jobbers, including Farwell, Ozmun and Kirk, for any shipments of SG&L lanterns to the Alexandria area. He said he should have a list of customers by tomorrow. Whether this will prove useful remains to be seen."

I now tried to sound Holmes out regarding other aspects of the investigation. I was especially anxious to hear more about the location of the rune stone, since Holmes had claimed to know its exact whereabouts. Unfortunately, Holmes showed no inclination to continue the discussion and soon slipped into one of those deep states of contemplation in which he was all but impervious to the larger sensations of the world around him. And so, with no prospect of conversation, I fell to gazing out the window at the dull countryside and the succession of small towns which seemed to so tenuously occupy it.

We traveled for well over an hour through gently rolling farmland dotted by lakes and wooded hillsides until we gradually came upon a vast plain—a landscape different from any other I had ever seen. Unlike the English moors or the deserts of Afghanistan, this expanse of flatland offered no distant prospects of hills or mountains and therefore no relief from its almost hypnotic monotony. Here and there a slender line of trees etched itself against the horizon, like a thin dark line drawn across a painter's canvas, but otherwise the vista in every direction was of a world without feature or end. It was as though the earth had been stripped of any comforting texture, turned and polished on some immense cosmic lathe until nothing remained but an elemental emptiness. Withal, I thought it the most melancholy place I had ever seen, for everything about it suggested the insignificance of man and the vastness of the natural world.

These unsettling ruminations must have been evident on my face, for a man sitting across from Holmes and me now said: "I take it, sir, that you have never been to the Red River Valley before."

"I have not," I acknowledged to the man, whose plain dark suit and sample case resting over his knees readily identified him as a drummer, no doubt on his way to do business somewhere out on the prairies beyond.

"Well, let me tell you, sir, the first thing you should know is that the valley really isn't a valley at all. What it is, or so they say, is the flattest place on earth. Why, I doubt there's ten feet of drop from here to Fargo. See that elevator over there?" he continued, pointing to the unmistakable silhouette of a tall structure off to our north.

"I see it," I said.

"Well, if you were to climb to the top of that elevator, you'd be on the highest spot for a hundred miles or more. You'd be king of the world, you would. Of course, you wouldn't be king of much except wheat. And the Red River of the North itself, why it's even stranger. Flows due north, you see, and it's the most fickle river on earth. In the dry season, why you could walk across it in your boots and hardly get your soles wet. But when it floods, well, sir, it's a sight. Turns into a regular lake, it does. They say that during the great flood of two years ago, it was thirty miles wide in places."[1]

I remembered now that Holmes had told me about the river, which was part of the route followed by the Viking explorers who had supposedly come south from Hudson Bay in the year 1362 and left the rune stone found on Olaf Wahlgren's farm. That journey seemed more improbable than ever to me now, for what could those Norsemen of old have been looking for amid these vast flatlands?

The salesman was about to continue his disquisition on the wonders of the valley when Holmes suddenly emerged from his reveries and said: "The gentleman is quite correct about the Red River Valley, Watson. The valley is really nothing more than the bottom of an ancient lake bed, as the late Professor Agassiz of Harvard was among the first to demonstrate.[2] It is also quite an appalling place, from what I can see. Man was not made to live in such terrible emptiness."

"Well, sir, I don't know about that," said the drummer, casting his sharp gray eyes at Holmes. "But it's the best damn wheat country in the world. I've heard some of the big bonanza farmers out here are millionaires already. Imagine that."

"I would rather be a poor man in London than a millionaire here," said Holmes, who then turned away and shut his eyes, signaling that his contribution to the conversation was over.

I continued to chat with the salesman, however, learning various details of the countryside and the wheat business until we at last reached the city of Moorhead just before four o'clock.

❊   ❊   ❊

Rafferty, dressed in a long topcoat of blue wool with a red bandanna thrown around his neck, was waiting for us at the station, and was much surprised to see George Kensington with us. Kensington no doubt was equally surprised to see Rafferty.

" 'Tis good to see you again," said Rafferty, who greeted Holmes and me with crushing hugs while settling for a firm handshake with Kensington. "But I'm wondering what you're doin' here, Mr. Kensington. Is there some trouble?"

Holmes at once described to Rafferty the circumstances surrounding the disappearance of Moony Wahlgren and her apparent flight to Moorhead. Rafferty was tremendously disturbed by this news, and I could sense a kind of terrible energy rising in him, like magma building in a volcano.

"We must find the child," he said, "and we must act quickly. If she's come to any harm, someone will answer to me, and I swear it will be the last answer they give in this world."

"I share your sentiments, Mr. Rafferty," said Holmes, "but we cannot act precipitously, as I know you would agree."

"You're right, Mr. Baker. I won't blow up on you, if that's what you're thinkin'. But I will see justice done."

"As will I," Holmes promised, adding: "Our first course of action is right here. We must see if anyone saw Moony arrive at the depot today. I should also be curious to know if anyone was with her."

"I'll handle that," said Rafferty. "I know a few fellows here."

"Somehow I knew you would," said Holmes.

It took Rafferty but fifteen minutes to complete his inquiries. When he rejoined us on the platform, he said: "She was here all right. One of the porters remembers her. Said she was wearin' a bright pink hat and carryin' a small bag. But he didn't see where she went from the depot."

"What time was this?" Holmes asked.

"The train got in around noon. And if you want to know if the porter saw anyone with her, he didn't. As far as he could tell, she was alone. But the porter did see someone else we know gettin' off that very same train."

"Billy Swift," said Holmes without hesitation.

"I'm afraid so, Mr. Holmes. What with his cowboy getup, Billy Boy stands out in a crowd. The porter saw him sashayin' down the platform not far behind Moony. It doesn't take much imagination to figure out what might have happened after that."

"Are you saying she was abducted by Billy Swift?" I asked.

"He'd be just the man for such a job," Rafferty replied. "But unless we can find someone who saw the two of them together, well, we've got nothin' to prove she was even abducted in the first place."

Holmes thought for a minute and said: "At least we know that she arrived here safe and sound. I am also inclined to agree with Mr. Rafferty. I think there is a very good chance that after leaving the station here, she either went or was taken to Fairview Farms."

"Then we have no choice but to go there at once and attempt a rescue," I said, my mind filling with grim thoughts of what could happen to the girl if she had indeed fallen into the clutches of Mrs. Comstock and a cutthroat like Billy Swift.

"I wouldn't be quite so anxious," said Rafferty. "You see, I was out at the farm this morning, Mr. Smith, and I doubt you have any sense of its size. 'Tis not like one of your cozy English spreads nestled along some windin' country lane. Fairview Farms is a full-blown bonanza operation, and that means it's like a small industrial city out there on the plains, for that is what bonanza farming is — an industry. The farm has three huge barns, a bunkhouse for the field hands, a cookhouse, various machine and storage sheds, and a grain elevator, not to mention the main house itself, where Mrs. Comstock lives. You'd need a good-sized team of men to search the place, and even then you might not find the girl, for there's twenty thousand acres out there and she could be hidden on any one of them."

"Mr. Rafferty is right," Holmes said. "There is no point searching for the girl unless we have a better sense of where she might be. Therefore, we must begin by narrowing the possibilities."

Turning to Kensington, Holmes said: "I will need your help, sir."

"Anything you ask," said Kensington. "No one wants Moony back more than I do."

"I understand," said Holmes. "That is why I think you would be the best person to notify the police and sheriff here that Moony is missing. Tell them all you know of her disappearance save for one thing: do not mention our suspicions regarding Mrs. Comstock, for the truth is that we have no concrete evidence of her involvement in this affair. The lady is nothing if not resourceful, and I have no doubt she has a story well prepared should she receive a visit from the local sheriff. However, make sure, Mr. Kensington, that you bring up Billy Swift's name. Simply say that someone saw him walking near Moony and that you believe he might know in which direction she went after leaving the depot."

"But if I don't tell the police about Mrs. Comstock, how will they know where to look for Moony?" Kensington asked.

"They will not know," Holmes admitted. "But there is always the possibility that Moony has not in fact been abducted. For all we know, she may be wandering around Moorhead at this very moment. If so, the police will be in the best position of anyone to find her. The fact that you are her guardian and can explain as well as anyone the peculiarities of her character will only help matters."

Kensington nodded and said: "I'll go at once. But I must ask you, Mr. Baker: Do you think Moony has been abducted or harmed in any way?"

"She will be just fine, Mr. Kensington, just fine," said Holmes. "Now, be on your way, sir, for we have not a minute to spare."

After giving Kensington instructions to meet us later at the Red River Inn, Moorhead's largest hotel, Holmes, Rafferty, and I began walking toward that destination.

"'Twas nice what you did for Mr. Kensington," Rafferty told Holmes. "The man is livin' on a diet of hope at the moment, and you went out of your way to heap a little more on his plate. I only hope he will not be left in the end with an empty belly. I don't mind tellin' you, Mr. Holmes, I'm terribly worried about the girl. Fact is, if she was abducted, I have trouble figurin' out a good reason why she'd still be alive."

I felt my heart sink as Rafferty uttered these words, and I asked why he was so pessimistic.

" 'Tis a matter of doin' the calculations, Doctor. I'd see no reason to keep her alive once I got those pictures of hers."

"But to kill a child in cold blood—"

" 'Twould not be the first time such a thing has happened, Doctor," Rafferty broke in. "If there's one lesson to be learned from this sorry life of ours, 'tis that cruelty is as natural to the human species as breathin'. I wish it were not so, but I know it is."

Holmes said: "I do not entirely agree with you, Mr. Rafferty, at least insofar as it concerns the Wahlgren girl. I can think of one very good reason why she may still be alive, and I believe we must pin our hopes to that possibility. At the same time, we must also realize that our situation has now become extraordinarily dangerous."

I waited for Holmes to explain this statement, but Rafferty jumped in first: "Ah, I think I catch your drift, Mr. Holmes. You're sayin' that the girl is bein' kept alive because somebody wants us dead."

"Exactly," said Sherlock Holmes.

Chapter Nineteen

"YOU CAN ANSWER A QUESTION FOR ME"

Holmes's one-word response to Rafferty's chilling statement made me aware, for perhaps the first time, that we now found ourselves in a situation of almost unprecedented peril. Holmes was, as I have often noted, the ultimate pursuer, a relentless hunter of men, from whom no criminal, however brilliant or ruthless, could hope to escape. And yet now, if I understood the implications of what Rafferty and Holmes were saying, the tables had been turned.

"Yes, Watson," said Holmes, noting the pallor which must have spread over my features, "there is now a real question as to whether we are the hunter or the hunted. Mr. Rafferty, I fear, is quite right. There is no reason for the girl to be alive, unless she is being used as bait to draw us into a trap."

" 'Tis worse than that," said Rafferty, "for we have no choice but to walk into it with our eyes open. I remember at Fredericksburg when we lay low to the ground, metal screamin' so fast and thick above us that liftin' your head was sure death, and yet there were all those fine boys in blue goin' up toward the long stone wall. They knew they could not get there—no men on earth could have done so—but up they went anyway, not because that butcher Joe Hooker commanded it but because they somehow knew that on that day, in that place, 'twas the thing they had to do.[1] Well now, our duty is plain. We must save the poor girl if we can, or die tryin' if we must. But in either case, we've got a damn sight better chance than those poor boys at Fredericksburg did, and I'll take those odds anytime."

"Well put," said Holmes in response to this stirring speech. "And I think our chances are indeed quite good, because we know something that Mrs. Comstock does not."

"And what would that be?" I asked.

"Let us find a place to sit and talk," said Holmes, "and I will explain everything to you, Watson. Besides, we have much to talk about with Mr. Rafferty."

"There's a good saloon over at the Red River Inn," Rafferty suggested. "That way Mr. Kensington will have no trouble findin' us."

"Lead the way," said Holmes.

It was a walk of but two blocks to the hotel, down a wide dusty street of the kind which appeared to be common to all the prairie towns of America. The usual dreary collection of small brick and wooden buildings overlooked the street, although from what I could tell Moorhead was already a larger and more substantial community than Alexandria or any of the others we had encountered west of St. Paul and Minneapolis. As we went along, I looked for the Red River of the North, which was supposed to flow past Moorhead, but I saw no evidence of the fabled watercourse during the short walk to our hotel.

The saloon at the Red River Inn—a plain brick building not unlike the Douglas House in Alexandria—was a dark, smoky room with japanned woodwork and heavy damask curtains. Taking a table at the rear of the room, we ordered drinks and sat down to talk.

"We have much other news to report, Mr. Rafferty," said Holmes, who then quickly sketched the events of the day: our visit to the bank and what we had found in Blegen's safety deposit box, our overheard conversation at the restaurant concerning Nels Fogel-blad's disappearance, and finally the discovery of what Moony Wahlgren had meant by "Rochester knows."

Rafferty reacted to this last revelation with a crestfallen air, bowing his head and emitting a long sigh. Then he said: "Well, you've stolen my thunder, Mr. Holmes. Yes, sir, you've taken it right out of my mouth and silenced it to a tiny peep. Fact is, I came to the same conclusion this morning right here at the hotel, if you can believe it."

"I would never doubt your word, Mr. Rafferty," said Holmes gallantly. "Indeed, the solution to the Rochester puzzle, as I came to call it, seemed so obvious in retrospect that I could only wonder that it did not occur to either of us sooner."

"I won't dispute that," said Rafferty. " 'Twas something I should have known, since I've dabbled in photography myself. But I'm still a glass plate man — I've never fooled with those new roll cameras.[2] As it turned out, what set me to thinkin' about Kodak and Rochester was a girl who was stayin' here at the hotel with her parents. When she saw me in the lobby early this mornin', she said to her ma, 'Look, there's Santa Claus.' "

"I must admit, there is a resemblance," I told Rafferty.

"True, but I'm fatter and meaner," he said with a grin, "and better-lookin', too. Well, this girl happened to have one of those box cameras, and she marched right over and asked if she could take my picture. I suppose you can figure out the rest, Mr. Holmes. I saw the nameplate on the camera, just as you did, and before long the whole thing started fallin' into place."

"Well," I observed, "it is said that great minds think alike."

"Let us hope that is true," said Holmes, "for we will need all the thinking power we can muster if we are to find the Wahlgren girl. But before we consider our strategy, I should like to hear what you have learned, Mr. Rafferty, since your arrival in Moorhead."

"All right, Mr. Holmes, here's the lowdown," Rafferty said, settling back into his chair and taking a drink from the glass of tonic water he had ordered. "I managed to get on the train last night in Alexandria without Mrs. Comstock seein' me, which was not easy, I

can tell you that. Tryin' to stay inconspicuous is not my strong suit—"
here Rafferty paused to pat his ample belly—"for it's like tryin' to
hide an elephant in a china closet. But I kept to the last car of the
train, which is where all the cigar smokers congregate, knowin' that
the lady's not fond of tobacco smoke."

"That was clever of you," I said.

"Also gave me a chance to smoke," said Rafferty, "so I killed two
birds with one stone. Once we got to Moorhead, I followed Mrs.
Comstock to this hotel, where she took a room for the night. I did a
little finaglin'—spread a few gold coins around, in other words—and
got the room right next to hers. Had a cup up to the wall half the
night, but nothin' happened that I could tell, and if she had any visitors they were quiet as mice at a convention of cats."

"Do you know if she left the room at any point during the night?"
Holmes asked.

"I don't think so. From what you've told me, Mr. Holmes, the lady
doesn't sleep alone very often, but last night I think she did. I finally
figured it was safe to go out at about six this mornin', so I went over
to the Great Northern freight station and checked on that crate Billy
Swift sent from Alexandria on Friday. A clerk told me that a worker
from Fairview Farms picked up the crate Saturday afternoon and
hauled it away in a wagon."

"I presume the clerk never examined the contents of the crate,"
Holmes said.

"He'd get in trouble for doin' that, Mr. Holmes. Of course, if I'd
been there when the crate arrived, I might have persuaded him to
violate company policy. Anyway, I went back to the hotel and waited
to see if Mrs. Comstock would check out. She did, at just after eight.
A fellow I didn't recognize picked her up in a carriage and they
drove to her farm, which is about five miles southeast of here. I hired
a rig and followed her out there, stayin' far back, of course, since
there's really no place to hide yourself on the prairies. I looked
around the farm a little—as I mentioned to you earlier, it's a huge
place with lots of buildings—and then came back early this afternoon to wait for you. And that's all I know."

"I am intrigued by something you mentioned earlier," said

Holmes. "I would like you to tell me all you know about the grain elevator at Fairview Farms."

Rafferty smiled and said: "I figured you might bring that up."

"And why is that, Mr. Rafferty?"

"Well, unless our supposedly great minds are in disagreement, then I think you already know that the elevator is where we'll find the rune stone."

As Holmes was wont to do when revealing some crucial discovery, Rafferty had delivered this remark in an almost offhanded way, as though it must be obvious to everyone where the rune stone was to be found. It had not been that apparent to me, of course, but as I thought back to the map I had found on Magnus Larson's corpse, I remembered seeing the letters "GE," among others.

Holmes now leaned back in his chair and said: "I see you have been thinking about that map, Mr. Rafferty. I did not think the map would present much of a challenge to a man of your acuity. And I agree that the grain elevator, as indicated by the letters "GE," must be where the rune stone is hidden. I also assume that on your expedition today to the farm, you checked the accuracy of the map."

"I did, Mr. Holmes, and everythin' lines up perfectly. The letters 'TR,' for instance, correspond to a township road that passes near the elevator, which is next to the tracks of the Great Northern Railway, as also indicated on the map. I believe I know what the other letterin' on the map means as well."

"As do I," said Holmes. "But that need not concern us until we inspect the elevator for ourselves."

"Well, that could be a problem, Mr. Holmes."

"Why?"

"The elevator, I found out today, is somethin' of a ruin. Part of its roof and headhouse got blown away in a thunderstorm a couple of weeks ago. The locals told me it was the worst March storm they'd ever seen. All the grain inside was spoiled, of course, and the structure itself is considered unsafe, accordin' to the lad who drove me out to the farm."

"In other words, it sounds like a perfect place to hide something," said Holmes.

"I suppose so," said Rafferty, "but we'll have to be careful. As you know, almost anything out there could be a trap."

"Of course," said Holmes, "but we may also have a distinct advantage when it comes to the elevator. That is where the answer to your earlier question comes into play, Watson. You see, I think it entirely possible that Mrs. Comstock is not aware that we have now pinpointed the stone's location."

"So you're sayin' she might not know anythin' about the map, is that right?" said Rafferty.

"Yes."

"Well, I'm not sure I agree," said the Irishman. "If she's the schemin' virago you've made her out to be, Mr. Holmes, then I figure she must know just about everythin' there is to know. At least, that's the way you've built her up. And to be honest with you, I'm a bit troubled in that regard."

"I am not sure what you mean, Mr. Rafferty," said Holmes.

"What I mean, with all due respect, is that I haven't seen any hard evidence that Mrs. Comstock is the villainess you say she is. Now, I know you have far more experience with the lady than I do, so I'm sure there are things I don't know about. She may be a female Attila the Hun, but I'm still waitin' to see the proof."

"You shall see it," said Holmes, fixing his magnetic gaze upon the Irishman. "I know the woman and what she is capable of."

"Then I'll take your word for it," said Rafferty. "But I'm not sure a court of law, if asked to bring her to trial tomorrow, would view things in the same light, and that is all I will say about the matter."

"Fair enough," said Holmes.

We spent the next half hour laying out plans, though in truth there were few options available to us. Or, as Rafferty put it: "If the girl is at Fairview Farms, then whoever has her will be waitin' for us, no matter when we come."

Holmes then suggested that we go to the farm before nightfall to make what he described as a "preliminary reconnaissance."

Rafferty, however, advised against the idea. " 'Tis now almost five o'clock," he noted, consulting his pocket watch, "and it will be dark by seven. We will need more time if we are to do any good. I'd also point out to you, Mr. Holmes, that there is no good way to reconnoiter a place like Fairview Farms except from a great distance, as I did today. If somebody at the farm is on the lookout, they'd see us comin' from miles away. No, I think we'd do better to go out there in the mornin', with plenty of weaponry in our coats, and have a talk with the lady."

"Why not go after dark?" I suggested. "It would give us a better chance if an ambush is waiting for us."

"Maybe, but the fact is, Doctor, it's pitch black out there, and we don't know where on the farm the girl might be. It'd be about as easy to find a certain grain of sand on Brighton Beach as it would to find the girl under those conditions."[3]

Holmes finally agreed. "Very well then, we will go in the morning, Mr. Rafferty, since it appears we have no other choice."

Not long after five, Kensington returned and met us in the hotel lobby, where we had gone to wait for him. He took a seat across from us and told us how he had been received by the police.

"They promised they would keep an eye out for Moony," he said, "but since I couldn't tell them where to look, that's about all they'd be willing to do. They told me children—especially of Moony's age—go missing all the time and usually show up on their own in a few days. I told them this was different, but they didn't sound too interested to hear any more from me. But I did mention Billy Swift's name, as you told me to, Mr. Baker. That got a little rise out of them."

"Ah, so the police here know Mr. Swift," said Holmes.

"They do. I guess he's got quite a reputation around town as a brawler. But the policemen I talked to said that didn't mean anything to them as far as Moony's disappearance is concerned."

Kensington paused before he suddenly began to cry. "I don't think they care," he said, trying to wipe the tears from his eyes. "I don't think they care one bit. I just want Moony back. If something has happened to her, what will I tell Elsie? It will break her heart."

"It will break all our hearts," said Rafferty, who went over at once and put a comforting hand on Kensington's shoulder. "Don't worry, we will find her, with or without help from the coppers."

Holmes, too, was obviously moved by this scene. Looking straight at Kensington, he said: "I can only imagine how you must feel, sir. Moony is indeed an extraordinary child, a gift to us all. That is why I now see that you are entitled to know the truth, since you have been of so much help to us over the past six days. Therefore, I must tell you that I am not a curator at the British Museum, nor is my friend. If you will give me your pledge that everything I tell you from this point forward will be kept in the strictest confidence, then I shall share our real identities with you."

Holmes had not told me of his intention to bring a fourth person into our circle, and I was as surprised as Kensington was by this announcement. Indeed, Kensington appeared so taken aback by Holmes's sudden offer that for a moment I am sure he suspected that he had fallen in with a den of confidence men. Rafferty, however, put him at ease.

Said the Irishman: "I know these gentlemen well, Mr. Kensington, and they are the best in the world at what they do. You have nothing to fear from them and much to gain, and if anyone can find your beloved Moony, they are the men to do it. Will you give us your word, sir, as I would not hesitate to give you mine?"

"Of course, of course," said Kensington, drying his eyes with a handkerchief. "I know you gentlemen are trying to help me. You have my word, which anyone will tell you is to be relied upon."

"I do not doubt that, sir," said Holmes. "Very well then. Mr. Rafferty, would you be so kind as to make the appropriate introductions."

" 'Twould be my pleasure," Rafferty said. "Mr. Kensington, I would like you to meet Mr. Sherlock Holmes and Dr. John Watson, of London, England. I imagine you've heard of them."

If it is possible for a man's jaw not merely to drop but to plummet like a lead weight, then such was the effect of Rafferty's announcement on Kensington.

"But I cannot . . . I mean, how did you . . . well . . . I am at a loss for words," he finally stammered.

" 'Tis an amazin' thing, I know," said Rafferty. "But it's true, Mr. Kensington. And that is why we asked you for your word. Mr. Holmes and Dr. Watson like to keep a low profile, as it were, and havin' their identities bruited about could harm our investigation."

"I understand, I understand," said Kensington, who stood up and shook Holmes's hand as well as mine. "I'm blessed, that's all I can say. I know now that Moony will be safe."

As Kensington made this confident assertion, I glanced at Holmes, whose features I had learned to read well during the course of our many years together. While I saw hope and resolve in his face, along with shades of doubt, the one thing I did not see was confidence.

After the four of us ate dinner at the hotel, we all retired to our rooms, since there was little else for us to do. As I sat in my room, making notes in the journal I had maintained since the beginning of the rune stone case, I felt rather like a soldier on the eve of battle, wondering whether dawn would bring triumph or tragedy.[4] My thoughts were soon interrupted, however, by a knock on the door. I opened it to find Rafferty.

"May I come in?" he said.

"Of course."

As there was only one chair in my room, Rafferty took a seat on the bed, which sank beneath his weight.

"What can I do for you, Mr. Rafferty?" I asked.

"You can answer a question for me, I hope. Is Mr. Holmes in love with this Comstock woman?"

I was, I must admit, shocked by this question, and I could scarcely believe that Rafferty had asked it.

"Why would you even think such a thing?" I said. "She is a criminal, and a very dangerous one at that."

"No need to take offense, Doctor. I was merely makin' inquiries, though I would note that love and danger often go hand in hand. Why, some would even say they're inseparable twins. After all, Cupid carries an arrow, or so the ancients tell us."

"Well, I can assure you that Holmes has never been stung by that particular weapon. There has never been time in his life for such a thing. Surely you must know that, Mr. Rafferty. Holmes does not have a romantic bone in his body. He is entirely a man of reason."

"Ah, now that's where you could be wrong, Doctor. You see, I've found that the man of reason is usually the greatest romantic of all, for who but a romantic could ever believe that the world is a reasonable place?"

I confess I had no answer to this conundrum, other than to tell Rafferty: "All I can say is that Holmes is most certainly not in love with Mrs. Comstock."

Rafferty now lay back on the bed, his feet dangling over the edge and his hands resting behind his head. Staring up at the ceiling, he said: "But you would agree, would you not, that he is obsessed with the lady?"

"What do you mean?"

"Just this, Doctor. To hear Mr. Holmes talk, the lady is nothin' less than evil personified. Now, as I said before, maybe he's right. Maybe she's as bad as he says she is. But as I also said, where's the proof?"

"Are you suggesting that someone other than Mrs. Comstock is behind all that has happened in this case?"

"'Tis possible, yes. 'Tis possible, in fact, that all she's guilty of is whorin' and then marryin' for money. Now, the first is an offense, to be sure, but not the worst in the world. And as for the second, well, the truth is, most rich men would die alone in their beds if some woman with an eye for the main chance hadn't picked them off like a clay pigeon at a shootin' match and dropped them at the altar. Now, as far as I can tell, that's exactly what this Comstock woman did. She found a rich man — or at least what she thought was a rich man — and went after his money, as any woman with aspirations would."

"So I take it you do not believe she killed her husband?"

"I don't know if she pushed him off the train, Doctor, and neither does anybody else, as far as I can tell. There's simply no convincin' evidence one way or the other. And the same holds true for this

whole crazy rune stone business. Did she arrange for the murder of
Olaf Wahlgren, steal the stone, and then kill Magnus Larson? Could
be. But again, where's the proof? If you've got any, I'd like to
hear it."

"That is a question you should ask Holmes," I said.

"I have, if you remember. All he said is that I'd get the proof."

"Why are you telling me all of this, Mr. Rafferty?"

"I'm tellin' you because you're Mr. Holmes's best friend, Doctor, a
man he trusts above all others, as he should. I don't want to compromise this investigation, and I certainly don't want to do anythin' that
would hurt Mr. Holmes or you. Remember that wall I told you
about at Fredericksburg?"

"Yes."

"Well, I'd gladly follow Mr. Holmes up there. Wouldn't hesitate a
second, even if I knew it was sheer suicide. But I just want to make
sure that Mr. Holmes is leadin' us up to the right wall, against the
right enemy, because if he isn't, then we've gained nothin' and that
poor Wahlgren girl will end up as a casualty of war. At least, that's
the way I see it. So all I'm askin' you to do, Doctor, as a friend of Mr.
Holmes's, is to think about what I've said and to speak up if you
have to."

Rafferty now got himself up from the bed, which creaked and rattled as he rose to his feet, and walked to the door. He opened it
slightly, then turned around and said: "Tomorrow will be a day to remember, Doctor. I can feel it in my bones. There's goin' to be big
trouble, somewhere, and we'll be in the middle of it. Don't forget to
bring your pistol."

And with that final caution, he went out the door.

Chapter Twenty

"I DON'T LIKE THE LOOK OF THIS"

E arly the next morning, which dawned cool and overcast, we ate a hasty breakfast at our hotel, after which Rafferty went out to bring around the wagon he had ordered from one of the local liveries. Only three of us, however, were to make the trip to Fairview Farms, for Holmes had decided that Kensington was to stay in Moorhead. This announcement precipitated a brief argument, since Kensington desperately wanted to accompany us. But Holmes simply would not hear of it, telling Kensington that he must remain in town "in the event there is some word as to Moony's whereabouts." This was not the truth, of course, as Rafferty and I knew full well. The real reason why Kensington was left behind was that Holmes did not wish to expose him to whatever dangers lay ahead at the farm.

After Kensington had reluctantly agreed to stay at the hotel, we walked outside and waited until Rafferty came down the street with our wagon, pulled by a two-horse team. Holmes had decided against hiring a driver, since he wished to visit the grain elevator in complete secrecy, and that meant Rafferty would have to handle the wagon.

He was more than capable of this responsibility—he had, after all, been a teamster at one stage of his adventurous life—and I noted how skillfully he managed the team as he pulled to a stop in front of us.

Once we had climbed up beside him on the seat, Rafferty said: "The spades and a couple of lanterns are in the back, Mr. Holmes, just as you requested, though I hope we won't have to do too much diggin' for that stone. I did all the diggin' I ever wanted to do in the Nevada mines, and I've been allergic to that form of exercise ever since. I also brought along that big piece of canvas you see back there, so we can keep the stone under wraps if we find it. Still, I'm a bit concerned about the stone's weight, especially if we have to pull it out of a deep hole. I've therefore taken the precaution of securing some rope and a winch in case we need them. Of course, if worse comes to worse, I'll pull out the stone with my own two arms."

"As usual, you have thought of everything, Mr. Rafferty," said Holmes.

"I hope so, but there's one other matter I must mention. Since I don't know what we'll find out there, I'm goin' well-armed to Fairview Farms. I trust the two of you are doin' the same."

"I am sure Dr. Watson has his trusty Colt revolver with him," Holmes replied. "That should be sufficient if trouble occurs."

"Ah, and what are you carryin'?" Rafferty asked Holmes.

"My walking stick," said Holmes. He then described the sleek cane with a hidden blade which he had used to great effect during our adventure in Hinckley more than four years earlier. "It is a most effective weapon," Holmes concluded.

Rafferty, however, shook his head vigorously and said: "No, Mr. Holmes, you'll want something more. This is rifle and shotgun country, Mr. Holmes. A knife is fine for slicin' a piece of sirloin, but it will do you no good in a gunfight. 'Tis my belief, based upon a lifetime of experience with miscreants of every stripe, that a man should not only be handy with weaponry but should always have plenty of it. I've got somethin' in back that should do the trick."

"Really—" Holmes began, but Rafferty cut him off.

"I insist," he said, reaching back under the canvas and pulling out the case where he kept his pocket rifle. "There'll be no arguin' on the matter."

Holmes looked at Rafferty, shook his head, and then said with a sigh: "Very well, Mr. Rafferty, I see it will be futile to resist. Let us inspect your arsenal."

"That's better," said Rafferty, opening the case to reveal the weapon he liked to call Mr. Stevens.

"I do not usually travel with a cannon," Holmes remarked as Rafferty removed the long-barreled gun and quickly assembled it.

"Well, this is not a usual situation, Mr. Holmes. Mr. Stevens here is a weapon that will make a man think twice before comin' at you with bad intentions."

Holmes examined the gun, which seemed far too large to be hidden anywhere on his person, and said: "Mr. Rafferty, I do not think—"

Rafferty, however, would entertain no discussion on the matter: "Don't argue, Mr. Holmes, because I'm not listenin'. You need some protection. Mr. Stevens will shoot the eye out of a grasshopper at a hundred yards, and that's fact!"

"I am sure that is true, Mr. Rafferty, but I shall be quite fine without such a weapon."

"No you won't," Rafferty said, setting the gun behind us beneath the canvas. "I've got a feelin' in my bones about today, and all of us need to be prepared."

"I suppose there is no point in arguing with you," said Holmes.

"None at all," Rafferty replied.

"All right, Mr. Rafferty, you shall have your way. I promise you I shall use Mr. Stevens if the need arises."

"I knew you'd see the light," said Rafferty, and gave the reins a shake.

As we made our way out of town, I debated whether I should mention, in some subtle way, the questions about Mrs. Comstock's guilt which Rafferty had raised the night before. But I finally decided against it, for I did not think Holmes would respond well to such questions, and I saw no point in bringing up such a potentially divisive matter at so critical a time. Indeed, I suspected that Rafferty probably felt the same way himself, which is why he had told me of his concerns rather than Holmes.

Despite these troubling thoughts, and the presentiment of disaster which both Holmes and Rafferty seemed to harbor about our visit to the farm, I was nonetheless pleased to be out in the open air and away from our cramped quarters at the hotel. I also sensed, as did my two companions, that the tantalizing mystery of the rune stone, which had occupied our every thought and prompted our every deed for the past week, might now be coming to its inevitable denouement.

Patches of morning fog—a rarity in so windy a place—lingered like ghostly ships over the prairies as we followed a die-straight road which seemed to lead to some incomprehensible infinity beyond the flat line of the horizon. As had been the case on the train to Moorhead, I was struck as we drove along by the alien immensity of the landscape, which seemed to reduce the affairs of mankind to small vanities and petty aspirations. Still, the human hand was visible, for scattered far to our south I saw the distinctive profiles of three tall grain elevators, rising out of the pancake-flat landscape like giant pencils thrust through a piece of paper.

"That one on the left is what's left of Fairview Farms's elevator," said Rafferty, who had noticed what I was looking at. "We'll start seein' the other farm buildings pretty soon, too."

Fortunately, Rafferty's natural exuberance was not dampened in the least by the daunting emptiness around us, and as we went along, he offered a running commentary on the operation of a bonanza farm such as Mrs. Comstock's.

"Now, her farm is actually modest by the standards of the Red River Valley," he pointed out, "for I've heard that some of the wheat barons still have fifty thousand acres under cultivation.[1] She's got about twenty thousand acres in all, accordin' to what I was told in town, and probably three-fourths of it goes to wheat every year. If the weather's decent, her crews might harvest twenty bushels per acre. That's, let see—"

"Three hundred thousand bushels of wheat," said Holmes, adding: "The last time I looked, top-quality wheat might fetch ninety cents a bushel in Chicago or Minneapolis. Subtracting various costs for labor, equipment, shipping, and the like, a woman like Mrs. Comstock might clear fifty thousand dollars or more in a good year, wouldn't you say so?"

"I'd not argue with those calculations," Rafferty said. "But if her husband left her under a mountain of debt, then most of that money would be goin' to the creditors, which means that the lady might have a lot of land but not much cash."

"And that is precisely why she must have been drawn to the rune stone," Holmes said. "The stone is a thing she can convert instantly to cash by selling it to that wealthy Swede in Chicago. After that, I believe her plan is to disappear."

"Why do you think that, Mr. Holmes?" Rafferty asked.

"Because that is her preferred mode of operation. When the situation in Hinckley became, quite literally, too hot for her, she simply vanished. I see no reason why she will not do the same thing in this instance, since I doubt she has any enduring commitment to her farm."

"Well, I guess we'll find out soon enough," said Rafferty.

We now came over an almost imperceptible rise in the flatlands, and far in the distance I could see the outlines of buildings, defiant splotches of red and white standing against the expanse of gray sky and brown earth.

"There it is, Fairview Farms," Rafferty announced. "By the way, I talked to an old-timer in Moorhead this mornin', before the two of you came down for breakfast, and he told me the place is quite notorious among the locals."

"In what way?" asked Holmes.

"Well, there were rumors that the Comstocks kept a statue of a naked woman in their bedroom. This unwholesome news scandalized every church congregation for miles around, or so I was told."

"I do not imagine sculptures of nudes are a common adornment in this part of the world," Holmes noted dryly.

Rafferty, whose tavern in St. Paul, as I recalled, featured a prominent painting of a nude over the bar, laughed and said: "You're right there, Mr. Holmes. Personally, I don't see anythin' wrong with a little erotic statuary in the bedroom, though it must not have been an inducement to slumber on Mr. Comstock's part."

"Tell me," said Holmes, "what did your old-timer have to say about Mrs. Comstock?"

" 'Hussy' and 'harlot' are two of the kinder words I recall, Mr. Holmes. The lady, it is safe to say, is viewed as a scarlet woman by the locals. She is therefore thought to be a danger to all God-fearin' adults and children and, for all I know, to household pets as well. Of course, when she comes into town and spends her money, the pious are happy to take it nonetheless. The old fellow I talked to also had lots of other gossip to peddle about Mrs. Comstock, though I'm sure you wouldn't be interested in hearin' it, would you, Mr. Holmes?"

"Try me, Mr. Rafferty," said Holmes, who in truth was a great consumer of gossip in all of its varieties. "Gossip," he had once told me, "is what drives the world, for if we had nothing to talk about save for what we know to be true, we should soon run out of things to say altogether."

"Well now," said Rafferty, "most of the rumors concern who she was supposedly sleepin' with in addition to her beloved husband. If even half these rumors are true, the lady must have been booked up every night. To my way of thinkin', a much more interestin' rumor concerns what she supposedly did after her husband died. It seems his body was hardly cold before she wired their bank in Moorhead with instructions to close their personal account and transfer everythin' to the Merchants Bank in Alexandria, where you and Dr. Watson staged your little performance in the safety deposit vault."

"How strange," said Holmes. "Why would she have done such a thing?"

"Don't know," said Rafferty, "but it looks like we've just about arrived. 'Twould be best if all of us stayed on our toes from now on."

We drew up to the farm's driveway, which was entered beneath a wooden archway emblazoned in red letters with the message WEL-COME TO FAIRVIEW FARMS. As I looked down the long driveway, I understood what Rafferty had meant when he described the farm as a "small industrial city" on the prairies. The immediate portion of the farm included three huge barns, all painted deep red; a scattering of equipment sheds and other outbuildings, perhaps ten in all; and the house itself—a large foursquare wooden structure of two stories with a steep hipped roof, large windows, and a porch wrapping around three sides, the whole of it painted a pure, shimmering white. A tall picket fence of the same color surrounded the house, in front of which two sturdy oaks—by far the largest we had seen since leaving Moorhead—arose in lonely arboreal splendor. It struck me as odd to see so large and stately a house in the midst of the prairie emptiness, but then I remembered Holmes's calculations as to the farm's annual income.

"Well, Mr. Rafferty, let us go meet the lady of the house," said Holmes.

Rafferty gave the reins a shake and we moved beneath the arch and down the long driveway. I became conscious now of the vast silence in which we found ourselves, for other than the clip-clop of our horses, the day was soundless. I heard no wind, no chattering birds, no human voices. As we neared the house, I noticed that the shades were drawn on every window, as though its occupants wanted no part of the limitless daylight beyond the glass.

"I don't like the look of this," said Rafferty, bringing our wagon to a halt well back from the house.

"Nor do I," said Holmes, whose voracious eyes consumed every inch of the house and its surroundings, looking for some evidence of life or movement. But nothing except dead calm and dead silence prevailed.

"Now what?" Rafferty asked.

"I see no choice but to knock on the door," said Holmes.

"All right, we'll watch out for you," said Rafferty, drawing a long revolver from beneath his coat and spinning the cylinder. I took out my revolver as well, though I did not know just what I was supposed to be guarding myself against.

Holmes jumped down from the wagon, walked straight toward the front porch and then up the two steps to the door. There was a large brass knocker on the door and Holmes struck it repeatedly.

The noise was almost deafening amid so much silence, but no one answered the door. Holmes waited a moment, then rapped on the door with his knuckles. This, too, failed to produce any response. As a last resort, he tried turning the knob, but the door was tightly locked.

Undeterred, Holmes walked along the porch toward the back of the house. Rafferty prodded our team and we swung the wagon around to keep Holmes in view. At the back of the house, Holmes found another door, as well as more windows holding their secrets behind drawn shades. Holmes knocked repeatedly on the door, but again with no result. This door, he discovered, was also locked. Finally, Holmes shouted at the top of his lungs: "Is anyone home?" Silence greeted this effort as well.

"Maybe the lady's already fled the jurisdiction, just as you predicted," Rafferty suggested.

"I doubt it," said Holmes, who stared down at the door lock. He said: "It would be an easy matter, Mr. Rafferty, to pick this lock."

"I'm sure it would," said the Irishman. "And while you're at it, I could find a rock and toss it through one of the windows."

Holmes gave Rafferty a sharp look and said: "What did you mean by that remark, Mr. Rafferty?"

"All I'm sayin' is that it's a little premature for breakin' and enterin', don't you think, Mr. Holmes? Maybe the lady is in one of those big barns over yonder. Or maybe she went off to town to have tea. I think we should do a little more nosin' around before we burglarize her house. It's a big farm and there's lots of places she could be."

"I agree," I told Holmes.

"Very well, I see I have been outvoted," said Holmes in a tone of voice which indicated that he was far from enamored of our democratic experiment. "By all means, Mr. Rafferty, let us do more 'nosing around,' as you so elegantly put it."

Rafferty rolled his merry blue eyes, as if to say what could we expect from such a difficult and opinionated man, and then set the team in motion after Holmes had climbed up to join us.

We went first to the closest barn, which was obviously intended for livestock. Rafferty kept his pistol at the ready as we slid open the main door and went inside. But we found no draft horses, cattle, or animals of any kind in the stalls lining both sides of the structure. Nor did we find Mrs. Comstock, Moony Wahlgren, or anyone else, despite a thorough search.

"When is wheat usually planted here?" Holmes asked as we emerged from the barn.

"Sometime in May," Rafferty said. "Strange, isn't it, that nobody's around. You'd think Mrs. Comstock would have folks gearin' up for plantin' time."

"You would," said Holmes. "Let us look at the other barns."

Again, however, we were to find nothing. There was no one in the barns, no one in the machine shed or other outbuildings, no one visible anywhere across the expanse of Fairview Farms.

We got back up onto our wagon and drove back to the house, where Holmes tried for a second time to rouse someone. But once again, he met with no success.

"We must talk," he told us as he climbed back up into the wagon.

"All right, but not here," said Rafferty, who had eyed the house's many shaded windows nervously all the while that Holmes was knocking at the door. "I don't like sittin' in front of this house not knowin' if there's somebody in there who's got a rifle trained on us. Let's go out around the other side of the shelter belt. We can talk there."

As I watched our backs, Rafferty expertly wheeled the team around and set off at a fast pace around the thick clump of trees on the northwest side of the house. Once we had found a spot he considered safe, we got down from the wagon and debated what to do next.

Holmes, I knew, had wanted to talk with Mrs. Comstock before going to the elevator, for he believed he could cause her to lose her composure, as she had during our last interview with her in Alexandria. And once that happened, Holmes felt, she might inadvertently give away useful information. Rafferty, on the other hand, was less interested in what the lady might have to say, since he did not share Holmes's conviction that Mrs. Comstock must be the criminal mastermind at the heart of the rune stone affair.

It thus came as no surprise that Rafferty pushed to go out to the grain elevator at once.

"The lady is not here, and we do not know when, if ever, she will be here," he told Holmes. "But we do know that someone has spirited away Moony Wahlgren and that we alone have a chance to save her. We also know that the stone itself may be in that elevator. There is no reason to delay, as far as I can see."

Holmes was silent for a moment and then said: "I believe, Mr. Rafferty, that you mentioned there is also a large bunkhouse on this farm."

"Yes," he said, pointing off to the west. "It's that long building over there, maybe half a mile."

"I should like to see it," said Holmes. "Then, Mr. Rafferty, you shall have your wish."

"Why not," said Rafferty with a shrug. "But I doubt you'll find anything at the bunkhouse. It's only used during threshin' season, when big crews are brought in to harvest the wheat."

"I know," said Holmes. "You will just have to humor me, Mr. Rafferty."

The bunkhouse, I saw as we drew near, resembled nothing so much as a military barracks. It was a long wooden building, one story in height, with rows of windows on one side, all built in the plainest and, presumably, cheapest manner possible. As he had done at the house, Rafferty pulled up well in front of the building, giving us time to look it over before coming too close.

"Looks empty, all right," Rafferty said, "but you never know. I'd be happy to take a look inside, Mr. Holmes."

"No, that is my responsibility," said Holmes. "I am the one who wanted to see it, so I must be the one who goes in."

"Then take this," said Rafferty, offering Holmes the pocket rifle. "Just in case."

"No thank you," said Holmes. "I see no need of it."

"I hope you're right," Rafferty replied as he moved the team forward to within ten yards of the bunkhouse. Holmes stepped down from the wagon at once and walked briskly toward a door at one end of the structure. We watched as he tried the door, pushed it open with little effort, and went inside.

We waited what seemed to be a very long minute, though I am sure it was less than that, without hearing anything from Holmes.

"I must go in," I told Rafferty, feeling a sudden moment of anxiety, for in truth the situation had begun to wear on my nerves. Perhaps it was the emptiness of the setting, or the nerve-wracking silence, or the sensation that we had nowhere to hide, but I felt as helpless as a patient prepared for surgery, strapped to a gurney and waiting for the scalpel to do its cutting work. I knew that I had to do something, anything, to break the tension, and so I jumped off the seat and followed Holmes.

"Be careful," said Rafferty, who got down and stood behind the wagon, watching intently for any signs of an ambush.

"I'm coming in," I said loudly as I started to open the door, only to feel my hand yanked from the knob. I stumbled forward and ran directly into Holmes, nearly knocking him off his feet.

"Really, Watson, you must be more careful," he said, and it was only then that I noticed the small hat in his hand. The hat was quite plain, with a wide brim and a simple bow attached to the front. It was also pink.

"My God, is that—" I began.

"Yes," said Holmes gravely. "It is undoubtedly Moony's hat. She was here last night, I am sure of it."

I called Rafferty over, and he soon joined us inside the bunkhouse, which consisted of one large room, with beds arranged along either side of a wide aisle. There was no linen, but there was a mattress on one bed at the far end of the room. Holmes told us he had found the hat beneath this bed.

Rafferty said: "Funny that her hat would be left behind, don't you think?"

"Perhaps she simply forgot it," I offered.

"In my experience with the female of the species, they do not forget their hats," said Rafferty.

"I have had the same experience," said Holmes. "The hat was left for us to find, unless I am mistaken."

"I'm likin' this business less by the minute," Rafferty said. "We are bein' led like sheep to the slaughter."

Holmes gave a solemn nod and said: "So it would appear, Mr. Rafferty. But as you yourself have said, we have no choice but to go forward."

Chapter Twenty-one

A s Rafferty swung the team around toward the elevator, which was a good distance away, I noticed that the wind had begun to pick up. The sky was still stretched like a taut gray tent as far as the eye could see, but here and there low black clouds scudded past, heading due south, as were we. It was also getting chillier, and I buttoned up my coat against the stiffening breeze.

"Mark my words," said Rafferty. "There'll be snow by nightfall."

We proceeded by due reckoning toward the stark, towering form of the elevator, much as sailors might navigate with the aid of a lighthouse. After making several jogs on the checkerboard of roads which divided the farm into mile-square parcels, we at last found ourselves near the ruined elevator, where we hoped to find the mysterious rune stone which had occupied our every thought and action for the past week.

"Stop here, if you would, Mr. Rafferty," said Holmes as we pulled to within several hundred yards of the structure.

"Do you see something, Mr. Holmes?"

"No, but I wish to be very careful," said Holmes, who removed a pair of binoculars he had brought along and trained them on the elevator.

"All right,'" he finally said. "You may proceed, Mr. Rafferty."

As we drew ever closer to the elevator, I was struck by its singular appearance. In its dilapidated state, the structure—which I judged to be sixty to seventy feet high—achieved a most strange and picturesque effect. It was a building without windows, ornament, or any architectural pretension, a giant container for the great valley's wealth of golden grain. A pair of railroad tracks ran alongside it, beneath a swinging conveyer which was obviously designed to pour stored grain into hopper cars.

Although constructed of wood, the elevator was covered by thin sheets of tin (a precaution against fire, Rafferty informed us). Large sections of this metallic skin had been peeled away by the storm, however, and flapped noisily in the wind. While the bottom of the elevator appeared to be in reasonably good condition, the upper portion told a different story, presenting a jagged profile of twisted metal and splintered wood. At the very top of the structure was its most curious feature of all—a series of circling metal tubes which resembled nothing so much as the legs of some monstrous insect.

"Well, we are definitely in the right place," said Holmes, pointing to a large red and white sign near the top of the elevator which read: FAIRVIEW FARMS, F. E. COMSTOCK, PROP.

At Holmes's insistence, we made a complete circle around the elevator, all the while poised for action, until we at last came to a stop near one of the two large doors at its base.

"Could both the girl and the rune stone be in there?" I asked as I gazed anxiously at the door.

"I do not know," Holmes admitted. "There is an excellent chance we will find the stone, but as for Moony . . . well, let us hope for the best."

"Must have been quite a storm, for it took the headhouse right off," Rafferty remarked as we all climbed out of the wagon. He had drawn his pistol once again and, like Holmes, he kept his eyes moving constantly, alert for the smallest sign of movement.

"What is the headhouse?" I asked.

"The topmost part of the elevator," Rafferty explained. "When a farmer comes in with his load of grain, it's dropped into a big pit beneath the floor, then it's scooped up by buckets mounted on a conveyer and lifted to the headhouse. Up there is a device for distributin' the grain to whichever bin it's supposed to be stored in. Those legs you see up there are what's left of the distributor. It looks like this elevator has eight or nine bins. That's about the usual size."

"Mr. Rafferty, you have again surprised me with your knowledge," said Holmes, who busied himself checking the wick of one of our lanterns. "Am I to take it you have some experience in the grain business?"

"Not much," Rafferty responded. "But in my wayward youth I did spend a summer once helpin' to build a grain elevator down in Iowa. 'Twas hard work, especially for a man such as myself who doesn't care much for heights."

"Well, we shall try to keep you on the ground," said Holmes, who set the lantern down while he made a final check of the map purporting to show the stone's location. Satisfied that all was in order, Holmes restored the map to his shirt pocket and lit the lantern.

"Now then, let us have a look inside," he said. "According to the map, the stone—presumably denoted by the letter 'X'—can be found at 'b number four, b-n-t-h c-h.' I translate that to mean 'bin number four, beneath chute.' Mr. Rafferty agrees with my interpretation, I believe."

"I do," Rafferty said.

Holmes then turned toward the elevator door, but was stopped by Rafferty, who put a hand on his shoulder.

"Aren't you forgettin' somethin', Mr. Holmes?"

"And what would that be?"

"This," said Rafferty, producing Mr. Stevens from somewhere inside his heavy wool coat. "You promised to bring it along."

"So I did," said Holmes, taking the pistol but looking none too happy about being burdened with such a large piece of weaponry. "Then I will have to ask you to carry the lantern, Mr. Rafferty."

"Be happy to," he said.

We found that both doors to the elevator were padlocked, no

doubt to keep out curious youngsters, since there was said to be nothing of value inside. One of the locks, however, was attached to a long, loose hinge which left a good deal of space between the door and its jamb. It was through this door that we decided to enter. Holmes studied the hinge and lock with great interest while Rafferty went back to the wagon, retrieved a crowbar, and easily pried off the hinge.

Exercising extreme caution, we stepped inside, startling a flock of blackbirds which objected vociferously to our presence before flying en masse toward the center of the structure and then disappearing out some unknown opening. The first sensation I had upon entering the elevator was a powerful odor—the sickening smell of thousands of bushels of spoiled grain. I also was struck by the large amount of dust which swirled through the air like thick, grainy mist.

"Whew!" said Rafferty. "The stink in here alone could kill a man."

As my eyes adjusted to the dim, shadowy light, I began to make out the details of the elevator. We were in a long, low room, a sort of tunnel obviously designed as a pass-through for wagons. The floor was dirt, the walls solid wood. Overhead, I noticed, were several large funnels, which I presumed were used to empty stored grain from the bins above. I found the elevator's walls to be especially curious, for they were made of long planks laid up horizontally somewhat in the fashion of an American log cabin.

" 'Tis known as cribbed construction," said Rafferty, noting my puzzlement.

"It seems an awful waste of wood," I noted.

"Not really," said Rafferty. "Grain is tricky to store, Doctor, because it's very heavy and flows like water when it's moved about. That is why these walls must be so thick, to withstand all that shiftin' weight. I remember back in the seventies there was an old elevator in St. Paul and it just burst open one day, like a tin can with a firecracker in it. The grain came tumblin' out and buried the shack some poor Swede had been foolish enough to build right next door. Luckily, he wasn't home at the time or he'd have been a goner."[1]

As we moved farther inside, the walls around us opened up until we found ourselves in a kind of central shaft, illuminated by a pool of light which poured down from a hole in the roof. The distributor legs were faintly visible at the top of this shaft, looking even more peculiar and menacing from this vantage point than they had from outside.

A series of rickety ladders climbed up one side of the shaft, which judging by the gross deposits on the floor was now occupied by a large community of birds. Next to the ladders I noted a roped conveyance which Rafferty informed me was a manlift. " 'Tis a nice convenience for fat men such as myself," he said.

"Ah, what do we have here?" Holmes said, tapping something with his feet.

" 'Tis the scale," said Rafferty, coming up next to Holmes and standing on a large wooden platform built into the floor. "Every elevator has one. Once his grain is weighed, the farmer gets a ticket tellin' him the exact amount he's storin' or sellin', whichever the case may be."

"So not all the grain stored here would have belonged to Fairview Farms?" I asked.

" 'Tis unlikely," Rafferty said. "Mr. Comstock probably bought grain from some of the smaller farmers in the area and hung on to it until he got a price he liked."

A violent gust of wind suddenly slammed into the elevator, and the entire structure shook and trembled.

"Lord," said Rafferty, "we had best be about our business here before this whole thing falls down on us. Trouble is, there's lots of places in here where that poor girl could be hidden away. Maybe we should look for the stone first."

"I agree," said Holmes. "What we need to do is find bin number four."

Overlooking the scale through a plate-glass window was a small room which Rafferty said must be the office. He went inside, shined his light around old piles of paperwork scattered around a battered rolltop desk, then stopped by the door, near which a sheet of paper was affixed to the wall.

"Ah, here's what we're lookin' for," he said.

"What have you found?" I asked.

" 'Tis the bin plan," said Rafferty, showing us the piece of paper, which to my surprise looked as fresh and white as if it had been posted only a day before.

The plan consisted of three rows of adjoining squares, arranged like a game of noughts and crosses, but with the outer squares numbered from one to eight. The central square, which bore no number, was marked along one side with the notation "OFF."

"Let's see now," said Rafferty, studying the plan. "Bin number four must be over there."

He then pointed toward the far end of the pass-through, opposite from the door we had entered. The light from the central shaft did not penetrate to this end of the elevator, which appeared pitch black.

"Maybe I'll just go have a look," said Rafferty, keeping the lantern in his left hand while in his right he brandished his pistol. As he walked off into the darkness, his lantern created eerie, wavering patterns of light and shadow. Perhaps it was the darkness or the pounding wind outside or the nauseating aroma of the rotting grain, but I now began to experience a palpable sense of dread, a feeling that we had stumbled out of the world of living men and into some dense, unknowable place from which we might never escape.

Holmes, who had been looking at the manlift, now came over to the office, where I showed him the bin plan. At almost the same instant I heard Rafferty shout: "My God, she's here! I've found her!"

Whatever joy I felt upon hearing this news was immediately dashed, for I saw a look of profound alarm flash across Holmes's face. "Wait, Mr. Rafferty, wait!" he yelled, rushing toward our friend.

Then I heard Rafferty say: "I've got you free, child, don't worry. You'll be all right."

I turned to follow Holmes, but just as I saw him enter the circle of light cast by Rafferty's lantern, there was a loud noise, a sudden sharp crack as of some huge branch being snapped in two. A moment later, the world came tumbling down.

❖   ❖   ❖

To this day, I can still vividly recall the sound. It was not a crash or a bang or a thud but more like a great rumbling whoosh, as though the very air had been sucked down from the heavens. Then came the sensation of some heavy liquid flowing past my feet, followed by billowing clouds of dust which left me blinded and choking for air. For a time I could make out nothing, but as the dust began to settle, I saw a gigantic pile of grain in the spot where Holmes and Rafferty had been standing only moments before. The grain extended nearly all the way up to the ceiling of the pass-through and for perhaps twenty feet in my direction.

It quickly became apparent to me what had happened. The bottom of the bin overhead must have suddenly collapsed (accounting for the loud crack I heard), sending down an avalanche of grain from within. Because I had been well back from Holmes and Rafferty, this avalanche had only brushed up against me. Light, presumably from a hole in the bin's roof, cast a faint glow over the heaped-up grain. This new source of light also revealed, poking out from the base of the pile, a section of the large funnel by which the bin would normally have been emptied. What the light did not reveal was any sign of either Holmes or Rafferty, and my heart began to sink.

"Holmes! Rafferty! Are you all right?" I shouted. There was no answer.

I ran into the pile and began trying to scoop away grain with my hands—a foolish and unproductive gesture, I soon realized. I called out the names a second time. Again, I received no answer. Instead, I received the shock of my life.

"You won't find them," said a voice behind me, and I turned around to see a man coming toward me, a pistol in his hand. "You won't find the stone, either."

Failing to understand the situation at first, I said: "You must help me. They will suffocate if we do not get them out."

"They're already dead," said the man, eyeing me coldly as he leveled his pistol. "And you'll soon be joining them, Dr. Watson."

I now experienced that terrible instant of recognition and betrayal—

"My God, it was you!"—which must come to so many victims just before the knife does its slashing work or the bullet explodes from the barrel or the poison induces its final agonized convulsion.

"You look surprised, Doctor," said the man as he stepped forward and put his gun to my head while he took the Colt from my jacket pocket. Then he stepped back, hurled my revolver into the pile of grain, and added: "But then I suspect that not even the great Sherlock Holmes himself had a clue, did he?"

"Do not flatter yourself," I said. "Holmes knows far more than you think. You will not escape."

"Really," he said insolently. "And who is to stop me? You? I doubt it. Holmes? Or your friend Rafferty? They're dead, Doctor, as you, too, will be soon enough. An old grain elevator like this is a dangerous place. The bin, damaged by the storm, suddenly gave way, quite by accident. That will be the verdict of the coroner's jury, I'm sure."

I sensed that he enjoyed this taunting, and I determined to keep him talking in hopes of buying as much time as I could.

"So you rigged the bin, I take it. That must have been quite a lot of work."

"It was, but I had help. A board cut here, another loosened there, a few ropes and weights in the right places, and we were ready. All we needed then was something to lure you here. The map we planted in that fool Larson's pocket did the trick, along with some live bait, of course."

"You mean Moony Wahlgren?"

"That's right. I've got nothing against the girl, but those pictures would have ruined everything. We couldn't let that happen. And it all would have worked just perfectly today if you hadn't been a bit slow afoot, Doctor. Perhaps I should have waited another second before pulling the ropes. But it hardly matters. Once I saw you were still alive, I came down the manlift, knowing you would be occupied trying to save your friends. You are nothing if not predictable, Dr. Watson."

"I would rather die trying to save my friends than murder in cold blood, as you have done," I said. "Tell me this. How much money do you stand to make from murdering so many people? Can whatever it is really be worth all of the blood you have shed?"

He laughed in a cold, unpleasant way and said: "You swells are all alike, aren't you? You're above worrying about money because you've always had it. Well, I haven't. There is twenty thousand dollars, perhaps more, Doctor, to be made from the stone, and I intend to put it in my pocket and leave this godforsaken wasteland. If you and Holmes and that damned Irishman hadn't stuck your noses in this business, then far less blood would have been shed, I assure you. But there is no going back now—not for me and not for you."

"I suppose not. But do you really think your lover, Mrs. Comstock, will be content to share the money? If you believe that, then you are the biggest fool of all."

"Ah, what a clever strategy," the man said, his eyes boring in on me, his voice dripping with sarcasm. "Create doubt in my mind, is that it? Well, Doctor, it won't work. Besides, don't you know it's impolite for a gentleman to talk about a lady?"

"I do not consider you a gentleman," I said.

"Oh dear," the man said, feigning insult. "Well, I guess I will somehow have to live with your distaste for my character. You, on the other hand, will not be living at all. But we have talked long enough, Doctor. There is work to be done. Now, I would like you to turn around, slowly, with your hands in the air."

"I will not," I said, knowing that to do so would mean instant death. I also realized that the man did not want to shoot me, since my death could hardly be explained away as an accident if there was a bullet in my back.

"You're a cleverer man than I thought, Doctor. You see my problem, don't you. But I am going to kill you, one way or the other. Now, if you turn around, I promise you that death will come quickly. If you don't, then I promise you a much more prolonged and painful end. Which will it be?"

Like most men, I have thought at times about what my last moments on earth would be like. I understood now that I had reached this point, and was surprised by how at ease I felt. That may seem an odd thing to say, for who — except perhaps for the occasional saint — does not gaze with trepidation upon the final darkness? Yet I believed that I had led a good and useful, if far from perfect, life. I also knew that I had enjoyed the supreme privilege of spending many years as a friend and companion of Sherlock Holmes. What man could have asked for a better fortune than that? And though my acquaintance with Shadwell Rafferty had been of much briefer duration, I felt privileged as well to have known him. My only regret was for Moony Wahlgren, who deserved a better and longer life than she had been given.

Staring now into the deadly eyes of the man who would shortly send me to my grave, I decided that I would die like a soldier, as I once had been, with my face to the enemy.

"I will not turn around," I said. "You will have to kill me as I stand."

"Suit yourself," said the man, cocking his pistol and aiming, I could see, for one of my legs. He had not lied about wishing to make me suffer.

I saw no choice now but to make a desperate attempt at escape, even though I knew it would almost certainly be futile. As the man cocked his pistol, I dove to my right, fully expecting to feel a bullet tearing through my flesh before I hit the floor. Instead, I heard from somewhere behind me the roar of a large-caliber weapon being fired. Almost at that same instant I saw come over the face of my tormentor a look of bafflement and disbelief as part of his neck tore away and blood squirted like a fountain from his carotid artery. He took one step forward, his eyes taking on the glaze of death, before his pistol fell from his hand and he toppled to the floor.

I turned around, imagining that Holmes or Rafferty must have somehow come to my rescue. But the only person I saw was Moony Wahlgren, the skeletal stock of Rafferty's pocket rifle resting against her shoulder as smoke curled from the gun's barrel.

She stared at the figure crumpled on the ground in an ever-widening pool of blood, carefully set down the gun, and said: "Bad man."

❀ ❀ ❀

I got up and went over to her at once. She had a large welt on one cheek but otherwise did not appear to be injured in any way. I gave her a warm embrace and said:

"My God, Moony, you have saved my life!"

"Bad man," she repeated. "He hurt me."

I now thought of Holmes and Rafferty. If Moony was alive, I reasoned, then perhaps they were, too. "Have you seen the men who were with me?" I asked.

"Back here," she said. "Come."

"Are they alive?"

"Come," she said again.

I followed her around the edge of the grain pile along one side of the pass-through. The grain was perhaps waist-high where it had come to rest up against the side wall, and getting through it was like trying to wade in thick mud. The light from above grew fainter as we slowly worked our way along the edge of the pile. My legs began to ache as I struggled through the damp, heavy grain, and I realized for the first time that there could be no possibility of survival for anyone trapped beneath it. Suffocation, from the pressing weight of the grain and from the lack of oxygen, would have occurred very quickly. I could only hope that Holmes and Rafferty had not met such an awful fate.

And then I saw them—two dark, immobile shapes tumbled together up against the side wall of the pass-through, not far from the elevator's rear door. I rushed forward, praying that I would find them alive. Rafferty was lying on his right side, his legs and lower torso buried in grain, his head pushed up against the wall. Next to Rafferty lay Holmes, his head resting up against Rafferty's right arm, which had been flung out as though in a protective gesture.

To my immense relief and joy, I was able to determine immediately that both men, while unconscious, were breathing. I could only assume that they had been knocked out when the weight of the cascading grain tossed them against the wall, much as if they had been struck by an enormous wave. It was also apparent that had there been only a little more grain in the bin, both men would have been completely buried and almost certainly would have suffocated before I reached them. The light was so poor that I could not tell whether either man had sustained broken bones or other serious injuries, and so I decided to force open the rear door to admit more daylight. Although the door was padlocked on the outside, it gave way easily enough after I put my shoulder to it.

The noise from my assault on the door, along with the sudden influx of light as it came open, was enough to stir Holmes. Jerking his head away from Rafferty's arm, he gave out a low moan and then began to blink his eyes.

"Holmes," I said, shaking him by the shoulders. "Wake up! Wake up!"

After several more blinks, he slowly opened his eyes, looked up at me, and said: "My dear Watson, is that you?"

"Yes. Are you all right, Holmes?"

"I think so," he said in a halting voice as he rubbed a bump on the top of his head, where he presumably had crashed into the wall. "What has happened?"

"I will explain later," I promised. "Why don't you rest for a minute, Holmes, while I attend to Mr. Rafferty. I fear he is badly hurt."

I bent over Rafferty and saw that he had a large gash on his forehead, a pair of black eyes, and what appeared to be a broken nose. However, I could detect no other obvious injuries.

"Mr. Rafferty, can you hear me?" I said, shaking him as I had Holmes.

There was no response.

In a louder voice, I said: "Mr. Rafferty, wake up! Please, talk to me."

For the next five minutes, I continued my efforts to awaken Rafferty, but as time went on I began to fear that he had suffered injuries to his internal organs which might put his very life in jeopardy.

I was therefore astonished when, after I had turned away for a moment to check on Holmes, Rafferty suddenly opened his blue eyes, coughed up several bits of grain, spat out a bloody front tooth, gave a slight shake to his head as though trying to clear his brain, stared into my anxious face, and said; "I'm thinkin' you're not St. Peter, and that's a fact!"

Moony, who had been anxiously watching my attempts at resuscitation, gave Rafferty a radiant smile. "The funny man is awake," she said. "I like the funny man."

"As do I," said Sherlock Holmes, slowly getting to his feet. "I thought we had lost you, Mr. Rafferty. But as you have told us many times, you are a hard man to kill."

" 'Tis true," Rafferty replied, sitting up against the wall. "But I don't mind tellin' you that my poor head feels like I just crashed head-on into a freight train."

"Well, I think you will survive, Mr. Rafferty," I said, looking into his eyes and then testing his reflexes. "But all of us have been very lucky this day."

Once Holmes and Rafferty had recovered their usual alertness, I told them everything which had happened since the collapse of the bin. I gave as complete an account as I could of my conversation with the man who had tried to kill us. Both Holmes and Rafferty expressed surprise — but not astonishment — when I gave them the villain's name.

"So I gather the two of you had some idea that he might be involved in this business," I said. "I must confess that I was caught completely unawares."

"He was one of several suspects," Holmes said. "But I would be dishonest if I told you, Watson, that he was my chief suspect."

"I was in the same position," Rafferty acknowledged. "There was somethin' suspicious, but I had no real evidence linkin' him to these crimes."

What did astonish Holmes and Rafferty, however, was the manner in which Moony had saved my life, and, of course, theirs as well.

"I always knew you were an extraordinary girl, Moony," said Holmes, "but today you have outdone yourself. And just wait until Mr. Kensington hears what you have done. He will be very proud of you, Moony, very proud."

"I would like some new paints," she said. "That would be nice."

"And you shall get them," said Holmes. "The best money can buy."

Holmes now explained how he, Rafferty, and the girl had come to survive the trap so carefully laid for us.

"It was only when I saw how fresh and clean the bin plan was that I knew at once something must be amiss," Holmes said. "The plan should have been old and yellowed, like all the other paperwork in the office."

" 'Twas incredibly stupid of me," Rafferty readily admitted as he used a handkerchief to daub at a trickle of blood still coming from his now misshapen nose. "I should have seen right then and there that we were bein' set up like a mark in a con game. But I was anxious to get my hands on that stone. Then when I found Moony here lyin' in the darkness, all bound and gagged, well, I couldn't stop myself. I got out my pocket knife and freed her lickety-split. The last thing I remember after that is seein' Mr. Holmes runnin' at me like a madman."

"Did you somehow realize that the bin overhead had been rigged to collapse?" I asked Holmes.

"No, but I did know that Mr. Rafferty and Moony were in imminent danger because someone had gone to great trouble to bring them to a very particular place in this elevator. As I ran toward them, I heard the cracking sound as the bin started to collapse, and so I simply tried to push them out of harm's way. From that point on, I remember no more than Mr. Rafferty."

Rafferty turned to Moony and said: "I've got a question for you, child. Where'd you find my pocket rifle?"

"There," she said, pointing toward a spot on the floor just inside the door. "You lost it."

"I guess you could say I did," Rafferty agreed. "It must have been knocked right from your hands, Mr. Holmes. Now, tell me, Moony, where'd you learn to shoot such a big gun?"

"Little Olaf," she said, referring, I supposed, to her brother. "He showed me. Bang, bang. I shot the bad man."

"Yes you did, child," said Rafferty with a grin, "and we're very all happy about that."

Not wishing to fight our way back through the grain pile, we now walked around outside to the main door, through which we had first entered the elevator, and then back to the place where the man who had nearly killed us all lay dead in his own pooling blood.

"How I wish I could talk to him!" Holmes said, staring down at the corpse. "Without his testimony, I fear that the person responsible for all of this will never be brought to justice."

"You must still believe, then, that Mrs. Comstock put him up to his crimes," I said.

"It can be no one else," said Holmes.

"Well, one thing's certain," said Rafferty, bending down to inspect the fatal wound. "Sheriff Boehm won't be runnin' for reelection."

Chapter Twenty-two

A s we stared down at the sheriff's lifeless body, Holmes said: "We must leave at once."

"Why do you say that?" I asked. "Shouldn't we notify the proper authorities of what has happened?"

Rafferty gave me a pat on the shoulder and said: "Doctor, you're far too honest a man for the detectin' business. Mr. Holmes is right. We're in a nasty bind, and the longer we stay around here, the more trouble we're likely to be in. Don't you see the problem? There's a dead lawman lyin' at our feet, with a bullet through his neck. Now, if we tell the authorities we're the ones who killed Sheriff Boehm, they won't be in a mood to shake our hands and pin medals on our chests. But they will toss us in the hoosegow and then take their sweet time tryin' to sort out what happened. No, all things considered, 'twould be wise to head back to Moorhead and keep our heads low. And if anybody asks about Moony, we could always say we found her somewhere in town."

"I agree," said Holmes. "We passed no other wagons on our way here, nor did we see anyone. The farm itself appeared to be deserted.

If questioned, we need only report that we went out for a drive in the country. There will be no evidence to the contrary."

"But what about Mrs. Comstock?" I said. "What do you intend to do about her?"

"I intend to find the lady," said Holmes. "I also intend to find the rune stone. The sheriff's remarks to you, Watson, made it quite clear that the stone was never hidden in this elevator. The map was merely a ruse to lure us into a trap."

"But where do you think the stone is?"

"That is a question we shall have to ask Mrs. Comstock," said Holmes. "Now, come along. There is no point in staying here any longer."

On our way back to Moorhead, Rafferty—who clearly had won Moony's affection—did his best to find out more about the circumstances of her disappearance. He sat with her in the back of the wagon while Holmes, who I must admit was no match for Rafferty as a driver, guided the team. Despite the girl's elusive and unpredictable way of responding to questions, Rafferty learned, among other things, that Moony had left Kensington's house of her own accord after being told her brother wished to meet her in Moorhead. Holmes, of course, had suspected as much, given the lack of any evidence of a break-in at the house.

Rafferty now asked the girl: "Who told you about your brother?"

"The gold-and-blue boy. He is very pretty."

"Ah, I see. Did he tell you his name, Moony?"

"Little Olaf was in Moorhead. That is what he said. I went to see him."

"Of course. So the gold-and-blue boy must have been a friend of Little Olaf's?"

"Yes. I like Little Olaf, but he left. Too bad."

Rafferty now had an inspiration. He said: "I bet those fringes on the gold-and-blue boy's jacket are also very pretty."

The girl nodded and said. "They blow in the wind. I like them."

There could be no doubt now that Billy Swift—he of the long

blond hair and blue eyes and fringed buckskin jacket—had been the gold-and-blue boy who lured Moony to Moorhead. He must also have been the person who had given her money for her photographs and train ticket.

Even by means of the most careful questioning, however, Rafferty was not able to establish exactly how Moony had been spirited away to the grain elevator or when Sheriff Boehm had first entered the picture. Nor could he learn how Boehm and Swift had found out about the photographs.

She did, however, tell us that the sheriff, in her words, "took the faces from the box."

"Ah, so he stole your photographs," said Rafferty. "That wasn't very nice."

"Rochester gave them to me," she said. "The bad man took them."

"Did he take all of them, Moony?"

"I have a secret," the girl suddenly announced.

"I knew you would, Moony. You have more good secrets than anyone I know. Will you tell me?"

"Maybe. I like secrets."

"I know you do. I like secrets, too. I have one for you right now. Can I whisper it into your ear?"

"Yes," she said. "I like secrets. Don't tickle my ear."

As he had done once before, Rafferty now leaned over and whispered something into Moony's ear, after which she broke out into an infectious giggle.

"You are funny," she said.

"I do my best," said Rafferty. "Can I tell you another secret, or do you have one for me? A really good secret?"

"Yes," the girl said, still giggling as she whispered into Rafferty's ear.

"That is a wonderful secret," Rafferty said after the girl drew away from him.

Not long after this, she seemed to lose all interest in further conversation, for something in the drab gray sky caught her attention, and she stared up at the clouds all the way back to Moorhead.

As Rafferty had predicted, a few snowflakes were swirling

through the air when we reached the Red River Inn. Kensington was waiting for us in the lobby, and there followed a tearful reunion with Moony. It was only later, after Kensington had gone up to get Moony settled in a room, that Rafferty told us what she had whispered to him.

"She told me she 'hid one,' " he said. "I may be wrong, but I'm guessin' she's tellin' us that Sheriff Boehm didn't destroy all of her photographs. If we can find the one she somehow squirreled away, we just might see who carved the stone after all."

After washing up and changing into fresh clothes, Holmes and I went to the railroad depot. Meanwhile, Rafferty—whose broken nose I had bandaged as best I could—decided to "jaw a bit with the local coppers," as he put it. He wanted to see if anyone had spotted Nels Fogelblad, Olaf Wahlgren's neighbor, who supposedly had come to Moorhead.

"Do you think Mr. Fogelblad is somehow connected with the trap set for us at the elevator?" I asked Holmes as we walked along Moorhead's main street. The snow had begun to fall more heavily now, in moist clumps which formed a heavy white mantle coating the ground.

"I am not certain why Mr. Fogelblad came to Moorhead," Holmes admitted. "It is possible, however, that he was lured here, as were we, in which case he may already be dead as we speak."

At the depot, Holmes asked if he had received any telegrams and was pleased to discover a message from Joseph Pyle, our able assistant in St. Paul. Holmes quickly read the message, pronounced a loud "I knew it!" to no one in particular, and passed the telegram on to me. I could see at once why the message had excited Holmes, for it concerned the outcome of Pyle's inquiries into whether any SG&L carriage lanterns had been shipped to the Alexandria area in recent years. By dint of an exhaustive check of the records of the FOK wholesaling firm in St. Paul, Pyle had discovered three such shipments—one of which went to a man whose name we knew very well.

"We are close now," Holmes said, folding the telegram and putting it into his coat pocket. "The last pieces are coming into place."

"Do you think he took the rune stone?" I asked, referring to the man who had been identified in the telegram.

"I think it very likely," said Holmes. "With any luck, we shall know soon enough."

Upon our return to the hotel, we waited for Rafferty in the lobby. I was anxious to eat lunch—it was now early afternoon—but Holmes would not hear of it.

"How can you even think of eating at a time like this?" he asked rather sharply.

"I have found, Holmes, that when I am hungry, I think of eating. It is, I believe, a very normal response, one which you would understand, Holmes, if you were only a normal person."

Holmes, who had just lit his pipe, arched an eyebrow and said: "Normality is overrated, Watson. The normal man spends far too much time filling his belly and not enough time thinking about the more important matters of life."

"If you ever became hungry, Holmes," I retorted, "you would understand that eating is a very important matter indeed."

Fortunately, this ridiculous little discussion soon came to an abrupt halt. Holmes, who was about to reply to my remarks, instead stiffened in his chair, his eyes locked on something behind me. I turned around to see Mrs. Mary Comstock, dressed in a long red coat, enter the hotel and walk toward the front desk. Before she could reach this destination, however, her eyes caught ours and she stopped as suddenly as if she had bumped into a wall of invisible glass. I caught a moment's hesitation in her gleaming violet eyes, but it was gone as quickly as it had entered, banished by the powerful will which controlled her every action.

"You!" she said, staring at Holmes as though he were a loathsome insect. "Is this absurd persecution never to end?"

Holmes stood up, went over to her, and said: "It will end today, madam, for your clever little scheme did not work, as you can see."

"I have no idea what you are talking about," she replied.

"We both know that is not true," said Holmes, taking her lightly by the arm.

"Let me go at once," she said through gritted teeth, "or I shall scream."

Holmes gazed into the lady's extraordinary eyes, twin sirens which must have sent many men hurtling up against seductive reefs, and said: "Very well, scream, madam, and we shall let the local police hear my story—and yours."

I now saw Rafferty come through the front door, his eyes opening in wonderment as he caught sight of the lady, who at this same instant removed her arm from Holmes's grasp and said: "What do you want?"

"I want," said Holmes, "to paint you a picture."

Mrs. Comstock sighed and said: "Very well. Since you seem obsessed by this matter, Mr. Holmes, it appears I have little choice."

The confrontation which followed was, I feel safe in stating, one of the most remarkable of Holmes's career. Holmes was very much like a thoroughbred who ran best when faced with the stiffest challenge, and in Mary Comstock he faced an opponent who was in every respect worthy of his supreme effort. Even Rafferty, who was a superb competitor himself, seemed content to sit back and watch the match, and indeed he told me much later that it was the most enjoyable contest he had witnessed in many years.

" 'Tis what I will always remember about this strange rune stone business," he remarked, "for if a man cannot take pleasure in seein' two fine minds locked in combat, then life is a pale and uninterestin' business indeed."

After we had all found seats in a quiet corner of the lobby, the lady removed her stylish fur hat, unbuttoned her coat, and stared at Holmes, a kind of dark amusement evident in the slight curl of her lips. I had a sense that she knew what lay ahead and that she gloried in the opportunity to take on the incomparable Sherlock Holmes.

"I have a picture I have been working on for the last week or so," Holmes began. "It is a most interesting yet disturbing portrait."

"Really?" said the lady. "I did not know you were an artist, Mr. Holmes."

"You might say I am an artist of ideas," he replied with a thin smile. "I draw them in my mind."

"How intriguing. Please, tell me about this picture of yours."

"It would be my honor, madam. The picture begins with a stone, a stone carved with runes telling of a voyage by Norsemen who centuries ago came halfway around the world to discover only death and misery. Now, as it so happens, this stone is a complete fake, as you are well aware. But it also happens that in Chicago there is a very rich man, a Swede by birth, who desperately wishes to believe in the stone. This man is willing to pay a fortune to whoever can deliver the stone to him."

"And who might this Swede be, Mr. Holmes?"

"His name is Karl Lund and he is reputed to be the richest Swede in America."

"I believe I have heard the name," Mrs. Comstock said. "I may even have met him. But then, I know so many men, it is hard to remember them all."

Holmes said: "I am sure you remember Mr. Lund, for he is the man you and your accomplices intended to defraud of twenty thousand dollars."

"You have an active imagination, Mr. Holmes," said the lady. "This all sounds like one of those lurid tales Dr. Watson is so good at writing for the popular magazines."

Although I bridled at this insult, I kept my tongue, knowing that Holmes did not wish to be interrupted. Rafferty, however, whispered to me: "The lady is an admirer of your prose, Doctor. You should be proud."

Holmes said to Mrs. Comstock: "What I have told you is no fiction, madam, for much real blood has been shed because of your ruthless pursuit of the stone. Now, let me reveal more of the picture I have in my mind. Its outlines begin, of course, with a poor farmer by the name of Olaf Wahlgren. His life is drudgery, and so one day he and at least one assistant decide to amuse themselves by playing a little joke on the world. They take a stone found in one of Mr.

Wahlgren's fields, inscribe it with a phony runic inscription, and then present it to the world as a genuine relic.

"At first, it is little more than a prank, something to laugh over around the stove on a cold winter's night. But then the unexpected occurs. A self-described runic expert named Magnus Larson appears on the scene. He is a man on a mission and, initially, he sees the rune stone as the opportunity of a lifetime to prove his theories about the Scandinavian exploration of America. So smitten by the stone is Mr. Larson that he even contacts the king of Sweden and offers to sell the stone to him. Mr. Larson then signs an agreement to buy the stone from Farmer Wahlgren for two hundred dollars."

Mrs. Comstock, stifling a yawn, said: "So far, I cannot say I find anything very remarkable about your picture, Mr. Holmes. I trust it will become more interesting before too long."

"It will, madam, it will," Holmes promised. "You see, at some point after Mr. Larson agrees to buy the stone, his plan begins to fall apart. First, he discovers new evidence which forces him to conclude beyond any doubt that the stone is spurious. We need not speculate on the nature of this evidence at the moment. What is important is that Mr. Larson is intelligent enough to realize that King Oskar's advisers, among them some of the finest runologists in the world, will inevitably come to the same conclusion. Are you following me thus far, Mrs. Comstock?"

"Perfectly," said the lady, looking serenely self-possessed, "though I would note once again that your picture, Mr. Holmes, is terribly slow to develop. I have always enjoyed an artist with a quick hand."

"Then I shall do my best to satisfy your wishes," Holmes replied. "Let us now consider Mr. Larson's situation. He has invested much time and energy in the rune stone, only to learn that it will yield him neither fame nor fortune in Sweden. Clever and unprincipled man that he is, he therefore decides on a bold new strategy: to wit, he will look for another buyer—one, I might add, without expert runologists at his disposal—who can be gulled into purchasing the stone for a large amount of money.

"Ah, but Mr. Larson soon encounters another unforeseen problem, which is that Olaf Wahlgren becomes suspicious of the deal he has been offered and begins to make it plain that he does not intend to honor the purchase agreement. And now, Mrs. Comstock, we have reached the point where my picture takes on an entirely new dimension, as it were."

"How intriguing," said Mrs. Comstock. "By all means, tell me about this marvelous new dimension."

"This new dimension centers on you, madam, for it is at this critical juncture that you come to Mr. Larson's rescue."

"Really? And just how did I do that?"

"It was quite simple. You, of course, had become acquainted with Mr. Larson because of your husband's interest in the stone. At the same time, you knew enough about Karl Lund to realize that he would be extremely interested in purchasing the stone. Perhaps you even visited Mr. Lund in Chicago and convinced him of the stone's authenticity. The result was that you were able to offer Mr. Larson a most attractive deal. He would continue to tout the stone in every way he could. I suspect you even had Mr. Larson send 'evidence' of the stone's authenticity to Mr. Lund in Chicago. Meanwhile, you would make arrangements to obtain the stone by whatever means necessary and then quietly sell it to Mr. Lund, who you knew would ask no questions about its provenance. I am certain Mr. Lund will confirm all of this when we talk to him."

Mrs. Comstock smiled and said: "Do you really think so, Mr. Holmes? I seem to recall hearing somewhere that Mr. Lund is an extremely private and secretive man. I wonder if he would wish to talk to you or the police about such fantastic and baseless allegations."

"We shall see about that," said Holmes. "But let me fill in more of the picture for you. Magnus Larson, it may be fairly said, was not your type of man. He was a blowhard and, even worse, a drunk. Therefore, in order to carry out your scheme, you needed a more reliable man, a man who could be counted on to act boldly and fearlessly. Sheriff Gustavus Boehm, I think, fit the bill. There is also the convenient fact that he was your lover, even though he was simultaneously blackmailing you in connection with your husband's death, which he knew to be a case of murder."

These last comments took me by complete surprise, and even

Rafferty, who had been uncharacteristically quiet thus far, cocked his head to one side as though in disbelief. Mrs. Comstock, however, remained secure behind the armor of her iron will.

"You have outdone yourself," she told Holmes. "You have not only constructed an elaborate fable about my supposed involvement in the rune stone affair, but you have also assigned me a lover who is at the same time my blackmailer. It is all quite ridiculous. Besides, as you well know, Mr. Holmes, my taste in men is highly discriminating."

The lady's use of the phrase "as you well know" struck me as a clear reference to the hour or so she and Holmes had spent alone together in Hinckley, and not for the first time did I wonder exactly what had gone on during their private meeting.[1] Be that as it may, Holmes now said:

"Your taste in men, Mrs. Comstock, is perhaps most discriminating in terms of their wealth. Frank Comstock must have been a grave disappointment to you in this regard, for he did not possess the fortune you had anticipated when you married him. Indeed, he was deeply in debt, a situation which no doubt led you to cut your losses, as it were, by pushing him from the train."

"That is a lie," Mrs. Comstock said, in the manner of a mother chastising a blatantly untruthful child, "but as there appears to be no calumny of which you are incapable, Mr. Holmes, I see no point in further protest."

"As you wish, madam. But the last elements of my picture are clear, are they not? You wanted money because your husband turned out to be a debtor. Sheriff Boehm needed money to support his gambling habit, or perhaps simply to increase his blackmail earnings. The rune stone offered a chance to make a quick twenty thousand dollars. Therefore, the two of you—along with young Billy Swift—conspired to steal the stone and sell it to Mr. Lund in Chicago. Unfortunately, Olaf Wahlgren disrupted your plan when he discovered the thieves in his barn. Was it the sheriff who planted the ax in Mr. Wahlgren's skull, or was it perhaps Billy Swift?"

"I would have no idea, Mr. Holmes," said the lady, "since all of this is a fantasy entirely of your own creation."

Holmes continued relentlessly: "And what of Magnus Larson? Did he become too greedy, perhaps, and want more than his fair share of the loot? Or was he killed simply to eliminate a witness to your murderous scheming? Or did his drinking make him too untrustworthy an ally?"

Mrs. Comstock now looked at Holmes with an expression of pity. Then, turning to Rafferty, she said: "Poor man. I believe he will next accuse me of being in league with Professor Moriarty."[2]

"Enjoy your amusement while you can, madam," said Holmes sternly, "for I have no doubt Mr. Boehm will have a most interesting story to tell when he is brought before the bar for the murders of Olaf Wahlgren, Magnus Larson, and perhaps others as well—murders which you planned and directed. I am sure Billy Swift can also be persuaded to testify against you."

Here was the moment of truth, for Holmes had played what he liked to call "the trump card of doubt"—a claim of some imagined evidence designed to create fear in the person being interrogated. It was a technique he had long ago mastered and often used to devastating effect.

I watched intently for some faint flicker of apprehension on Mrs. Comstock's elegant features, but the lady was truly magnificent, conveying not the slightest suggestion of worry or fear. Instead, she stared coldly at Holmes and said:

"Whatever Mr. Boehm might tell you would be a lie. It is true that after my dear husband's death, the sheriff made certain allegations against me. These were totally false, of course, but he nonetheless thought he could blackmail me. It was not money he wanted. When I refused to give myself to him, he became very bitter and abusive. If he is now speaking against me, it is for that reason and that reason alone. As for Billy, I do not believe he would tell lies about me. He is a fine young man. Indeed, I was supposed to meet him this afternoon at the hotel. I do hope nothing has happened to him."

There was something ominous in the way Mrs. Comstock spoke these last words, as Holmes understood at once.

"You have killed him, haven't you?" he said.

"I have killed no one," she replied calmly, "nor would I ever do so.

I am merely concerned about young Billy. It is not like him to be late."

She now rose from her chair and slowly began to button her coat. Holmes, Rafferty, and I stood as well, surrounding her like bodyguards. I sensed that Holmes wanted to stop her from leaving but knew that he could not. It was only then that I realized the terrible truth: Mrs. Comstock would in all likelihood escape her crimes now, just as she had nearly five years earlier in Hinckley.

As though to confirm her triumph, the lady said: "We are finished here, Mr. Holmes. Indeed, I trust we are finished for good. Still, should you wish to continue pursuing me, I would advise you to be very careful. I understand you were out at my farm today."

"You are mistaken, madam," replied Holmes coolly. "And what about you? Were you at home this morning?"

"I came to town early this morning to do some shopping," she said. "There are many witnesses who will testify to that. There is also a witness—a servant girl at the farm who does not answer to strangers—who told me over the telephone that three men pounded at the door this morning. As she described them, they were identical to the three of you. I do not know what you were doing at my farm, Mr. Holmes, but if any foul play has occurred, you may be sure that I will contact the county sheriff and tell them what my servant girl saw."

Rafferty, who had begun to smile as the lady delivered this thinly veiled threat, jumped in before Holmes could make a reply. Addressing the lady, he said: "I doubted you, madam, but I see now I was wrong. You've dealt the cards like a regular mechanic and prepared yourself for every hand that might be played, includin' the one Mr. Holmes tried out a minute ago. Fact is, you're everythin' Mr. Holmes said you were, and more. 'Tis rare to see such a deep talent for villainy in a woman, especially in a woman as beautiful as you are."

But Rafferty's compliment, if it could be called that, now turned into something much different. He continued: "But hear this, madam: you came very close to gettin' a beautiful girl killed this mornin' and I don't like you for that. I don't like you at all. So, I am tellin' you that I don't want to see you, ever again, here or in St. Paul or anywhere in Minnesota. If I do see you, if you even so much as brush across my path, then you will become my life's work from that moment forward, and I will not stop until one of us is dead. And I warn you, I am a very hard man to kill. Have I made myself clear, Mrs. Comstock?"

The ferocity of Rafferty's comments startled not only Holmes and me, but Mrs. Comstock as well. She snapped her head back, as though trying to escape Rafferty's wrath, and replied:

"You have made yourself perfectly clear, Mr. Rafferty, and I assure you that I have no desire to stay in Minnesota any longer than necessary."

Then she stepped forward, gave Holmes a quick kiss on the cheek which took him completely by surprise, and said: "Perhaps we will meet again, Mr. Holmes, but somehow I doubt it."

And with that final comment, she donned her fur hat, adjusted the collar of her coat, and then proceeded at a stately pace through the lobby and out the door. I caught a final glimpse of her red coat just before she disappeared into a white wall of swirling snow.

Holmes stared into the snow and said: "I wonder what it is like to live without shame or conscience."

" 'Tis probably very comfortable for the lady," said Rafferty, "for unlike you and me, Mr. Holmes, she is prepared to take the world as it is and not as it should be."

Rafferty paused before adding: "By the way, I didn't get a chance to tell you earlier, Mr. Holmes, but the coppers here had a very interestin' piece of news. It seems Einar Blegen and Nels Fogelblad have been found."

Chapter Twenty-three
"YOU WILL TELL US WHAT YOU HAVE DONE WITH THE RUNE STONE"

Five days after our memorable encounter with Sheriff Boehm in the elevator, a small gathering took place at the home of George Kensington in Alexandria. Besides our host and his wife, the company included Holmes, myself, Shadwell Rafferty, and Einar Blegen. Among the surviving principals of the rune stone affair, everyone was accounted for other than Nels Fogelblad (who declined an invitation to attend), Moony Wahlgren (who preferred the serenity of her own room), and Mrs. Mary Comstock (who presumably had more pressing business to attend to).

We had come together to hear Holmes's final summation of the rune stone affair, which by this time was becoming a sensation in the press, with newspapers as far away as New York expressing interest in the case. The discovery of the bodies of Gustavus Boehm and Billy Swift in the grain elevator at Fairview Farms had set off the publicity furor. An anonymous message (sent, of course, by Holmes) had directed authorities to the elevator two days after our fateful encounter with the sheriff. Boehm was found where he had fallen. Billy Swift's corpse was discovered in the elevator's pit, buried beneath grain and debris. An autopsy would later reveal that although his body was badly bruised, he had died of suffocation, as a result of either falling into the pit or, as Holmes believed, being pushed into it by Boehm.

But the most interesting news, from Holmes's point of view, concerned Blegen and Fogelblad. The two men, it turned out, had gone into hiding—at an abandoned farmhouse just south of Holandberg—because of fears for their life. But on the day of our visit to Fairview Farms, they had been spotted by an alert boy from a neighboring farm and later brought into custody, where Blegen told a most interesting story. Fogelblad, by contrast, had remained as uncommunicative as ever.

The two men had been released only after the discovery of certain items in Boehm's house which established his guilt. These included a letter to Karl Lund promising delivery of the stone, chits and letters showing that he owed nearly ten thousand dollars to gamblers in St. Paul, and—most convincingly—Magnus Larson's missing notebook. What the authorities did not find was any evidence linking Mrs. Comstock to the crime, although she was brought in for questioning.

With nothing to point to the lady's guilt, the official version of events centered on the activities of Sheriff Boehm, who was believed to have collaborated with Billy Swift in murdering Wahlgren and Larson as part of a plot to obtain the rune stone. The two men, it was thought, subsequently had a falling-out while meeting at the elevator, presumably to discuss the stone, which had not yet been found. It was assumed that Swift shot and killed Boehm, a theory bolstered by the fact that a .44 caliber pistol with five spent rounds was found on Swift's body. And how had Swift died? The prevailing idea was that due to simple carelessness, or perhaps after being startled by the bin collapse, he accidentally fell into the pit. Although his injuries proved fatal, Swift was able, before he succumbed, to fire off several more rounds from his pistol in hopes of attracting help. This accounted for the fact that he had fired five shots in all.

"I could not have invented a tidier scenario myself," Holmes said to me after learning these details from Rafferty, who had befriended the Clay County sheriff in Moorhead and so kept us apprised of all developments in the official investigation. "I have no doubt, for example, that Mr. Swift did indeed fire his pistol after being pushed into the pit by Sheriff Boehm. We will never know exactly when Mr. Swift met his end, but he probably was killed not long before our arrival on the scene. It is our good fortune that his pistol and Mr. Rafferty's pocket rifle are of the same caliber."

Now, as we enjoyed coffee, tea, and excellent sugar cookies baked by Mrs. Kensington, the events in the elevator had already begun to seem like an old nightmare—still disturbing to the memory, to be sure, but very much in the past. The entire case was to be our focus on this afternoon, and Einar Blegen was the star witness. The lapsed minister had spent four days with Fogelblad in the county jail while authorities tried to sort out the events surrounding their disappearance. Released only the day before, he had been summoned by Holmes and Rafferty to tell his tale. Blegen had been reluctant to attend our meeting, but after what Rafferty called "some not entirely friendly persuasion," he agreed to join us.

Standing in the middle of the Kensingtons' parlor and facing us all rather like the conductor of a small orchestra, Holmes said: "Let us begin, Mr. Blegen, with the rune stone itself. Tell us, if you would, when and how you and Mr. Wahlgren carved the stone."

Blegen, who had been nervously rubbing his hands together, looked up at Holmes with his owlish eyes and said: "It was just a prank, you know. Just a prank. It all got out of hand."

"That may be the understatement of the century," said Holmes. "Now, give us the details, please."

"Well, it was the winter before last when Olaf got the idea. He just thought it would be funny to 'pull one over on everybody,' as he put it. Since I have some knowledge of runes, Olaf asked if I would help him. I saw no real harm in it, so we took a stone he had found earlier out in his pasture and started working on it. I wrote an inscription that seemed suitable and made a template of the runes so Olaf could do the carving with a chisel."

"The runic writing we found in your safety deposit box was, I take it, your first draft of the inscription," said Holmes.

Blegen was so astonished by this matter-of-fact statement concerning his strongbox that he was temporarily unable to speak. Finally, he sputtered: "But how—how did you get into—"

"It hardly matters," Holmes interrupted. "Suffice it to say that I know everything about you, Mr. Blegen, and you would be wise to remember that. Indeed, knowing things is my business, sir. Pray continue."

Blegen shifted in his seat and adjusted the collar of his rather threadbare coat, looking very uncomfortable as he did so. Then he said: "Well, last spring—that would be the spring of 1898—we hauled the stone up to the hill on his farm, dug a big hole, and slipped it between the roots of a small polar tree."

"And just how did you do that?" Rafferty asked.

"Olaf had a kind of jack he'd built—he was a very good mechanic—and he used it to pry apart the roots so we could insert the stone. It was hard work, but Olaf thought it would all be very funny when he dug up the stone in the fall."

Holmes asked: "Did anyone other than you and Mr. Wahlgren know about the prank?"

"No, it was just the two of us. Not even Nels knew, and he was a good friend of Olaf's."

"Very well. Proceed."

"Well, I guess you know most of the rest. After Olaf dug up the stone, thinking he'd just have a little fun with the folks around here, along comes Magnus Larson and starts talking up the stone."

"This came as a complete surprise to Mr. Wahlgren, I take it?"

"Oh, sure. He was flabbergasted, especially when Larson offered him two hundred dollars for the stone. That was a lot of money for a man like Olaf."

"Since you acted as notary for that sales agreement, Mr. Blegen, I assume you thought you were entitled to half the money. Is that correct?"

"Yes. It was the fair thing to do in my mind."

"Even though you knew the stone was a fraud?"

Blegen said: "I was wrong, I admit it. But Larson was such a loudmouthed, obnoxious man that I guess I didn't feel too bad about it."

"All right, let us move on. Why did Mr. Wahlgren refuse to honor his agreement with Mr. Larson?"

"He got greedy, that's all. He figured that the way Larson was talking up the stone, saying it was the greatest find of the century and whatnot, that maybe it was worth a lot more than two hundred dollars."

"I see. Magnus Larson, I imagine, was not happy to learn that Mr. Wahlgren intended to renege on their deal."

"Oh, he was furious. Olaf told me he came out to the house one night with a pistol, making all kinds of threats. But Olaf was about the most stubborn man in the world, and he couldn't be budged. He was worried about Larson trying to steal the stone, though, so that's why he hid it out in the manure pit. I helped him move it, since he had a bad back."

"I am curious about something," said Holmes. "Just when did Mr. Larson first make you aware that he knew the stone was a fake?"

Blegen hesitated. "Well, I'm not sure about that."

"Do not lie to me," Holmes shot back, glaring at Blegen. "I have seen the note in which Mr. Larson advises you to 'play along.' Or have you forgotten that item?"

"No, of course not. He sent that note after, well, after I had voiced some doubts, I guess you could say, about the new arrangement he had in mind."

"This 'new arrangement' was, I presume, the plan to sell the stone to the rich Swede in Chicago. What was to be your share of the proceeds, Mr. Blegen?"

Looking more uncomfortable than ever now, Blegen cast his eyes to the floor and said in a barely audible voice: "They promised me five hundred dollars."

"Ah, I see. And what about Mr. Wahlgren? What was he to receive?"

"I'm not sure. The same, I guess."

Rafferty said: "You are about the poorest excuse for a liar I've ever seen, Mr. Blegen. Every time you launch a whopper your eyes go to the floor like they've been pulled there by a magnet. So why not try honesty for a change? It'll be easier on you and we'll all save a lot of time. The fact is, Mr. Wahlgren was to get nothin' from this new arrangement. The fact is, you're the one who told Mr. Larson where to find the stone. Do you deny it, Mr. Blegen?"

"No," he said, his eyes still fixed on the floor. "But I had no idea he would be killed. You must believe me."

"I believe you," said Holmes. "You do not strike me as a man with the nerve for murder, Mr. Blegen. It is obvious the sheriff and Billy Swift carried out that horrendous deed, though I doubt that even they had murder on their minds when they entered the barn. But once Olaf Wahlgren caught them at their work, they had no choice but to kill him. Now then, Mr. Blegen, let us discuss what happened after Olaf Wahlgren's murder, when I imagine you came in for a rude surprise. Was it Sheriff Boehm who delivered the threats which caused you and Mr. Fogelblad to flee?"

"Yes," admitted Blegen, who seemed to have abandoned all attempts to resist Holmes's persistent questioning. "He came to my apartment the night after Olaf's body was found. Until then, I'd known nothing of his involvement in any of this. All of my dealings had been with Larson."

"What did the sheriff say?" Holmes asked.

"He accused me of taking the stone and threatened to kill me unless I turned it over to him and kept quiet. I was terrified. I don't know how well you know the sheriff, sir, but he can be a very frightening man. Very frightening."

As he spoke these words Blegen steepled his fingers as though an expression of religious sentiment might protect him from the memory of his encounter with Boehm.

Holmes asked: "How did you respond to the sheriff?"

"I told him the truth," Blegen said, "which was that I had no idea what had happened to the stone. I think he believed me, but I'm not sure. Thank God, he finally left, but not before telling me that if I was lying he would slit my throat."

"Am I correct in assuming that he repeated this threat, perhaps with even more vehemence, after the stone failed to turn up at Fogelblad's farm?"

"Yes. I guess by then he thought the two of us must be in it to-gether. He'd also threatened Nels before we all went out to the farm. So, as you can imagine, when the sheriff told me that he and Mr. Larson would visit me late Sunday night, I decided it was time to leave. I took out my buggy and went over to Nels's place. He knew about the abandoned farmhouse, and we decided to go out there and stay until things calmed down."

"A wise decision," Rafferty noted. "I imagine the sheriff was plan-nin' to beat the truth out of you if he had to. Instead, he must have taken out his frustration on Mr. Larson."

Holmes said: "I think the sheriff intended to kill Magnus Larson all along, though perhaps not at your apartment, Mr. Blegen. With his love of drink and his fondness for loose talk, Mr. Larson was, from the sheriff's point of view, a liability who might compromise the rune stone scheme at any moment. But I agree with Mr. Rafferty. Something must have happened at the apartment. Perhaps it was a sharp exchange of words, or it may have been something Mr. Larson inadvertently said which caused the sheriff to react violently. We will never know for certain."

"I feel fortunate to be alive," Blegen said.

"As well you should be," Holmes replied. "By the way, did you leave a message at the Douglas House two Sundays ago asking that Mr. Smith and I come visit you in Holandberg?"

"A message?" Blegen repeated, sounding baffled. "No. I left no message."

"I thought not," said Holmes, confirming what he had suspected. The message, we now knew with certainty, was simply part of the elaborately constructed trap by which we "found" the map that led us to the ambush at Fairview Farms.

After questioning Blegen at some length about Mrs. Comstock and learning—to no one's surprise—that he professed no knowledge of or involvement with the lady, Holmes said: "I have but a few more matters I wish to clear up with you, Mr. Blegen. To begin with, I should like to know why Mr. Fogelblad, before going to your hide-away, left a note stating that he had traveled to Moorhead?"

Blegen shrugged and said: "He told me that he just picked a place at random. He thought maybe the note would throw the sheriff off our scent."

Here was another coincidence, I thought, in a case rife with them. Of all the false destinations Fogelblad might have selected, Moorhead was the most troublesome for us, leading us to believe for a time that he, too, had been lured into a trap.

Holmes appeared to take this newest revelation in stride, remarking on it only by means of a slight shake of the head, as if to say: "Of course! I should have expected that Mr. Fogelblad would pick Moorhead by sheer coincidence."

After pausing for a moment, Holmes now said with a kind of dramatic flourish: "Very well, we have now come to the point where we must consider the one great mystery which remains before us. Where is the rune stone? It is, after all, the object upon which this entire case depends — the sun, as it were, in a veritable solar system of crime. Yet it has remained in eclipse, hidden from our view. Or, to use an image favored by Mr. Rafferty, the stone has been like a pea in a shell game, one we seemed always to be a step away from uncovering. As I recall, Mr. Rafferty also theorized that 'a regular little elf' might have taken the stone from Mr. Fogelblad's woodlot and left for us that memorable note which read: 'Fooled you all.' What we need to know is where that elf hid the stone."

"But isn't it possible that the stone is somewhere at Fairview Farms?" asked Kensington. "Wasn't there a crate of about the right size shipped out there?"

"There was," Holmes acknowledged. "However, Mr. Rafferty has since determined through his contacts with the authorities that the crate did in fact contain a tombstone for Frank Comstock, just as his lovely widow told us. We must look elsewhere for the rune stone. Now, let me show you something."

Holmes took from his coat pocket a document which I recognized to be the telegram he had received in Moorhead from Joseph Pyle. Holmes said: "I have in my hand a message regarding the sale of a certain item by the FOK firm of St. Paul. FOK happens to be the sole distributor in the Northwest of carriage lanterns manufactured by the now defunct Steam Gauge and Lantern Company, based in Syracuse, New York. On September 13, 1896, according to FOK's records, a No. 0 Safety Tubular Hood Reflector Lantern was shipped to this area at the request of a customer."[1]

I could tell that Holmes was enjoying himself immensely, for there was nothing he liked more than snapping a case shut as tight as the lid of a coffin. He was now near the point. First, however, he walked over to the front hall and retrieved a large bag he had brought along. Returning to his place in the center of the parlor, he slowly opened the bag to reveal a lantern with a silver-glass reflector, a clear glass globe, and a pair of sturdy side tubes. A piece of glass was missing from the globe. Holmes set the lantern on a side table, took from his jacket pocket a glass fragment—the very piece he had found at Nels Fogelblad's farm,—and carefully slipped it into the damaged portion of the globe. It was a perfect fit.

Then, turning around as swiftly as a pirouetting dancer, he said in a commanding voice: "And now, Mr. Blegen, you will tell us what you have done with the rune stone."

Two hours later, we found ourselves at the base of a wooded hillock less than a quarter of a mile from where Olaf Wahlgren and Einar Blegen had first planted the rune stone. This particular hill—where Blegen had told us we would find the stone—was on Nels Fogelblad's farm, within eyeshot of his woodlot. Upon being confronted by Holmes, Blegen had agreed at once to lead us to the hiding place, for he finally saw that further resistance was futile.

The outlines of Blegen's story were simple and, in a way, unsurprising. He admitted that on the day after the discovery of Wahlgren's body, he had learned of the stone's new location in the woodlot at Fogelblad's farm. This information had come in a telephone call from Fogelblad himself.

"Nels wasn't real happy about being a party to the whole thing," Blegen told us, "and he felt that he had to tell somebody what had happened just to protect himself if there was trouble. So he left a message at the depot in Holandberg for me to call him."

"And he told you about the stone's hiding place because he thought he could trust you?"

"We were friends," Blegen explained.

"I should hate to think what you do to your enemies, Mr. Blegen," Holmes remarked.

In any event, Blegen—believing Fogelblad would never share the proceeds from any sale of the stone—decided to take matters into his own hands. And so he had gone out that night in his buggy, dug up the stone, lifted it from the ground with a small winch, and then reburied it some distance away.

"Now, let me get this straight," said Rafferty. "You moved the stone on Friday night, just a day after Olaf Wahlgren had been murdered and Sheriff Boehm had threatened to take a knife to your throat if he discovered you were hidin' the stone from him. That was a mighty brave thing to do, Mr. Blegen, especially considerin' how frightened you were of the sheriff, or so you told us. Just what was your game? Or are you a man who simply enjoys lyin' for its own sake?"

"Oh, no, I really was afraid," Blegen insisted. "But I thought that, well, I would be safe as long as the sheriff didn't know I had the stone. Besides, if I had turned it over to him, well, he probably would have killed me, too."

As Holmes looked on in amusement, Rafferty shook his head and said: "I am wonderin', Mr. Blegen, if you learned any of the commandments while you were studyin' to be a minister. You see, I think you were plottin' to the very end, tryin' to figure out a way to sell that stone and keep all the money to yourself. Maybe the sheriff would have done the world a favor by slittin' your miserable throat after all."

Rafferty's comment—with which I could not entirely disagree—was still fresh in my mind when we arrived at the stone's final hiding place.

"Dig," Rafferty instructed Blegen after we had all gotten down from our wagons. "You might as well do at least a little honest work in your life. And if the stone isn't here, then I just might slit your throat myself."

Looking suitably chastised, Blegen did as he was told, and it was only a matter of minutes before the hard spring soil yielded its treasure. I could not but think, as we gathered around Blegen, how far we had come to investigate the stone and how elusive it had proved to be, and I felt an odd sense of disappointment, for I sensed that actually seeing and touching the stone would forever diminish its magical hold on my imagination.

With Rafferty doing much of the heavy lifting, we pulled the stone from the ground and lifted it into one of Kensington's wagons. I was struck by how unprepossessing the stone was. Yet this dark gray tablet with neatly incised runic characters marching across its rough face had cost four lives, and could easily have claimed ours as well.

Holmes, eager to study the artifact, climbed up on the back of the wagon and for the next half hour examined the stone in minute detail. He went over every inch of it with his magnifying glass, measured it with a ruler, ordered it turned over so that he could inspect it from every possible angle, and rubbed his hands across it.

"So what do you think?" Kensington asked when Holmes had finally completed his inspection.

"I would say it is, at best, a fair piece of forgery," said Holmes. "For one thing, the inscription's characters are all precisely one inch high, which suggests the use of a modern, as opposed to medieval, chisel. I would also observe that the apparent freshness of the chisel marks does not indicate great antiquity. What a pity that so many lives were consumed over such foolishness!"

On that solemn note, we put a canvas wrap over the stone and made our way back to Alexandria in the light of a brilliant orange sunset. It would be our last night in town, for we planned to begin our long trip back to England the next morning. Rafferty would be leaving as well, to return to his saloon in St. Paul.

Before returning to our hotel, we stopped again at George Kensington's house to bid our final farewells. We chatted amiably with Kensington and his wife before going upstairs to see Moony. She was sitting, as always seemed to be the case, at her desk, working on another beautiful drawing. This time, the picture showed billowing white clouds sailing through a deep blue sky. A girl who looked very much like Moony was floating atop one of these clouds, golden hair streaming behind her.

"Is that you, Moony, up in the clouds?" Rafferty asked.

"Yes. I like the clouds. Clouds are soft."

Rafferty smiled and said: "I'm glad you found your way to the clouds, Moony. You belong there, with the angels."

"I have a secret," she announced, continuing what had now become a kind of ritual between her and Rafferty.

"I knew it," said Rafferty with a clap of his hands. "All right, do I go first or do you?"

"Me," she said.

I expected her to whisper something into Rafferty's ear, as she had several times before, but instead she opened the center drawer of her desk, reached inside as far as she could, and brought out a small photograph. "Pretty picture," she said, handing it to Rafferty.

The photograph, which looked as though it had been taken from a barn loft, showed two men — one clearly Olaf Wahlgren, the other Einar Blegen — standing in front of the rune stone. Wahlgren's right arm was swung back, preparing to strike the chisel he held against the stone with his left hand. Blegen, meanwhile, looked on as though supervising the work.

"Oh, that's a fine picture, Moony," said Rafferty. "I bet it's the one you hid from the bad man."

"Yes. I hid it. The bad man is dead, just like Papa. Too bad. Tell me your secret."

Rafferty leaned over and whispered into her ear. As he did so, a radiant smile spread across her face.

"What did you tell her?" I asked Rafferty when he had finished.

"I told her she has a new uncle — me — and that I will visit her from now on every chance I get."

The girl suddenly rose from her chair and gave Rafferty a big hug. "I like you," she said. "You are funny."

"And you are the bravest girl I know," said Rafferty, engulfing her in his arms. "And the prettiest, too. We will always be friends, Moony, always, no matter what happens, and that's a fact!"

Epilogue

"WHO IS TO SAY WE MIGHT NOT MEET AGAIN?"

Upon our return to London, at the end of April 1899, Holmes at once became enmeshed in a series of difficult cases so sensitive in nature that I am not yet at liberty to present them to the world. Holmes, however, did find time to deliver a complete report on the rune stone to Erik Ohman. Citing "incontrovertible evidence" that the stone was "a modern forgery," Holmes told the professor that "King Oskar under no circumstances should invest in such a spurious artifact." The professor wrote back to tell us that he was extremely grateful for this information and that Holmes's report "convinced His Majesty that the stone has no place among Sweden's runic treasures."

There was other news of the stone as well. In early June, George Kensington, who had promised to keep us informed of events in Alexandria, reported in a long letter that the stone had been put up for auction as part of Olaf Wahlgren's estate. The artifact had by then become completely discredited as a result of Holmes's insistence that Blegen confess publicly to his role in the fraud. Blegen had made his confession several days after our departure, and

Kensington sent along a copy of the Alexandria *Clarion,* which reported this signal development under a banner headline reading: RUNE STONE FAKERY EXPOSED.

Even so, no criminal charges were ever filed against Blegen, since his duplicitous conduct, however distasteful, did not meet the standards required for prosecution. Blegen, however, was so reviled for his behavior in the community that he soon left Holandberg and was never heard from again.

Kensington said in his letter that after Blegen's reluctant confession, there was little bidding for the stone at auction. As a result, Kensington had been able to buy it for only twenty dollars. "It will look very nice in our county historical museum," he wrote, "and will be quite a conversation piece, I think. P.S. Moony is fine and still talks of you and Dr. Watson."

We also received frequent correspondence from Rafferty, who informed us that he had indeed kept his promise to visit Moony Wahlgren as often as possible. "Took the girl fishing over at Osakis," he reported in June, "and she caught the biggest, fattest pike I've ever seen. I swear the child has magic in her fingers. Will send you photos as soon as they're developed." Rafferty went on to tell us that he had begun to spend more time in the "detecting business," as he called it, and was already hard at work investigating "an ugly case involving the lynching of a man in Minneapolis."

"I can only imagine what strange conversations must take place when Mr. Rafferty and the Wahlgren girl get together," I said to Holmes after putting down the letter.

"Well, at least they seem to understand each other perfectly," said Holmes, "and that is what really matters."

But of all the letters we received that summer, none was more interesting than the one which came from Mary Comstock. Dated August 10 and addressed to "Mr. Sherlock Holmes, the world's greatest consulting detective," the letter read as follows:

I am writing to you, Mr. Holmes, because I know you will be interested in the latest chapter of my life. Indeed, I often think you are far too interested in me, yet what woman would not want to have the attention of so famous a gentleman as Sherlock Holmes?

Hard as it was for me, I recently sold Fairview Farms, for without my dear Frank, what life could there be for me in such a lonely place? The sale was not quite sufficient to pay off Frank's debts, but I was able to secure a handsome loan from a businessman in Fargo to make ends meet. Of course, I will not be able to repay the loan, but I think the businessman will nonetheless conclude that he got his money's worth.

Now that I possess at least some money, I have determined to begin a new life elsewhere. I have been thinking for some time that New York City might appeal to me. It would afford an ambitious woman such as myself many opportunities, don't you agree? Then again, I could end up somewhere else, as circumstances dictate.

I have no doubt you remain convinced that I had a hand in the unfortunate deaths of Olaf Wahlgren and Magnus Larson. While I continue to have the utmost respect for you, Mr. Holmes, I also believe that it is cruel and unfair to make accusations unsupported by proof. Indeed, I will always be disappointed that you would attribute evil conduct to me without, dare I say, a single shred of evidence. Still, I am hopeful that in time you will come to see me in a different light.

You will note that I have enclosed a small item which may be of some interest. I came across it quite by accident while cleaning out poor Billy Swift's room. Because you are such an intelligent and insightful man, you may, I fear, come to some wrong conclusion about how I happened to obtain this item. Then again, perhaps your conclusion may not be so wrong after all. But as I have always said, doubt is what makes life interesting, for if we were certain of everything in the world, how dull life would be!

Well, there is little more to add, other than to say how intriguing it was to meet you for a second time in Minnesota. And given the coincidences which mark the lives of us all, who is to say we might not meet again, in another place, at another time? I should like that, for I have always regarded you as the most fascinating man I know.

The "item" which Mrs. Comstock enclosed was another photograph, undoubtedly taken by Moony, which showed Olaf Wahlgren and Einar Blegen at work on the rune stone.

After placing the photograph on his desk, Holmes crumpled up the letter from Mrs. Comstock and threw it into the fireplace grate. Then he said: "There is no end to the woman's cheek, Watson, no end. How I should like to one day see her standing before the gallows, for there is pure evil lurking behind that beautiful facade! But I fear I will not live to see that day."

I thought now of what Rafferty had said to me, in the hotel in Moorhead on the night before we went out to Fairview Farms. Could it be true that Holmes secretly loved Mary Comstock even as he depicted her as the epitome of evil? It seemed unlikely, but I also recalled what Rafferty had said about the connection between love and danger.

Whatever his true feelings for the woman, Holmes had become too agitated to continue. Taking one last glance at the photograph, he said: "Come along, Watson, let us go for a walk. I feel the need of fresh air."

In December of 1899, not long before the dawning of the new millennium, we received another, and very surprising, letter from George Kensington. He passed on the unbelievable news that a second rune stone had been found, near the shores of a small lake about ten miles north of Alexandria. The message on this stone told of a visit by Vikings in the year 1358. Initially, the stone was universally dismissed as another fake, Kensington told us, but then something strange had happened. A highly regarded professor of Scandinavian languages from Stockholm had, quite by chance, been visiting relatives in the area and agreed to examine the stone. To everyone's surprise, he concluded that the stone was almost certainly genuine.

"I don't need to tell you how excited folks became after that," Kensington wrote. "I guess we're in for rune stone fever all over again. More experts are supposed to come out from New York this week, and the whole town can talk of nothing else."

After Holmes had finished the letter and shown it to me, I asked him: "What do you think? Could there be something to what Mr. Kensington is saying?"

Holmes sighed and reached for his briar pipe. He filled the bowl with tobacco, applied a match, and said: "I do not know, Watson, I do not know, though I must always remain a skeptic. But I am inclined to think that a hundred years from now, people will still be debating the authenticity of this latest stone, and what the world will think of it then, I cannot fathom. Perhaps it will be a mystery for the ages."

Notes

INTRODUCTION

1. Little is known about Albert Carlson other than that he was editor of the Alexandria *Clarion* from the early 1890s until about 1930, when he apparently retired. Of the many stories he wrote about the rune stone mystery, the most complete can be found in the *Clarion*, April 12, 1899, p. 1. Like other accounts of the case prior to the publication of this book, Carlson's version of events is accurate only insofar as it goes, since he was not privy to the inside information available to Watson.

2. One of the most famous of Watson's unchronicled cases, the story of the giant rat of Sumatra is mentioned in "The Adventure of the Sussex Vampire."

3. Brief accounts of the rune stone case may be found in the Chicago *Tribune*, April 16, 1899, p. 21; the New York *Sun*, April 24, 1899, p. 16; and the London *Daily Telegraph*, April 29, 1899, p. 32.

4. For more information on my procedures for authenticating manuscripts, see Dr. John H. Watson, *Sherlock Holmes and the Red Demon*, ed. Larry Millett (New York: Viking, 1996), xi–xii.

CHAPTER 1

1. Unfortunately, the case of "Pemberton, the Ipswich Strangler," is one of all too many that Watson never recorded for posterity. As a result, nothing is known of the "amazingly fortuitous circumstances" that led to Pemberton's capture.

2. "The Milverton blackmail affair," as Watson calls it, is a reference to one of his finest stories, "The Adventure of Charles Augustus Milverton," which recounts events that occurred in January 1899. According to Watson, Milverton was known as "King of All Blackmailers" and was considered by Holmes to be "the worst man in London." Watson did not publish his story about the case until 1904, well after *The Rune Stone Mystery* had been written.

3. I was unable to locate the tale of the "diplomat's stabbing at Kings Cross Station" in *The Times*. It is possible Watson's memory failed him and that the account of the incident actually appeared in another London newspaper.

4. The Cardiff Giant was a famous hoax perpetrated in 1869. The giant was supposedly a ten-foot-tall "fossil man" discovered by well diggers on a farm near the town of Cardiff, in central New York State. Large crowds turned out to see the amazing petrified figure, which created a sensation in the press. The farm's owner, William C. Newell, and a relative named George Hull soon raked in a small fortune by charging admission to the site and selling food and souvenirs. Although experts dismissed the figure as a hoax from the start, it took several profitable months before Hull came forward with the truth. He admitted that the "petrified man" was actually made from a block of gypsum purchased in Iowa, carved by artisans in Chicago, and then secretly buried on Newell's farm. Even so, the huge figure proved to be such a lucrative scam that P. T. Barnum, an acknowledged genius at snookering the public, offered to buy it for $60,000. When he was rebuffed, Barnum had his own copy of the "giant" made and put it on display in New York City. There is an account of the hoax in Stephen Williams, *Fantastic Archaeology: The Wild Side of North American Prehistory* (Philadelphia: University of Pennsylvania Press, 1991), 87–90.

5. Holmes's observation that Minnesota is "a thousand miles from salt water" is not quite accurate. The northeastern part of the state is within six hundred miles of James Bay, the southern extension of Hudson Bay. However, the water route supposedly taken by the Viking explorers on their way to Minnesota (up the Nelson River in Manitoba, across Lake Winnipeg, and then up the Red River of the North) would indeed have involved a journey of close to a thousand miles. The article regarding the rune stone may be found in *The Times*, March 15, 1899, p. 5.

6. The revelation that Holmes performed a "small favor" for the king of Sweden will be of interest to Sherlockian scholars, since there is no mention of such a case in any of Watson's other writings. Exactly what this favor might have been is a mystery. Also of interest here is Holmes's statement that he adopted the alias "Sigerson" at the suggestion of Ohman. In "The Adventure of the Empty House," where Holmes recounts his three years of travel after his final battle with Professor Moriarty, he tells Watson: "You may have read of the remarkable explorations of a Norwegian named Sigerson, but I am sure that it never occurred to you that you were receiving news of your friend." It may seem odd that Ohman, a Swede, would have suggested a Norwegian alias for Holmes, but it must be remembered that Norway in 1899 was still under Swedish rule and did not secure full independence until 1905.

7. Oskar II (usually spelled "Oscar" in English) ruled Sweden from 1872 until his death in 1907 and thus was king of Norway as well until 1905. Sweden already had a parliamentary system of government at this time, but Oskar nonetheless was said to be most distressed when he was forced to abdicate the Norwegian throne. In addition to performing his royal duties, he wrote plays, poems, and several works of history.

8. Carl Christian Rafn (1795–1864) was a Danish philologist whose book *Antiquitates Americannae* (1837) was an influential early study of Viking exploration in North America.

9. Holmes discusses Rosander's popular book, *Den kunskapsrike Skolmästaren*, first published in 1854, in chapter 4. Carl Jonas Love Almquist (1793–1866) was a popular Swedish writer whose work included novels, stories, plays, and poems in addition to the grammar book mentioned by Ohman.

CHAPTER 2

1. All of the artifacts mentioned here by Holmes are regarded today by most scholars as either archaeological hoaxes or, in the case of Dighton Rock, as the work of Native Americans. The Davenport Tablets were two stones with hieroglyphic marking found in 1877 in burial mounds near Davenport, Iowa. The Newark Holy Stones, dug up from Native American burial mounds in Ohio in the 1860s, were carved with texts supposedly in Hebrew. The "Grave Creek controversy," as Holmes calls it, centered on yet another burial mound, this one in West Virginia, where a tablet with three lines of writing (in an unknown style of hieroglyphics) turned up in the 1820s. Dighton Rock, a fortyton boulder in Massachusetts marked by numerous inscriptions, was first noted in the 1680s and was later cited by Rafn, among others, as evidence of early Scandinavian exploration in America.

2. Hill, who had always been interested in farming and livestock, began in the 1880s to build a herd of cattle and sheep imported from Scotland. He even went so far as to make his best bulls and rams available to farmers who had shown particular skill in improving their herds. Berkeley Duke of Oxford was a prize Scottish bull Hill purchased for $5,250 in 1883. See Albro Martin, *James J. Hill and the Opening of the Northwest* (New York: Oxford University Press, 1976; St. Paul: Minnesota Historical Society Press, 1991), 309–314.

3. Holmes's description of the circumstances that led to the creation of the so-called bonanza farms is correct. The most complete account of these gigantic wheat farms is in Hiram Drache, *The Day of the Bonanza* (Fargo, N.D.: North Dakota Institute for Regional Studies, 1964).

CHAPTER 3

1. The three ethnic groups mentioned here by Kensington accounted for almost all of the immigrant population in Douglas County at this time. According to 1895 census data, the county had over 2,800 immigrants from Sweden, over 1,400 from Norway, and about 900 from Germany.

CHAPTER 4

1. This is the first reference I have been able to find in Watson's writing to the "extraordinary" skill Holmes possessed for making "quick searches." But given Holmes's long practice in examining crime scenes, it comes as no surprise that he had become extremely proficient at this particular task.

2. George Cruikshank (1792–1878) was a leading English illustrator and caricaturist. He was especially well known for his satirical drawings and for his book illustrations, which included the first edition of *Oliver Twist* in 1836. Sidney Paget, of course, needs no introduction to Sherlockians. A talented artist, Paget illustrated many of Watson's stories for *Strand Magazine*, which published its first Holmes adventure in 1891. The public's visual image of Holmes was shaped in good measure by Paget.

CHAPTER 5

1. The official canon of Sherlock Holmes adventures, as established by Sir Arthur Conan Doyle, makes no mention of Sigmund Freud (1856–1934). However, the famed psychiatrist does play an important role in John H. Watson, *The Seven-Per-Cent Solution*, ed. Nicholas Meyer (New York: E. P. Dutton, 1974). A number of Sherlockian scholars have also speculated that Freud and Holmes—with their shared interest in the dark secrets of the human heart— may well have met at one time or another.

2. Holmes's expertise in handwriting analysis is well known. He used this skill to great effect in a number of cases, including "The Adventure of the Norwood Builder," "The Naval Treaty," *The Valley of Fear,* and *The Red Demon.* His most thorough discussion of the topic, however, appears in "The Reigate Squires," where he notes that even a person's age can be deduced from his or her handwriting.

3. Lake Osakis, about ten miles east of Alexandria, is one of many large lakes in the west central part of Minnesota, where retreating glaciers left behind numerous bodies of water. Resorts and cabins now ring the lake, which remains a popular destination for anglers.

CHAPTER 6

1. Watson, while serving in the Royal Berkshire Regiment, was wounded at the Battle of Maiwand, in Afghanistan, on July 27, 1880. He says here he was wounded in the shoulder, which was most probably the case, although in another story he claims to have been hit in the leg. Curiously, there appears to be another bit of confusion in this paragraph, since Watson refers to "young Stanford" as the person who introduced him to Holmes. In *A Study in Scarlet,* however, Watson identifies the man as "Stamford." Since Watson's memory of the events was undoubtedly fresher at that time, "Stamford" is in all likelihood the proper spelling of the name.

2. Watson's uncomfortable encounter with the jack pine twins can be found in *The Red Demon,* 100–105.

CHAPTER 7

1. What Rafferty calls a "stand-up joint" was the most common kind of workingman's saloon of the time. There were few if any tables in such establishments, which meant that customers did their drinking while "standing up" at the bar. Rafferty's own tavern in St. Paul was a far larger and more elaborate kind of saloon, with many tables in addition to its long mahogany bar.

2. St. Brendan was a sixth-century Irish monk long reputed to be a great explorer. Among his many journeys was a voyage to unknown "western islands" in the Atlantic Ocean sometime between the years 565 and 573. Despite much speculation as to exactly where these islands might have been, there is no proof that the monk ever reached North America.

308

CHAPTER 8

1. Holmes and Watson first met Clifton Wooldridge in January 1896 in Chicago, just before they went north to St. Paul to investigate the case that became *The Ice Palace Murders*. A highly capable police detective, Wooldridge was an even better self-promoter, who later described his many adventures in *Hands Up! In the World of Crime; or 12 Years a Detective* (Chicago: C. C. Thompson Co., 1906).

2. The Comstock lode was discovered on Mount Davidson in western Nevada in 1857 and turned out to be the richest silver strike in American history. The "Big Bonanza" mentioned by Rafferty was an especially rich vein of ore found a thousand feet underground in 1873. The Comstock lode continued to produce ore until 1898.

3. So-called pocket rifles were produced by a number of manufacturers in the nineteenth century. Among the most popular models were those manufactured by the Stevens Arms Company. The model Rafferty acquired in the 1870s must have been the "Hunter's Pet Pocket Rifle No. 34," which was introduced in about 1872 and came in a variety of calibers and barrel lengths.

4. Harry M. Pope of Hartford, Connecticut, was a highly regarded riflesmith who was employed by a number of arms manufacturers during his career. However, he did not work for Stevens Arms Company until about 1901 (and then only for a year or so), which means Rafferty's "special model" pocket rifle could not have come directly from the factory. The best guess is that Rafferty's "special" weapon was a Stevens "New Model Pocket Rifle No. 40" (introduced in about 1896) that Pope then fitted with a "screw-on barrel" and other custom features.

CHAPTER 9

1. This is Watson's first and only reference to a specific crime reporter with whom Holmes maintained a good relationship. Despite Holmes's harsh words about the press in general, it is likely that he knew reporters from many of the London dailies and perhaps even relied on them for occasional tips.

2. "The Rathburn and Son swindling case" is, alas, yet another of those adventures that Watson did not find time to set down on paper.

3. Rafferty was a member of the famous First Minnesota Volunteers, which fought at Gettysburg and many other major battles of the Civil War, beginning with First Bull Run. His military career is described in more detail in *The Ice Palace Murders*, 155–157. For a history of Rafferty's regiment, see Richard Moe,

The Last Full Measure: The Life and Death of the First Minnesota Volunteers (New York: Henry Holt, 1993).

4. What an extraordinary coincidence this is! Harry Sinclair Lewis, who would have been fourteen at this time, did indeed became a famous writer and world traveler. As a young man, Lewis liked to hang out at Sauk Centre's railroad depot, perhaps because he saw it as the place from which he might eventually escape the small-town conformity he found so stifling. Later, of course, he would transform Sauk Centre into the fictional community of Gopher Prairie for one of his most popular novels, *Main Street*, published in 1920.

CHAPTER 10

1. Frank Woolworth (1852–1919) was one of the most famous and successful retailers in America at this time. After opening his first store in Pennsylvania in 1879, he gradually built a national chain of "dime stores" in cities across the United States. There was no Woolworth's store in Alexandria in 1899, but there would have been one in St. Paul where Rafferty presumably purchased his phony badge.

2. Calamity Jane (born Martha Jane Cannary) was a legendary frontierswoman who settled in 1876 in Deadwood, South Dakota, where she reportedly took up with the equally famous Wild Bill (James Butler) Hickok. Their relationship was short-lived, however, because Hickok was soon gunned down in a Deadwood saloon by a gambler named Jack McCall. Watson is wise in doubting Rafferty's story that he "stared down" Hickok, although there is no way of knowing for certain whether the two men ever met.

CHAPTER 11

1. Rafferty's attribution of a do-or-die mentality to the First Minnesota Volunteers is not an overstatement. The regiment, among the first to be recruited for the Union cause, was famous for standing its ground, a characteristic evident from the very start of its military service. At First Bull Run, in July of 1861 in Virginia, the regiment was among the very last to leave the field and also suffered more deaths—forty-nine—than any other Union regiment in the battle.

CHAPTER 12

1. Contrary to Rafferty's claim, tornadoes can and do occur in Minnesota in early spring, as demonstrated by a series of especially violent series of twisters that struck the southern part of the state on March 29, 1998. But the majority of Minnesota's tornadoes — the state averages about twenty a year — do indeed occur later in the season, with June usually being the stormiest month.

CHAPTER 13

1. The "sawbones" referred to here by Rafferty were the brothers William and Charles Mayo, who along with their father (William Worrall Mayo) developed the medical practice in Rochester that is known worldwide as the Mayo Clinic.

2. Developed by George Pullman (1831–1897), Pullman cars set new standards for railway sleepers when they were introduced in 1865. The first car built by Pullman became especially famous after it was used to transport the body of President Abraham Lincoln on the last stage of its journey to Springfield, Illinois. By 1899, Pullman sleepers were featured on virtually every railroad in the country. The cars were unique not only for their high quality and innovative design but also for the fact that they were leased rather than sold to railroads. Pullman staffed the cars with his own employees, collecting a premium directly from passengers for this service.

3. The "Colt Frontier" was a double-action revolver made from about 1878 to 1905 by the renowned Colt Firearms Company in Hartford, Connecticut. The revolver came in a variety of calibers and barrel lengths.

4. John J. ("Bull") O'Connor was the corrupt chief of police in St. Paul in the 1890s. His encounter with Rafferty is described in *The Ice Palace Murders*, 91–96.

CHAPTER 14

1. A. D. Jorgensen and J. Steenstrup were Danish historians who wrote in that language, which suggests that Blegen must have been well versed in Danish as well his native language (presumably Norwegian). C. F. Keary was an English historian and the author of *The Vikings in Western Christendom*, published in 1891. Holmes's familiarity with these writers suggests that his study of runes had been both wide and deep.

2. Holmes's "special instinct" for locating hidden safes was more than matched by his ability to open them. For a demonstration of his talent, see *The Ice Palace Murders*, 122–127.

3. The Minneapolis, St. Paul and Sault Ste. Marie Railroad, better known as the Soo Line, was founded in the 1880s by Minneapolis milling interests. By the 1890s it was one of several major railroads that competed against Hill's Great Northern.

CHAPTER 15

1. The image of Watson portraying a "dissolute county squire" is wonderfully appealing. Unfortunately, the doctor left behind no account of the "murder case involving Lord Claverton."

2. The manufacture of lanterns was a big business before the widespread introduction of electricity toward the end of the nineteenth century. Kerosene, which became available in the 1850s, was the preferred fuel for lanterns, which in 1899 were still extensively used, especially in rural areas. The Steam Gauge and Lantern Company was founded in Syracuse, New York, in 1881, and made more than twenty types of lanterns. The company was purchased in 1897 by the R. E. Dietz Company of New York City, which by that time was the nation's largest lantern manufacturer. For more information, see Anthony Hobson, *Lanterns That Lit Our World* (Spencertown, N.Y.: Golden Hill Press, 1991).

3. The Farwell, Ozmun and Kirk Company was incorporated in 1887 in St. Paul, evolving out of a number of smaller wholesale hardware firms dating back to 1859. For many years, the company was best known as the distributor behind the chain of "OK Hardware" stores.

CHAPTER 16

1. Chemistry was one of Holmes's specialties, as Watson noted in *A Study in Scarlet*, where he described Holmes's knowledge in the field as "profound." Much to Watson's dismay, Holmes conducted frequent chemical experiments at 221B Baker Street on an "acid-stained" table. All told, there are at least ten cases, including *The Red Demon*, where Watson mentions Holmes's interest in chemical experimentation.

CHAPTER 17

1. The Kodak box camera was introduced in 1888 by what was then known as the Eastman Dry Plate Company, founded by George Eastman (1854–1932). It was Eastman himself who invented the camera, which was the first to use roll film as opposed to glass plates. "You press the button, we do the rest"

was Eastman's advertising slogan for his easy-to-operate camera. Quickly improved upon over the next decade, the camera revolutionized amateur photography by making it much cheaper and easier than it had ever been before.

CHAPTER 18

1. The salesman in this case did not exaggerate the unusual qualities of the Red River of the North, which begins in western Minnesota and flows to Lake Winnipeg in Manitoba. The 545-mile-long river is prone to disastrous flooding because of its direction (it flows almost due north, and its headwaters region experiences spring melt before the downstream area) and because the flatness of the surrounding terrain allows the river to spread for many miles once it jumps its banks. The 1897 flood mentioned by the salesman was equaled only by the flood a century later that devastated Grand Forks, North Dakota, and a number of other communities along the river.

2. Louis Agassiz (1807–1873) was a Swiss-born scientist who taught at Harvard for many years and was noted for his studies of glaciation in Europe and North America. Glacial Lake Agassiz, named in his honor in 1879, at one time covered an estimated 80,000 square miles in Minnesota, North Dakota, and Canada, making it larger than the current Great Lakes combined. Large remnants of the lake (most notably Lake Winnipeg in Canada) still exist. As Holmes points out, the so-called Red River Valley is not a valley at all but simply the flat bottom of the ancient lake.

CHAPTER 19

1. The Battle of Fredericksburg, on December 13, 1862, was a disaster for the Army of the Potomac, in which thousands of men were sacrificed in a series of hopeless attacks against Confederate forces entrenched behind a stone wall atop a bluff known as Marye's Heights. Rafferty's regiment, the First Minnesota Volunteers, was held in reserve during the fighting and escaped the slaughter, although he and his fellow soldiers had a clear view of the disaster from their position. Rafferty's reminiscence of the battle is incorrect in one important particular, for it was General Ambrose Burnside, not Joseph Hooker, who ordered the futile assaults. Hooker, however, was a corps commander at Fredericksburg, and he subsequently took command of the Army of the Potomac, only to suffer a devastating defeat of his own at Chancellorsville in the spring of 1863.

2. The use of glass plates made early photography a cumbersome affair, requiring large cameras and other expensive equipment. As a result, most early photographers were either wealthy amateurs or professionals who could

charge for their work. That Rafferty was able to indulge himself in this hobby before the era of cheap roll film suggests that he must have earned a handsome income from his saloon.

3. It is unclear whether Rafferty is referring here to the beach at Brighton, England, or to a place of the same name in Brooklyn, New York, near Coney Island. My guess is that Rafferty means Brighton Beach, New York, since I have found nothing in his personal papers to indicate that he ever traveled to Europe. He was, however, raised in Boston, and it is therefore very likely that at some point he became familiar with New York City and its environs.

4. The only other mention of Watson's journal is in *A Study in Scarlet*, but it is hardly surprising that he maintained a careful record of his experiences with Holmes. It is likely that the bulk of Watson's published writings derive from material he had first entered in his journal. Sadly, Watson's journal—which would be of immense value to Sherlockian scholars—has never been found.

CHAPTER 20

1. A farm of fifty thousand acres was unusually large even during the bonanza era. In 1880, there was only one farm of that size in the Red River Valley. The valley's largest farming complex appears to have been assembled by Oliver Dalrymple and his family, who reportedly had sixty-five thousand acres under cultivation in the 1890s. See Drache, *The Day of the Bonanza*, 71–82.

CHAPTER 21

1. The year 1899 was crucial in the development of the grain elevator, a type of structure that, as Rafferty notes here, presented difficult structural problems. Cribbed wooden elevators, like the one at Fairview Farms, were first developed in the 1860s and did indeed provide a strong container for grain. But they also posed a persistent fire hazard, even when clad in metal. As a result, elevator builders experimented with other materials—steel, tile, and brick— before finally turning to concrete. The breakthrough came in 1899, when Minneapolis engineer C. F. Haglin designed the first workable concrete grain elevator for grain merchant Frank Peavey. Haglin's experimental elevator still stands in a Minneapolis suburb and is a National Historic Landmark. For an interesting look at the subject, see Lisa Mahar-Keplinger, *Grain Elevators* (New York: Princeton Architectural Press, 1993). Incidentally, Rafferty's tale of the "Swede" whose house was buried by grain from a collapsed elevator is true. An account of the incident can be found in the St. Paul *Dispatch*, May 19, 1876, p. 4.

1. Watson's stated curiosity about what Holmes and Mrs. Robinson (as she was then known) may have done during their "private meeting" in Hinckley is rather odd, since Holmes gave an account of their activities in *The Red Demon*, 112–115. It can only be assumed from Watson's comment here that, for whatever reason, he did not believe Holmes had told him the whole story.

2. Moriarty made his first and most notable appearance in Watson's stories in "The Final Problem," which concerns Holmes's celebrated duel with the evil genius in 1891 at Reichenbach Falls in Switzerland. That Mrs. Comstock would use Moriarty's name in such a casual manner suggests that she followed Holmes's career more closely than he followed hers.

CHAPTER 23

1. The No. 0 Safety Tubular Hood Reflector Lantern was introduced by the Steam Gauge and Lantern Company in 1888. It was sold until 1897, when SG&L was taken over by the R. E. Dietz Company. For an illustration of the lantern, see Hobson, *Lanterns That Lit Our World*, 139.

Author's Note

READERS FAMILIAR WITH MINNESOTA HISTORY WILL RECOG-
nize a good deal of fact in this story, which is based on a real
event: the discovery of a stone with runic writing near the small
railroad village of Kensington (Holandberg in this book) in November 1898. The Kensington rune stone, as it is commonly called, has
been a highly disputed artifact since the day it was unearthed, inspir-
ing both impassioned defenders and ardent debunkers. And even
though the bulk of scholarly opinion holds the stone to be a modern
forgery—and not a very good one at that—there are still enough dis-
senting voices to make the debate interesting.

For the purposes of my tale, I appropriated the actual inscription
of the Kensington stone and used one of the many modern English
translations (all quite similar) that are readily available. My fictional
stone is also of the exact same size, shape, and composition as the
real one. In addition, I've used a number of surnames for my characters (Ohman, Wahlgren, Blegen, Fogelblad, and Kensington) that
are the same as those of real people or places connected with the actual stone. Even the name of Holandberg is derived from the real

rune stone saga, since an amateur scholar named Hjalmar Holand was for many years the most outspoken champion of the stone's authenticity. Finally, the circumstances surrounding the discovery of the Kensington stone, which was found on a wooded hill entangled in the roots of an aspen tree, are virtually identical to those described in this book.

Most of the book's settings are also genuine. Alexandria, Minnesota, is indeed a real city and is home to a museum where visitors can see the Kensington stone, proudly displayed in a glass case. The city even advertises itself as the "birthplace of America"—a claim not universally accepted in scholarly circles but one that many folks in town are more than willing to defend. As for the farm where the rune stone was found, it is today a handsome little county park that becomes especially inviting in autumn, when the wooded hillsides turn gold, orange, and red. I've also tried to depict the great flatlands of the Red River Valley accurately in this book, even though the day of the bonanza farms is long gone, and wheat no longer reigns as the valley's dominant crop.

Of course, the murder mystery I've spun from the basic set of facts surrounding the Kensington rune stone is entirely fictitious, as are all of the characters in this book with the exception of James J. Hill, Joseph Pyle, and Sinclair Lewis. As far as I know, the Kensington stone never inspired any murder or mayhem, nor was it ever coveted by a wealthy man like Karl Lund. In fact, Olof Ohman—the farmer who found the stone—reputedly sold it for ten dollars after using it for years as a stepping stone to his granary. Although Ohman has been implicated by some scholars as the man who fabricated the stone (perhaps with help from others), he insisted it was genuine until his dying day and never appears to have earned more than ten dollars from his famous discovery.

The continuing debate over the Kensington stone (now conducted on the Internet, among other places) is itself a fascinating story, one that over the years has pitted mostly amateur investigators against a skeptical scholarly establishment. For those interested in learning more about the stone, I suggest the following books:

The Kensington Rune Stone: New Light on an Old Riddle, by Theodore

Larry Millett is the author of six Sherlock Holmes mysteries. He is an architectural historian whose books include *Lost Twin Cities*, *AIA Guide to the Twin Cities*, and *Once There Were Castles: Lost Mansions and Estates of the Twin Cities* (Minnesota, 2011). As a reporter for the *St. Paul Pioneer Press*, he covered many beats and had the honor of writing clues for the newspaper's legendary Winter Carnival Medallion Hunt, which annually attracts thousands of treasure seekers. He lives in St. Paul.

Blegen (St. Paul: Minnesota Historical Society, 1968). This book offers a good account of the historical debate over the stone and is skeptical as to its authenticity.

The Kensington Stone: A Mystery Solved, Erik Wahlgren (Madison: University of Wisconsin Press, 1958). Wahlgren was an expert in Scandinavian languages, and he concluded that the stone is undoubtedly a fake.

The Kensington Rune Stone: Important and Authentic, Robert Hall (Lake Bluff, Ill.: Jupiter Press, 1994). Hall offers by far the most cogent defense of the stone in print, using sophisticated linguistic analyses to buttress his arguments.

Today, the debate shows no sign of diminishing (one recent publication, for example, purports to show that the stone's inscription contains secret codes). This suggests that Holmes may well have been right when he observed that the stone could prove to be "a mystery for the ages."